School for Tricksters

School for

TRICKSTERS

A NOVEL IN STORIES

Chris Gavaler

Southern Methodist University Press
Dallas

Copyright © 2011 by Chris Gavaler
First edition, 2011

Requests for permission to reproduce material from this work should be sent to:
    Rights and Permissions
    Southern Methodist University Press
    PO Box 750415
    Dallas, Texas 75275-0415

Cover art: "Jim Thorpe in His Carlisle Indian School Football Uniform," by Ben Wright, Sage Creek Gallery, Santa Fe, New Mexico.

Jacket and text design: Tom Dawson

Library of Congress Cataloging-in-Publication Data
Gavaler, Chris.
    School for tricksters : a novel in stories / Chris Gavaler. — 1st ed.
        p. cm.
    ISBN 978-0-87074-563-8 (alk. paper)
    1. United States Indian School (Carlisle, Pa.)—Fiction. 2. Off-reservation boarding schools—Pennsylvania–Carlisle—Fiction. 3. Indians of North America—Cultural assimilation—Fiction. 4. Buffalo Child Long Lance, 1890-1932—Fiction. 5. Thorpe, Jim, 1887-1953—Fiction. I. Title.
    PS3607.A984S36 2010
    813'.6—dc22

                                                                        2010022462

Printed in the United States of America on acid-free paper

10   9   8   7   6   5   4   3   2   1

For Madeleine and Cameron

The Indian may shed his outer skin, but his markings lie below that and should show up only the brighter.

ANGEL DeCORA, 1911

Trick plays were what the redskins loved best. Nothing delighted them more than to outsmart the palefaces.

GLENN "POP" WARNER, 1931

Twine
    Your anatomy
       Round the pruned and polished stem,
    Chameleon.

MARIANNE MOORE, CA. 1914

Contents

Nov 10, 1911, *Red Man*

THE MASQUERADE BALL

The masquerade ball given by a party of girls in the gymnasium on the evening of October thirty-first, was, according to a statement made by Supt. Friedman, one of the finest "getups" ever given by the pupils. The ball started at seven-thirty, when figures garbed in costumes of varied and fantastic appearance marched into the gymnasium. Clowns prevailed and amused the lookers on by playing pranks with what appeared to be a stuffed dummy representing a scarecrow; but soon the dummy became animated and walked around. He proved to be not a dummy after all, but was senior Sylvester Long Lance who portrayed the character with great exactness.

There were pretty maids dressed in costumes representing Red Riding Hood, Gypsies, Swiss girls, Scotch girls, and many other quaint characters. The boys represented Indians, monkeys, girls, darkies, tramps, rustic lassies and happy sons of Erin.

After several dances, the revelers unmasked and each found out who his partner was. After having found their right partners, refreshments consisting of pumpkin pie, apples and coffee were served. Good behavior was observed throughout the evening and after the "Home Sweet Home" waltz all adjourned carrying with them the memories of one of the most enjoyable social events in the annals of Carlisle. The prize for the best dressed couple was given to Miss Moore and Mrs. Deitz who graciously chaperoned the event. James Thorpe and Iva Miller were the winners of the prize-waltz.

EDUCATION **One**

Sylvester Becomes an Indian

The rest of the passengers are dozing, lulled by the rattle and drone of the tracks. Sylvester sits upright. He is watching the landscape shift behind his reflection. Outside, the Mason-Dixon is an invisible fissure sutured by rail lines. He watches until the blackness slows, then trembles, and then hangs in his window, motionless except for the engine's hum. The train pauses as he counts seconds, a full minute, two minutes, three, before he stands, grips his sack, and slips out to the platform, just as the rear car is churning forward again, before the conductor can correct him, call to him, Carlisle another forty miles yet.

He changes at the border, in an alley facing the one-building depot in State Line, Pennsylvania. It's barely a town. A few clapboards slouch two-dimensionally in the half-light, with a wall of flattened hilltops circling them. A quarter moon hangs above the buzz of the platform lamp. It's midnight. Sylvester folds his best cotton shirt into a square on the edge of a shopkeeper's rear stoop and steps away smelling of strangers.

His mother salvaged the cast-offs from the Baptist church basement, from a box marked "furnace." The trousers—a restitched flour sack—chafe where the reversed letters curve into the seam. The left and less ragged hem reaches mid-calf. Sylvester hopes it will make him seem taller, give him that extra inch he has never stopped believing he will grow into. The chambray shirt exposes a gash of dark flesh between the missing buttons. His fingers press at it. He is eighteen. He is done growing.

The night air is cooler here than in Winston, or Sylvester wants to believe that it is. He is in the North now. He imagined how the day's sweat would evaporate from his skin, leaving a light smooth chalk to brush away like sand, but already the new shirt is clinging to his ribs. His scalp is damp. It's summer here too. At least no stink is blowing in from any tobacco factories or warehouses. And the vegetation—those woolly branches bobbing against the rooftops and the shorn weeds at the black edge of the street—does smell crisper, a bluer flavor, not that acrid rot of home.

Sylvester takes his first step across a patch of shattered bricks and flinches. The moccasin soles are thinner than slippers. He found them himself, two weeks ago, on the top shelf of a Salem pawnshop, more decoration than sales display. The owner charged him double the price on the yellowed tag Sylvester found in the toe when he slipped them on again in the kitchen at home. The checkered bandanna, his girlfriend Lovie's contribution, he knots under his chin the way Whippoorwill and the other horse handlers at Robinson's Wild West Show tied their bandannas. Masks to be pulled under eyes for the stagecoach robbery act. That was a year ago. They knew Sylvester was no Indian, not really, but they didn't care. Everybody wears costumes.

Sylvester slouches half the night on the depot bench, ankles crossed far in front of him, and watches the tree line detach itself from the hills as the field deepens. When the next train huffs and stills against the shivering planks, the sun is raging in its windows.

He sits nears a white man who studies his profile but does not speak the whole hour. A fold of newspaper rests on the seat between them. Sylvester does not reach for it. There must already be a scent of ink on his fingertips. Some mark, some residue of evidence lingers on everything he touches. It is not enough to be Indian. You have to prove it. He wants the ponytails that drummed against his shoulders when he rode bareback for the circus, with invented symbols etched across his chest and arms in pretend war paint. He tucked the wig and the feathered headdress into the props trunk every night, never certain whether he wore another man's braids or woven hairs chopped from a dead horse's tail.

Forest walls give way to meadows and herd-spotted pastures, then to the slant of farm rows and the islands of whitewashed houses, and then to spaced oaks and the gingerbread of porches and storefronts. The blur of the signs slows—Wagner Hardware Co., Cornman Printing Shop, Western Union Telegraph. Sylvester toured half the South last year, face streaked with greasepaint and burnt-cork, while his older brothers stayed home watching other Negro families crowd 4 ½ Street and the whites flee from Fifth. But he has never seen a northern town. He has never seen a colonnaded cupola on a corner courthouse, or the spired shadow it cuts across a wagon-etched intersection. If not for the web of trolley cables overhead, this might be the old Winston his parents abandoned their plow for. If his mother had moved here after the war, moved north instead of marrying an ex-slave, instead of wasting those years sharecropping, she could have been a white woman. His mother could be a white woman right now, a white woman with the rustic tale of a Croatan grandmother. Not the bastard grandchild of a gentleman farmer and his favorite house slave.

According to the pamphlet Sylvester left folded in the drawer of his attic nightstand, the school entrance is a mile-and-a-half walk from the town center. But which direction? He pivots on the thin of a moccasin heel while squinting at street signs. He shields his eyes as though saluting the silhouette of the clock tower. Its shadow is slanting behind him, so his train must have come in from the west, not the south. But the tracks, he can't remember them bending. He can't remember the sun ever leaving his cheek.

"Lose your way, chief?" The ticket cashier cups one hand between his mouth and the round hole in the counter window. The other is pointing at the north line streetcar.

Sylvester looks, nods, and grunts. It's his imitation of the noise Whippoorwill used on brats between shows. The ones who kept pestering him, kept war-whooping, their daddies grinning wide-jawed behind them.

The trolley runs every fifteen minutes. Sylvester clomps up the metal steps and clinks an Indian-head nickel into the change slot—too boldly—before skulking to the rear seats—another mistake. Moments before, he stepped into the gutter for a pair of white ladies, stepped from a brick sidewalk wide enough to drive three carriages. He sits, head down, fingers laced, until the car grinds forward.

Outside, the sidewalks recede under tree shade as porchless brownstones press toward the street and ebb back again. The gaps between them widen into lawns and then orchards. When the conductor calls Diffley's Point, the other passengers are already standing, bracing their hips against the backs of seats as the brakes curve their spines. Outside, a Negro woman in a laundry dress trudges across the intersection. Sylvester does not look at her, does not want to look at her, as his window rattles, his neck turning then straightening, turning then straightening.

His mother—the only midwife in Negro Salem who can fill in a birth certificate—wears the same apron on washdays. He pictures her kneading the denim of his father's new overalls. The old pair he passed down to Sylvester after getting him the janitor job at the library. Sylvester had promised his circus days were over. He was supposed to be happy reading titles from leather spines while mopping floors. Better than shifts his brother Walter wastes behind a sales register, or a bar counter like Abe. Abe's wife opened a hair-straightening boutique in their basement. She is dark-skinned, but Abe's face is as fair as their mother's. A move of a few miles might wangle Abe a listing in a white directory. An Italian or a Greek or even a Turkish overseer, anything to explain the soot of their father's complexion, a hue that darkens every time his father bends to kiss their mother's cheek. All of their Negro blood comes from their father, probably all of it; that's what he kept telling Lovie.

Sylvester leans with the bridge tracks as the car curves between a pair of gateless pillars. It slows with a grinding metallic chord. He is the last passenger. He doesn't notice "Indian School" bolted below the trolley's single headlight until he is standing at a railway plank marking the tracks' end. The words shrink as the trolley hums backward.

Sylvester is alone on a dirt lane between white cottages and—what is it pretending to be, a castle? A one-story cement square of a building with a crenelated rooftop and fake turrets. He hears barking—no, it's baying. Deep elongated howls that come from no dog Sylvester has ever seen before. The gray-furred animals—their pen spreads behind the last cottage as he follows the lane—snarl and eye him through wooden slats.

He has never been on a reservation, never seen more than two, maybe three Indians in one place, begging Mr. Robinson for circus work he would never give them. Whippoorwill was plenty. Sylvester wants to go back, jog to the depot, ask for better directions. The cashier must be a prankster. Maybe he hates the Indians here. Maybe the whole town does. It isn't too late. Sylvester could go back, buy a second ticket with the last of his dollar bills. It might get him halfway home, halfway somewhere.

The lane ends at the edge of a wide square of grass. Sylvester tells himself it looks familiar. He's seen it before. He studied every newspaper photograph, the same lime-gridded football field over and over. There could have been one of this parade grounds too. A gazebo sits at its center. Sylvester decides he recognizes the roof, the way it curves and points into a spire. Or maybe he's thinking of that Turkish temple he drew from an encyclopedia while the rest of his class kept diagramming the same sentence again and again. It's supposed to be barracks here, army barracks, the ones Confederates torched on detour to Gettysburg. He read that in the book the Winston library special-ordered for him. It was a parting present.

The grass is yellow-green but for weedy tufts. A boy is pushing a mower across a shaded corner. Voices and cutlery blend in the windows of the corner hall. Sylvester squints through a row of oaks at one of the blocky buildings bordering the edges of the grounds. They all look the same, thin white pillars descending from red tin roofs. The one behind the gazebo could be a plantation house. The sun is hovering above it. Its roof burns like a mirror. He could be back in his parents' old county. If they had stayed sharecroppers, if they had raised him where they had been raised, Sylvester would have known this view every morning of his life.

"You got to go see Mr. Henderson."

A woman, a Negro woman in a laundress uniform—the one the trolley passed?—points over the roof of the building where she's standing. Her other hand yanks at the door. Sylvester blinks as though stung with bleach.

"Down in the Large Boys' Quarters," she yells. He nods. When he thinks to wave a thanks, the door is closing at her back.

He follows dried wagon ruts past a white-bricked building with GYMNASIUM chiseled into its granite arch. The dormitory emerges behind it. Its three-storied rows of windows stretch the length of a Salem block. Sylvester paces in place, denting a patch of onion grass, wondering which door to knock on. He counts them instead. Twelve. Talidu. He is imagining his brothers' laughter, the way they will tease and cuff him when he goes back home, no more an Indian than they.

He is picturing the gray wires of his father's moustache, the way his face hides all but the darkest disappointments—when a man's head appears from a propped window.

"Who are you?"

Sylvester swallows before cupping a hand to his mouth. "Sylvester Ganvhidv."

"Who?"

"It means—it's—my name is Sylvester Long."

The man reappears downstairs. His shoulders fill the doorway. He looks dark too, probably an illusion of the shadow of the second-floor balcony cutting him in half. He isn't wearing a uniform. Sylvester thought everyone had to wear military uniforms here.

"Semester started last week."

"I came as soon as the superintendent wrote me. My application—"

"I know, I know," he says. "You're on the list."

The man looks at the hand Sylvester offers before returning a weak shake, fingers limp around Sylvester's. He expected a firm grip, painful, the way his brothers grind knuckles. The man's ironed shirt bulges in the sleeves and chest. He could twist Walter to the floor. Sylvester asks if he is Mr. Henderson, the head disciplinarian. Sylvester's letter told him to report to Mr. Henderson.

"I'm Denny."

First or last name Sylvester does not ask as they climb a flight of wooden stairs. The high cheeks and flattened eyes confuse him more. He is too old to be a student, even one of those assistants Sylvester heard the football coach sneaks into line-ups, to keep competitive. They stop at a locked shelf of folded uniforms as Denny judges his size with unnerving accuracy. Then Sylvester is standing at the threshold of his new room, a square barely twice his height in any direction.

"Washroom's in the basement, but you should get to classes. The towel is to last the week. Don't share it. Mr. Henderson will be up in a minute."

Two of the metal beds are made, mostly. The third is sheeted, with a pillow and blanket folded at its center. Sylvester sits, surprised by the thinness of the mattress. He lifts the sheet edge to find there are two mattresses, neither thicker than his thumb. He fights an urge to seal the door before splashing his face with pitcher water. He fingers the red clay dust in the folds of his wrist. It's a marking as familiar as his tattoo, or the scar on his back, the one he touches often but never sees. He dresses facing the door.

The wool underwear he doesn't like, no one would, but the school uniform is better than he hoped, that darkest of blues, the feel of it on him, masculine yet elegant. He's taller now. It's the angular cut and the column of brass buttons. The cloth, though worn, is crisp. It smells of soap. The rags of his clothes rest at the foot of the washstand. He knots the trouser legs into a ball, the moccasins at the center, and hides the mound under the bed. He will be indistinguishable from the hundreds of other students now, the other Indians.

He looks up at the washstand, at the wall behind it, expecting a mirror. A crack descends the plaster like a river etched across a map. It changes angles, turns crosswise, dives again, flattens, descends more. He parts his hair with the comb from the pouch he carried under his shirt like a smuggler, feeling his way by fingertip, until the pink line across his scalp is perfect, what Sylvester imagines to be perfect.

After knocking at the teachers' dormitory—a round pale woman shooed him away—he finds what must be the Academy building. It's true, it's impossible to miss, even wider than the Boys' Quarters, and older. Brick and wood shades darken in subsections, evidence of expansions, renovations, decades of them, the stonework the grayest above the center doors.

The air is still and warm inside and cavelike in its dimness. No breeze follows him into the windowless cross point where the arms of the hallway open. Mr. Henderson told him the room number of his first class. "Ten," he said, all of his fingers in front of Sylvester's face as though deciding which ear to box first. "Ten," Sylvester repeated.

The tap of his shoes echoes down the tiles, grows tangled in the upper hallway, and peters back to him. A mechanical drone filters through an open transom. Though rhythmic, like a grinding wheel in a river mill, it is human. Voices drag through a choral chant. Stray syllables, an alto, now a tenor, separate from the garbled whole, which cranks for a dozen beats before halting. A woman claps, "Again!" The class begins over, the stanza repeated in unison, except for a lone voice faltering, the precision of the wheel always ruined.

An "X" hangs above the next door. It's closed. Sylvester taps his knuckle against the pebbled glass and waits. Inside a single voice recites. Sylvester knocks again, not louder but higher on the wood. The voice stops, then a distorted shadow congeals in the glass, before becoming a woman, hair in a bun, throat behind a high collar in the widening doorway.

"What do you want?"

Sylvester inhales. His shoulders are straight. "I am Sylvester Long."

The woman continues to stare at him.

"I'm supposed to be a student."

He remembers the schedule Mr. Henderson folded into his breast pocket. The woman reads it. She is not an ugly woman, but not pretty, someone who may have recently been young but is no longer.

Shoes move from Sylvester's path as the teacher directs him to the heat of the last window. He wiggles into the attached desktop seat. Over his shoulder the woman's hand lowers a textbook with frayed edges and a split spine. She opens it to a crinkled page and taps a fingernail at the top of a paragraph. He does not look up until she is behind her lectern again and the rows of heads have turned away.

The bow of a pinafore dangles over the next chair back. Another girl fidgets with a skirt, her pendant necklace holding a shard of sunlight. The boy beside him removes a pair of horn-rimmed glasses and twirls the lenses clean with a paisley tie. The Windsor knot clashes with his collar. Sylvester is one of two students in uniform. The rest could be mannequins in a clothing store window. Sylvester smooths his hands over his sleeves, stops, then smooths them again.

"Why don't you read next, Sylvester."

He clears his throat, and a thread of sweat, impossibly cold, skitters down his ribs. He opens his mouth, but the teacher interrupts. He stands. The book is pinned against his chest. "While the tribes differed from one another, all the Indians were in some points alike. They were brave, but they were—" He stops. He is reading too quickly, too competently. The letters quiver.

"Spell it."

He looks up.

"Spell the word if you cannot pronounce it."

Sylvester entered first grade able to recite the letters of his full name. He knew his numbers to one hundred. He could point at himself on a globe. "T," he says, "r-e-a-c-h-e-r-o-u-s."

"*Treacherous.*"

He repeats the word, then churns out the remaining syllables in a deliberate, unvarying march: "They could bear hun-ger and tor-ture in si-lence, but they were cruel in the treat-ment of their cap-tives. They were a si-lent race, but of-ten in their coun-cils some of their num-ber would be ver-y el-o-quent."

The teacher calls on a tall boy in a varsity sweater, a massive "C" across his chest, to finish. His accent is peculiar, but his reading is flawless. Sylvester wonders what sport he plays. Football tryouts must be soon. Sylvester will go for a backfield position, running back maybe, quarterback even. Don't hide your talents, his mother warned. His father said stay in the open. It's safer. Nobody will think to look for you there. When a bell chimes, the teacher dismisses everyone but Sylvester and the tall boy.

"You did well," she says. "You must have had a perfectly fine teacher at your reservation school." The corners of Sylvester's smile twitch. The tall boy is named Samuel. He is to show Sylvester upstairs to his typing class. "Samuel's Cherokee too," the teacher says.

The hallway is smaller with moving bodies. The light from the open doors shimmers on the high polished bricks. Sylvester watches eddies of students halt in conversation, hover, and spin off, all indifferent to him. Twice, three times, he glimpses his uniform in the rush, like a reflection breaking on a surface of water. The tall boy waits until the teacher has strolled back to her desk.

"You're supposed to be Cherokee?" Samuel's face is creased, surveying Sylvester's. Their eyes meet without meeting. "How much?"

Sylvester knows to say quarter, half at most, but his hands are clenched. He can't prove a word. He can't prove anything. One drop and you're a nigger.

"Full blood," he says.

The boy grimaces. "*Tsalagi udo.*" Then he plunges into the stream of strangers alone.

Miss Moore teaches typing. She is young and thin-boned and wears her red hair in an elaborate nest. Sylvester likes the precision with which the black bow hangs from the collar of her white blouse, the ironed waist of her black skirt tight under her ribs. Her style is exacting, masculine.

He sits at an Underwood frontstroke machine—not one of those blind writers with the carriage blocking every word you type. The kind that squatted on the secretary's side table in Winston's all-white West End School. Sylvester used to poke at letters as the squeak of his father's janitor cart grew distant. This keyboard is similar, four rows instead of three, but only one shift. Sylvester works the letters in a flurry of jabs. When two typebars wedge midstroke, he pries them back and smears the evidence between his thumb and fingertip before Miss Moore can turn around. He types better with his eyes closed.

Rows of machines rattle around him, some steady, most halting, the taps merging like rain on the tin roof above his old attic bedroom. Or against the classroom windows his father still swabs handprints from. Sylvester looked into those double panes every day for six years, a pause on the two-mile walk to his Depot Street school. When he came back, bored by his fourth tour with Robinson's Circus, his father enrolled him in a private school, in the seventh-grade room where boys a foot shorter gawked and whispered. His father added a year to the birth date on the Carlisle application to keep Sylvester below the cutoff, but some of these students look three, four, maybe five years older than him. Some of them don't even look like Indians.

When the floorboards creak beside his desk, Sylvester opens his eyes. Miss Moore is standing at his elbow. She curls a tendril of rust blonde hair behind her ear and bends to read the sentence repeating across his platen: *The quick brown fox jumped over the lazy dog.* He has typed it ten times without error.

"Very good, Sylvester. Why don't you go to the next test?"

"Yes, ma'am."

He flips to the page, memorizes it, and closes his eyes. He improvised harder lessons at night in the West End office. His mother made his father lend him the school keys after Sylvester dropped out of school again. He could learn more on his own, he told them, and then recited the months, days, and numbers in Cherokee, in Whippoorwill's accent, even his lazy r's.

He was inventing an obituary for himself—world-renowned inventor dies at one hundred—when the principal found him. If Sylvester hadn't left his father's key chain on the blotter, he could have run for the window when the doorknob jiggled. The principal ordered him from under the chair well and exhaled his relief when he recognized Uncle Joe's boy. The darky janitor's boy. He had seen him that Saturday, bent over a history book, while his father was smearing the dates of the Spanish-American War from a blackboard.

When the principal raised the telephone from his desk, Sylvester knew the operator would connect him to the Winston police. But the man asked for the Joe Long residence instead. The only house on 4 ½ Street with a private line. The conversation was short and one-sided. The principal hung up first. Breathless, with a shirttail loose under his best jacket, his father was standing in the doorway before the minute hand above the secretary's desk clicked a fourth time.

The principal sat with a folder in his lap. A pen twitched in his fingers. When he spoke, it sounded like small talk, quizzing Joe about his family, making Joe repeat tales the principal had obviously heard before. Everyone in town knows the Longs are descended from Indians. Slavers plucked Joe's mother from a papoose board. The principal dragged open a side drawer and handed his janitor a pamphlet. Sylvester's father reached far over the desk to take it, then opened the cover in the fold of his palm. He kept blinking.

"Can you read, Joe?"

"Yes, sir."

Sylvester could only make out the bold red lettering of the frontispiece. *The Red Man.* It was upside down. He wished his father would lean closer to the lamp.

"Any boy willing to risk jail in order to teach himself to type," announced the principal, "deserves more schooling."

Sylvester's brothers had heard of Carlisle. Walter lost money betting against them in the football pools at Abe's bar. Sylvester's father mailed an application request on West End Grade School stationery while waiting for the first coat of paint to dry on the walls of the principal's office. His next two Sundays he hauled a decade of water-damaged files from the basement, a penance his son, now barred from school grounds, was not permitted to share.

Under "Nation" Joe Long printed "Cherokee." Once the most populous people of the region, so maybe it was true. Joe had met his mother only once, and she was certain she was a Cherokee, or a Catawba maybe. Joe's father was a white man. She swore it. Joe added "Eastern," the small mountain band of hold-outs from the forced exodus a century before. That was possible too. He moved Sylvester's place of birth to the southwestern tip of the state. That made Joe a wayward full-blood, lured by the prospects of city life. Listing Sylvester's mother as half-Croatan more than doubled the one-quarter requirement. Fakes, his father explained, congregate near borders.

Sylvester's third-grade teacher—he'd given Sylvester high marks for an essay embellishing the Long family tree—signed the first witness voucher. The second line needed a white man's name. The principal had never seen a plantation ledger with Joe Long's name on a purchase, birth, or marriage description, so Sylvester had to accompany his father in their Sunday best to the rear door of the Winston Clothing Store and wait an hour in the hallway by the toilets until the proprietor welcomed them with fatherly swats on the shoulders. Mr. Harrison called Sylvester's father Vet, for Sylvester, his middle name, what he'd been known by growing up in the county. Mr. Harrison, a known officer of the Winston Klan, regretted that he could not help the rest of the family too. The Longs were better than the average nigger those damned factories churn out.

Joe Long swore to the accuracy of the application before a realtor friend who freelanced as a notary public. Sylvester sat at the receptionist's desk typing the Carlisle address onto the envelope. The real estate office used a damaged Underwood No. 4.

Miss Moore pauses at Sylvester's other shoulder. He has been tracing the movement of her heels up and down each aisle, waiting to impress her again. When he opens his eyes, he fights to keep the corners of his mouth even. She leans over him, the columns of blue window squares framing her head. She's frowning. Sylvester looks at the paper. He has typed a dozen lines with his fingers misaligned:

%y3 178di g492h g9s u7k03e 9g34 5y3 oqa6 e9tl.

The teacher says nothing and continues to the next desk. Sylvester unrolls the sheet, folds it into rough squares, and wrinkles it into his pants pocket to shred in the wastebasket later. He glances up, twice, but no one is looking at him. The mechanical rain keeps clattering. No one is paying any attention to him at all.

When a whistle blows at the end of Mr. Mann's mathematics class, the student body assembles in twos along the central hallway of the first floor. A trickle of scuffed light splits the tiles between the rows, except where Sylvester is hesitating. A teacher points at him.

"Where do you belong?"

Sylvester does not know.

A student with military insignia on his sleeves waves him to the rear. First battalion, Company F. Sylvester imitates the column of puffed chests and raised chins. The boys' formation threads through the double doors and follows a wide arc across the parade grounds to the dining hall steps. Out of speaking distance of the girls stopping on the opposite edge of the entrance. They stand motionless. A student captain snaps his fingers at a pair of whispering boys. They ignore him. Their eyes are on the matron on the shaded porch. She is squinting at them, at the sun-bright grass, and fingering the metal whistle around her neck. Sylvester's shadow puddles at his shoes. His scalp pricks.

The bread bowl at his table is emptied before he sits. The other boys pocket what they are not chewing. Sylvester cannot tell their faces from those he has seen in his classes. Each is crowned by the same straight black hair. The ears of the boy diagonal to him were once pierced by something heavy. The holes are the diameter of Sylvester's pinky, the lobes now loose and flabby. Sylvester pictures railroad nails. Another two have the same squint, the same bloodshot eyes, the thick droopy lids. Most of their fingers are lighter against the soiled tablecloth than Sylvester's. He folds his hands in his lap as a teacher mumbles a prayer, and then a bell chimes. The steamed beef is dry, the bacon gravy broth-like. Sylvester eats with his fingers like the boy beside him. Their utensils are missing too.

He waits a half hour in Mr. Denny's office after his battalion ignores their captain's last command and dissolves across the lawn of the Large Boys' Quarters.

Sylvester unfolds the slip from his pocket and points. Wagon Making. The one to five o'clock slot.

"I asked for Photography."

"That got canceled." Denny gestures at the open window, at the horseshoe building beside the stables. It looks like a factory. "How about Telegraphy? The teacher only comes in for an hour in the afternoon and you get the rest of the afternoon off."

A cluster of students in grease-stained overalls pass under the window. They look like the Negroes outside the brick warehouses any day in Winston. The air shifts, and the scent of the stables blows in warm. Sylvester spent his first summer at Robinson's on manure and feeding duty, till he could distinguish between the horse and elephant and bear excrement he dug from his boot soles before bed.

"They keep all the shops over there?"

"All but the new printing office," says Denny. "You want that?"

A hand-written sign, DO NOT SPIT ON THE FLOOR, hangs by the door. No one looks up. Sylvester studies the web of pulley lines and electric cords strung to the ceiling from the four cylinder presses dominating the floor. The noise is bearable when all four aren't running. The printing teacher pairs him with another new student, Robert Geronimo—Sylvester wonders but does not ask. Sylvester blows dust from the rack of type cases with a bellows as the teacher studies his profile.

"What are you supposed be again?"

"Cherokee." It's a mumble.

The teacher makes a complicated noise under his breath. "Well, keep clear of Ned Wilnotah." He jerks his chin at the other side of the presses, at a face framed by the flywheel. "He's Cherokee," the teacher says. He doesn't say "too." "Father died at Richmond. Under Jackson."

By the end of the afternoon, Sylvester is arranging type on a composing stick and adding white material, quoins and hair spaces, so the letters don't slur under the rollers. The teacher keeps looking at him, keeps saying he's a fast learner, even after Sylvester drops a drawer and scatters metal letters across the cement. He has to scrape them out from under the cabinets with a broom handle. Next week's *Red Man* will feature a student article about the Croatan tribe, a peculiar people of mixed race believed to be descendants of Sir Walter Raleigh's lost colony. Sylvester assembles one line at a time:

separate churches and are given privileges not granted to the

At dinner, he slips a knife from a neighboring place setting before the seat is filled. But the meat is spoiled. He swallows canned peas and watery coffee colored with a dollop of milk. For his hour of cleanup duty in the basement washroom, he mops urine between the exposed toilets and hoses mud down the trough sink under the cold-running spigots. Quiet hour starts at seven. The reading room is nearly empty, with the newspaper racks jumbled and the pages folded to cartoons. He spreads the local *Sentinel* and the *New York Times* across a far table. There will be a piano recital this weekend at the Thudium House and a suffragist meeting to discuss the legal status of women. The record-breaking London heat wave is over, and a team of Norwegians is making an attempt at the South Pole after a sunless summer at their supply camp. He is sitting with his back to the door and so does not hear Mr. Henderson enter.

"Says here you live in Winston." Sylvester half stands, but the head disciplinarian is already dragging a chair out for himself and opening a folder across Sylvester's newspapers. Sylvester recognizes the handwriting and his father's upside-down signature. "You got two city men saying you're Eastern Cherokee." His tone is casual but loud. "You ever live on the reservation?"

"No, sir."

"But you were born there?"

"Yes, sir."

"Your father's family?"

"Yes, sir."

"You a relation of Charles and Rachel Long?"

"Not that I know of."

"You know Elmer Coates?"

"No, sir."

"Never heard of you either. How about William Baldridge? Or David Gilstrap? Adam Tewatley? Luther Crowe?" Sylvester's neck jerks sideways after each name, and back, like a gear. Mr. Henderson scratches at the bars of his blond moustache. "You know how many new students we got?"

"No, sir."

"Almost three hundred. And I'm on the admission committee for over half. You know how much white trash we already got in here?"

"Sir?"

"Kids with barely any Indian blood. Trying to steal an education from the government." He leans his chest against the table. "*Tla-i-go-li-ga, o-gi-na-li?*"

Sylvester has never heard anyone speak Cherokee but Whippoorwill. Henderson's attempt is clumsier than Sylvester's history recitation. He probably cribbed the phrase from a student—an unofficial infraction of the no-Indian-language rule. From his inflection, he meant to say, "Understand, my friend?" but he butchered the verb, added an "I don't."

Sylvester rattles off a few rudimentary sentences. He comments on the weather, on the dining hall food, on the length of Mr. Henderson's nose hairs. A laugh sounds behind him, and Sylvester turns to recognize Ned Wilnotah, the Cherokee from the printshop, seated at the table behind them. He must have entered at the same time, a spy to verify the imposter's speech. Perhaps he went to Henderson first.

Sylvester answers a few more questions, in English, before the folder closes. The man is annoyed but busy. A three-hundred-mile trip to verify a single student is not happening.

Wilnotah is still sitting after the reading room door clatters behind Mr. Henderson. Sylvester smiles at him, an expression the Indian mirrors. Sylvester begins to stand, his open hand forward.

"You no Indian, Cherokee. You a nigger. My daddy owned some of you. Whipped them when they got mouthy like you. Would of lynched them if Union hadn't marched up and down his fields."

Wilnotah leaves the door open behind him. His footsteps grow distant, then merge with others. Sylvester skims random paragraphs. The Mexican Civil War is over, but the one in China is heating up. The Nationalists want to abolish pigtails. He reads until taps sounds on a bugle on the lawn, and then he jogs up the empty staircase to his room. He stares at the moonlit cracks on the ceiling until midnight.

Ivy Stands on a Bridge

vy tightens her collar against her throat. The breeze is light but cold, colder than any wind she ever felt in Oklahoma or Kansas. The cries from the skaters below crack the thin blue air. A Sioux boy, Loud Bear, digs his blades into the ice as he clacks his stick and skitters the empty condensed milk can toward the far goal. Ivy feels the spray of crystals prick her cheek. But that is impossible. The boys' shouts are distant. Snatches of Cheyenne and Iroquois go unnoticed by Mr. Stauffer. The bandmaster is leaning his gut into the bridge railing, reading the town *Sentinel*, angling the pages to catch the last of the light. The sun is tangled in the orchard across the fields. The steeples, the city clock tower, a few nearer rooftops jut through the fingers of red-lined branches. The game is scoreless. Mr. Stauffer thrusts his left arm into the air, bends it to study his wristwatch, and then squares his newspaper to a new page.

Ivy does not like Mr. Stauffer, but he is a fool and probably suspects nothing. Ivy has told no one, not even hinted, but she wonders how many of the teachers and students know, or suspect at least. They must. They've had since September to study her. She knows it is wrong, dangerous, for her to think like this. Her sister, Grace, would scold her. Ivy isn't allowed to write a word about it. What if someone opened the envelope? What if she misplaced a sheet of half-used stationery? She's not a child anymore. This isn't Chilocco. It is no accident she is here.

The morning Mr. Whitaker of the Whitaker Orphan Home dropped Ivy and the rest of his half-breeds at the steps of Chilocco, her first Indian school, Ivy had nothing to hide. The superintendent accepted Mr. Whitaker's signature as evidence of the children's ancestries and reimbursed him the cost of the bank loan he had borrowed to rent the wagon. "Take a good look at these pupils," he told the matrons sorting them at the prairie steps. "You will see that they average up pretty well with Indian blood." He stroked Ivy's dark head as proof. Ivy's friend, a one-eighth Cherokee, had taught her how to divide and braid her hair in four plaits with strips of calico the night before.

Ivy did not know why she was an Indian. A Shawnee. No one had ever called her that before, but Mr. Whitaker had said so, and Grace had reminded her, had whispered the word to her again while pulling her down from the wagon. Ivy still stammered, her mouth too small for her tongue and teeth plus all those words when the lady with the enrollment book made her say them, Margaret Iva Miller, age nine, Sh-Shaw-Shawnee. That was years ago. She was a child. Ivy is almost sixteen now.

She watches the other girls, the Indian girls, cut slow figure eights along the stream edge, snapping the stems of frozen weeds. The assistant matron—a violent woman who hoped to restrict skating privileges to alternating evenings, to reduce fraternization—trudges along the bank, fists deep in her apron pocket. The boys flooded the field before Christmas, improvising a dam of broken bricks and carpentry scraps, but the stream was so shallow the superintendent had to telephone the Carlisle Fire Company to pump more water. Mrs. Denny, the head matron, says when she was a student the LeTort surged like a river along the school's western edge, threatening the warehouse and water tank. She found Ivy a pair of broken skating boots. The loose blades could be refastened and filed in the harness shop, but Ivy does not want to go on the ice. Some undetectable fault will splinter and drop her through its shards. She didn't say that to Mrs. Denny. It is a mistake to say it to herself. Ivy will have to repair the skates. She will have to go on the ice, soon, before someone else notices.

She doesn't like winter here. This morning she woke with the window chattering, her two blankets and a borrowed shawl around her. She misses Oklahoma, not just the warmth but the dryness and the blue and the open flatness. Her shoulders are always clenched here. The sky sits like a clouded jar on the shelf of the roofs. There are no sunrises, just a slow thick glow, sometimes an ember caught in a basin between hills. One of the new girls, an Aleut transfer who shares Ivy's washstand, says they're lucky. There was no skin of ice in the pitcher to crack with the hairbrushes this morning. Ivy is just thankful to have a small room, only two roommates to hide from. She likes the Aleut girl and hopes she might not care when she does find out.

A school to make you white, their father wrote Grace days before Mr. Whitaker carted them to Chilocco. What could be easier? His postmarks were from Muskogee then. The paper was fancy stationery from a hotel he said he managed. Grace showed it to her, and Ivy pretended to look. After the funeral, their father told Mr. Whitaker they were orphans. He said he was their uncle, their dead father's brother, and so not responsible, and then Mr. Whitaker shook his hand again. Their father let Grace keep the daguerreotype of their mother, the one in the rust-colored frame from on top of their old bureau. It was pretty, he said, but didn't look like her. He said she would always be watching them. Ivy couldn't imagine such wakefulness, eyelids that cannot close, that cannot rest so long as Ivy is there to be seen, her mother studying her through the eternal but inaccurate eyes of a photograph. Ivy's father told Mr. Whitaker their mother had been a half-breed, so they were probably half-breeds too. That's what he said.

On the north side of the entrance bridge, local kids are hobbling through a game of their own, loping between crags after their zigzagging puck. The smoother south field is reserved for the school, and the Indian boys always chase them away—kids they sing beside in St. Patrick and Second Presbyterian choirs every other Sunday—whooping with their sticks raised in parallel fists, until the townies scramble back up the banks of Judge Miller's property. They are poised at the edges of the bridge now, waiting for the chapel clock in the schoolhouse to strike.

Girls are already scaling the path below Coach Warner's house. Some stop to pry at laces, while others stump ahead, ankles bent sideways from the skate blades. A threesome, on a dare, giggle barefoot down Pratt Avenue toward the third floor of the Girls' Quarters rising behind the laundry building. The boys play to the seventh knell, the last drive orchestrated as both teams step from the ice in lazy unison before jogging through the mesh of girls. Ivy keeps to the center, a trolley track at each side, as she passes between the gateless posts. Mr. Stauffer rolls his newspaper into a tight rod. He prods a pair of Sac girls to their feet before the last of the boys vanish at the corner building. The boiler house smokestack juts above the eaves.

Ivy walks by herself. She is used to that. She's never had many friends. When their mother died, strangers came to look into the casket in the corner of the front room. Their family hadn't gone to any services, but ladies from the Pryor Creek Presbyterian Church helped with the body anyway. Ivy nodded when they described heaven, the brightness and the sweets and the happy organ music, knowing they had sponged her mother clean on the kitchen table and wrestled her into her Sunday dress that morning. Her left eyelid would not close. A slit of white peeked out all day.

Ivy stares into the blackness between the teachers' cottages, but sees nothing. The Deitzes' hounds are sleeping, or pretending to sleep. The art studio is dark too, but for a row of classroom windows nearest the back. The crenelations and turrets look real, or almost real, in the half-light. Ivy does not know why the Commissioner of Indian Affairs thinks Zuni pottery and elk-tooth necklaces belong in a cinder block castle, but the school named the building after him and stuck it at the entrance to trick visitors into buying mementos on their way to the athletic field. The moon hangs just above its roof. Ivy didn't notice it before, or the pinpricks brightening around it. The moon is nothing more than a shaving. She imagines a hole closing, a crack of light thinning behind a lid.

The art teacher told the matrons Ivy was to report to the studio for study hour. Ivy does not know why. The teacher is a Winnebago, a full-blood according to Ivy's other roommate, but Ivy avoids her the way she avoids the cliques of Cherokee girls.

Ivy looks at Mr. Stauffer and points at the art studio. "I'm supposed to—"

"I know what you're doing, girl." He waits for Ivy to trot ahead and watches as she shoves at the swollen door. She can feel him watching. "One hour," he calls. "Lights out at eight for you, same as everybody." Ivy nods and vanishes.

Inside, it is dark and still, and she stands a moment breathing and waiting for the walls and floors to emerge. She's only been here once before, and that was last semester. Each week Miss Moore escorted their Commercial English class to a different industrial shop. They wrote essays using thirty-word vocabulary lists. They learned what leathers are used in the tannery and which animals they come from. They learned how much ink costs. They learned how many coats to varnish a wagon. They learned that twelve thousand garments are scrubbed and wrung and dried and ironed every week. They learned four kinds of sentences: declarative, imperative, exclamatory, and interrogative.

When they visited the studio for the first time, Ivy expected chipped straight-edges and water-thinned paints. Instead she found rugs and pots and necklaces and baskets, each a maze of color, simple until her eye caught in the intricacies. The designs were tiny and geometric—a horse, a woman, a bird. They were those things without having to look like them. The other students improvised rug patterns on strips of paper while the art teacher paused at each desk with Miss Moore's roster book. Miss Moore was gone. Ivy sat at the back near the door. The teacher made Ivy's tongue swell. The simplest words came out thick.

"Margaret Iva," the woman said, reading Ivy's real name, her legal name, what only strangers ever called her. "That's pretty. Mr. Deitz and I named one of our Russian wolfhounds Ivan. It means 'God is gracious,' doesn't it?"

Ivy thought it meant John. She did not say that. She did not say anything. At least her mother had not saddled her with Fiona, after Ivy's father, Finis. Ivy used to look up words in the Whitakers' dictionary and then make Grace explain them to her. It said *Finis* meant "the end," but Ivy knew it really meant "white," even if it was in some language Ivy didn't know about. Her mother had told her so.

If the art teacher recognized her that morning in class, the woman betrayed nothing. Ivy only realized it after she had moved on to the next student on Miss Moore's roster. Then Ivy's heart pricked and something cold spilled through her. At first she thought Chilocco—but there were never art classes there. Then she remembered the mural, a whole wall in the foyer of the St. Louis Indian Building. Ivy had done so well her first year at Chilocco, high marks in all her courses, smiles from all her teachers, that the superintendent chose her to join the exhibition school at the St. Louis World's Fair that summer. Grace wasn't picked, or any of their brothers, only Ivy. She was a model Indian. She passed the art teacher in the Indian building hallway every morning during the Fair, stepping around the edge of the drop cloth and the older students stretching on chairs. Sometimes the teacher would look down and smile at her, or almost smile, and Ivy would tighten her books against her chest and trot away.

Ivy didn't know the art teacher's name then, and she still doesn't know how to address her now, which of her names to use. Mrs. Denny calls her Mrs. DeCora, but DeCora is her maiden name, what she must have been called at the Fair. Some students call her Angel when other teachers—white teachers—can't hear, but Ivy can't use her first name, wouldn't dare. She wonders if it is a distortion of some real name or just another one plucked from a chalkboard list. Grace used to laugh at their Chilocco schoolmates, George Washington, Julius Caesar, Rip Van Winkle, jokes played by Indian agents herding enrollees into reservation day schools. Teachers prefer them over the spill of syllables of a Ruth Nantasnaggil or an Owen Woothahewaitty, names that if translated would be no more remarkable than Susan Little Shield or William Looks Twice. Miller, the name Ivy's great-great-grandfather carried over the Atlantic, is just as literal.

Winding through the display room, past the abandoned photography studio, down the rear hall, Ivy imagines a chorus of pottery wheels humming from the last door. It's open. The classroom air is warm, warmer than the metal and dust of the radiators. Angel DeCora sits, her neck bent over her great oak desk. She smiles before she looks up.

"Hello, Ivy."

"*Si-yo*, Mrs. Deitz."

It is Cherokee, and forbidden, but Ivy knows the teacher likes to hear a word now and then. Not to is more dangerous.

DeCora gestures that she will be with her in one moment. Her other hand stabs at an inkwell. Her braids, a black rope over each shoulder, graze the edges of the paper. Her part, usually a perfect taut crease across her scalp, betrays a crook at the back, as though a painter's hand had faltered while stroking the bright line of flesh dividing the skull in half.

Mrs. Denny likes to say how Mrs. DeCora studied with important artists. She illustrates stories in magazines that look just like illustrations in other magazines. Miss Moore says that Angel DeCora is good, but not as good as Miss Moore's neighbor Mr. Plank who draws covers for *Vogue* and gives lectures in town. Everyone, even Ivy, knows that Angel DeCora is friends with Colonel Pratt, the school's founder, even though the colonel disapproves of Native Arts and the rest of the new curriculum. Kill the Indian, Save the Man. The motto from Chilocco. Grace had to explain it to her then, but Ivy understands it now.

"You don't like to skate?" DeCora's eyes flash toward the windows, and Ivy turns. She sees her reflection, blinks, and sees the entrance bridge floating behind it in the center pane. It looks posed, like a painting, or a memory. Anyone could have seen her standing out there, not noticed her necessarily, but seen her. DeCora speaks before Ivy can invent an excuse. "I liked your essay."

Blood, like steam through the boiler house pipes, rises to Ivy's face. "Miss Moore showed you my essay?" Ivy had only parroted DeCora's lecture, platitudes about cultural preservation. Chilocco students would have been expelled for it.

"Miss Moore showed me everyone's essays. Yours was one of the best. Your English is excellent. Where did you transfer from?"

"Chilocco." She pronounces it like an incantation, an off-reservation school almost as prestigious as Carlisle, but the teacher is shaking her head no.

"I mean after that."

After her second three-year term at Chilocco—all any student is permitted, even full-bloods—Grace put Ivy in a convent school, temporarily, she promised, though Ivy liked it fine, would have stayed there. Ivy describes the tiny town where the sisters taught, halfway between Chilocco and Pryor Creek, where her mother died. Ivy could walk from the orphan home to the tombstone any Sunday.

"Was that difficult for you there? Being the only Indian? I graduated to a girls' school in Massachusetts, then to Smith. Not another Indian face for miles."

Ivy's father didn't allow 'skins in his hotel, even though Indian Territory was printed on all the envelopes. The Millers were Sooners, one of the families who snuck onto unassigned lands before noon the day the border opened. Ivy can't remember much from their Arkansas home before their father claimed a stake in the Territory. He never ranched it before selling to neighbors and carting the family to town, where he took a job behind a hotel counter. He's somewhere in California now, still a hotel man according to Grace, and Grace has no reason to lie about it.

"No," says Ivy. "They thought I was white."

It's the safest thing to say. Students brag about their white blood all the time. At least here they do, to teachers. Grace called Carlisle a finishing school, a place that accepted only the cream, those in step with the larger and guiding Christian society.

Ivy cannot look the teacher in the face, so she looks above her, at the painting hung cockeyed above the blackboard. She knows why she has been summoned. A boy, a part-Negro boy, was nearly expelled last semester. His name is Sylvester. Ivy knew to sign the petition rather than draw suspicion. She knows to avoid the clannish girls too, the Poncas and the Kiowas mostly, and to mix only with Civilized Tribes. Their family trees are already so cross-hatched. There are other girls who look as white as Ivy, or nearly. She wonders how many were expelled before her.

"Do you like that one?" DeCora throws an elbow over the chair back as she looks up at the painting, the one Ivy is looking at. A figure peers forward on horseback, off center, studying something outside the frame. The animal's shadow waits beneath it as it breathes its own fumes, the white almost indistinguishable from the white of the snow, the barely differentiated gradations sweeping toward the horizon where they lift into cloud haze. "It's William's favorite, but I think the face lacks soul. Too 'stoical' as they say. But at least it looks like an honest-to-God Apache. Remington doesn't blend features. You can tell an Ottawa from an Oneida, or a Cherokee from a"—her pause is almost imperceptible—"Shawnee."

Ivy blinks. When Mr. Whitaker heard that Chilocco had to take any child of one-eighth ancestry, the Whitaker Orphan Home cleared a twenty-five-bed room in one afternoon. Ivy's Chilocco records say one-eighth Shawnee. But her brothers enrolled there as part Cherokees. She doesn't know why, and she doubts either is true. None of her grandparents were Indians. Grace said Cherokee is better, easier to fake, so that's what Grace wrote on the Carlisle application, "Eastern Cherokee" in firm black letters, "one-quarter," before running the envelope flap across her tongue. Carlisle requires one-quarter. Ivy knows all of this, knows that anyone could see the truth if they looked at it, but Grace said it didn't matter. Secretaries make mistakes all the time. That's what Ivy is supposed to become here, a secretary. Or a nurse maybe. Ivy doesn't know what she is, not for sure, so it's not lying, not really. That's what Grace says.

DeCora is staring at her. The beaded threads of her earrings sway as she speaks. "Don't you think so?"

She means the painting. Ivy says, "Yes."

DeCora squares her papers and stands. She is shorter than Ivy, a fact Ivy forgot. "But it's a burden too," she says. "Authenticity." And then she lifts a smock from the chair back, the left sleeve less fabric than paint crust. It crinkles as she threads an arm through. The pretend armor a pretend warrior would wear on the auditorium stage. The colors change, the splotches separate, as she nears Ivy. "I had the worst trouble finding a Lakota model for my last commission. It turned into a composite because none of the boys would sit long enough. And I had to finish it with a photograph anyway."

She looks at Ivy, eyebrows raised, so Ivy has to say something.

"Why didn't you ask Mr. Deitz?"

"Billy? Billy looks more like Kaiser Wilhelm than Sitting Bull. He's three-quarters German."

Ivy repeats the last word, the two syllables rising like notes on Mr. Stauffer's piano. She remembers how one of the tall kids, a boy Grace's age, almost twice Ivy's, barked that he was white when a Chilocco matron tried to coax him from Whitaker's wagon, holding out stick candy as she would to lure a dog. The disciplinarian dragged him by the collar while Whitaker sputtered. An understandable lie, he insisted. When these mixed-breeds live too long with white children, they start thinking they're white too. Who can blame them? The others learned to keep quiet after the boy was carried bloodied to the infirmary the next morning. A gang of Hopis cornered him behind the storehouse. Hopis don't like whites. Ivy got off easy, shoved into the crusted barrel she was scouring. The kitchen matron asked how and Ivy flushed, revealed nothing. That was important too. It still is.

"Billy was at Chilocco too. Did you know that?"

Ivy nods. She rooted for Lone Star Deitz from the football stands—although he had already earned a diploma from a white high school, they said. Ivy didn't understand that. Now he is somehow a lineman on the Carlisle team, and an art teacher too, or an assistant in his wife's program, now that the football season is over. She thinks he may have been one of DeCora's students painting the mural at the Fair, but she can't be sure. The Fair was so long ago. She was ten. Rich white ladies doted on her, said she was precious, said they wanted to take her home. One almost did, but Ivy's father refused when they wrote to him. No adoption, he said. He was still their father. You can't change blood. Ivy hadn't seen him in years, still hasn't. When she tries to picture his face, she sees Mr. Deitz instead, the shock of black hair parted to one side. But his features are shifting. The cheeks flatten as if by the pressure of two thumbs on drying clay. Mr. Deitz is twenty-five, more than a decade younger than his childless wife. Miss Moore likes to repeat the fact during business class to favored students. Ivy was standing near one.

Ivy will be expelled. She knows that, expected it from the start, despite what Grace promised. DeCora will ask her, and then Ivy will answer. She could lie first, but Ivy is not good at lying. Secrets she can keep, but lies are a different art. Grace could do it. No one will dig up those old records, she said. If only her father had said yes, had let Ivy be adopted, she would be someone else by now. No second term at Chilocco, no year with the nuns, none of this waiting to be found out. It wouldn't matter that she hadn't completed her Carlisle business certificate yet. She wouldn't need high marks in shorthand and bookkeeping to answer secretarial ads, or have to settle for work as a laundress like Grace. Ivy rubs at her knuckles, where flatiron burns tattoo her sister's. She closes her eyes, and breathes. DeCora is saying something.

"I use photographs or written descriptions when I have to, but like Remington, I prefer live models. I hate generalities." She points over Ivy's shoulder without looking. "But I find myself stuck with the same props. I've used those moccasins a dozen times now."

Behind Ivy rests the model's platform, a tiny stage, a crate lid commandeered from the quartermaster's storehouse. She cannot imagine what once was stored beneath it. Something monstrous. A pair of stretched hides balances between two easels. The dried skin is etched with paint and pierced in quillwork. A beaded cradleboard leans between them, and a deerskin dress folded in a square, as though just scooped from a chest of drawers. The moccasins sit on top.

Ivy wonders why DeCora is delaying. She does not seem a cruel woman, never strikes with her ruler or the long wooden brushes like Mr. Deitz. She wonders who shared their suspicions with her, who on Ivy's floor guessed first, whether Ivy is a topic of jokes in the Teachers' Quarters yet. Imagine, trying to defraud the government with a family legend, hearsay from her mother's line. Her father didn't even know what tribe to name when he abandoned them at the orphan home—Shawnee, Cherokee, he didn't care. Ivy could have been a Gould. That was the rich lady's name at the Fair, the one who wanted her, said she was adorable, a precious little thing.

Ivy studies the moccasins, imagines the papery hide on her skin, on the tops of her feet. It would be easier to confess, but she waits, fills the silence:

"What are you working on?"

"A story for *Harper's*," says DeCora. "About a Cherokee girl deciding to go to boarding school even though her family doesn't want her to. It took some effort, but I got the right costume from a collector in Raleigh. It's an historical piece." DeCora steps beside Ivy and presses the hollow of her back. "I think it will fit you," she says.

Ivy blinks. And then she says, "Oh."

Her face is still, her face is always still, but she keeps her eyes on the costume, afraid to raise them, to meet the teacher's, while trying to adapt quickly, imperceptibly. The pottery kiln radiates behind the hides. She does not know what is baking inside its mouth, but she feels its heat escaping. She is flushed again.

When DeCora asks if she minds, Ivy says, "No." She says, "No, of course not," and the woman's hand falls away as Ivy steps onto the platform. Her foot makes no sound, as if weightless, but the wood still creaks. It bends under her. She changes between the easels, aware of her reflection in the window, a smudge of yellows and browns and pinks beside the dark of the chalkboard. Anyone can see her. Ivy can see nothing but a sliver of moon. The outside is invisible but for the wink of its dozing eye.

Sylvester Loses His Virginity

She makes noises for him, little coaxing whimpers, as he clutches her knees, pulls them to his armpits, so her lower back lifts from the cushion each time he pushes his hips into her. Twelve thrusts, she counts them, and he's done, face clenched up, fingertips digging into the meat of her thighs. He's a virgin—was.

For a dollar he can sleep the night with her, Hazel Myers, on the couch in the basement of Lily Stackfield's house. Carlisle police don't care what happens in the Negro quarter. One dollar could buy him a bottle of rye at the Pennsylvania House, or the Thudium, even the saloon in the lobby of the Congressman's hotel, but he came here instead, another Indian boy from the Indian school. He's a pretty one too.

His stomach, legs, ribs even, his whole body is quivering now, every muscle spooled up. Hazel wriggles her knees free, presses the small of his back so he knows it's okay, ease down, rest here, on her. He lets go a long, knotted breath, sucks it back, then out again, the snags coming loose. She should prod him, worm a thumbnail between their hips till he rolls, but she doesn't. Most are stringing up suspenders by now, tucking at shirttails, the way they do at her toilet when they leave her door wide. This one settles his temple against her ear.

Yuda sent him. Said she'd know him before she saw him, skulking up the back porch, worrying the hat in his hands like he'd been sent up to the massa's house, and then Yuda laughed the way Yuda does, his nose flaring out. The lady working in the Indian School laundry—only Negro in the barracks according to the government—she told Hazel about this boy too, how the Cherokees got up a petition against him, want him out, say he's fake, but his grades are too good.

Superintendent might send him to Dickinson to study law, what he promised Yuda once. His name's Long, they said.

When he starts sliding out of her, wincing as he goes, Hazel shifts her hips, cups it all inside her. It doesn't matter. By the calendar in the table drawer—one of their little black pocket schedules with the Indian face on the front she found wedged in the cushions last summer—she should be bleeding already. Lily would scold her, talk up those scars again, the ones on her insides. Hollowed me out, Lily says. Hazel doesn't care. She likes the smell of the boy, the soap in his hair, not the burn of lye she expected. Even the roots are rigid, all the way down that perfect part. She doesn't know how he does it. His shirt hangs on the chair back, his trousers folded over them, the pleat flat. He emptied the pockets first, paid her all in coins, four bright quarters. She likes him better this way. Her skin burns brighter in the curtain light than his. The moon, a fat one, is chopping their bodies into window squares.

The boy stirs, scoots his chin up her neck. He would climb off, she thinks, but it would mean defying her and the play of her fingers on his spine. There's a spot on the back of his hip she likes, a scar, the skin puffed up, puckered, like a kiss. He doesn't like her touching him there, her pinkie creeping where he can't feel. It doesn't hurt, she can tell that, no nerves. There couldn't be. When he's about to move, she speaks:

"How'd you get it?"

He rolls onto an elbow and tries to look, but can't, the scar moving with him, moving into shadow as his neck twists. "A horse," he says, then clears his throat, feels for a lower note. "A horse," he says, "at a county fair. I was, I don't know, maybe ten I think. Came up on me out of nowhere, knocked up the hip pretty bad." He keeps his head turned, as though he can see the mark or the palm Hazel settles over it.

"Musta hurt."

He doesn't answer, like he's thinking about it. She can't see his eyes in the shadows of their sockets. Hazel's used to talkers, men who brag, tell her tales, but his shrug could mean anything. Last month the Indians' coach flashed her the wad he quadrupled scalping comps and playing his boys light the second quarter to run up halftime odds. Hazel gets lots of traffic from the Indian School, a lazy walk past the flophouse on Bedford and through the old graveyard. She lives just the other side, where Confederates hunkered behind headstones on their way to routing the barracks, Lily tells everybody. Torched it all. Like she knows. Hazel wasn't born yet either.

"You're a quiet one," she says. "Real Indian."

That gets him sitting up, which is fine by her, since her leg is going tingly from the weight. His sweat is pungent, or maybe Hazel is smelling herself. She's happy enough Lily sent him down here, though he'd probably hoped for something nicer: pine floor, not just a throw rug and all that cement, maybe a picture on the paneling, some of those curtain frills they got upstairs. There's only the one window, way up where mud from the yard spatters when it rains. At least it's a big room, same fat square as the parlor upstairs, only with none of the furniture. Just the necessities, Lily said. Hazel scoots herself against the sofa arm.

"So, you a Cherokee, huh?"

"Blackfeet."

She thinks he's funny, laughs almost, then swallows it, like something's gumming up her throat. Not a ladylike noise, she thinks, but she makes it again.

"Yuda said you were Cherokee."

"I'm a Blackfeet."

He's found his underwear where he tucked it beside the sofa leg. He couldn't bear walking the last yard naked to the sofa with her sprawled there watching him. She'd snuffed the light without his asking, which he wouldn't have, dragging his eyes around the rug, the red glass of the lamp on him like a shaft of church light. He vanished with a flicker of the kerosene, but emerged again, larger somehow, his body more itself in the half-light. She can see him fine now and rubs a toe along his rib.

"Wanna drink?"

She points behind her, at the end table and the gin flask she knows is on it. He has to press against her to reach it, which she didn't think he would. She likes the little shiver his body gives after he swallows too, and the way he holds his face rigid on the second swig, to show he can.

"You know," she coos, "it's federal crime giving alcohol to an Indian."

He smiles, politely, and not because she smooths her fingers around his when he hands the flask back.

"I'd like to see Detective Shuler bust in here, huh? Or Bentley. You know him, big tall redhead? One of my regulars. They took Charlotte out of business."

She keeps eyeing him even as she tilts her chin up and drinks.

"Is she a . . . ?"

His chin rises a little too, at her. It's not that he can't think of the word. There are too many of them, all on his tongue at once.

"No," she says. "Bootlegger. Too many saloon men in this town to have a Negro cutting in. They don't even keep them from selling to you boys. Yuda tell you how that Jew of yours tried to catch them up once? Sent out a bunch of them white Indians, you know the ones? Only they're supposed to get caught, so the police can fine the owners or close them up or something. Only the police chief, he doesn't like it with the Congressman liable to get snagged, the headlines and all. So he has all the barkeeps tipped off. Only night a Indian couldn't get served in this town."

She laughs, loudly, head back, and straightens a leg across his lap. He's too far forward on the cushion to fit the other.

"You know Yuda that well?" she asks.

"Not really. I bought ice cream at his wagon sometimes. He graduated before I enrolled."

Hazel snorts. "Graduated. Boy was expelled. Moses had it in for him."

"Superintendent Friedman?"

"For coming here nights, and passing Charlotte's hooch around the Boys' Quarters. At profit too, a dime on every fifty-cent jar. Yuda's no fool. He'd still be there if he'd cut the Jew in."

She studies the boy's face, how it stays flat, while working underneath, thinking the facts through. She likes the profile best, how the purse of his lips is as full as hers almost.

"That," she adds, "and Friedman got wind of talk. About Yuda's daddy's tribe." She holds the last syllable, trills it almost.

"What tribe?"

She grins, waits for him to look at her, grins. "Quadroon," she says. "Same as mine."

That, she thought, would get him standing, tugging those trouser legs up, but he stays perched there, her foot on his thigh, his eyes on her. She doesn't know what he can see, how much of her face is shadow. She thinks about the rouge Lily makes her rub in thick, the too dark tufts of her eyebrow, how stiff her hair gets from bleach, how the roots have already gone black again. He probably can't see all that. When he parts those lips of his, it's not even her he's thinking on.

He says, "I heard Yuda started a petition against the school administration and rode three hours down to D.C. to hand it himself to the Secretary of the Interior."

"Oh, see now, you know all kinds of things, don't you?" She plants a heel against his hip, the good one, and shoves, playful kind of. "That's right. Yuda said Moses was stealing checks, opening student letters, but nobody believed it, not the fine upstanding Mista Friedman, only a half-Jew anyhow, and a praying member of Second Presbyterian. Then, after he boots Yuda, he wants him fired at the ice cream shop too. So Yuda hires out his own wagon and horse, and his boss sells him the ice cream at cost or something, and Friedman can't boycott the shop like he said. He goes in with lawyer papers, but the cops don't do nothing."

Hazel grunts, the sound she makes when she's supposed to sound disgusted, but it comes out funny, like her throat's all gummy again. She hates her voice, how she talks, nothing silky about it, nothing good about it at all. The boy is still looking without looking at her.

"But his wagon is gone."

"Oh, well, yeah sure. But he's got a deli he's going to open across the tracks, he says. You'll see." She pulls her leg away from where the boy's hand has settled on it and winds the other out from behind him. He should be gone, for his own sake, not just because Hazel likes to pee alone. "What would they do to you if you got caught?"

His body knots up, from his stomach out, every thread caught and thinking to snap.

"I mean sneaking out like this," says Hazel.

It takes him a moment to nod, another to pretend he'd no reason to. "Guard-house probably."

"Been in there yet?"

"No."

That she believes. Yuda lost weeks straight in lockup, but no strappings, what the Jew called spanking. The government doesn't fool with its Indians, herds them from their wigwams and freights them all the way out here to Pennsylvania, the smack-dab middle of civilization. Built them a three-story schoolhouse, chapel, gymnasium, and two farms and that row of shops, plus three dorms not counting the teachers' and the superintendent's, the big house in front of all that mowed grass the size of a Negro block. Hazel has been out there, at night. She knows what the government can do when it wants.

Sitting up now, next to the boy, their legs not quite touching, Hazel wiggles her slip back down. The window slat draws a shadow between them, almost, the line slicing into his half, part of an arm, a hipbone, his knee, nothing essential, nothing he couldn't go without if he had to. The other slat cuts them horizontally, though the shadow's all wiggly up and down their thighs and the cushions. The cross in the center of the glass is perfect.

He's started talking about how the student watchman owes him a favor, but she cuts him off. "My grandfather was supposed to be Shawnee. My mother's father. Makes me quarter, right? That school got lots of those."

White trash, Yuda told her, what the teachers call them, boys so pale a bar-keep doesn't think twice tilting them a shot. Like white men, getting their liquor uptown, don't cross South Street but for one reason.

"Some I guess. I don't know. I'm half."

"And the government," says Hazel, "they pay for it all, have to, right? It's in some treaty or something, a law, they got to take you."

"If you have signed vouchers."

"Don't sound so hard."

"From witnesses, respectable ones, from the community in which you live."

His voice marches up and down like poems Hazel used to read aloud in the Negro Public School, in the basement of the African Methodist Episcopal, except without the words rhyming, and he's not standing at a school desk bending a broken spine in his palms, nose to the page because hardly any light comes in those windows way up along the ceiling.

She asks, "Who'd you get for yours?"

When he stands, the sofa darkens, her half too. He's not so tall a boy, but he is long-limbed, with some good meat gripping the bones. For a moment the window's gone, and the moon inside it, swallowed up in the width of his back, or the outline of it, his insides gone as well, deep as water, and blacker. Then he steps toward his clothes, and she can see her own legs again, and the cross flattening against the cushion back next to her.

"Besides," he says. He's stringing his arms through his shirt, filling the white fabric, talking to her sideways. "You don't look it enough. That's genetics. Indian features don't show up after two generations. That's why the government says eighth-bloods aren't Indians anymore, not unless the Commissioner in D.C. signs off on them."

She can't really see his face now, the hook nose, the cheekbones, none of that coppery skin. With the lamp snuffed she can't see the room behind him either. There are no walls.

"Genetics is a science," he says.

"That in the books they teach you?" She crosses her arms under her breasts and watches him with his trousers, the way he can balance on one leg at a time, effortlessly. He's good at what he's doing, she has to admit. Probably she couldn't lie half as smart. "I bet they got you reading all sort of pretty stuff like that. Say something pretty, Indian boy. Go ahead."

He looks away, then mumbles something about not being a man, bleeding if you stuck him. He trails off as he fusses with his fly.

"You're too old anyway," he says. "It's a sort of high school. The cutoff is eighteen."

"That what you are?" She laughs, or pretends to, shoves air out her lungs. "I have players in here older than me. Twenty-five some of them look. Hell, thirty maybe."

"That's football. Football is different."

Hazel's got nothing to say to that. It's true. The town loves its Indians. She hears the parades at the depot every Sunday, the mayor up there at that little podium they truck around for him. The players come through Lily's every home game, always a rout. Any night of the week the backfield can strut in, drunk or sober, with their tailored suits from Wardecker's, shoving a fancy ring under her nose like she's supposed to sniff it or lick it. That coach is worse, spewing his Turkish cigarettes, one after the next, the last smoldering over the table edge while he's on top of her. Wanted to burn her once, brand her, he said, his personal mark. Not that he would have, but still she had to tell Lily to keep him off her couch, or he'd ruin it.

Hazel snatches her dress from the floor, starts wrestling her head through. Not midnight yet, probably somebody else sitting up in the kitchen for her, wincing down a shot of Lily's while he waits. The boy's by the chair, with everything but his shoes laced up neat.

"My foster parents were Cherokee," he says. Then a little softer, he adds, "That must be what Yuda meant."

She nods, doesn't look. "That so?"

"My real parents are Blackfeet, from out in Wyoming. That's where I grew up. Our clan was some of the very last Plains people, the real ones, living on the land, following the buffalo. That's what I remember. The trampled grass under my blanket, the smoke smell of our teepee. My father and uncles used to dance and chant all night before leading scalping parties against the Crow. Did you ever hear a real Indian war whoop?"

Hazel is fixing her sleeves, getting the cuffs right, tucking back the torn lining, for no particular reason. "Oh, I make Indians whoop all the—"

The sound jerks her neck around, the movement independent, as though her spine, the marrow in her legs, are alive, animals frightened in prairie grass. The boy is screeching, head back, throat tall and flat, as this sound comes up and out of him, rattling through his spread legs, from the cement floor, from what must be earth under it somewhere. Hazel reaches a hand out to touch something, anything. The wall throbs.

She's staring now, waiting for the air to slot back into its old shape, which it doesn't, even after his chin slumps and he gives a little cough. He wrings his hands too, like this next part is going to be harder.

"But see, I'm ashamed of my father, some of the things he's done. He wouldn't listen when the chiefs signed the last treaty. He said it was wrong. The ancestors would punish us all. So he became a renegade, an outlaw, wanted up and down all Wyoming, farther even. So see, if I'd told the truth on my application, I would be known as his son. They might not have taken me, or taken me the way Joseph Geronimo got sent, to keep his father off the warpath."

She's thinking how old he looks, and how long ago the last railroads must have been strung anyway, and how it might all fit, maybe—until she hears herself thinking it. Then she wrinkles up her mouth, sets her whole face lopsided, the way Lily tells her not to. Nigger ugly, Lily calls it.

"So them Blackfeet," says Hazel, "they get a lot of fairs out there?"

She flips her chin at the boy's hip, though it doesn't seem like the same hip now, even when he touches it, through the fabric, to feel it, hide it maybe, the mark nobody can see.

"No, no, that happened in Winston. That's where the Longs lived, my foster parents. I was coming through with a Wild West show, the Robinson's Circus. I joined up when I was a kid, to get away. Our clan was broken up, so my aunt took some of us to the city to beg. Mr. Robinson let me carry water pails to the elephants."

"And that circus just happen to bring you all the way around to Carolina?"

"And past, Texas, Florida, we went everywhere. You should've seen them, Oriental acrobats, Arab tumblers, Mexican rope walkers, we had everything."

"Wild Indians too."

Hazel is fussing with her dress again, twisting her arms behind her to reach the buttons. She would turn, but he might think it an invitation, a lady's plea. And she just has to take it off again anyway. He's pacing in place, left foot shuffling against his right, right foot against his left.

"I'd still be there if that horse hadn't trampled up my leg. It was the Longs who took me to the hospital, and took me home after Robinson left town."

"The Longs, huh? See now that don't sound enough Indian to me. Long. You should fix it up some, Long Arrow, or Long Spear maybe. Long Lance. I like that, you my little Long Lance."

She's sniggering, but he speaks over it. "I'll tell you a secret if you want." He tenses up before the words are out, shoulders shifting over his spine, like this is the big one, what he's never told anybody. He takes one more breath first, pulls her in with it. "I was nineteen when I applied."

The sound she makes, she doesn't know what to call it, gasp, snort, air going both ways. "So what?" she says, louder than she expected. The things Lily must be hearing, her and the other girls shushing each other at the top step.

"So it's worth maybe you typing up an application. Can't hurt. I mean I didn't make cuts on the football squad, but the coach saw me, told me to come back for track in spring. That's something that wouldn't have happened if I hadn't tried, see?"

Hazel pads barefoot to the toilet, still working the front of the dress in place, her slip bunched up. She says, "I don't know how to type."

She leans the door shut with her elbow, doesn't slam it, but gets the satisfaction of the click, and the least effort it takes to make it. Only good thing about Lily sticking her in the basement, Hazel has a toilet to herself, more than any of those Indian School squaws can brag about their government quarters. She pees, thinking about Yuda and how he's with a new girl now, nowhere near the Negro quarter. He's got no business sending her Joes, even Injun Joes. Next he'll be wanting a cut. Yuda with his bad leg, getting tramped on by his own damn wagon horse, the fool.

Before Hazel pulls the flush cord, she hears something, under the door, breathing, grunts, but not the kind she can hear most nights under any door upstairs. This is slower, more syncopated, no wincing in the high notes. She tilts her ear to the frame before touching the knob. It's breathless, a kind of singing, the way the preacher barks amens from his gut every Sunday, only she can't make out the words, unless it's the same one, broken up, snagged on a syllable. The wood is cool against Hazel's cheek.

Opening the door will end it, she thinks, get the boy gabbing again, how his people danced this song all night round their pretty campfire. What's the Negro still got to hustle her for? She isn't anybody. Superintendent is never going to care what a darky whore thinks about his star Indian pupil. Hazel is nobody. Same as him.

Before she can notice the trouser legs twisted on the rug, or the white shirt dangling its ghost arms over the cushions, she sees him. He's bent up, shuddering, lurching in a half circle, but not naked, not quite. The breechcloth, it's the towel from under the sofa, knotted with his belt. She wants to laugh, but she can't. His feet are moving so intricately. She can't find the pattern, where the next beat will land, only that it will, the bellows of his lungs building. It is a song, getting frenzied, panicky. His jaw keeps widening, blowing out impossible sounds, shrieks now, but chopped up like they're too big to come out at once, but bigger than he can hold in.

She wants to touch him, feel the burn of his skin where the moonlight slaps it, but he's spinning too fast. She'd have to throw her whole weight just to slow him. Outside feet are padding down the wooden steps. There's a banging at her door, the knob jingling, Lily's shout, but Hazel doesn't turn. She can't. She doesn't want to. The show is too good. He looks so real, all that sweat, his face bunched up, spiritual-like, his people, his people, the dance of his people. Even now she wants to believe. If this boy can fool her, if he can trick one of his own, then he can trick anybody, himself even. That's what Hazel is thinking. This fool will trick us all.

Ivy Works for Strangers

The Maxfields took their first Indian girl the May Henry turned ten. Henry's aunt, who lives in Carlisle and lauds the government for providing a civilizing environment for the offspring of an incorrigible race, told Henry's mother it was cheap summer housework. The monthly seven dollars, what a white girl earns in a week, is wage enough considering the moral and practical benefits afforded the pupil. The first girl was called Mary, though once when she walked Henry to the ice cream wagon and back, she said her name was something else, something Henry couldn't pronounce then or remember now. The second, a sulky, big-boned creature, he spied licking her thumbs from the sugar jar. Then her black eyes were always on him. The third spring came Lucy Hummingbird, whom Henry sometimes still dreams about, the olive smell of her, the splay of her fingers when she tussled his hair. She giggled whispery things while he watched her scour the dishes his family had just eaten from.

Ivy is the fourth. Her hair is not as long or as perfect a black as Lucy's, but she is pretty, her pupils green-ringed, almost blue. A promising sign, his mother says. A mixed-blood. Henry asked her the first day, breathless after watching his father hoist her trunk over the top step to her attic room, "Did your people name you Ivy 'cause that's your plant spirit that watches after you?"

The boards above them creaked with his father's weight.

"It's short for Iva," said Ivy.

It took Henry a while to notice how that isn't even true—"Ivy" is no shorter than "Iva." It was odder her last name being Miller, same as Henry's cousin's family, but there is logic there too, her living in Carlisle like them, learning the white ways. Someone named her that, Henry figures, to fit her in better, because her real name is too wild-sounding, or dangerous, Miss Ivy Geronimo maybe.

They sat, chair tops touching, in the basement of the First Episcopal Church the first Sunday, then with Henry's parents between them during the sermon afterward. Ivy they placed at the aisle end of the pew for the congregation to admire. It is only a block's walk, but Mrs. Maxfield stopped five times and introduced their new Indian girl, a Cherokee would you believe, to anyone willing to watch her curtsy. She wasn't as much of a curiosity as their past girls. The Carlisle Outing Program placed a second Indian student in Moorestown this summer, another sixteen-year-old, over with the Heatons. That, Henry figures later, was the root of the problem.

He lingered on the landing again as Ivy continued up to change from her Sunday dress before starting on lunch. His mother's voice rose through the porch windows, still talking to neighbors about the Heatons, a perfectly respectable family, but whose girl, the neighbors agreed, was not as lucky as the Maxfields' girl.

"My cousin," said Henry, "he lives in Carlisle, you know. I've been there. His name is Billy Miller, just like you. Some coincidence, huh? How'd you get a name like that?"

Ivy stopped and looked down the attic banister past him. "From my papa."

"But how'd he get it?"

"From his."

Her hem brushed the base of the railing before the attic door clicked.

Ivy works as hard as she is told to, but, the Maxfields discovered, she does not keep accurate accounts of her earnings, even though the Indian School issued her a little black calendar book for precisely that purpose. Mr. Maxfield attributed the negligence to a racial deficiency, though none of their past girls had shared it. Henry volunteered to help with the addition. His teacher always gives him high marks in arithmetic.

"I know how to count," said Ivy.

Henry wants to know about her tribe. Lucy's uncles killed General Custer at Little Bighorn. He sat in the threshold, propping the door for her, for the breeze, while Ivy scrubbed herself into the opposite corner of the kitchen.

"Hotels," she said. "My papa runs a hotel."

"An Indian hotel?"

Her lips curved, and she exhaled hard. Her eyes were not kind, but they paused a moment on Henry.

He keeps a can of arrowheads on his dresser, but she didn't want to see them. You can pick them up anywhere around here, he told her, fields, along roads, bones too. He knows a place just the other side of the north creek where you just about tripped over them still, piles almost. They had battles there once.

"Were your people great warriors?"

"Scotch-Irish," said Ivy. "My papa's side."

She explained the history of the ethnic term while polishing Mrs. Maxfield's wedding silver, an annual chore now reserved for June. When the king took away land from the Irish rebels, he gave it to some English families who'd been living over in Scotland, so they weren't really Scots either. And they ended up living in Ireland is all. Her fingers worked up and down the prongs of a dessert fork, mechanically, like the needle on his mother's treadle sewing machine. Strong hands. Lucy, the last girl, said they used brick dust for polishing at the school, for when important people visited the dining hall, politicians.

"I'm no more Irish than I am Hindoo," said Ivy.

The fork clattered on top of the others, the shiny pile.

"But your mama's a Cherokee?"

"My mama's dead."

When she moved on to the spoons, she told him how she'd almost been adopted by a family of railroad tycoons at the 1904 World's Fair, but Henry said he didn't believe that. He said it twice, but she just kept rubbing a handle up and down in the rag in her fist.

Henry saw the Heatons' girl buying chops at the butcher's the next week. He knew she was an Indian because she wore the same ugly black shoes as Ivy, same as all the Carlisle girls do, plus he'd never seen her before, which is why he followed her past the rail station and to the shop door. Her hair was black but all in a bun like his mother's, so he could imagine it any length he liked. Sometimes his mother combs hers out past her elbows, but the ends are all scraggly, like a horse's tail. The Indian girl counted her dimes and nickels and pennies into rows before sliding them across the counter for Miss Seehorn, the butcher's unmarried sister, to drop into the register. The bundle she carried from the chopping room even Henry, squatting in the doorway petting the Seehorns' mutt, could smell.

"What," she said, "not good enough for you?"

The girl hadn't said anything but maybe a thank-you, though she might have made a face, couldn't help it. Henry was watching the pleat of her skirt swish, tracing the shapes behind it.

"Maybe you'd like my brother to go and chop up that dog for you? Can't get fresher than that, can it?"

Both the girl and Miss Seehorn looked at Henry then, at the black bitch and its red tongue lapping pastry sugar from between his fingers. He'd spent his Friday treat money already. He didn't stay to see what happened next, but he told Ivy the first half, while holding two corners of his parents' bedsheet up high for her to line up with her end.

"I hear the Heatons' girl is part Delaware and part Shawnee."

"Her name's Edna," said Ivy. "Edna Shingas." Her fingers were warm, even the callused tips.

"Delawares used to live right here," Henry said. "You know that? Lost all their land on a trade. The settlers said they just wanted a patch the size of a buffalo hide, but then they got scissors out and cut the hide into a long long strip and made a shape the size of New Jersey."

He took the bottom ends again, and Ivy's elbows touched his through the fabric, until she took it all, the sheet lessening by halves until it was a flat, taut rectangle in the crook of her elbow. She and the Heaton girl went out that afternoon, to the nickelodeon, for a half hour nearly. There was dinner preparation, but Mrs. Maxfield was gone too, bicycling with the neighbor, which involves long stops by the pond and talking hushed about things nobody else could ever care about. Henry watched them pedaling back between dried puddles from his window, while downstairs Ivy had the kitchen thick in smoke and flies, and the table half set. Mrs. Maxfield scolded her good-naturedly and told Henry to put her bicycle in the shed.

Sometimes Henry goes to the nickelodeon by himself. When he presses his cheeks and forehead between the metal blinders, trains and clowns and ships and soldiers flicker up at him. He went after school every day for two weeks after his cousin visited. Billy said motion picture men had filmed at the Indian School again. Usually they set up in the bleachers for a scrimmage or down by the track hurdles, but this time Billy said they staked their tripod in the crabgrass in front of the Large Girls' Quarters. They'd come for a fire drill. They have them all the time, Billy said, and he would know living across the creek, across from all those wooden buildings three stories high and a block wide. When the Maxfields visited Carlisle last Easter, Henry listened for the rattle of the fire bells and watched the electric lights through the orchard branches as his cousin snored beside him. Billy said you could see the girls' calves. Their dresses balloon up as they slide down the iron posts, one floor at a time, two, three hundred crowding out in rows.

The next time his mother was out, Henry asked Ivy if she wanted to go to the nickelodeon with him, but she said she was busy, though he could see she was only sitting there writing something at the board he'd helped his father brace between a pair of crates in front of the attic window. It wasn't her little black book either but a letter, the fancy stationery from her trunk. She carries an envelope around the block to the post office two or three times a week. When Mr. Ravenel, the postman, knocks, he hands Henry envelopes from Philadelphia and Pittsburgh and Harrisburg, all of them with girls' names in the corners. Julia. Mary. Sarah. Friends, Ivy says. Other girls in the Outing Program. There is no better education, Mrs. Maxfield tells the neighbors, than hands-on experience in a moral and instructive family environment. The Indian Problem must be solved, Mr. Maxfield declares, one Indian at a time.

Whenever Edna appears, she and Ivy stroll out for pastries and a stamp. "Tell your mama I'm gone to the post office," Ivy yells.

He followed them the third time. The Heatons live ten blocks down, so he can't understand it how they know when the other can get away, especially with Henry's mother's comings and goings on no set time May to August. They walk in step, a firm, fast marching step, the way they drill them at the school. Henry has seen that, the Sunday regiments coming from the gate past Billy's house, twenty girls at a time, headed toward town, to First Presbyterian, St. Patrick's, St. John's Episcopal. Two perfect rows, joints synchronized under woolen pleats, the red of their cape linings swishing in and out. The boys' regiments they release fifteen minutes later, or used to, Billy said, till the superintendent started alternating

Sundays, all-boy, all-girl. Too much "fraternizing," the word that won Henry his class spelling bee last year.

Cutting behind the rail and through the Wilsons' thicket got Henry to his bedroom window before Ivy mounted the porch steps. The Heaton girl kept going. She is taller than Ivy, ganglier, something birdlike in the way her body works under the skin. He was glad he got Ivy. He waited before going down and then didn't say anything a full minute while poking for sweets and not watching Ivy stir up the coals under the soup pot.

"My cousin in Carlisle knows where there was an old Shawnee village," he said. "Not in Carlisle exactly, but a little north I think, where the village was. That must be weird for Edna, huh? Going to school right where her people used to hunt and all?"

Ivy didn't look up, so Henry hovered by the cabinet, scattering crumbs from a stale cookie, one of the last with the burnt bottoms from before Ivy got the knack of the oven.

"My people used to hunt there too," she said.

"In Carlisle? You part Shawnee?"

"My papa's great-grandfather lived in Carlisle. His stone's in the old grave-yard. Lots of Millers are."

"Billy says Uncle Miller's people founded Millersburg."

"The one in Perry County or Dauphin?"

Henry didn't know.

"Brothers," said Ivy, "or uncles maybe. They all came over together before the war."

"The Civil War?"

"Independence."

"So you and Billy could be related?" asked Henry.

She stood and wiped coal grime on her apron, the fabric already cross-hatched and crusted with finger streaks. Her hands rested there, on the curve of her hips, the bones. She looked at his face as a big weird smile bent up half of hers. "Then that'd make you and me cousins too then, don't it?"

Henry had to think about it in his room awhile before figuring it isn't true. Billy is his cousin, but Aunt Claire could have married anybody she wanted, so

Billy's dad isn't related to Henry at all really, just to Billy. Still, his stomach hurt at suppertime, and he stayed upstairs by himself after his mother said he could, and spread his tin of arrowheads across the blanket on his bed. Four he found himself, plus the fifth from Billy. He traded his cork gun for it and got a strapping from his father for being so foolish. He had a bone once too, a forearm it looked like, though maybe a thigh, a child's thigh. He kept it under the dresser until his mother found it. In the county over, they dug up a mammoth in the basement of their new post office. They hung it on wires in the lobby, like a marionette, only real. Henry's father hasn't taken him to see it yet.

He thought the footsteps he heard on the stairs were his mother's until the door opened and Ivy walked in with only a little of the ham soup lapped over the bowl rim onto the tray.

"Your mama said bring this up to you."

There was nowhere else to set it, so she lowered it to the blanket by his leg, which he didn't move as he watched her bend, her hair trying to slide out of its string.

"Wanna see something?" he asked.

He waited till her hands were free, then tossed an arrowhead up high. She caught it by reflex, that part of the brain more animal than human. It's the human part that made her roll it around her fingertips, a half foot from her nose.

"Would of gone on the end of an arrow once," Henry said. "Could be a thousand years old." He pictured the sliver of wood rotting in a mammoth's gut, the carved stone clattering through the cage of ribs when there was nothing left to hold it there. "Found that in a grove not a mile from the end of the Wilsons' lot. It's real pretty up there, especially this time of year, all the blossoms and all. I go sometimes, by myself, and just sit. It's real pretty. We could pack a lunch if you wanted."

Ivy kept staring at the arrowhead, but her fingers weren't moving anymore. It was just balanced there, between her fingertips. It was the best of the five, Henry's favorite, the one he found by the pond last year, when he wasn't even looking for it.

"You like that?" he asked. "You can keep it if you want."

Ivy blinked, turned the chiseled rock over in her palm, and then set it soundlessly on the dresser. "Okay," she said.

She was on the steps before Henry called back to say that he would bring the tray down himself when he was done, that Ivy didn't have to worry about getting it for him. He slurped his dinner, then tried to help her with the other dishes, but his mother called him out of the kitchen twice. When Ivy finished her evening chores, she went to her room early, and Henry said he wanted to go to bed too. He was tired. His mother felt his forehead, though he insisted he didn't feel sick anymore, and then he allowed her to kiss him on the cheek before he took the steps two at a time.

Ivy's door was closed. He imagined her stretched out above him in the attic on that cot he helped his father carry up and arrange in the corner, right over where Henry's own bed is, only a room higher. Their two bodies hung in darkness, as though doubled two deep in graveyard dirt, hers motionless but for the green-blue eyes skittering under the lids.

It was another week, a bad one, his mother grousing up and down the back stairs, before they went. The grove is a little farther than he'd said, but Ivy was good on the loose shale, could tramp down her own brush, though she scowled and hissed when slashed by thorn branches. Henry didn't look when she lifted her hem to step across the dry stream, mud mostly and a few wide rocks.

"Why don't you ever talk about your mama?" He was smoothing out the picnic blanket, the stained one from the back of the shed. He lugged it himself.

"I don't remember much," Ivy said. "I was five when she died."

"Was she born on the reservations?"

"That's what it says in my records." She folded her legs up under her when she sat, ladylike, the hem of her skirt splayed around her, floating down all natural on its own. "How about you?" she asked. "Where your people from?"

Henry can name half his dead grandparents and the state where his mother was born, Connecticut. His father doesn't talk about those things. He's an orthodontist. They were eating the sandwiches now, the ones Henry had made all by himself while Ivy was finishing the dusting his mother said she hadn't done the day before. She leaned on one arm at first, then slumped down to her elbow, behind him slightly, the sun working up her dress. If he'd moved his knee at all, it would have touched her, her shin, might have been touching it already, but he couldn't be sure through his trouser leg. His mother had patched the knee again.

She says the sewing machine is too sophisticated for Indian girls. They might run a finger through and bleed over everything.

When Henry turned his head, Ivy was staring at him, had been the whole time. Her eyes were even greener than his mother said, like shards of church glass twisting sunlight. Her fingers wandered the folds of her dress before slipping to the blanket by his hand. When she moved toward him, her whole arm and her face too, Henry stood up, by reflex.

"You want to see the bones?"

He started kicking at the mat of last year's leaves. He found the first a few yards away, then worked his way back, pawing with both hands, finding bits of gray, then larger chunks, pulling them up long and porous under skins of dirt. The best were scattered only feet from the basket, a rib, and a whole shoulder blade, maybe the cap of a skull, a chunk of it. He wiped them half clean and arranged them in an evenly spaced row, digging grit from the joints and cracks with his fingernails. He found four pieces in all. The shoulder blade was his favorite, he said, his favorite ever, even though it wasn't all that big, a girl's probably.

Ivy stayed at the center of the blanket, her arms knotted around her knees.

"Don't you want to finish your sandwich?" he asked.

Henry's palms were brown, the creases black. He wiped them on his patched knees before reaching inside the basket again. He should have brought napkins.

"No thank you," said Ivy.

She snuck out all the time, so it isn't Henry's fault she got caught coming back. When they rounded the neighbors' house, they saw Mrs. Maxfield's bicycle leaned against the porch rail with the front tire flat and some of the spokes funny. Ivy doubled around to the kitchen door while Henry clattered up the front, but it didn't matter. His mother had been home an hour, and not happy about it.

Ivy's voice was not loud, but not soft either. "Why do you want to know?" She kept her back to the room as her fingers struggled with the apron strings. Henry's mother eventually noticed Henry in the hallway and made him say that the girl had gone out not a minute after she had.

How Mrs. Maxfield tells it to the school agent who came early because of the letter Mrs. Maxfield wrote and posted herself is mostly true, if you include Ivy's fib. Mrs. Maxfield says, "I left her in charge of the house, and she spends the entire morning at the nickelodeon, and I have to shame the truth out of her. All bold about it too. I don't see how a one could keep such a girl. Above work, she is. I don't know what you teach that kind of child at your school, but send this one back to her teepee, I say."

The school agent, a tall middle-aged lady whose squint never lessens, even now after she came in from the porch, keeps writing, speaking the last words under her breath: ". . . neither truthful nor trustworthy." She flips back a page in the notebook she holds open on the table beside the basin where Ivy and sometimes the washwoman take meals. "When the last school agent visited on the thirty-first, she wrote here you were satisfied with the girl: 'quick to learn,' you said, 'a refined girl.'"

Mrs. Maxfield rolls her eyes so high her pupils quiver under the folds of her lids. "'Refined.'" She coughs a sort of laugh through her nose. "I hadn't had her but ten days. How was I to know how fool she was? So refined she can't help with a package to the streetcar, because she was in her work dress she says. As if her suitors might see." Mrs. Maxfield's nostrils flare again.

Henry slouches against the cabinet and watches the lady's pen flick. "Was the dress neat and clean?" she asks.

"It was."

His mother plumps up some other gripe, something about Ivy's backtalking, and adds, "Isn't that so, Henry?" Henry grunts his agreement while worming the edge of his shoe against a loose screw in the door hinge. When he looks up his mother is eyeing him over the rims of her kitchen spectacles—the only room in the world she wears them—so he adds a "Yes'm." He feels his face warm, but no one is looking at him anymore.

When his mother's back is turned too much for him to ask to be excused, he drifts up the rear stairs, minding the creaky boards. He hesitates on the second landing, below the attic loft Ivy hasn't left since taking her breakfast, a slice of toast and the remains of the strawberries not fuzzy with mold. Her heels make no sound through his bedroom ceiling either. He studies the back of the steeple through his window, the same view as hers only wider and better hinged. The steeple's shadow is working its way across the church roof, like the hand of a clock, not the minutes just the hours. His father said all the girl needed was a tighter leash, meaning supervision, the bicycle better off in the shed where it belonged. That quieted Mrs. Maxfield enough to get through supper that night and for Mr. Maxfield to retire with the newspaper in his chair after. When she brought him his evening coffee, Mr. Maxfield told Ivy he would miss her.

Henry turns when the attic step thumps. Ivy is wrestling the trunk around the banister, slanting it to fit. No one called for her, but she's coming down. Behind her the attic door hangs open, her room the way Henry remembers it the month before, the sheet tucked along the edges of the cot the way his mother makes Henry's bed.

"Can I help you do that for you?"

She looks at him, full in the face, before rolling her eyes. "Think you're old enough?"

When he reaches to tilt her end up, she grips her handle harder. It is awkward, but they manage the corners together, and even find a kind of rhythm by the bottom step, their legs synchronized, her knee in, his knee out. He smiles at her. He keeps trying to smile at her.

The school agent is standing in the foyer, squinting down at Mrs. Maxfield. "When I entered Carlisle, the Outing Program was just started. I spent my first summer with a farming family not so far from here. Bordentown, have you been there?"

"You," says Henry's mother. "You . . ."

"Class of '90. Whole other world then. These girls come in now with such airs, sometimes I don't know what to think. Ivy, the way she plays sonatas, you would think she was born a baroness. I'm so glad Superintendent Friedman reinstated the Saturday recitals. Has she had a chance to play much for you?"

Mrs. Maxfield follows the agent's gaze to the piano, an ugly little upright that collects dust and picture frames in the parlor corner.

"Well," says the agent, "she applied to Carlisle for the nursing program, but now she's one of Miss Moore's top accounting students, business law too, if you believe it. The things they learn now."

Ivy and the school lady carry the trunk the rest of the way, after Henry's mother sends Henry to signal the streetcar. He stands on the car runner and helps with the trunk, which somehow seems heavier between the three of them. Henry's mother stares from the porch.

The agent says, "Thank you," and seems about to tussle his head, but offers her hand instead. Thin fingers, like his mother's, the joints round and hollow-feeling. Ivy shakes Henry's hand too. He prefers the meat of hers, the way it grips his in return, the muscles working under the sleeve. The skin is warmer too. He has to let go when she lets go. It's a shame for the Heatons' girl losing a best friend this way, but it will work out for the better probably. Henry already knows Edna's hours, trips to the bakery Monday and Thursday mornings. His mother will have a dozen errands for him now. He would say something to Ivy, but next thing she is inside the car, behind glass, not looking at him, except once maybe. With the clouds and the blue and the corner of the sun reflecting off the window, he can't say for sure what she can see of him.

Sylvester Runs in Circles

By the third lap he's leading. The top Hampton runner, a spare, tawny-skinned Negro, hangs two, maybe three strides behind. When the track veers away from the grandstand, Sly can't help himself, his head twists, at Tewanima and Gus pacing each other, elbow to elbow, and Big Jim lost in the dark clutter of the Hampton boys. Jim's legs and arms flash in the churn of limbs. Sly tilts forward. His heels barely touch the cinders as his shadow pivots in front of him, a black splotch jerking along the margin of the grass. He ignores it. He's never led before.

Deitz, the assistant coach, squints from the bench, digs at his scalp, laughs.

His first October, before he got too paranoid to pen a Winston-Salem address on the face of an envelope—only Negroes live on 4½ Street—Sylvester lied to his parents. Most touchdowns on the printshop squad, top intramural fullback at the boarding school. No time for varsity, he wrote Lovie, the virgin he'd left waving from the station platform. Studies are too important.

The student officers, those sergeants in their ironed uniforms inspecting rows of spine-straight classmen, impressed him at first. Then he noticed the training table in the dining hall, the trays of bakery loaves and second pudding bowls carted to the players. The athletic dorm glowed after lights-out. Sylvester watched it through the cracks of the branches outside his window, watched the rows of lit squares suspended between the black of the ground and the black of the sky. It was all doubles inside, even singles he heard, while Sylvester and his roommates knocked knees every time they rolled out from the pits of their mattresses.

The first day of sophomore tryouts, Sylvester tossed his shop apron on the printing bench, the way varsity boys did all season, two hours before the school bell rang, if they showed to class at all. He hung the apron on a hook when the teacher shouted. The coach—Pop, they called him, though Sylvester's father looks twice his age—paced a strip of white chalk framing the trampled grass. It was a slow, rolling walk, his eyes bobbing, player to player, as though counting them, pausing, losing count, counting, pausing. The tip of the cigarette wobbling from his lips brightened then darkened.

"Can you do that?" he drawled.

Sylvester looked at the—were they scarecrows? At each whistle blast, boys crouched, arched their spines, dove shoulders into the bulging, headless uniforms. Flakes of pillow down plumed and settled on the grass, on the patches of gouged dirt, on the scarecrows' jointless arms.

"Can I . . ."

He didn't even make the scrub team, the benchmen varsity fooled with, gag plays mostly. Sylvester watched from the bleachers during band breaks, while blowing grit from the mouthpiece of his clarinet. Varsity massed around the punted ball, then scattered, with their helmets cradled in their arms, while the band laughed and pointed. Big Jim jogged for a touchdown, open-handed, with the ball tucked hunchback under his shirt.

It was Mr. Deitz who took care of Sylvester. Off-season Deitz taught in the art building, with his wife, full salary plus coaching. Indian Arts, she taught, even though the school was supposed to be erasing all that. September through November, Mr. Deitz worked in the backfield, the only twenty-five-year-old on the government enrollment sheets. Sylvester called him "S-Sir."

"All you got to do," Deitz said, "is catch the ball."

Gus, the new quarterback, rested the ball against his hip, his weight on his other leg. "Hike," he said.

Sylvester lunged, turned, but Deitz's arm reached between his, slapped the pass away. Sylvester cut left the second time, faked right the next, spun, sprinted deep, rolled wide. Deitz was there, plucking the ball, hardly grazing him sometimes, sometimes wedging his body into Sylvester's ribs, his hip, his chest. Sylvester lay on his back, unable to breathe, open-mouthed, like a fish.

Gus waved the next guy over, but Deitz shook his head, pointed the kid back, watched Sylvester hobble to the scrimmage line. Gus coached him some, where to turn, where the ball is going to be, dead into his gut, but Sylvester couldn't catch those, with or without Deitz hurdling over him. The boys were grinning now, shaking their heads, even Big Jim. Deitz let Sylvester catch a few, or nearly. The ball sprang loose before Sylvester struck ground, before Deitz's body dropped onto him, into him. The coach wasn't watching. Assistants weed the scrubs.

"Where you going?" yelled Deitz.

Pop was pointing a cigarette at another boy, hollering at him, you stupid son of a bitch. Sylvester kept his head down. The grass wasn't trampled so much as stunted, grown that way. The blades spread low.

"Come back for track cuts," Pop said. "Distance maybe. You might be good at distance."

The smell of the bakery wagon tightens Sly's stomach. The town kid is selling pies from a basket. Behind him, the stubbled fields of Farm 2 recede toward the tree line. Students clump around the bakery horse, lean against the great wooden spokes of the wagon wheels. Others are loitering at the bottom of the grandstand. Sunlight on the rows of dented metal shimmers and then flattens with Sly's approach. Nobody's watching him. The ninth lap, Sly leads, and they're not watching.

It's not a real meet. Hampton's barely a team, except for the long runner, the Negro at Sly's back. Sly sees him on the turns. His bony hands jounce with his footfalls. Sly's are fists. Pop books the college circuit—Georgetown, Johns Hopkins, Syracuse—not local teams, not some backwater Negro school from Virginia. Big Jim, Gus, even little Tewanima, they're going to Stockholm in June, for the world games. Jim's All-American. But the Commissioner in D.C. thinks it's good policy for government schools to compete, a show of support for Hampton's fledgling track program, especially with Hampton thinking to shut its Indian dorm. Good idea, agreed Mr. Friedman, though he and Pop didn't bother showing up. Deitz is running it.

The next time Sly passes the benches in the infield, Deitz looks past him. His fingers are in the air, all ten. That's halfway. He cups his hands, calls something to Gus and Tewanima. They're still holding back, slotting into line on the curves, Tewanima first. Tewanima will take first, the gold. Everybody knows that. He's a Hopi. Gus always settles for second, silver. Third place, it doesn't matter where they compete, how good the other team is, the other school's top distance man always gets third, the bronze, leaving fourth to Sly. Sly is pointless, literally pointless, every meet.

Deitz shouts at Big Jim. Big Jim nods, flicks sweat off his chin. He never runs the miles. Dashes aren't his best either. At Lafayette he swept six golds, both hurdles, both jumps, both throws, but he needs distance experience. Races, roared Pop, not jaunts through town palling with the team. Fifteen hundred meters, a mile almost—you can't win a decathlon without it. I'll pace you, Sly offered. Running partners. Jim chuckled, pulled a towel from his neck before stepping into the shower spray. "Sure," he said. His big-jawed grin wrapped halfway round his head, could have meant anything.

The Hampton boy tightens his gait on the straightaway. His shadow jabs at Sly's ankles, thrusts beside them, between them, ebbs back. Only yards before the next turn, not enough to dare a pass, but Sly surges anyway, pushes off the balls of his feet. The Negro's head bobs, eyes downcast. He keeps his own pace.

If Sly had listened to Lovie, the Hampton runner would be his teammate. She said Sylvester belonged there, first school for ex-slaves, opened right after the war. She was applying the next fall. Booker T. Washington's school. She wanted to be a teacher. So did Sylvester, or a lawyer maybe, maybe write for a newspaper, a colored paper, though everyone knew Sylvester's parents were whites practically. The neighborhood adored them, sought their advice, offered favors, hoped for a good word in exchange. The Longs were royalty.

Sylvester's mother used to pass the old Cowles mansion and admire the gardens through the iron fence, imagining which third-story window her father, Senator Cowles, hid behind. Her father was her cousin too. He'd taken a liking to his uncle's plantation and one of his daughters, one of the light-skinned slaves who came out of his uncle's concubine, a Croatan Indian, Sylvester's great-grandmother. They kept the children outside all summer, to darken them. Sylvester's mother was born the month the war ended. She had to draw on a piece of paper for Sylvester to understand, the family tree jutting in and out of itself.

His father's is simpler, all blanks mostly. Forty years he searched before finding his mother, Sylvester's grandmother, in a sharecropper's shack in Alabama, dying. She said her parents were no niggers. A white man, she told him, and a Cherokee woman, or maybe the mother was a Catawba. Sylvester's father was born a slave.

"Well Hampton's got Indians too," wrote Lovie. Booker T. taught some himself. A hundred of them still, she figured. Hampton had started a program for them before the government opened Carlisle, the first nonreservation Indian school. Carlisle was an experiment. There had been no line for Sylvester's signature on the application.

The Hampton boy gains on the straightaway again. He is plunging in and out of Sly's periphery. Sly sees the sweat on the Negro's arm, the skin like mud, the huffing of that squashed nose, the lips bobbing. Sly can't see all that. Rivulets splay the dark hairs of his own wrists. His own jaw sags.

The printshop intramural team finished four losses, one win, and a tie, worse than Sylvester's first year. He tried to talk girls from the seamshop into sewing leather patches on their jerseys, football-shaped, like the ones Pop used before the collegiate association outlawed them. Sylvester promised cakes from the downtown bakery, but the head seamstress said no; his printing teacher too.

So Sylvester focused on grades, high marks even in mathematics, his worst subject. The shortest distance between two points, Mr. Mann droned, is a line. Sylvester liked English. He recited Shylock's part in class. He liked *Ben Hur*. A noble Jewish slave saves the Roman fleet commander, becomes his adopted son. Miss Moore drew tall white letters across her blackboard: The first thing in my life that I can remember is . . .

a dull, deep bluish gray. That was the color of my early world. Everything I saw was tinted with this mystic grayness. I do not remember anything more until I was four. And then I came to life again one day in mid-air. I was in the act of falling off a horse. I do not remember sitting on the horse's back, but I remember falling through the air, hitting the ground and lying there on my back, looking up in bewilderment. . . .

In Debating Society, he argued that Lee was a better general than Grant, that country life is better than city life, that the Indian should not become a citizen of the United States. He sang at Bible study meetings. He knew the hymns from Big Meeting, the Baptist festival his family attended every October. An hour in the Jim Crow car, two more by wagon, along fields his parents once cropped, the late corn, the unshorn cotton, the scent of grinding cane, the weave of his mother's dress, the crevices in the joints of his fingers, everything veiled in that fine fine red dust, same red as the leaves overhead. What a friend, what a friend we have in Jesus. Black voices, and the whites too, rhythm of neighbors at harvest, and the preachers and the heavenly rewards.

When Joe Long moved his wife Sallie to Salem, just a county over, hardly a city yet, their new white congregation got word from their old plantation town. The Longs were Coloreds. Joe lost his counter job at the grocery. He kept to mopping and singing Sundays at the Negro Baptist, that same boasting bass Sylvester would grow into, the same hymns, always the same hymns.

Winter track was monotony, rattling the wooden planks along the gym walls, circling, never moving closer to any center. Pop noticed him though, told him to pace himself. Stick with Gus. Outside ice hung on the windowpanes. Inside, the air was thick with sweat. The glass turned translucent, with the day brighter through the drips and streaks. They looked like cracks.

Sylvester sidled closer, scissored his legs in sync. "Why they call him Pop?"

Gus exhaled as he shook his head. It was a laugh. "He's the Old Man. *Na'pi.* Sly Fox. *Phneefich.* The Coyote!"

Sylvester recognized some of the names, the codes Gus shouted from hurdles during scrimmages, gibberish to white teams. Pop would get himself thrown out for calling plays from the sidelines, then hunker in the stands, scribbling cigarettes in the air, smoke signals Gus ignored half the time. Gus was honor roll, the only brains out there. A full-blood, somebody said.

"I love that pass you threw." Sylvester was yelling, trying to be heard over the roar of the boards. "I mean that one to, who was it? Ran out of bounds, behind the benches, then cut back in. That was great! They got to rewrite the rule book every year just keeping up with you guys!"

"Hey," said Gus. "Sly. That's your name, isn't it? You're Sly too." Gus was exhaling hard again, laughing.

Tewanima nods as he passes. It looks friendly enough. He's all bones, nothing to hold him down. Gus says he's a political prisoner, that his dad led some uprising out west, on the reservation, but Sly doesn't believe it. Gus says all sorts of things.

Sly squints to count the three fingers Deitz is holding over his head. The number doesn't seem right, high or low, he isn't sure. Deitz raised the same fingers minutes ago, but he's counting laps down now, as if the track reversed itself, flung Sly in the opposite direction. He's moving backward.

Students in the stands, girls mostly, are perking up, clapping. Some shout. Tewanima's name maybe, but Sly can't make it out, or their faces. He feared Lovie would emerge with the dozen Negro boys at the town depot. But Hampton doesn't ship its players around with carloads of fans. Carlisle students vie for seats to away games, crammed in with the marching band, not first-class like the team, and three to a hotel bed. Lovie wouldn't do that. She stopped writing before Sly could ask her to. The return address was too dangerous, a Negro dorm, worse than Winston. It was just small talk anyway. She wasn't waiting anymore.

"A couple dozen or so," she answered in her last letter. "They stick to themselves."

Deitz pulled Sly aside before the meet. The discus sack swung against his back. He pointed at the shot puts on the closet floor. It was hours yet, too early to be placing equipment.

"You know, my wife," he said, "she went to Hampton, before art school."

Sly trudged beside him. It was uphill. He was nodding.

"Five years she spent with them, all kinds, mulattoes, quadroons, octoroons," he said. "Hated it." His eyes ran along the side of Sylvester's head, where sweat pricked his scalp. Deitz kept slowing down, was hardly walking at all.

The sun smoldered behind a haze of cloud, low still, but burning through. Sly squinted. He kept following.

"Teachers mocked her, all the Indians. See how much the darkies know? Aren't you smarter than a dumb darky?"

He was squinting at Sylvester, as if waiting for an answer. Sylvester swallowed. "So she'd hate the darkies instead? Not the—the teachers?"

Deitz dropped his mesh sack. Metal rattled against metal then stilled. They were yards from the field edge.

"She can still spot them," he said. "Even the white ones."

Sly asked him where he wanted the other sack, and Deitz shrugged, told him to walk it back to the dorm. They didn't need it.

The footfalls at his back aren't the Negro's. Gus rounds his elbow, hovers there. The *C* on his Carlisle shirt jounces against his chest, spotted with sweat, but more white than gray, not soaked through like Sly's, not clinging like sloughing skin. Gus waits till he is holding Sylvester's eyes.

"Bronze," he says. He's nodding, so Sly nods too. "You're bronze, Long."

"Bronze," he calls back, or tries to. It's air mostly. Sly keeps nodding, his whole body is.

Gus hangs another moment next to him, like a bird, then pushes off. Tewanima is already in the turn. All those level plains out west, horizons of it. It's not fair.

They're closing the program there, Lovie wrote, for the Indians' good. The teachers say it's bad mingling races. Poor Injun getting dragged down. Good riddance. That's what she wrote.

On their last night in Winston, Sylvester strolled her down Fourth, toward the theater where Sylvester's brother took tickets at the stairs to the Colored balcony. Four years, he was saying, I'm home again. We'll be married. When a white couple turned the corner of Main, heading the opposite direction, Sylvester stepped off the sidewalk. His hand rose and clutched his cap. Lovie still held his elbow, still smiling. The heel of her boot shattered a puddle. Sylvester looked at the white girl. Her eyes were the blue of her pale dress, and her skin almost the same shade as Sylvester's mother's. Not like Lovie's, whose face could spill into a shadow, her cheek or throat bleed into shade.

He remembers Lovie in the train window, the engine smoke unraveling gray between them. It's not moisture from her kiss drying on his cheek now. His face is streaming with sweat.

The heaving behind him, it's the Negro. Sly feels him. So stupid, the creature jockeys out of the lane, the inner lane, before the track straightens. Twice as far. You learn that in Geometry. Sly looks back, once, twice. Third time his neck barely swivels. He doesn't look at the face, only the shoulder, how it jerks. The rhythm is even. Sly isn't moving like that. The sweat blurring the track, it's water Sly is pushing through. His lungs buoy him. They're too big to hold under.

He shoves against the cinders, watches the player's heels, shoves more. Next Big Jim swerves to miss him, doesn't look back. The lane is moving too fast. It's a circle, a globe, spinning under him. Something else shudders past, a runner, two others. What lap? His body is filling with water. He can't find Deitz, or the stands. The grass veers up at him, at his face. He holds it back with both hands, all ten fingers. Metal in his throat constricts, widens, constricts, until his stomach opens. The spasms shove him forward. He's being struck, from inside, his own muscles, his own body. Webs sway from his lips and nostrils. They're translucent. Is he crying?

Sylvester wipes at his face, wipes his hand on the grass. There's someone there beside him, a coach, a Hampton coach. The ankles are dark above the dirt-stained socks. "You okay? You gonna be okay, son?"

Sylvester feels the hand between the blades of his shoulders. It's a light touch, fingertips, but he can't shake them free. He can't rise. He can't speak.

Ivy Is Accosted

"A priest and his nuns," her teacher says. Ivy keeps her face forward, eyes on the music, as Mr. Stauffer's callused fingertips graze her knuckles. "It's a harem really." He stops her. She is rushing the bridge. "Begin again here."

Ivy withdraws her hands from the piano, curls and splays the fingers twice, and arranges them across the keys again. The rectangles of sunlight paling on the band room floor have left the air cool and brittle.

"What is that?" she asks. "A 'harem.'"

Mr. Stauffer chats too much during lessons, but if ignored he grows testy. Last week he caught Ivy's pinky as he slammed the piano closed. He is grinning in her periphery now. The bench creaks as he leans his gut toward her.

"You don't know?"

Ivy does not turn. It isn't a question meant to be answered. Mr. Stauffer always grins at her. He started calling her "Countess Giulietta" the afternoon he unfolded the new pages on the music stand. He waited two weeks to tell her that the composer had dedicated the sonata to a seventeen-year-old student, a countess, his lover. Ivy knows the first movement now, though Mr. Stauffer still sighs and scowls over her execution, the nuances, the color of the notes. Her hands remain on the keys.

"Begin," he says.

He is not much of a teacher, and, even Ivy can see, less of a musician—his career spent clapping rows of teenagers into order, parading them around football fields, berating them for the same missed beats and false starts. He is handier with a paddle, or the block of wood he used on Ivy's best friend, Julia, while the matrons held her on the storage room floor last month. Julia showed her the bruises up her back and her shoulder and her arm. Still, when Mr. Stauffer played the sonata for Ivy that first time, something in her rose with the top notes, that queer third voice that wafted between his stumpy digits. When her own fingers tap the same keys, she thinks of Miss Moore's typing drills.

Mr. Stauffer strokes the air between them, slowly, urgently, pushing back her rising cadence. "Foolish," he says, "to think a man's not a man under the cloth. Priests have needs too, only they lie, and the Catholics are children enough to believe them. Adagio, Ivy. Adagio."

Her left hand, the weaker hand, stumbles but does not stop. The run is difficult. She is picturing Father Stock, the way his gray moustache curls over his pink lips. Every fourth week he takes his turn leading nondenominational prayers in the school chapel while Ivy's knees shift in the wooden pews. He wrote to Washington and made the superintendent release the Catholic students to Mass at St. Patrick's every Sunday, with or without a teacher chaperone, the way the football players can go to town anytime they like. Mr. Stauffer leans forward as Ivy pushes through the bridge, those treacherous triplets, and exhales.

"You lived in a convent, didn't you?"

Ivy is staring at the yellowed sheet, at the creases crisscrossing the staves, but she does not read the notes. She knows them. "Yes," she says, quickly, as though breathing between gasps through a flute. One year, ninth grade, she spent at the Pawhuska mission school in the Saint Louis Convent, before transferring to Carlisle.

"Sostenuto," he says. "The notes must resonate beyond their value." Ivy's foot presses the pedal harder. Her left foot keeps time. "That must have been difficult for you. The hypocrisy. The other students were probably too naive." His fingers slip through a gap in his shirt and scratch between the buttons. "What are you again?"

He knows this too, has quizzed her before, but he nods as though newly pleased when Ivy mumbles, "Episcopalian."

His chin rises and drops in time with the half notes. Most of the girls at the convent weren't Catholic either, but Grace told her to pretend. You'll need high marks when you apply to a real school, a school with boys. The nuns like believers. It's easy. Go to the back of the communion line and watch what they do. Orphan instinct, Grace called it. Ivy did not like the way the wooden door of the confessional scraped shut, the next girl in line always too distant to eavesdrop. There must be codes, mores, notes more nuanced than Ivy's ear can detect. Grace is lucky. She graduated. She married someone. Ivy's brother-in-law is a perfectly nice man. He is in telephones or appliances or something. Grace says Ivy will be lucky—no, blessed—to steal a man half as decent.

Mr. Stauffer turns the page before she completes the bottom measure. It is an awkward break, one that used to make her falter as the melody shifts to the bass notes. Mr. Stauffer is watching the paper, not her hands. "The priest beds a different sister every night," he says. "They have orgies on holy days, worse than any brothel. Thank God you escaped when you did."

She strikes the wrong note twice, thrice, yanks her hands back in tiny fists. It is a lie of course. The nuns were good to her. She looks up at Stauffer's stubbled jowls. His shirt collar is open under his tie.

"They didn't give music training," she says. That's what Grace printed on Ivy's application, the excuse for transferring to a better high school, practically a college. Ivy is learning a trade here, a livelihood. Grace's husband couldn't keep supporting her. "Or nursing," she adds.

Mr. Stauffer raises first his right eyebrow and then his left. "Nursing?" His laugh is so loud, so mirthless, Ivy knows it means something else, a reference to something she does not, cannot know. When he closes his eyes and rubs them, Ivy imagines the tug of his pocked cheeks under her fingernails. She looks at her hands, at the nails' spoon-round edges, filed every evening with the emery board she found on the floor of the reading room. She hopes they are pretty hands. She keeps them soft with the jar of Vaseline she purchased with the first of her summer earnings, not the lard she used to massage into her knuckles during kitchen detail.

Mr. Stauffer reaches for the middle sheet, flips it, and taps. "Here." Ivy squints and finds her place. Stauffer watches her face. "You're Welch's girl, aren't you, his new one?"

Her fingers lift, hang an instant, then drift down again. Stauffer means Gus Welch. The football captain. Gus walked right up to her and Julia in front of the chocolate shop last Saturday, a girls' Saturday in town, and bought them both dipped pretzels, because strawberries are out of season. They smiled and swayed in identical uniforms—Mr. Friedman requires them off-campus. Gus's collar was unbuttoned, and the button beneath it. Gus had been admiring them, he said, from down the block. Ivy glanced toward the corner hydrant. He couldn't have told them apart from that distance, the same height, the same dark columns of hair. On Monday Gus moved his seat between theirs in Commercial Law. He had trouble seeing the board, he said, a joke even Miss Moore smiled at. He had thrown a forty-yard pass the day before. Gus could choose anyone. Any of those boys on the team can.

"He's Catholic," says Stauffer. Ivy is straining not to rush the bridge again, not to stab at each key. "And a brainy one too, honor roll. You can be sure he knows what goes on in a rectory at night. Welch is the sort of boy who would end up in the priesthood. I mean, if it weren't for football. The privileges they get in that dorm. Believe me, you don't need to know."

Ivy's foot beats randomly, but her hands keep in time, like waves on a moonlit lake, Mr. Stauffer told her. Big Jim, the new halfback, is Catholic too. Ivy knows that. He made All-American again. He and Gus will be on the Olympic track team next year. Everybody thinks so. Last week when the carpentry teacher spotted Jim swinging drunk beside Gus in the bell tower, cause for expulsion, Mr. Friedman did nothing. Instead, the coach put Jim in Miss Moore's classes to keep him with the rest of the backfield. A row of blanks hangs from his name in the grade book. But he is very polite, knocks that smart-aleck Loud Bear in the back of the skull whenever Miss Moore looks away. They aren't bad boys. Gus says only the prettiest girls get into business classes, girls like her and Julia, though Julia wasn't there when he said it. Julia is still in lockup in the Girls' Quarters. She and three of her friends will be there all week. Julia won't see Gus play this Sunday.

Mr. Stauffer's finger rises, and his lips part. Ivy's rhythm isn't right, she knows that, but he says nothing, just sighs through his nose again. His hand lowers, incrementally, as though by gears, as Ivy keeps playing.

The grandstand couldn't fit the free-admission crowd for the final home game last week, but the business girls always get seats. Dickinson lost by forty-three points. Jim and Gus made the most of their first quarter, stoking the bleachers into chants as they ran consecutive touchdowns. Ivy does not understand the school cheer, some amalgam of Indian words, but she shouted it until her throat burned. She pastes the articles into her scrapbook every Wednesday after lunch, after Miss Moore is done with the business department's copy of the town newspaper. Big Jim's name always comes first.

The bench creaks as Mr. Stauffer leans back again, his arms folding above his paunch. "Mind you," he says, "I support the team. They bring a great deal of honor to this school. And champions are entitled to certain liberties. I've turned a blind eye more than once myself. But what's good for a school isn't always good for a young lady such as yourself. You know that, don't you?"

Because her face is supposed to be rigid with concentration, Ivy does not have to answer. She realizes now Mr. Stauffer introduced the topic of priests so he could use it to describe the team. And he brought up Gus so he could talk about her. Mr. Stauffer always wants to talk about her. Ivy is the goal of all his digressions. It surprises her how easy it is to see through others, their variations, their rote melodies. It is not necessary to enter the small room of their thoughts. It is not necessary to hear their confessions. Ivy knows Mr. Stauffer would rather have bedded Julia than beaten her. Ivy knows Mr. Stauffer would rather bed her than keep listening to the plunk of these ill-tuned keys. She keeps squinting at the paper, at the blur of notes.

"You know that," repeats Mr. Stauffer. "A beautiful girl like you must be very careful."

Ivy's face warms, and she smiles, unwillingly. Her fingers keep pressing keys. Pretty, she suspected. But beautiful? It is dangerous to stand out. Grace taught her that. Miss Ridenour—now the head matron—slapped a senior at inspection this morning, not for scuffed shoes or grimy palms, but for the cut of her hair, the newest fashion. Ridenour yanked the strip of calico free and knotted the locks into a frumpish bun. When the girl descended the stairs again minutes later, her hair tied in a French braid as before, the matron swung so hard only the balustrade kept the girl from tumbling. The girl is rich. She was wearing the new dress her parents shipped her last week. Ivy doesn't have that problem. Ivy knows how to keep on Ridenour's good side, but without snitching, even when a student officer dunked her towel in toilet water and a dead mouse stained the bottom of her trunk. That was her first year. This is her third now, her last. Other girls smile at her, enviously. She still avoids the clannish ones, and if she thinks a teacher favors her for her fair skin or green eyes, Ivy is the first to mock her, imitating the queer way Miss Moore enunciates, as if holding a pebble on the back of her tongue. The other business girls laugh.

"I'm sure," says Mr. Stauffer, "you know about the ruined girl."

The flat note is not Ivy's fault. The piano has not been tuned this semester, not this year probably. She knows which keys stick, which to work lightly.

"Mr. Friedman is making arrangements to have her shipped to a Philadelphia hospital. She's due at Christmas." He sniggers before repeating the joke Ivy has heard already. "Maybe it's immaculate."

Ivy sometimes speaks to the ruined girl in the infirmary, where the girl is living now. She is barred from the dorms and the school building, and from the socials obviously. The other girls say it is a disgrace to allow her in the open where visitors could see her. Their petition says so. Ivy signed it when Julia handed it to her. The girl came back from the summer Outing program heavier but not showing. She was not the only one. Father Stock married a boy and girl in the chapel last month—the pair that used to meet at the dispensary, a daily four o'clock coincidence. They used an empty room on the side wing. Ivy told no one, even when asked, even by Mr. Friedman.

She completes the final measure, allowing the last isolated notes to linger, but Mr. Stauffer is not listening. He is tilted toward the door. Ivy didn't hear the next student, a girl named Agnes, enter. Agnes does not wear the heavy black government shoes Ivy wears. Agnes snuck out of the dorm with her eyebrows blackened too. Once the superintendent's wife was seen in powders and paints at the first gymnasium social, Ridenour gave up, or nearly.

Mr. Stauffer stands and greets her loudly. He likes Agnes. She has a beautiful voice. Even Ivy can hear that. Agnes does not wade through the same piece week after week. He asks about the soreness in her throat she suffered the day before, while Ivy stands and gathers her books. Harem. Of course she knows the word.

"Did you hear," says Mr. Stauffer, "Agnes is going with us to the Georgetown game next weekend? She's going to sing for the mayor and deacon."

Ivy says she did not know, congratulations, and then the two girls pretend to smile at each other. Ivy will have to purchase her own ticket and cram in with the other students, though at least the business girls always claim a separate section for themselves, nearest the Pullman car when possible. Gus says Agnes is a whore. All the boys do, all but Jim. Jim is never mean about any girl.

"You sound very nice," says Agnes. She means the piano. Ivy thanks her, while trying to muffle the beat of her heels as she walks. Her black stockings bunch and droop under her dress. Government issue is cheap.

Mr. Stauffer is speaking as Ivy rounds the band room door, and Agnes's laughter, a bright affected trill, follows her outside. Triplets ring between Ivy's steps. She prefers a marching cadence, curt, unadorned. The sonata composer, Mr. Stauffer told her more than once, did not choose the title. The sonata was not moonlight when he wrote it. And the girl, the countess, was an afterthought too. Mr. Stauffer guffaws every time he repeats the fact. Foolish, he called him, lusting after girls above his station. The composer died alone, in a thunderstorm, shaking his fist at God. Mr. Stauffer tells all kinds of stories. It annoys Ivy when they are true, especially ones about Gus. Mr. Stauffer understands Gus.

Students crisscross the wooden walkways as the sun slumps behind the gymnasium roof. Another group huddles in the gazebo. The bell to release the afternoon shops was rung early again, by one of the older boys, a bored officer probably. Ivy steps through a drift of leaves swirling on the steps and paces toward the Girls' Quarters, past Mr. Stauffer's house. He lives alone in a two-family faculty bungalow overlooking the school lawn, his because Mr. Friedman values his half-time and commencement spectacles, the pomp of his parades. His band blares battle tunes while students pull the football team in farm wagons, victory chariots they call them, around and around the dirt track. Ivy applauds until her hands throb, bruised almost. Everyone does.

She enters the dorm by the door nearest Ridenour's office. The hour before the dinner bell is Ivy's only free time. She usually stops at Miss Moore's room or the superintendent's building, to help with paperwork, the government attendance sheets the clerk falsifies with truants' names. The business girls did office work unchaperoned until a new girl was caught talking with a boy, a student janitor, alone. The others knew when to risk it, for how long. Other days Ivy visits the grandstand to watch practices with Julia, when Julia isn't in lockup. They sit on the bottom bench, and Gus strolls over and talks to them. He slouches with his elbow on the wooden slats, and their knees tighten under their dresses, level with his chin. Big Jim smiles and waves, but he stays at the benches.

Ivy knocks at Ridenour's open door. The matron's dark head bobs up from her desk then tilts back down as she keeps scribbling. "What do you want?"

Miss Ridenour does not like business girls. They get too many privileges over there in Miss Moore's department, she says, an imbalance she likes to correct. Julia takes the brunt. Ivy knows when to smile, when to nod blankly. She always says "Thank you" in a high soft voice. The worst she receives are demerits. Two points this morning for improperly tied shoelaces. She did not protest, not like Julia would have. Ivy had laced them intentionally crooked. She explained it to Gus in the note she passed to him that morning while Miss Moore was diagramming sentences on the blackboard. Gus didn't need to know all the details, just the timing, the place, but Ivy wanted to appear smart to him, smarter than she needs to be, than Gus wants her to be.

"Miss Ridenour?" she says. "I was wondering if it would be okay if I could work off those demerits now? Would that be allowed?"

Ridenour squints. Her eyes would not be ugly otherwise. That is the thought Ivy is focusing on. Ivy keeps her own face open and attentive.

"Toilets," says Ridenour. "You like scrubbing toilets?"

Ivy curls her mouth into a glum smile. More than two demerits and you risk losing a Saturday in town or an evening at a social. Talk in line and you could spend an hour standing at attention. Sassing could put you in lockup. But two points are nothing. Only Ridenour assigns bathroom detail. Ivy knows that. She says, "Yes, ma'am."

"Supplies are in the back hall."

The matron reaches for her hip and rattles a ring of keys onto the desk. The dorm knows the sound, a warning shudder. Ridenour muffles them sometimes, when she caught a pair of girls in the same bed, strapped them both. They were only sleeping. Most of the girls grew up in boarding schools, two to a bed, the way Ivy and Grace used to sleep at the orphan home. They are all orphans here.

Ridenour unstrings one key and sets it at the desk edge. "This opens the closet only." It is worn and coppery, almost black. Ivy steps forward, retrieves it, and steps back. "If you're done before a half hour, I won't count it."

"Yes, ma'am."

A clock ticks on the desk where Ivy cannot read it, but Ivy knows the time, not a quarter past yet. On Tuesdays the team breaks into running squads by four o'clock. They loop around the school graveyard and the north farm and down into town. They won't be seen again until the five o'clock bells. There will be just enough time.

Ivy trots through the rear parlor to the closet beside the uniform room. Ridenour's key quivers in her fingers. She uses her other hand to guide it into the lock. Her stomach churns. She is humming staccato notes under her breath. When she hears a voice, a muffled voice from behind the adjacent door, she falls silent, her spine tight. The voice shouts: "Who's that?"

Ivy's face is blank again, or almost blank. Her reflexive smile remains. A different voice, a different girl, calls through the uniform room door: "Come on, who's out there?"

Ivy looks behind her, toward the front hall, toward the head matron's office. They know she isn't Ridenour. Her gait is too light, her hesitation too long. "Me," says Ivy.

There is a scuffling behind the wall. It's Julia's voice now. "Ivy, is that you?"

Ivy nods, to no one, before trying the knob. It is never locked. No one wants more uniforms, not when their parents cram their trunks with such pretty things. The door scrapes the jamb as Ivy pushes. "Don't yell," she whispers.

The lockuup is a cramped corner room made obsolete by renovations. Its single window faces not outside, but into the uniform room, a room inside a room. The window frame is nailed with a four-inch gap at the top, for air. Ivy closes the door soundlessly. Heads vie in the window squares, as Ivy's own face warps in reflection. Ivy wonders what Father Stock sees through the tiny window in his St. Patrick's confessional. She assumes it is Father Stock inside. She never saw the priest at Pawhuska enter or leave that closet of a room, but she glimpsed inside it once when the door was left ajar—just a bench, hardly the width of a person's body, like an outhouse.

Julia shoulders to the front and touches her fingertips to the glass. "We're dying in here." Her hair separates from the darkness when she moves, then sifts back. "Get water before Ridenour comes."

Ivy has never been in lockup, but she understands. Ridenour keeps the girls day and night. They can't go work at the laundry the way Mrs. Denny allowed when she was head matron. Their dining hall plates come an hour late dolloped with portions more meager than the kitchen staff dare serve in person. They pee into a pitcher. Julia and the others were caught by Ridenour in an empty third-floor room with a group of boys after lights-out. That's what Ivy heard, not from Julia but from the other business girls. Julia hasn't spoken to Ivy about it. Mr. Friedman confined two of the boys to the guardhouse when they weren't shoveling coal in the boiler basement. The band captain was in there already, for not leading the anthem at the last game. The boys couldn't have broken in if Julia hadn't removed the hasps from the side door. The other two boys are on the team. That's what Ivy heard.

"Hurry up," hisses a girl. She is a shimmer of gray behind Julia's head, almost invisible in the dark box of the room. The nuns told Ivy no one but God can see those who confess. The opening between the booths was masked in lace. The priest can see too, of course, but he doesn't count.

The pail from the closet swings in Ivy's fist as she trots down the basement steps two at a time. It is a risk. Ridenour wouldn't bother recording demerit points in her green booklet. She would shove Ivy in with the others. It doesn't matter what the student court-martial board ruled later. No one cares what the officers think anymore. Ivy only has to worry about the popular girls. It is necessary to be liked by the right ones, and the right teachers, and disliked too, just enough. Ivy understands the balance, which surprises her, the way compliments surprise her. Sometimes Julia says Ivy's eyes are too far apart, or her cheeks are too flat, exaggerations that make Ivy blush. Gus said he likes her eyes. Jim did too. But Jim compliments everybody, dances with all the girls in the gymnasium each month. He doesn't pick favorites. Jim could have anyone, even one of Gus's girls, any of them, even Ivy maybe.

Ivy glances into the tub and shower room, then turns toward the row of seats along the metal trough. The basement is empty. It isn't four-thirty yet.

"Hello?"

Her voice echoes and dips into the dark spaces. She worries it sounds flirtatious, cheap.

The pail clanks under the first tap as she twists the valve, then she can hear nothing else. Leaning into the mirror, she pinches her cheeks, hard, what would make her gasp if done to her by someone else. Her hair is still neat, but she fusses a moment with it, with the ribbons, before sliding her hands down her ribs and hips. It is her newest dress, her best, the one she saved the longest for. It is not as nice as some of the other girls', but Ridenour could have noticed, still could, another risk. If Ivy had been adopted, all of her dresses would be nicer than this one. She would be better than the rich girls. She used to work so hard to stand out in a parade of children through a banquet hall or down a carpeted staircase. The trick was pretending you already knew that someone had picked you. It was just a matter of recognizing them, searching each pair of eyes, asking, is it you? Are you the one I'm going to love?

After working the wrinkles in her stockings to the tops of her thighs, Ivy tears an arm's length of paper towel from the roll on the ledge and listens again after twisting the spigot off. Her ears can detect nothing. She probably has time.

Upstairs the hall is empty. Ivy slips into the uniform room and seals the door behind her. Julia is at the inner window. "Roll the towel into a funnel," Julia says. Ivy already is. Then she unloads a stack of skirts from a low cabinet before pushing it under the window and climbing up. Julia is standing on a stool on the other side of the glass with her face at the opening along the top. She has to bend. The pail sloshes as Ivy lifts it.

"That's too much. You won't be able to pour it."

"Don't you have a cup or something?"

Julia says something to the other girls, who laugh. They don't have a cup. "Just tilt it to my mouth." Ivy balances on the cabinet while other hands hold the paper funnel in place. Julia half-kneels. The palm of her right hand presses flat and pink against the glass. Her mouth is open. "Go ahead."

Ivy begins with a trickle, then a gagging rush that makes everyone giggle, even Julia, after she curses and mops her neck. Ivy apologizes. For the next girl she does better, but still splashes at the end when she pulls away, the girl's eyes wide from choking or the fear of it. When the sisters in Pawhuska took communion, their eyes always closed that instant when the priest placed the wafer on their tongues. When Julia takes her last turn, Ivy tilts the pail back at just the right moment. They spill nothing.

As Ivy steps down from the cabinet, Julia asks, "How's Gus?"

Ivy returns the stack of skirts, presses them flat and even. "Great," she says. She can't see Julia now, not really. Almost all the light is gone. Soon it will be pitch-black in there, not a glimmer till morning. "He's great," she says.

Miss Ridenour nearly catches her in the hall, as the uniform door clicks behind her. Ivy smiles sheepishly. "I forgot the brush." She reaches for the scrubber on the open closet shelf. "I was using rags," she says, "but I couldn't get the mildew along the bottom edge." She illustrates with her hands, bending to show the angle.

Ridenour nods, smiles almost, then gestures at the lockup with her chin. Her fingers are splayed on her hips. "They making any noise in there?"

Ivy turns to look. "A little, I guess," she says. "Laughing about something."

Ridenour regards the uniform room door, then rattles her keys, unconsciously, probably unconsciously. When she holds out her hand, Ivy places the blackened copper key into her palm. "You go on down now," says Ridenour.

The basement has darkened over the last fifteen minutes. Ivy pulls the light cord and pictures streetlamps blinking on across town. She does not know where exactly the boys run on Tuesdays, only that they are unsupervised but for the assistant coaches, former players themselves, some dating students too, secretly. She heard Gus was one of the boys found in the dorm with Julia, but Ivy doesn't know if it is true. It's a rumor. That's what she said when one of the first-years told her. You can't trust rumors. Ivy tilted her neck when she said it, her half smile at just the right, knowing angle. The coach might have suspended Gus for Georgetown, maybe, but after that it's Harvard and Syracuse, the toughest games of the season, according to Mr. Stauffer. Gus is their most valuable player, everyone says so. Next to Jim of course.

With the bulbs humming, no light escapes the edges of the boarded windows along the ceiling. It could be midnight out there. The boards were nailed in place before Ivy arrived at Carlisle, for the girls' protection, but there are a dozen ways into a dorm. The matrons can't be everywhere.

As Ivy refills the pail, the water splashes in triplets, and her left hand fingers notes on the sink edge. The sisters said she would be good at piano, perhaps very good. Her thumb and pinky stretch an octave. According to Mr. Stauffer, she will never perform in anything but school recitals, though she does have other talents. She is pretty. Imagine, he said, that poor little countess wooed by a bore, a slob. The man dunked his head in a bucket before composing. The piss pot beside his pedals brimmed.

Ivy hears something, turns, but the room is empty. Puddles on the cement floor ripple where she stepped. She twists off the spigot and dunks the sponge and runs it along the metal shelf before the mirror. Mr. Stauffer's voice drones in her head. The composer was deaf. The composer was in love. He hated that sonata. He hated performing it, always suffering the same compliments. Surely, he railed, I've written better. Surely there's more than this.

When she looks up, Gus is standing in the mirror. He is smirking. Gray stains press his shirt against his chest. Ivy startles, for no reason. Such a pretty boy, she thinks, practically as handsome as Jim. She likes Gus, though she wishes she liked him more. Then Ivy shapes her mouth into her favorite smile and turns her spine like a corkscrew, her shoulders balanced. She waves at him, shyly, waves as though fingering a run on Mr. Stauffer's piano.

Sylvester Pretends to Search for a Missing Child

The Arnolds' neighbor drives the Indian to their house, or as near as he can. He knots the reins on a low branch and walks him the last quarter mile past the other wagons and carriages cramping the lane. "Must be two hundred men in those hills now." He raises his chin at the tallest peak and squints. The Indian—he said his name was Long Lance—doesn't look. A black-and-white pinto slashes its tail against the front of the judge's buggy, while gnawing the weeds at the road edge into a sickle of dirt. The neighbor imagines what the road will look like with all the wheel ruts after the searchers have given up, and the mounds of evenly spaced droppings, except where the automobiles are standing now. He's never seen one of them out here before.

"My father," says the Indian. He stops to run his hand across the pinto's jaw, sliding his fingertips under its halter. "He rode a horse of these markings. Rode into last battle against the palefaces." The neighbor recognizes the buggy, all leathery and polished and those frilly spokes, but has never regarded the animal before, the strips of black across its ribs, the dark wedge high in its white neck. The flies grazing at its eye ducts disperse, buzz, return. "Good omen," says the Indian.

The neighbor touches the Indian's sleeve—a cotton shirt, same as store mannequins wear downtown, only with an ironing burn along one shoulder. "Way I see it," he says, "the fifty dollars the commissioners raised for the reward, half that's mine, since you wouldn't even be here if it weren't me bringing you. That's fair, see?"

The Indian is young, twenty or so, if you can judge by the swarthy skin, the queer skull under it. Maybe his shoulders widen, slightly, as he listens. He blinks.

"The money. You understand what I'm saying?"

Probably that Indian school only teaches practical things, hammering nails and sawing boards, leave the financials to the white man. The neighbor climbs the porch steps first. The front door hangs wide. Inside a child, a boy, shirtless and wet-haired, crouches on the top stair, eyes the newcomers, and flees. The neighbor watches the Indian watch the ceiling as the footsteps rattle to the back of the house. A chair leg scrapes behind the kitchen door, muffled by bodies and a hushed murmur of women. Only the archway to the sitting room is open.

The reverend is stalking behind the rocking chair by the window. "Did the state policemen, did they tell you to go see that fortune teller?" His collar, the brightest square of white in the room, in the house, vanishes in the glow of the glass.

Mr. Arnold, the missing girl's father, perches at the edge of the rocker, tilting it almost to the points of its curved bottom boards, and stares into the rug. "I didn't see her, Albert did. And why—" He twists, lets the chair roll back. "Why the hell shouldn't we?" He's never sworn at a preacher before, not before today. You can see that, and how good and ugly it feels. "Been searching since Monday and nobody's found a *damn* thing."

The judge reaches across the arm of the sofa. Mismatched afghans drape it, cover everything but the corner of stuffing blooming at the foot. "Can I see that again, Bill?"

He is pointing at the scrap of paper in the father's hand. Arnold gives it to him, and then he rubs the stubble of his chin against his empty palm, in circles, his fingers twitching. The reverend studies the porch through the window and the pillars buckling in the warped glass.

"I mean, look at these numbers, Bill, five hundred and sixty-seven feet from house, one thousand three hundred and sixty-three feet from field, which field?"

"The pasture where she was."

"Is it some kind of grave she's telling us to look for?"

"No. No, it is not. She said Alice was definite, definitely alive."

"Excuse me, Your Honor?" The neighbor raps his knuckles against the wallpaper before stepping to one side. His other hand is open, gesturing like a magician's. "I would like to introduce you here to Mr. Long Lance. Mr. Long Lance is agreeing to join in on our search. He's a skilled tracker, from way out west, maybe the most skilled woodsman ever attended the Indian school down in Carlisle. Thought he just might be able to turn up something finally."

The judge climbs out of the sofa, notices the paper in his hand, and pockets it in his vest. He would offer the hand in welcome, but the Indian does not step nearer, does not bend in acknowledgment, does not move. The father rocks forward again.

"We are obliged to you, sir," the judge says. "Any help, any help whatsoever, is mightily obliged."

It's the reverend who shakes the Indian's hand, says how he didn't know students were permitted so far from school grounds unchaperoned. He hopes the young man is not risking expulsion on their account. They have some mighty strict rules down there in Carlisle, he hears, for their own benefit of course, for the students' benefit. The reverend's arm has stopped pumping, but he's still gripping the Indian's coppery hand. What brings the young man up to Ickesburg anyway?

"Ah, now," says the neighbor, "I'm sure his principal won't begrudge Mr. Long Lance using his natural abilities to do some good for his fellow man, now would he?"

All four men lead the Indian across the pasture, to the juncture of cow trails where the girl's eldest brother and the sister said they'd seen Alice last, standing there by the big rock, just standing there, after the boy had yelled at her to go home, after maybe switching her once with the stick he was prodding the heifer with, not that hard though, across the shoulders maybe, 'cause she wouldn't listen, three times she wouldn't. The rest is hearsay. The sound of a child crying, a stranger in the woods with a girl at nightfall. The men look toward the hill slopes, the trees, the sun squinting back.

"She wasn't gone fifteen minutes before we got after her, the six of us scattered all over here, yelling after her and all."

"Probably fifty men by noon," adds the judge. "Two, three times that by morning, and more than that now still."

"How many?" asks the Indian.

"Well, hard to say, but I would have to estimate almost three hundred in all, if you count—"

"How many days?"

"Monday," says the reverend. "Four days." The reverend describes the search procedure, the lines of men, no more than a yard between them, pushing through brush, vines, rock, all of it now trampled, uprooted. They had to crawl at times, beat snakes with clubs, scramble up boulders. At night their lanterns swarmed the hillsides. Four days.

"I suppose it's pretty hopeless," the judge says, but the Indian is crouching, inspecting a curve of heel in the soft dirt, a large one, one of the men's. The father watches.

When the Indian rises and, without another word or glance at the men, strides up the hill, the neighbor trots after him, waving over his shoulder as the grass thickens and parts at their knees. The judge volunteers to lead a few men around to the place the soothsayer instructed—to be prudent, he says, to the father, though of course he doesn't believe a word himself, he reminds the reverend. No one moves until the Indian ducks beyond the deepest branches.

May 14, 1912
The Longs
4 ½ Street
Salem, North Carolina

Dear Mother and Father,

I'm afraid that the Pennsylvania track and field meet I wrote to you about last month turned out a disappointment. I hope that you are not too disheartened to hear that I did not qualify for any of the finals. The competition was high, even though neither Swarthmore nor Washington and Jefferson attended this year. Penn State was also away. Of course my Carlisle teammates are competition enough for any runner, especially a bookish son such as yours. I am sure you would agree that my time is better employed writing my commencement speech than running in circles like my Olympic-bound teammates. Superintendent Friedman says that he looks forward to hearing my words of wisdom and encouragement to my peers, and I do not intend to disappoint him.

Despite my ill sporting luck, I can report that my brief sojourn from Carlisle was an unexpected educational experience, perhaps my most personally rewarding since becoming a student. There was a great deal of talk and commotion regarding a child who had wandered into the Tuscaroras. She was but three or four. Of course I volunteered my services when I heard and joined the many dozens of dedicated men already in exhausted search. I imagined you, Mother, the stricken look upon your face if one of my brothers or I should have vanished at so tender an age. I remember well the tears I brought to you when I left our home, and I regret the pain I caused you still, despite the vast world it continues to open to me. I would still be in Winston-Salem today, swabbing library floors with Father, instead of drafting the pages that may someday sit upon those shelves. How, by the way, are my brothers? Are they still taking tickets and serving drinks in the Colored hall?

Late spring, the hillside is thick, but a young green, the leaves bright around their veins. Some lower branches swing broken, but the damage is worst where the child could not have gone, over crags and through nests of brambles. The Indian keeps to the path. Creepers line its edges but do not venture across the strip of dry dirt at its center. The neighbor follows, watching the Indian's shoes, the way he steps heel to toe, like a tightrope walker, and wondering what mark a child's shoe could leave. Those aren't moccasins he's wearing. That Indian school doesn't allow things like that, the neighbor knows that much. They might bring them in wild as cattle, but a good shearing and shoeing and they're halfway to civilized right off. The outside half anyways. He's just hoping those teachers didn't scoop all the Indian out of his insides too.

When the Indian crouches again, with his hand on a shelf of rock, his face near to it, close enough to lick the crumbled edge, the neighbor stretches. His calves tingle. They have kept a trotting pace, the pauses unpredictable, fleeting or lingering depending on how the Indian hovers over a twig or a tuft of dirt or, it seems, nothing at all, like a dog scenting air, weighing a wisp in its lungs, the way he is now. The neighbor stretches again, and yawns.

"That state trooper, Sergeant Markley, he got himself bit poking like that.

Copperhead. He's laid out up at the Lesh house, where they got all the police quartered, just the lane down from me." The neighbor taps a knot of clay from his boot, leans his shoulder against a tree, and fingers the tread. "More excitement than we've had round here since the War."

The neighbor doesn't have to squint when he follows the rattle of a branch and a squirrel's plunge. Not much past noon, but the light is changing with all the clouds wheeling over the treetops. Rain maybe. The leaves are shuddering. It sounds like water, a waterfall, or an ocean, far off somewhere, up near the top of that next ridge maybe, toward where the Indian is walking again.

Yesterday, when the neighbor went out, after sleeping a good night in his bed and eating the second plate of eggs his wife scrambled, for his strength, it was a corpse he was looking for. He's stopped picturing that funny little Arnold girl, stout they called her, big-boned, the three feet of her, and the blunt haircut her mama always gave her with their kitchen shears, all four of those kids. He is watching for turned earth. A body that size needs a hole.

He wants to tell the Indian that. The girl's dead. Somebody buried her, probably had his way first. But the Indian keeps moving, urgent, but calm too, and with all those thoughts pedaling behind that face of his. He must know things, see things the neighbor doesn't, standing right there over his shoulder, as if he and the Indian aren't in the same place at all, the one of them only a flicker on a screen or in a nickelodeon. The way those faces can stare into yours, and then you blink, and step back, and it's just you there, and the burn in your eyes. He thinks of bats too. They can hear things a person can't even think about.

When the Indian pauses again, this time looking up, curving his back into a wind that rattles down the slope, the neighbor imagines him as the hide-dressed heathen that must have huddled in front of a teepee fire, stripping half-raw meat from a buffalo bone with his teeth. He has seen photographs. They come as youngsters mostly, only way to save the race. Any older and there'd be no digging out the animal parts.

"So," he says, "that school of yours. You'd be in some trouble, wouldn't you, if they saw you like this, sniffing around and all? I mean, it must a relief, getting out, into your natural habitat. You got to hate being caged up thumbing Bibles all day. That's what it's like, right? Reading grammar all day?"

He tries to imagine the Indian bent into one of those little school desks he used to sit in himself, all those runty letters swimming under his eyes and the ruler bruises pulsing across his knuckles, his right knuckles. The teacher swatted the same hand every time. He wouldn't have minded being an Indian himself back then, burrowing around in the woods, splashing in the creek. This one must be longing for it right now. Take his eye off him, and the town might have two vanished children in these trees.

When the silence gets too much again, and the Indian still isn't moving, the neighbor chuckles, loudly. "The judge, you know, he considers himself something of a woodsman himself. He headed out this way Wednesday on horseback, that pinto of his you liked back there. He was out half the day just looking for the road again. Come sunset he had to shimmy up one of these pines to figure out what's where." The neighbor chuckles some more, thinking of that tubby judge clinging like a cat.

"Yes," the Indian says. "Passed his hoofprints quarter mile ago."

By way of conversation, it is the most the Indian has mustered in an hour, so the neighbor makes the most of it. It was just ten, no, twelve years ago, he tells the Indian, they were out hunting up another girl, another Alice in fact, Alice Rachel Peck, same age even. Though that was down in Franklin County. She'd wandered out after her mama had gone off, a butcher's errand if he remembers correctly, and the girl, she found her way up an abandoned bark road, what was left of it, climbed all the way into the mountains, shoeless too, and no bonnet, nothing but huckleberries to munch. They searched three days. He saved the walking stick he used, a souvenir, everyone did. Three days and they figured it would be a clawed-up corpse they'd literally stumble over, a blind thing staring up at the sun. The girl didn't smile or cry or do much of anything when the men hoisted her up and the whoops started down the hills and back in echoes, till every bird in the county was in flight. Five miles the child had wandered. It wasn't the neighbor who found her.

"No reward that time," he adds.

Through the branches he spies wings circling, buzzards. A pair of them is riding a spiral of warm air down into a gully. From thirty miles they can scent a kill. Yesterday, wherever one dipped, men scrambled, but it was always a snake that sagged in its talons when the scavenger rose again.

"Now forty years ago," continues the neighbor, "it was a Snyder girl. They live not eight miles from me and the Arnold house. She was a teenager then, like me. She just strolls out of her house one afternoon and no one ever sees her again. Broke up the family pretty bad for a while. I had a little something there with the sister too, though she wasn't the sort you marry."

Because of the rumble of his own voice, he doesn't hear the tramping along the upper path. It is on top of them before he turns. The Indian jerks too. Three men, three searchers, cutting through the brush toward them. From their looks, they are the ones in need of finding. One is shirtless. Another strides in front, halts, swipes at his face. Thin clean streaks have rinsed his cheeks, before he smears them again. The third is breathing hard, but not from running. Between the knots of muscle twisting his face, black streaks run, thumb streaks, like war paint. The man's hands are blackened too. The shirtless one cradles a bundle, a checkered shirt, but not big enough, nowhere big enough to wrap a body, even a child's body.

"We found her," he says. "We found her bones."

The man bends forward, almost to his knee, as though genuflecting. The hollow of his shirt is smeared with ash and something darker. One sleeve falls open. The girl's bones are nestled inside, a dozen of them, in a sheath. Each is black and charred, but whole, and much thinner than the neighbor imagined possible.

My search partner revealed a great many things about the quaint Pennsylvania town where the lost girl lived. It seems those dark hills swallow up a child every few years, like a cannibal god who can never be appeased. I am reminded of your folklore, Mother, the stories Grandmother told of her people, the Croatans, and how the first white settlers vanished so mysteriously from their settlement centuries ago. How strange for the sailors to find the houses gone, and only rain-spoiled maps and armor rusting in weeds, but no hint of massacre, and the families never heard from again. It is queer to imagine their blood in my own veins now, but of course

Grandmother's people must have adopted them. Though painful, perhaps it is best that their English relatives stopped searching. After so many years, would their own parents have recognized the white-skinned savages and their half-breed cubs? Better to believe them dead and allow the wounds to scar.

As far as little Alice, we found no traces either. And there are no kindly tribes left in these mountains to adopt her. Better she lived out West, where my own heart longs to roam, and where perhaps some wild remnants of my distant tribal cousins might still take a wandering child into their fold. Some believe her not lost but kidnapped. After the papers published a description, a man telephoned from a depot town fifty miles west. I read the description myself, brown eyes, yellowish hair, the gingham dress I can see twenty times a day. The caller did not mention the scar on her forehead, only that she was in the care of a family of Coloreds headed out of town. He thought they had abducted her. Imagine the confusion these northerners would suffer if they ever witnessed one of our Carson Town reunions. They would call you a kidnapper, Mother, with your milky arms around one of my brothers' little black boys. Others suspect the child's own family of doing her harm. They demanded a search of the house, and the barn, in case the girl's brother had attempted to disguise his crime. That is nonsense of course. No child could be so cruel to his own kind. However roundly my brothers once boxed my ears, I know the love they always concealed from me. I am thankful to them for remaining close to home, so that my absence has not been so severely felt by you. I would not wish all of your children scattered into the wilderness.

She could have stumbled into the flames. Hunters are known to frequent the spot, only about a mile from the Arnold house, and camp, keep a log glowing most of a night. It could have kindled up on its own maybe. That or the murderer burned the body when he was done with it. Sergeant Markley, who is mostly recovered now, tells reporters assembled on the Leshes' porch that a snake bite was likely, that in a state of delirium produced by the reptile poison, Alice Arnold may have fallen into the campfire and in her weakness been unable to roll free and douse her dress in the dirt before the flames consumed her. That or they are some animal's bones. Dr. Bryner will make his determination.

This, the reporters agree, beats the rumors from the lumber camp. A pair of dogs vanished Monday night, returned Wednesday, vanished again, returned yesterday. Preparations have been made to track the mutts when they wander next, but neither has left its kennel. Were there bloody tracks? Scraps of meat in the canines' teeth? Burnt bones are better. They will type their notes for the local editions. Include the Indian too, red man versus white in a race of wits to save the child. The neighbor lures the *Sentinel* man to the Arnolds' yard for an exclusive. The Indian is an orphan, renegade father slain in war party, mother lost to smallpox, left wigwam behind, adopted white man's ways. A couple of paragraphs, more if you puff up the Indian school bit, government dollars civilizing the savage, etc.

After giving his own name and making sure the newspaper man spells it down right, the neighbor takes the Indian back inside, through the Arnolds' front door, without knocking again. On the porch the other sergeant stands assuring the reverend the police disapprove of mediums meddling in criminal investigations and he most certainly had not suggested Mr. Arnold, the uncle of the lost girl, visit another such hustler this very noon. Beyond them, the lane has emptied but for a few stray wagons spaced as if their owners were attending to matters of private and unrelated business. No automobiles remain.

Inside, the father's voice pitches against the foyer walls. "Why they calling off the search? Who told them she was dead? Who called it off?"

The judge is seated, in the sofa corner as before, losing his belt under his gut as he leans forward. "No one told them, Bill, but they've been through those hills two and three and some of them four times over. She's not up there."

"Madame Black said she's alive. Alice is between two currents of water. That's where they should be looking."

"But what's that mean, Bill? Rivers? Streams? Water pumps? There're a thousand springs in the county alone. And you said it was gypsies before, that she said it was gypsies who took her."

"That's right, and if there's a big enough reward they're going to return her. Unharmed, she said. If the newspapers don't scare them off. She said all those reporters could wind up killing my Alice."

"But the police had to publish a description so if there are kidnappers they can't move her around without someone seeing her. That's the whole point.

You think I like reading how that card at the *Telegraph* wrote me up?" He is waving his hand around, as if there were something in it, a gavel probably. Both men have noticed the neighbor, but neither turns toward him until now. "Any word, John?"

"No, sir," says the neighbor. "Nothing from the police doctor yet."

"They're not hers. They're just wasting time. She's out starving somewhere, and they're—" The father chokes off his words. The neighbor thinks he remembers seeing an actor on a stage make the same gesture once—the fist, the teeth. Only he can't think when, what stage. What play has he ever seen?

"How about you?" The judge is tilting his chin at the Indian. "You find anything at all out there?"

The Indian's spine tightens. Like his teacher just called on him while he was only pretending to be reading along with the rest of class. Nothing else about him changes. It doesn't seem he is going to answer, then he speaks, in that sluggish rumble of his. "A thousand trails," he says. Maybe it is softer than before.

The judge slinks back, hands on his knees. His face is blank too.

"Might have found child if called in soon."

"We'll wire you next time, chief."

The neighbor's hand rises, chest high, like a student's in the front row. Then he points toward the kitchen. "Think we could get a bite to eat still?"

The judge looks away, at a bit of pretty glass on the mantel, a horse, or a unicorn. It catches a splinter of light from the window. "The ladies should have some sandwiches left."

The neighbor walks in on the wife telling about Mr. Arnold's dream. Her husband isn't one for believing dreams, she's explaining, but this was different. Only one he's remembered in months, years even. The wife is sitting in the corner of the kitchen, on the only chair missing from the table, opposite the Indian. The neighbor didn't see her at first, or recognize her, with all her hair loose like that. Her husband dozed off in the rocker, after midnight again, she says. She swallows.

"And Bill hears the window opening in the next room, this room, that one right there. And it's Alice calling, 'Mama, Mama, let me in, Mama.'" She does the girl's voice high-pitched and quavery. "And she's banging on the door, banging on it, shouting." Her hands have floated off her lap, and the flesh of her arms flaps as she mimes with both fists. When the husband pulls his revolver, the one he's kept tucked in his trousers since Tuesday, she squeezes her hands around the invisible handle and curls out one finger, aiming at nothing particular, though nearer him and the Indian than the neighbor likes. The father's gonna kill the man who took his baby. But when he thuds through the door, a real thud, a real door, he's awake. Her arms spring out, open-handed. Alice is gone!

There is a pause, a kind of silence, so the neighbor stops chewing. He looks at the Indian, but the Indian is staring at his plate. Probably confused by the sandwich. God knows how they feed them at that school. Maybe they got him so trained up with silverware he doesn't know to pick a thing up with his own two hands anymore.

"It means something," says the woman by the sink. The neighbor doesn't know her, so she's a relative probably, distant. He tugs at the Indian when he hears the front door and the sergeant's voice.

The five men—the other officer followed his partner in with the reverend— stand in a lopsided circle in the entranceway, with the reverend edged against the grandfather clock. It is the kind the neighbor's wife is always wishing after, a dark-stained heirloom taller than a man. Only she wants one that works, it being a crime the way the Arnolds gummed up the pulleys.

"Couldn't possibly be a human child," the sergeant is saying. "Definitely a dog."

"See now," says the neighbor, shouldering around the judge, though not brushing him, not hard, "that's exactly what Mr. Long Lance here said to me when we first saw them. No way those scraps belonged to no girl. He was dead sure of it. He'd still be out there looking if those lumber boys hadn't dragged us back with them."

The state policemen, both of them, shake hands with the Indian, while the neighbor repeats the best tidbits the newspaper man scribbled down. The neighbor sticks his hand out there too. "John Wise," he says, and then he sets his hand on the father's arm, and pats it, saying how long he and the Arnolds go back, fought in the War together, their two families did.

"Will you be sticking around?" Markley asks the Indian. "I can't say exactly, but there may be a possibility or two we wouldn't mind your taking a look at."

The neighbor's smile displays gaps along both rows of teeth, before he sees the Indian shaking his head no.

"I leave now," he says. "Before the sun is gone." He turns his head toward the window, but does not look through it, at the yellow glow leaning not low in the pane, but not high either. The clock reads quarter to four, which could be right, by chance. The pendulum hangs straight.

"What," laughs the neighbor, "you got a spelling bee or something? 'Rithmetic? This is this man's little girl we're talking about, not some report card. I'm sure these fine officers here can send you back with a note for your principal if you're a little late."

The Indian points at the slope of green filling the glass. "I will find her."

The father's lips make a wet sound when his mouth opens, a suction breaking. He doesn't close his jaw until the Indian is on the porch steps. Arnold grabs the neighbor's elbow, holds him there. "Madame Black," he says, "the lady my brother talked to, over in Waterloo." He glances at the reverend, the only other man not watching the back of the Indian's head. "She said he'd be hurt, the Indian trailer be hurt bad hunting Alice. She said that."

The reverend smiles, or he curves his lips at least, before parting them. "I'm sure Mr. Wise's friend does not concern himself with superstitions. It's Christianity they teach them in Carlisle."

The neighbor promises to pass on the warning, before weaving out between the sergeants, apologizing. He'll get that Indian back soon as he can.

I am so sorry for my few letters these past three years. It is only now that I am nearly graduated, that I feel confident enough to write. I regret that it is still not safe for you to respond, for I would so love to hear word from my home again, but it must be enough for me to imagine your slight pleasure in these musings. Superintendent Friedman is known to intercept letters both from afar and those leaving the school in order to control the spread of untruths about himself and Carlisle. This I write in private and will mail myself in town. I am in good standing with the administration so of course our Superintendent would suspect nothing of me. Nonetheless, I would be undone should he read what I must say next.

As you know from the article in the <u>Washington Post</u> I clipped for you, President Wilson accepted my application to West Point. The novelty of a full-blooded Cherokee was too much to be ignored. I had to adjust my age again, but Mr. Friedman's recommendation was the strongest possible. Sadly, however, the publicity has produced an unexpected danger; the War Department has contacted Mr. Henderson, the man who originally questioned my application here. He is now the superintendent of an Indian school in Cherokee, North Carolina, where Father claimed to have been born and where no residents acknowledge our family. Had Father thought to name a more distant and less domesticated tribe of the Western Plains, I might be safe today, but with the government so close on my trail, I had no choice but to fail my West Point entrance exam. I averaged ninety-five in algebra and geometry all winter, only to score a thirty-seven. The football coach here, the highest-paid employee at the school, almost twice Mr. Friedman, failed it too once, so I do not believe this will result in further scrutiny.

One of the lumbermen and a reporter tag along, so there are three of them shuffling a few yards behind, giving the Indian space. The reporter talks the most, saying how those state police don't exactly take you into their confidence, though he does know for a fact they are out of the Lesh house and staying in town the night, though why, who can say?

"Suspects are under surveillance, they told us, but what's that mean? They went through the uncle's house yesterday, and there's no sign of the kid, and the other uncle, the younger one, there's something weird there. He's gone all week, around Pittsburgh somewhere, and gets back this morning, knows nothing, he says, but then he says he does know she's missing, that his mother wrote him about it, but then where's the letter? No letter, and why's he changing his story?"

The neighbor eyes scraps of gray-blue overhead. It's dark, darker than it should be. Leaves curl their bellies over, trembling all in a direction, like weather vanes. He doesn't want to get caught out here in a downpour.

"And the buggy from last night, now that was something else," the reporter continues. "A big white horse pulled right up near the corner of the Arnolds' lane. A couple men followed the tracks into a forest trail, toward Shenandoah. That's where the kidnappers must have her. If it weren't for all the gawkers around the Arnolds', they would have let the girl loose in the grove behind the house, pretended the searchers missed her somehow. That or bury her. Make it look like the family done it."

When the Indian bends over again, the neighbor sighs and rakes his scalp. With his knees up and his back down like that, the Indian looks like a frog, a freak-sized bullfrog in people clothes, like in a traveling show.

"You got something there, Mr. Lance?"

The Indian doesn't answer the reporter—no surprise there—but his arm rises. Over his shoulder he displays a leaf. He holds the pose until the reporter scrambles over and plucks it, gingerly, as if something that bright a green could crumble and blow away. The reporter is wearing city shoes, and they are looking pretty scuffed now, all those dark red and brown slices along his suit slacks too.

"Is that blood?"

The neighbor has to go around to his other shoulder because the lumberman takes so much room. Two dark spots, reddish if not red, and dried. He would tap a fingertip against it, but the reporter keeps angling the leaf, trying to catch what light there is.

"So," says the reporter, "she must be injured then, right? Is she injured?"

The Indian says nothing.

"Well, this is great," announces the neighbor. He reaches for the leaf again, but the reporter is pocketing it. "Gives us something concrete to impress those constables." He goes on, pointing at what is left of the sky, saying they'd be lucky if they make it down with any light at all. They don't want to lose the trail, get gummed up in these trees worse than the judge did. The lumberman agrees.

"What do you say there, Mr. Lance?"

The Indian stands off, arms akimbo, staring at nothing. "I will sleep here." He indicates the spot where the leaf rested. "At dawn, I pick up tracks."

No real attempt is made to dissuade him. The reporter is grinning, delighted by the notion and the prose he can put to it. A few yards and the Indian's graying form filters out of sight. The reporter is chuckling.

"Crazy," he says, "him being the best chance that girl's got." He turns around, as though to look at the Indian, but doesn't. "If it is kidnappers, they're fools to stick their heads out now."

The neighbor remembers something now. It was weeks ago, more than a month, that he was sitting over a mug in Paul Stohr's tavern. Who was it he was talking to? He recognized the one fellow, from one of his father's Blue-Gray reunions. It was Stohr who said afterward, from behind his bar, that the other had lost two years in the state penitentiary for something, didn't know what, couldn't remember. They were asking all kinds of questions, about his neighbors eventually, so maybe he talked them up some. What kind of money the Arnolds got, how much land, how many kids? It probably didn't matter, and folks would call him a liar if he brought it up now, say he was trying to show off.

When the rain starts, it is only sound. The wind has died back, so there is only the clapping of water against leaves overhead. The neighbor feels no drops until they make the clearing. He looks back then, at the closing maw of the trees, wondering if he'll ever see that red boy again. He wonders what his Indian family must be feeling, even now, their flesh and blood lost to them, kidnapped practically. How many years for a hole like that to scar. There's nothing left of him, just the black beyond the gray trees, and the roar of the falling sky.

> *I must take time now to work further on my commencement speech. Just as my teacher Miss Moore told us how Mr. Poe penned his great mystery tales, I have begun at the conclusion. I know that I will end with these words: "When we pass through the brick portals of this institution for the last time, we do not leave as Cherokees or Sioux or Pawnees; we leave as members of that one, great, universal tribe of North American Indians, a tribe sharing one language, and one chief, our great White Father in Washington. We leave as <u>Carlisle</u> Indians." I hope that it will draw some applause. I regret that you will not be there to add your approval, but of course the risk is too great. Coloreds never attend commencement, and of course you would have to pretend not to know me. How painful it would be to walk past each other, feigning to be strangers. I would rather never see you again than suffer that wrong.*

> *The police have given up the case of Alice Arnold, this despite a town petition headed by a prominent judge and reverend. There is simply not enough manpower to trace every criminal to his rightful end. The poor child will remain lost forever.*

I can't tell you my disappointment in returning to school without locating her, but what chance did I have after so many had failed before me? At least I afforded her family a moment of hope and possibility, which is the most that any man can do for another. Only a fool would expect more. I will write again after graduation. I leave for Calgary the week following. The managing editor of the HERALD *there was impressed by my application and has agreed to start me at thirty dollars a week, a fine salary for a cub reporter born on a reservation blanket in Oklahoma! My new boss knows a good story when he hears one, and he is pleased to find a child of such humble and barbaric origins ready to ascend into the larger White world. I have assured him that I have abandoned my Western ways and will never return to my forgotten people, especially when Alberta is just the sort of open frontier my spirit craves. Carlisle has taught me so much. Who can foresee where I will find myself next?*

Your Loving Child Always,

His wife is still reading in bed when the neighbor wrenches his boots off at the foot of the stairs. The kerosene lamp flickers on the ceiling. It's late. He and the lumberman stopped at the tavern, to get out of the rain, which never did let up much. She isn't angry, or pretends she isn't, since she expects him to mount her before rolling over to sleep. The woman is how old and still pretending a baby could come? She prays for it, coaxes him to, but he isn't one for lying, not to himself anyway. The lamps at the Arnolds' place are still burning. He can see them through the branches.

When he wakes an hour later, sweaty, he is dreaming about the Indian still sifting through twigs and pebbles up there. Shouts echo between lower trees, but the Indian pays no heed, and the neighbor can't make out what they're saying anyway. The girl crouches on the edge of the path. The Indian sees her. A ball of a girl, black with mud or soot or God knows, curled smaller than she could be, blinking out from two animal eyes. It doesn't look like her, but it's a dream, and he knows that's who she's supposed to be. He wants to cry out, holler the news, but his lungs push back, sink him into the down of the mattress. In the morning the dream will be gone, the memory of it, everything.

Ivy Wants to Go Home

vy runs the scissors just above the top letters of the headline. Otherwise the article won't fit in her scrapbook. They've been getting so much longer, all front-page columns now. Thorpe Wins Second Gold. She dabs the back with glue, but doesn't see that the strip is too long until she's pressing it down, trying to smooth the bulges flat. She'll have to snip off the bottom, move it to the top of the next page, unless she can angle it, or maybe cut it into more pieces, a row of squares along the margin. Her scrapbook is such a jigsaw. It's mostly all sports, has been since she fell for Jim.

The breeze is hot through the open window, and the scraps of newspaper lift, flutter a few inches, and rest on the desk again. Ivy has the office to herself again this morning. Most of the other buildings are empty too. The students—those who didn't graduate in May, or get expelled, or receive train tickets from parents with letters of permission to visit home—are gone on the Outing program. Hershey's and an automobile factory in Detroit are the two big employers this summer. Ivy was allowed to stay an extra month, two almost, to help with administrative work and stray hours in the infirmary. They're not paying her, just room and board. Miss Moore arranged it.

Ivy blows on the strip of newspaper, rubs her fingers over a spot that has turned translucent from the glue, and shuts the scrapbook. Oak leaves rustle against the window glass, and she stares a moment at the shifting sunlight, the play of cloud shadow over the grass. It's hot. Not as hot as Oklahoma this time of year, or California her brothers tell her, but it's enough to dampen the sides of her dress. It's enough to make her sit whole minutes staring and breathing and thinking of almost nothing at all, except the weight of her hair, the way it tugs at her scalp and presses against her back. She could go over the parade list again. Mr. Friedman dictated it to her last week, after news of Jim's first medal came over the telegraph. The mayor telephoned minutes later. They want the celebration downtown, full band, streamers on the lampposts, new bunting on the platforms. Even the governor wants to speak now. Mr. Friedman says it's going to be bigger than all the football celebrations combined—all of the town, the whole county, folks from all over the state coming right here, to his school, coming to see his Indian boys, to see Carlisle's James Thorpe, Mr. Friedman's very own Olympic star.

Ivy wishes she could see him too. She's written Jim twice a week since he left for practice with the U.S. team three months ago. He writes back sometimes, or he did until they sailed for Sweden. Ivy knows her last letters won't make it over in time, will end up in basement bins, will be burned in some post office furnace maybe a year from now, an annual bonfire of the undeliverable and unreturnable. Still, she likes writing them. She likes watching her thoughts scroll out in pretty looping script. When she was little, she used to write to pretend people, made-up names and streets. She would spell her full name, Margaret Iva Miller, and the school address in perfect round letters in the top left corner of the envelope, exactly the way the teacher taught her class to. None of those envelopes ever came back either.

There are footfalls on the porch steps, and she sits upright, squares the blotter on her desk. She tries to arrange the newspaper too, but it's bent out of shape now, the sheets won't align, so she creases a new center and then a second before folding it all into the metal trash pail by her knee. She's not doing anything when Mr. Friedman walks under the transom, so she pulls the desk drawer out, finds something, a pad, a broken fountain pen. Mr. Friedman is grinning at her.

"Good morning, Miss Miller!"

He grins all the time now, and not just at Ivy. She glimpses the corners of yellowed incisors through his goatee as she smiles up at him.

"How are you today, sir?"

"How am I?" he asks, and then he asks it again, more loudly, with his thin arms spread, looking around the office as though at an audience through the invisible walls of a stage. "Just look out that window. Sunshine, everything in bloom. I am telling you, Iva, I've been superintendent of this school for how many years?

Eight? Eight years? I've never seen a day like this. Reminds me of how blessed we are, how blessed to have this school as our home."

"Yes, sir, Mr. Friedman."

Ivy watches him stare at the window, his eyes myopic in thought. He cheered up at this time last year too, after the students and teachers had thinned out. Ivy should be down at the main school building, helping Mrs. Denny and the other Outing coordinators type their reports, but Miss Moore said it would be better if she could say she had worked directly under the superintendent. Secretary to the superintendent. It would impress the hospital administrators at her new job. It might get her away from bedpans and urine-soaked sheets and in front of a type-writer where she belongs. The hospital is in California, just a town away from one of her brothers, so Ivy can stay with family, in their attic loft, as long as she needs to. It's a good job. Grace got it for her.

"Iva?" Mr. Friedman's chin has drifted from the window. "Is that my *Sentinel*?"

Ivy looks at the trash pail and watches her hand jerk toward the mangled newspaper. "No, sir," she says, "I put yours on your desk, sir."

He nods but his smile is weaker now. It doesn't take much to remind him of the government inspector, the student petitions, the runaways. That's what Miss Moore told Ivy. Mr. Friedman doesn't tell Ivy anything.

"Tomorrow I want to go over the parade list with you again. The auditorium podium is a disgrace, and with the wood shop closed for summer, we may have to splurge."

"Sir," says Ivy, "I won't be here tomorrow."

"Then Thursday. Make sure you have the new speaker order. I am not going after—"

"Today's my last day, Mr. Friedman."

He squints at her, as though he is considering whether to contradict her, or is uncertain if he has been speaking to the right person this whole time.

"Oh, of course," he says. "You graduated, didn't you?"

Ivy remembers how heartily he shook her hand in both of his after she and the rest of the business department finished their song and skit and exited the commencement stage while the band started blaring the school anthem again. He called her Julia—well done, Julia!—as his eyes found the next girl in line.

"Well," he says. "We will certainly miss you here." Ivy smiles up at him as he says how invaluable she has been, how really very indispensable. Mr. Friedman is certain her parents are very proud of her too, all of her people are. They must all be so happy to be finally getting her back again. Ivy's hands are folded on the desk blotter as he steps into his office and pulls the door closed between them.

She looks at the window again, and she thinks of Oklahoma, the clean heat of it, her mother's tiny grave marker sunk in front of a wide and unbroken horizon—and then she thinks about commencement instead. It really was very grand. The marching and the applause and the bleachers overflowing. Her favorite was the valedictorian's speech. That Sylvester Long Lance looked so bold in his blue suit and paisley tie, a regular entrepreneur, a self-made man. He was addressing the whole world up there. He said there was but one race, the race of Man, and no borders between the territories of the spirit. There are no reservations that can hold back the will if the will has no reservations. Ivy stood to applaud as Miss Moore prodded the other girls. Ivy envied Sylvester, with his endless future, all of the world his home now. He has so many places to go.

When she hears the mail wagon loping toward the porch steps, Ivy stands and walks to the entrance. She greets Mr. Stehley by name and accepts an armful of letters. They're bound in a string. During the semester, the office receives sometimes two canvas bags, not counting the packages and trunks. Ivy thanks him, says his name again, and Mr. Stehley nods without looking at her. He has no idea who she is. For six days of each of the last seven weeks, Ivy has met him at the porch steps of the administrative building, and not a flicker of recognition has ever warmed his face. She's just another Indian.

Maybe it's the sound of the mail truck as it grinds forward, or the sudden sway of her hair as she turns, but Ivy is remembering the morning her family first arrived in Oklahoma. It was still called the Indian Territory then. Ivy hadn't seen one yet. An Indian. Their father's wagon lurched on its bad wheel, and Grace kept pointing out of the rear flap, saying Injuns are comin'. Once when they stopped to water the horses at a scribble of a creek, their mother dragged Ivy back under the tarp before she could worm herself over the rear board. There was some kind of burial ground across the water. Ropes stretched across pole tops with their ends staked in the dried mud. A dozen scalps swayed. Some looked like animal skins, pelts of rodent fur. Ivy stared at a wave of blonde curls that hung down almost three feet from the hunk of blackened skin gripping the roots. Ivy had never seen hair so bright. She wanted to try it on.

It's a silly thing to be thinking about, and so she stops and goes inside again. She doesn't start reading the envelopes until she is sitting down. There aren't that many, and she doesn't have anything else to do when she's finished. She doesn't expect there to be one from Jim. He is much too busy to be writing anyone, let alone her. It's not as if they are a couple. Jim danced with lots of girls at the socials, not just Ivy. It's true he always sat beside her in Miss Moore's class, after she and Gus broke up, and he did say he wanted to see her again, after he got back, but none of that means anything. He's a celebrity. He can have his pick, he always could, but Ivy won't be there to compete anymore. It doesn't matter how smart she is, how pretty, how light-skinned. She won't be there. She won't exist.

Her hand stops above the largest stack, the principal's stack—he does all the real work at the school. The envelope in Ivy's fingers is addressed to her: Miss Ivy Miller. She flushes, then realizes there's no airmail stamp, no Swedish postmark. It's not from Jim. It's from California. She thinks of her brother, but the handwriting is wrong, too cramped, too ragged, and then she sees her father's town name in the corner, just his address. He didn't write his name. He knows better. He keeps writing to her, wanting her to live with him. He can get her work at his hotel, a real job, not linens and toilets, but bookkeeping. She'd be a bona fide clerk. That's what Grace's letters say. Ivy's never opened one of his.

She leans back, with the envelope corners balanced between her fingertips. It's light. Probably a single sheet inside. The first few were heavier. Grace says she's being childish. It was years ago, he couldn't afford them all, he had to give them up, or some of them at least, and wasn't it better their all being together at Whitakers', better than starving? And if Ivy's still sore about that adoption, well, that's just proof he still loved her, isn't it? He couldn't bear to know that his own daughter was someone else's. He couldn't give her up completely, even if it meant giving Ivy a new mother, a home somewhere.

Ivy's never told anyone that story, not anyone at Carlisle. It would sound like bragging. It sounds like a lie. I was almost adopted by a millionaire spinster. She tried to tell Gus once, but then he proposed, and then she couldn't tell him anything. Even Jim might laugh at her. Isn't it enough being white? Isn't winning the star player for a whole semester enough for the white girl? Does her whole life have to be pretend?

When the telephone on the desk rings, Ivy startles, then she drops her father's envelope into the trash pail before picking up the receiver.

"Superintendent Friedman's office, may I help you?"

It's Coach Warner at the athletic building. He asks for Friedman, tells Ivy to hold on a sec, inhales a long breath through what she has learned to recognize is a cigarette, and asks for him again.

Friedman is delighted. His voice booms through his closed door. He only whispers when it's bad news, when D.C. calls, when the police chief telephones from the town lockup. He and Pop—he's started calling Mr. Warner "Pop" like everyone else—are making plans for next year's season, expand the grandstand for home games, the gymnasium too. There's a rumor—or a joke, Ivy can't tell— that they're going to rename the gymnasium in Jim's honor. Name the gym after Jim. Friedman's laugh is a high, thin rattle.

After he hangs up, his door opens. "Do we have James's parents on the invites? Telegraph them. It'll look good. Show how far you can go in one generation."

Ivy almost doesn't call after him, almost doesn't speak as he begins to turn away. "They're dead."

Friedman looks at her, seems to consider contradicting her again, then doesn't. "Does he have any family?"

"Just siblings," says Ivy. It sounds like an apology. "His half-brother is enrolled for the fall."

"Is he now? Good for him. I bet he'll hold up the Thorpe tradition, don't you?"

Ivy says she bets Jim's brother will hold up the tradition too.

After Mr. Friedman's door closes again, she takes another ten minutes sorting the mail into piles and then placing the piles into department slots. She would offer to carry the batches down to the school building, but Mr. Friedman doesn't like her to leave before her shift ends. She has another twenty minutes. She could lie. She could say that Dr. Butler at the infirmary asked her to come in early today. She could say anything she likes, but she doesn't. She waits until the tip of the minute hand splits the twelve and then she walks out onto the grass.

She sticks close to the circle of oaks, looping the long way across the grounds to keep in their shadows, but she's in a sweat before she reaches the Girls' Quarters. The heel of her hand leaves a damp spot on the scrapbook cover when she sets it on her bed. The other two beds are bare, no mattresses over the metal springs. A decade of government schooling and she finally has a single, no roommates, no one to hide from, no one to fool. When she closes the door she's completely alone.

Her trunk is packed, all but the clothes she's wearing and the scrapbook. She kneels, lifts the lid back, and places the book across her winter coat. She started assembling it her first semester, almost three years ago, though it seems much longer. She can't remember when she stopped expecting prairie dirt every time she glanced at a window. It's been four, no, five years since she saw her mother's grave. It might not be there anymore. Grace is always writing about new roads coming through, railways, buildings, floods sometimes. Ivy won't recognize the place. There wouldn't be anything left of her mother anyway, not even the bones. Her mother died in the last century. Ivy doesn't remember her, not really. Grace kept the only photograph, and then lost it somewhere, scolded Ivy for crying when she finally told her.

Ivy opens the scrapbook and flips backward until she finds her favorite *Red Man* clipping, the Halloween social, the prize waltz with Big Jim. She hardly knew him then. They had never danced before. Anything was possible. The next page is a football article, a victory against Army. The sheet is thick with glue. She keeps flipping, but there's so little there, a paragraph on the business department, a sentence on one of her piano recitals. Then two more pages of football. It's a queer history, hers, one she's barely in. It's all gaps and random facts, the wrong facts, each bit of newspaper scissored into its own jigsaw shape, no two connecting. She thinks of the necklace she made in Arts class, how high the beads bounced and scattered when the string broke, what they looked like in her palm when she gathered the few she could find. She wonders what a stranger would make of her book, whether someone could recognize her from it. Someday she will be old and this will be all she has to remember herself by. She will be somebody else, and this will be all that is left of her.

Ivy wedges the scrapbook along the trunk's inner edge, pinning it against the soles of her good boots. She checks that her train ticket is still in the envelope under the strap. One-way to Chicago, then a changeover, and out to California, all prepaid by the school. Miss Moore made sure of it. It's policy to cover the cost of returning home, but Ivy was worried because she doesn't have family in Oklahoma anymore, and she is eighteen now and so her sister isn't her guardian. No one is. But Miss Moore said the school is still responsible for her. Right up until she steps onto the train. Then she's by herself. She's a free woman. That's how Miss Moore said it. She looked happy for Ivy, proud of her, one of her best students ever, she said, going out into the wide-open world. Miss Moore lives in town with her widowed mother, in the house she grew up in. She never goes anywhere.

Ivy changes into her nurse's uniform and stands at the mirror with her brush. Her hair has grown very long again, longer than it was the morning when she arrived at Chilocco, the morning she became an Indian. The matrons led her to a dorm wing and tugged and snipped fistfuls of her hair with a pair of sewing shears before scrubbing the roots with kerosene. Ivy remembers how impossibly light her head felt, as though her scalp were lifting from her skull. The assistant swept and carried the severed braids at arm's length, like dead things, snakes, the bowels of a pig, as the head matron shaped the remains, rounding it above Ivy's shoulders with a bang high above her eyebrows. When Ivy leaned forward, the sides closed in, concealing her face. Ivy liked that. The matron handed her a wooden brush and Ivy pulled at a tendril of hair woven into the base of its teeth, before running it behind her own ear. Her hair was shorter, shorter than her mother had ever allowed, but tangled and damp. She pulled with both hands. Ivy is pulling with both hands now.

Her hair is black and straight, but the ends are ragged. She would snip them with the shears in her trunk, but she can't see behind herself. She can't trust herself to cut evenly. If Julia were here, she would ask her, but Julia left after graduation like everyone else.

Ivy misses lice check. Carlisle is lax these days, but at Chilocco it was weekly. The matrons sat them in pairs and they would take turns fingering and combing each other's scalps. Ivy would run a brush over another girl's head, gentle with each tangle, until the hair spilled like water through her fingers. Her mother used to comb her hair that way, stroking it long after the need had passed, while Ivy slumped, wrapped in towels and dozy from the woodstove. The other girl would sit, arms knotted, while Ivy enjoyed the tug of the teeth through thick locks. She was surprised how white, how literally white, a scalp could be. When ordered, the other girl would perform a grudging job in return, while Ivy stared at the window, at the stars perforating their reflection. Two girls sitting on a bed. The glass was always blurry. They might be any two girls in the world.

Ivy knots her hair into a heavy bun at the base of her neck and pins the nurse's cap through it. She leaves through the rear of the dormitory and ducks along the gymnasium for its strip of shade. The infirmary is a new building, financed by football revenue, so there are no trees along its entrance, nothing to block the heat. It's cooler inside, with the windows propped for the cross-breeze. She stands a moment, feeling the sweat chill on her neck, as she knots her nurse's apron behind her back. Dr. Butler isn't at his desk or in the pharmacy vault, but the other nurse, the one student in the nursing program who didn't get an Outing placement, nods at Ivy. Ivy is early. It's only quarter past, but it's good to start the patients' lunches now, so she and the other girl can eat before they're weak. Her name is Malinda.

When the beds are full, they have to cart trays over from the dining hall, but it's summer and the second floor is empty. It's just the lingering cases along the front rooms. The other girl starts ladling soup into bowls in the corner of the tiny kitchen. She's new. She keeps looking at Ivy but not saying anything. Ivy is rolling utensils into linen napkins.

"Gus is better," the girl says. "Doctor Butler says he can go home whenever he likes now."

Ivy arranges the tops of a fork and a knife and a spoon so that their tips jut evenly from the cloth. "That's great," she says. Gus caught the flu days before the U.S. team met in New York for final cuts. He was supposed to run the distance meets. He is better than Jim at distance.

"Do you want to take his tray in?" asks Malinda.

Ivy has barely spoken to Gus since he was put on bed rest. He was infectious. She barely spoke to him all year. He used to propose whenever they were alone, laughing when she said no. Julia said she was a fool, once Julia started talking to her again. Ivy will never find someone better than Gus. Miss Moore is recommending him for law school, at Dickinson, after he finishes an extra year on the team. He could be the next valedictorian, plus football captain again, if Jim doesn't want it. Any girl in the world, said Julia, even a girl like Ivy, would be lucky to have him. Ivy knew she was right. So did Gus. He kept cornering her between classes, in hallways, in the backs of rooms, asking why not. Until she danced with Jim at the October social. He stopped after that.

Gus is sitting up in bed reading when she walks in with his tray. The *Sentinel* is spread across the sheet on his lap, open to the sports page. There was a follow-up article Ivy decided not to clip. She pauses at the foot of his bed, but he doesn't look up from the pages, so she walks the tray to the beside table.

"Can you believe it?" he says. "The Decathlon too?"

His hair isn't combed, so black tufts jut from the top and sides. Otherwise he's as handsome as ever.

"It's really a freak event, you know? They're probably getting rid of it for the 1916 games. He's the champion of a dead event."

Gus lifts his head when Ivy turns toward the door.

"Why don't you stay? I got no one to talk to all day." There's a chair next to the table, and he looks at it. "It's not like you have anything better to do."

Ivy says something about needing to help the new nurse, as she sits down. It's so easy to do what Gus tells her to, what anyone tells her. She never imagined he would propose. She had no idea she would ever be liked here. The white girl tricking the government. Gus loved that. She's still not sure when he found out, whether he always knew. He raps the newspaper with his knuckles.

"He almost slipped up on the jumps, but he pulled it out. You have to give him credit. I would have beaten him on a couple of the runs, but he can do it all, can't he?" He goes on awhile, talking up Jim's strong and weak points, how lucky the team will be to have him back in the fall, how proud he is of his pal, showing the white world what a red man can do. Ivy keeps nodding, agreeing.

"Though it would be too bad if it all came back at him now," says Gus. "Once you're on top like this, you're exposed, no one at your back. You know he played minor ball, right? On a summer team."

Gus is staring at her, waiting for her to answer, for Ivy actually to say something. "What's that have to do with—"

"He's not amateur, not technically. He got paid."

"I thought lots of players spent summer—"

"Sure, but how many are all over the front page? I bet there are photos out there. All it takes is one guy with an old team photo and everybody knows."

"Who would do that?"

"It's like you," says Gus. "You only made it through here because no one said anything. No one told. But everybody knew. Anyone could have got you thrown out."

Ivy doesn't know if that's true. Sometimes she thinks she's fooling everyone, herself practically. But it's lucky Gus saw through. Gus would never have bothered with her otherwise. She assumes Jim knows too, but she can't be sure. If he does, he doesn't care. Ivy was the one who asked him to dance. She invited him to the social. She wasn't special. He didn't fight to win her. She wasn't his trophy, not really.

"So are you going to stop dyeing it when you get home?"

Ivy's hand stops. She didn't realize she was running her fingers through her hair, tucking a strand behind her ear. Her arm hangs there as she stares back at Gus. He's pointing.

"I would have loved to have seen it all golden."

She tries to smile. But Gus isn't looking at her, just her hair, seeing something that's not there, that will never be there. She tries to ease her hands back to her lap, to lace her fingers there, to wait for what happens next. Tomorrow she is leaving. She will never see Gus again, or the school, or anyone. Tomorrow she leaves her tribe forever.

ASSIMILATION TWO

Ivy's Father Tells the Truth

Miller starts writing, longhand, on one of those hotel pads he keeps crammed under the front desk, the night he sees Ivy and her Indian husband done up in grainy lace and bow tie on the bottom fold of the sports page. He knew it was coming. His oldest daughter wrote to warn him, but still, to see it, his flesh and blood wed to a fraud. Best athlete in the world according to the King of Sweden, but that Thorpe boy isn't what he said he was, so the Olympics took their medals back, same as Miller would have. Worst was how Ivy didn't have to, wasn't pregnant by him or anybody else after working her year after graduation out here in California, not living with Miller though but her brothers at least. They stole her letters, the Thorpe boy's love letters, and lit them for kindling, same as Miller would have. His daughters are no Indians.

Miller keeps the wedding article in his room, with the others, a little wrinkled but all the edges scissored straight. The photograph doesn't show Ivy's green eyes, a shade paler than her mother's, the only part of her mother that didn't pale and shrivel at the end, skin tented on ribs, lungs spitting her up in pieces. Ivy is prettier anyway, and smart too. She weaseled all those nursing and typing classes out of the government, a decade's room and board almost. That was the point of it. She didn't have to go and marry an Indian. It probably makes her one now too, finally, with her Indian diploma and a priest's signature saying how God doesn't mind mongrels. Nobody asked Miller for her hand. Thorpe didn't write him or telephone or come knocking at his door in person, the way a white boy would know to, showing the rightful respect due to a young bride's father. His daughter beds a savage, a famous one, and so now she's a little famous too, he supposes. But that doesn't change where she comes from and who it is she's supposed to belong to. That's what Miller is writing these nights, a history, for posterity, he tells himself, the truth and anybody willing to pay him to print it.

Starting a story is hard, so he's starting in the middle, after his wife's funeral, after Ivy and her sister and their brothers already found themselves in the Whitaker Orphan Home in Pryor Creek, in what was not yet the fine state of Oklahoma. Mr. and Mrs. Whitaker were much admired across their county for doing God's work, and being blessed for it. The roll of fat along Whitaker's wrist jiggled when he shook hands, how he shook Miller's that once. The man may even have believed Miller's fib about Ivy and them being part-Shawnee blood, long before Whitaker unloaded her and all his half-breeds on that Indian school up along the Kansas border. Miller never saw Chilocco, but he's been told it looks like a lighthouse, a prairie lighthouse, for Noah and whatever ocean he comes riding in on next. On the wagon Mr. Whitaker rented and the United States government paid him for, Ivy's brothers connived to bunk with some of their Indian pals and so converted to Eastern Cherokee. It wouldn't work out like planned, but that's the tribe they told the lady sitting outside the school steps with the book and pen. Miller knows how important that is later.

There are all kinds of stories he could tell about Ivy, how she later faked her way into that Pennsylvania school, switched to Cherokee like her brothers, because it's easiest, the most civilized of tribes, the one fraternizing with Christians longest. But he picks a tale he knows a newspaper man would have to stop and read, with a prize location, and a celebrity, and a mystery only a father can undo. It's set at the Louisiana Purchase Exposition in St. Louis in 1904, spring to fall, and it's about how little Ivy almost hoodwinks a rich lady, Helen Gould, daughter of the dead railroad tycoon, into adopting her. It's about a good deal more than that, more than Miller is willing to acknowledge just yet, least of all to himself. He did not attend the Fair, but he found some used postcards from a bin in a bookshop near the train station and bought them, The Palace of Electricity at Night, The Esquimau Woman and the Baby Carriage, A View of the Grand Basin from the Central Cascade. That last is in telescopic 3-D. He remembers reading some newspapers at the time, but he didn't keep them. He has never been very historically minded.

But a story needs facts, true or not, and Miller reads as fair as the next man, better than the Mexicans trying to rent rooms on his late shift. The library's only twelve blocks over, and they let him take books home, books that give off leathery fumes on the pine board he fitted over his radiator, a desk if you hunch and twist a bit. He penciled out a map, the Palaces, the Pike, the Canal, Monuments, but nobody needs to see all that. The Indian Building was over to the side on a hill. As he understands it, Indians were part of the Anthropology Exhibit, a Record of the Development of Prehistoric Man. Inside there's cavemen and stone hammers, Egyptian tidbits, a bunch of cracked pots it sounds like. The good stuff is outside. At the gully along the base tattooed women squat in front of thatch huts and carve up scraps of wood. From there time marches uphill past real-live Pygmies and Patagonian giants and a genuine teepee village with around-the-clock war-whooping and rug-weaving, till up at the very top you got the model Government Indian School, where little Indian grammar pupils nail farm wagons and bellow "The Star-Spangled Banner" through brass horns. That's where you would have found his Ivy.

Turns out the superintendent at Chilocco, where Ivy was a couple years after the Whitakers washed their hands of her, was put in charge of the Expo's Indian Building. Miller never met him, but he knows the type, government man, all ironed creases and moustache scissors, a set of ivory teeth to chew his sausage. He gathers a boatload of child breeds to fill his exhibit, from Walapai down the bowels of the Grand Canyon to Esquimau up top the frozen scalp of the world. These are the good ones, no runaways, no still-makers, none of the girls that get themselves shipped home big-bellied or in boxes.

Ivy's a good one, what you would have called talented. She's ten about. She can play piano, like the upright in Mrs. Whitaker's sitting room, though Ivy never got to lay fingers on those keys being only five when her mother put herself under a gravestone and so only eight or nine when Chilocco had to take her in. That was later, probably, with the nuns or in Pennsylvania, that she learned the piano. She was just the little actress now. Downstairs in the Indian Building they put on plays, *Hiawatha* by Mr. Longfellow. Ivy knows the words by heart. She says, "On the shores of Gitche Gumee," and she says, "Of the shining Big-Sea-Water," better than any real savage girl, and the tourists grin and clap and see how smart and pretty she is in her white ironed dress with the frills and piping.

She dances too, Indian dancing, not that they teach it at the school, only waltzes, but they got that wild Apache chief Geronimo downstairs, in a guarded booth, opposite the children sewing handkerchiefs and harnesses. He's a prisoner of war. For a dime he'll scrawl his mark on a postcard for you. He dances for nothing, lures little Ivy into his booth, hunches around a circle with his headdress feathers slithering over her toes, the two of them jiggling to his drummer's tattoo. Ivy can learn anything.

There's eight months of this, six o'clock bugle, flag salute quarter of seven, then breakfast and class work, three R's, handicrafts, all the parading and reciting. The lady art teacher, a civilized Indian herself, and her boy assistant pencil up a wall's length of plaster, so the youngsters can paint in the shapes, arrows and faces and feathers and fires. The superintendent calls it a mural. Some of the parents are right there, stealing up from those wigwams or across the main hallway where the superintendent has them whittling whatnots on pony rugs, the old ways. Imagine the pride their little papooses wrench out of them, their civilized calflings, and what shape hole that leaves in their gut. Their own aren't their own anymore, never were.

Miller does not care to think how that feels. Ivy didn't have to trouble herself though, with her mother dead half her life already. What could she have remembered about family, about the old cattle farm and the hotel where she and her sister made themselves a nuisance running and getting underfoot? Ivy's a heathen now, a practical illustration of the benefits possible when society directs its maternal instincts toward a malleable and appreciative recipient, what it says right here in one of Miller's library books. He has it wedged up between the pine board and radiator grill. The pages feel milk-white and smell like they have never been alive.

Miller looked up some things to say about Helen Gould too. Born 1870, third of six children, one of two daughters, named after her mother, family called her "Nellie." Her father you should have heard of, gobbled up railroads and telegraphs and newspapers, rigged stocks, left it all, seventy-two million, to his brood, and not so much as a Geronimo-scribbled postcard to charity. His mother died when he was five. Miller figures that's one of those coincidences a historian is supposed to plump up, like it means something, the way this line happens to rhyme with that one. It's just words. Nellie read Dickens and Twain aloud from the Windsor chair she scooted up against her daddy's deathbed, 1892. She's the do-gooder's do-gooder, Fundamentalist, anti-Marxist, Bibles to Baghdad, missionaries to Morocco, plus the Temperance pamphlets, YMCA branches, memorial libraries. Letters pile up like kindling, the pleas, the scams, the one-paragraph tragedies. She took up the charitable work after her mother Gould's stroke. If Miller got the arithmetic right, she's thirty-four the night she meets Ivy.

Reading what he's written so far, Miller can see it doesn't take long to get here from where you start, nothing compared to what it took him, these nights hunched up breathing kerosene smoke, the shadow of his hand quivering along cracks in the plaster. Another Miller is doing the same in the window glass. He suspects anyone could see him from the street, framed up like a painting, though there's none down there to do the looking. He also suspects it won't take a person long to get to the end of all this either, though he's got a living to finish between the punctuation marks, up and down Main to the Prescott, a once-fine hotel establishment where the lobby chandelier still catches what light there is mornings, double shifts sometimes, and then there's meals and cigarettes and pretty girls behind the store and library counters. He could be here a while yet.

Unlike old man Gould, Miller has no lawyer to write down his last will and testament, billing by the hour, by the lifetime, an eternity—even when the devil never takes off his coat and shakes your hand goodbye before you can heat up a tin for tea for him. That was ten years ago. Helen Gould's lawyer sat in this same chair Miller is sitting in right now. It creaked less, didn't snag your pocket on the loose nail head then. The room's not changed much otherwise, least of all the view. How the rascal found him, that's money for you, all the way out here in California. If he pranced through that door again, the thing might play out different, what with the can of rat poison in the closet crate, and that's an authentic antique Confederate revolver on the mantel, loaded, and enough hemp under the bed to hang a man twice over. It should be a Sherlock Holmes that Miller is penning, even if nobody dies right off, and what he did is done whether he tells it or not.

Back at the Fair, Ivy is munching squaw cake and chumming around with the little Esquimau girl "Columbia" christened at the 1894 Chicago Expo, still a draw for the passing reporter. Ivy knows how to stand for a photograph too. Same as she sniffs through a crowd, finds where to sit herself, what hand to brush her black locks back, delicate, silk to the touch, dark as Miller's when he washes it. She's no Nellie Gould, sheltered child princess sick with shyness. She holds on to what's worth holding. Both the doll and the dish set, souvenir gifts at Miss Gould's Expo party she gets herself paraded at. The other girls, the little Japs and Swedes and Spics, girls from every color of the globe, they just get the one or the other, the dishes or the doll. It was pretty, a blonde thing, probably real hair maybe, and eyes that blinked blue when you tilted her back up. Miller never saw it, but he knows ones like it, from store windows, decked up in velvet and frills and things Ivy and her sister could never have worn themselves. Once, not long before her mother died, or right after, Ivy clung at a shop window blubbering for all the town to hear, smearing tears and snot on the glass, her fingers going white at the tips from pressing the glass so hard, until Miller yanked her inside and held her on his lap and the damn doll on hers. To hell with the store lady glaring. So when someone handed Ivy the toy dishes, Ivy's free hand grabbed for that porcelain head too.

Miss Gould hosted her party in the Administrative Building overlooking the basin and fountains and the lights of Festival Hall and the Palace of Transportation twinkling off the shallow water. It was just tree and meadow before St. Louis loosed an army on it a couple years before, and Miller heard they toppled it when it was done, a Mid-West Babel, only all spread out to begin with. The girls were the entertainment, beaming, curtsying in pairs, while the rich ladies clapped, their rings making little muffled clinks. Probably Helen got up and said something about the Lord God and capitalism. Miller has never seen a photograph of her, which says something right there, but he will bet every face moved with hers, ugly or not, every wrinkle in her gown a tremor in someone else's stomach. Ivy would have done her Gitche Gumee for half a dime. Probably she did, while casting her mother's green eyes at anyone willing to peek into them, green like the belly of a leaf or the bud on a flower stem before it undoes itself. Those Christian ladies never had a prayer. Miller doesn't know how for a fact it was Ivy who snagged the top prize in all that circus, she wouldn't tell him, but that spinster was all she ever dreamed, gracious and proper in her simple gown, a year's rent if she hocked it to Miller's landlady. Good Works, that's just chopping up a camel to cram it through a needle's eye.

Mattie, Ivy's mother, she knew some things about Our Lord Jesus too. She'd allow no Dickens at her bedside, just her Bible, mostly Job at the end. Miller would have to mumble it aloud with the kids bickering and sniveling through the crooked door while his finger stumbled under the words so damn small. Mattie was a proud thing, a Knox, as in Knoxville, and a Denton of Tennessee. She didn't care for the old Indian Territory, or the stink of Miller's herd when the family got there. Open pastures, what the tribes called hunting ground, before the government herded them out. Miller sold his shares off, though it wasn't town life that satisfied her either. Mattie looked down on him some, he knew that, so maybe it was from spite he told Mr. Whitaker that yarn about her grandma, wild Indian he told him. The granddaddy had to truss her to a pole, wrists and ankles, to haul her home. It would never have occurred to Miller he could write a letter to a millionaire's daughter back then, though it's a fortune buying milk and eggs year out, keep five growing in pants and dresses, rent on a whole house when all he needs is this one room.

He's kept up on them though, even before Ivy got herself in the newspaper. That cigar box on the nightstand shelf, it's all full of letters, from Grace mostly. She got work laundering at Chilocco after finishing her terms, then teaching, drawing only sixty dollars less than what they call the white staff. The cigars Miller didn't smoke himself, but it was a fine box before the lid tore.

Grace wrote him about Helen Gould. Except for her brother, Grace is oldest, seventeen when the wagon clattered through the Chilocco gate, and so guardian to the rest, legal-wise. Helen Gould knows what that means. Her sixth of the seventy-two million came lawyer-tied to the family mansion and guardianship of two baby brothers. She'd picked up a few from orphanages since and thought little Ivy, a bona fide green-eyed Injun, would fill out her sideshow. A governess for each is how they do it. Grace said yes. Miller didn't father fools, save for the boys. But adoption, that's more than a note on Prescott stationery, even a good sheet from the back drawer, under the yellowed ones. It's lawyer words and big looping signatures and a notary stamp witnessed in flesh and blood.

Helen Gould was no fool either, her father's girl. Instead of slicing, the father left the whole pie to the six, as one, a unit, no spouses, no fortune grabbers, not that actress little Howard would have married but for Helen's veto. They voted on everything, said so in the will. Dead and gone or in between, a father's a peculiar thing. You can't hate a man for needing to keep hold of what he's lost, even if it's just pride making him do it. Gould dictated from his deathbed, signature no prettier than Geronimo's. Miller's has gone a little shaky too. When he shucks off his blanket mornings, he doesn't look back at that shallow dent in the mattress, at that old man's missing body.

Nellie learned from her father. Being the homebody meant hiring legs, not just lawyers and accountants, but men with grime under the nails, ex-cops, ex-cons some of them, Burns men. You don't just sing the lady a number and she wires you the cash. There's investigating. They found Miller before Grace's letter did.

"James Finis Miller," the man said at the front desk, not "Mister Miller" like the maids, not "Fin" like the boss. "Father of Miss Margaret Iva Miller?" His forearm jammed in his coat sleeve as he slid the envelope across the wood. Not all that bigger than Miller, younger though, nose set by a quack. The St. Louis return address is preprinted, GOULD etched like tombstone letters. Miller still has it with the others.

The Orange County lawyer took four days more, but he telephones first, made Miller shout in the hall in his socks, nodding, "Tuesday? Yes, Tuesday's fine." It meant losing a day shift, and pacing the length of his bed half the morning, because the man's train is late, and he insists meeting him at Miller's resi-dence, he says, three clean syllables, like at a spelling bee.

Miller has been up and down this conversation some thousand times since, preamble to what's in store when he's dead, so he's not saying every word is the word that was said, the way men in history start talking in quotation marks with the writer crouched behind a gooseberry bush hacking up a shorthand note-book. It's not like that. If Mr. Winslow, that's the lawyer's name, if he reads what Miller's been writing, he'll tell you it's all true too, mostly. Not that he has cause to remember. Miller doubts old man Gould could have listed half the men he shoveled under, much less conjured their faces in the half-light of his bedroom curtains, after his Nellie stole off, thinking him asleep, relieved, her bookmark slipped between his pages. Men aren't words until they're dead.

He was at the window when Winslow knocked. Landlady sent him up. He doesn't know how he missed him on the street in that suit. Miller's is all loose threads and elbow-thin even then. Winslow took the chair before Miller offered it, bent his leg into a desktop, and leaned his briefcase open against his other shin. Miller sat on the cot, leaned really, and tried to keep his hands from fluttering, two birds.

"Your wife was Martha Michael Denton." Winslow was reading from a piece of paper, talking to it. Miller answered the bald patch on the crown of his head.

"Before I married her."

"And she bore six children to you."

Miller supposed these were questions, a species, and so expecting something in the way of answers. "No, there's just the five. Gracie, and Ivy of course, and then there's their three brothers."

"Not four boys? Clyde Bryan, Greene Barrie Denton, Lloyd George—"

"Oh, well now, Georgie, haven't heard that name in, I don't know, see, he died about, what, he couldn't a been much more than one was he?"

"Pneumonia."

"That's, yes, that's probably right."

"The death certificate for Mrs. Miller indicates consumption."

Miller didn't say anything to that, nodded, and a second time when Winslow looked up.

"And your second daughter Margaret Iva, she suffered a mild attack of smallpox in 1901."

First Miller heard of it. Ivy'd already been a couple years in the orphan home then, so he repeated, "Mild," unwinding the "i," and that was good enough for both of them. It went on like this awhile. Miller found himself poking around the kettle when the lawyer got to the parts about the Whitakers, more surprised than he should have been someone dug them up.

"Your four youngest children enrolled at the Chilocco Indian School on September 2, 1902. They arrived with a group of twenty-four other mixed-breed children, including the Whitakers' adopted son and daughter."

"I wouldn't know much about that."

"Margaret Iva and her siblings were listed by Mr. Whitaker as one-quarter Shawnee, the minimum for government enrollment. That was on the 31st of August, 1902."

Miller's back is to him, the spoon clicking the kettle, goading it to boil. He asked Mr. Winslow if he wanted tea. A jug of milk kept cool on the ledge outside the bathroom window, where the sun still doesn't shine more than once a day.

"What I find difficult to understand is why two days later the two Miss Millers remain Shawnee, while Denton, age thirteen, and Clyde, age six, are recorded as one-quarter Eastern Cherokee. It's a peculiar inconsistency and one that is repeated on the school's list of students whose three-year terms will expire on June 30th, 1905."

"Bookkeepers," says Miller. "You wouldn't believe the bunk I turn up in the Prescott register. One time there was this man, stayed maybe two nights, but the date—"

"Was Mrs. Miller born on the Indian reservation in Cherokee County, North Carolina, or in Jefferson County, Tennessee, as indicated on her birth certificate?"

"I wouldn't know about that, but her father's parents, the Knoxes, they go back to North Carolina I'm pretty sure, before the War of Independence, Mattie always said."

"And did she also say whether her mother was a full-blood Shawnee or Cherokee?"

"Full-blood something, maybe, I don't know. They're all Indians."

"But your wife was one-half Indian."

Now see how Winslow didn't put a question mark at the end of that one again, so Miller knows it's not a question exactly, not the kind that's looking for an answer any different from what it's already got. Winslow's goading him, sure, but it's mainly the t's he's crossing, getting all the words spelled out for his lady boss. He's not here to sniff out a fraud. He doesn't suspect Miller's little girl is a fake. Nobody does. Miller knows that. Winslow just wants to be rid of him and slurping cocktails in his Pullman car back to civ-i-li-za-tion. You can see it in the way he's breathing, sucking air between his lips, what Miller does when the stink of a poncho wafts over the check-in desk before the Mexican wearing it comes anywhere near. All he's got to do is nod, grunt, do nothing at all, and his little girl has a millionaire for a mama. It's just a matter of deciding what kind of man he is.

"Her?" Miller says. "Nah, but her grandma, she could have been part something or other, I guess. It's possible. But my wife, I wouldn't marry no Indian, understand? Mattie she was white as me. She was American." He said it again, "American," and Mr. Winslow didn't say anything at all for a long time. An eternity you could call it.

Miller didn't do anything wrong, not according to any law. Defrauding the government, that's a federal crime, and the Whitakers', as Miller sees it. Whitaker rented the wagon. Miller dropped Grace and them off to him clean and proper. Another man might have left them unprovided, slunk out with them balled up and snoring, or trucked them places no child ought ever go. He didn't do that.

Things get garbled up next, with the kettle shivering on the flame, and Winslow's bag zipping up. Miller said he thought there would be something for him to sign. Winslow didn't say anything, at least not anything Miller can recall now, though he imagines the letter Winslow wrote next, or, no, the lawyer would have telegraphed, told his boss to call it off.

Miller has to give Helen Gould credit, some kindness in her, godly or otherwise. Superintendent would have chucked all four children on St. Louis, beggars and whores, worse off than the half-men chewing bark at the foot of school hill. Instead she told Ivy her old man refused, no adoption, which Miller said himself when Grace wrote him again, not right away, but eventually she did.

You got to be proud of those two girls of his. He didn't want any of them re-enrolling after their first term, but they went on ahead, the girls did. Then Gracie finds herself a man and then a spot in a convent school for Ivy, before Ivy snuck herself into Carlisle, the Red Man's College, where she found herself a man too, or a part-man. He hears Thorpe's got some white blood at least. Miller might understand it if she'd said yes before the scandal, before Thorpe dropped out of the school and went pro because he couldn't go anywhere else. He's a fake, and the whole world saw it in black-and-white. Ivy was a fool for marrying him. Their kind are liars by birth, and so Miller told her he was denying his consent. That's the word he used, consent, same one as was on Mr. Winslow's form he never showed him. But this time there is no piece of paper wanting his signature, which isn't more than a scribble anyway, in blood or the ink just faded rusty that way. It's a sort of consolation prize, the fame, some money, and all that traveling up and around the globe that way, the real globe, scandal or no. Next thing she'll be pregnant too, little half-breeds coming. Ivy's mama loved babies.

Helen Gould married last year as well, forty-four years of age by Miller's arithmetic. The librarians help him with newspapers from all over parts, but he has to read them there. It wasn't a missionary or a railroad president—it was a railroad president's assistant she married, after the two met in a train wreck, if you can believe it. Miller imagines the wedding must have been pretty fancy, same way he imagines Ivy's. He can't blame her for not inviting him. A man only gets to give his daughter away once. Papers claim Thorpe can play anything, so he's started up baseball now, honeymooning off-season, postcards from London, Cairo, Tokyo, every month or better. The cigar lid's torn up pretty bad. Hardly a sentence on a one of them though, like to an acquaintance, Mr. J. F. Miller on the front. Same as Mr. Winslow said was written in the Chilocco book, the blank space beside "Parent."

Ivy was never untrue though, not even to Nellie Gould for almost doing what she almost did. She was a kid. Miller suspects she'll squeeze out the same allotment of tears for him as Nellie saved for her old man. You give what you got, owed or not. He could twist this all up and around nooselike, say how his holding back on Winslow saved Ivy for her Indian brave. How the boy could never have asked her to dance in any Indian school gymnasium if she'd been plunking out piano keys for her mother Gould's dinner guests. The funny truth is Miller's granddaddy, Ivy's great-granddad, was a BIA man, Bureau of Indian Affairs, and he may have gotten a little too comfortable around that kind of people. Miller's mother said hers was one, and that's probably blood enough for Chilocco's minimum. Can't prove it, so it probably wouldn't have been enough for Winslow if Miller had gotten around to saying it. It's just words now, and all Miller will have left, after the landlady cleans up, and his month's pay shovels a spot for him, a thousand or so miles from Ivy's mother's stone, which he figures is fair too. Half-men they get dug along the bottom, like they're accustomed. The good ones, the Matties and the Georgies, go right up top the hill, but just as dead.

He'll mail this all to Gracie before long, though there's not much she hasn't heard or guessed at, Ivy either probably. He'd like to think it belongs in some leathery book, up on a good varnished shelf, when it's done and everything spelled proper, all the t's, what could be a while yet. He's in no hurry, no train to take him back to anywhere he can go. There's tonight's shift coming, and books to drop off, a pretty girl to wink at, green-eyed like Ivy and him. It's the yarn a fellow tells himself at the end that counts. The last one should be writ up tall so God doesn't have to squint too hard, slouching over that Book of His when the next wagon clatters through. God can smell Miller coming. Miller knows He does. Miller can picture Him, the way He's breathing through his lips, the question already on them. "What are you?" The only question He asks anybody.

Sylvester Makes a Name for Himself

The clock on the nightstand clacks to a minute before six, before his hand rises and clicks the alarm switch down. It never rings. He's awake, has been, since before the lid of the open suitcase took shape on the radiator and the window lace kindled from gray-pink to pink. It's a big day. Mrs. Vahey is below in the kitchen, clattering the coal stove, the metal of the iron pot against the metal of the iron stove top. She's cooking his last breakfast.

A rubber mask droops empty-eyed from the post of the desk chair in his room, where he hung it the night before. A swarthy face, with crooked, bulging teeth and a hideous, pimpled nose. He stares at it as he dresses. He folded the Palm Beach suit over the chair back the night before too. It's thin for February, much too thin, but he is sentimental. It was his first purchase, from down on Eighth, years ago, just two blocks from the boardinghouse, his first morning in Calgary. Everything else is packed. The Carlisle uniform—a tailor widened the shoulders, tightened the loose seams along the pant cuffs—is tucked into a neat blue square in the center of the open suitcase. The scrapbook sits on top of it. He presses the cover flat and smooths a stray page edge. It's ready too. He considered faking some articles, laying them out after hours in the *Herald* basement. Nothing extravagant, just a piece or two to fill gaps. There are so many gaps. That's what a scrapbook is, a story of gaps, what his life is, any life probably. He squares the book again, before closing the suitcase lid, leaning his weight down until both latches click.

Downstairs, Mrs. Vahey has the table set, plates at each chair, but a napkin and cutlery only at the far seat, his seat. It's early still. The rest of the family is sleeping. He touches his hand to his suit pocket, the one bulging from his hip. The rubber mask crinkles.

"Morning, Mama," he booms, but not too loudly. His fingertips pat the faded petal cut off in the shoulder seam of her bathrobe. "You shouldn't have."

"Oh, no trouble, Chief. Couldn't let you sneak off without something in the gut." The smile is real enough. The lines around her eyes crinkle, but she has already turned to the pot in the sink soaking from last night. He listens to the splash and scrape of the scrub brush as he chews his eggs.

Normally it's a two-block jaunt to the *Herald* office. His long coat, the gray one with the imitation fur, is hanging in the hall closet. He would be off in a dash. This morning he has to listen for the a-ooga of Howard's roadster and eye the half of the porch window visible from Mrs. Vahey's table. He doesn't work at the *Herald* anymore.

According to the clock tapping from the hook above the kitchen arch, Howard isn't late yet, but Mrs. Vahey doesn't wind that clock, not daily. It's too high without dragging a chair over, which he sometimes does himself. No one else seems to appreciate the effort of a weighted pulley, of small gears grinding against smaller gears.

After the automobile warps to a stop in the glass, and he stands and announces, "Well, I must be off," and then pushes in his chair, his fork and knife crisscrossing the empty plate, Mrs. Vahey still hasn't turned to him.

"You have a safe trip now," she says to the draining sink. "Best of luck to you out there. I'm sure we'll all miss you."

He thanks her again and assures her he will miss the entire family very much too. He's in the archway now, under the clock. "Oh," he adds, as though he nearly forgot, as though the thought were just striking him again this moment. "I have something I thought Jonathan might like."

The mask is already in his hand. Mrs. Vahey turns and blinks at it. She blinks at it again. He knows if he waits she will recognize it eventually. He is almost certain she will recognize it.

"Remember? The night I—"

But her head is thrown back now, mouth wide, cackling at the cracks in the ceiling. "Oh, you devil! You devil!" When was it, a year ago almost, they were all sitting there, the family, the lid of the soup tureen barely lifted, when the dining room door creaked, and that hand appeared, gun barrel raised at them all, and the figure from the shadow behind it, that horrible mask and voice, that voice of a killer—"Stick 'em up!" Oh my how they laughed! That big, sweet Indian grinning when his other fist yanked the rubber face away. The gun was real though. He never told them that, a .45. It's at the bottom of the largest suitcase.

She hugs him one-armed now, pats the small of his back with her dry hand, almost the way she does Jonathan's before school. "You take care now. You do."

Howard is standing at his back bumper, smiling, the mouth of the trunk waiting. "Morning, Chief!" That's what Howard calls him. Chief. The Chief. Everybody does. It's his name.

The Chief takes his last look at the Vahey house from the passenger window. The white frame, and the deep porch, pickets fencing the frosted yard. It's a cliché really, a lovely cliché.

They turn onto Centre, and Howard guns around a slowing streetcar. The sun is staining the bricks of the Hudson's Bay Building orange, but the electric streetlights haven't clicked off yet. The closest glows no brighter than—he weighs the simile as if his finger were poised above a row of typewriter keys—than a match through the bottom of a whiskey tumbler. He can't help but steal a final glance at the *Herald's* facade of window squares, and at the Grand Theatre next door. Their editor treated the whole staff to seats at the annual minstrel show there last Christmas, a hundred Rotary Club bigwigs clowning in blackface—his very own boss up dere a-grinnin' as big moufed and white-eyed as dey come.

Calgary is really too small for him. Sixty thousand people, barely a third of Vancouver, plus Vancouver is younger, his own age practically, a real railroad town. The frontier. He will have no trouble keeping himself in newspaper work there. The *Sun* loved the clippings he sent, the special interest pieces, the Blackfoot Reserve, the Sarcee Reserve, his best out-of-town assignments. Uplifting, the editor called them.

When they pass the last traffic light and the road bends south past the mills, he thanks Howard again for driving him such a long way. It really wasn't necessary. There's a depot just fifteen miles off the Blood Reserve, where he's stopping tonight. The reverend with the English accent invited him.

"Hey, it's my pleasure. You know that," Howard says. He turns his whole head to say it. "It's completely my pleasure." On cue, the roadster bucks. Something under the hood flap clacks a measure of sixteenth notes, rests a measure, clacks another. A kid with two hammers and a dented pipe. Howard is gripping the wheel in both fists. "Bet you'd prefer Margaret's Rolls though, huh?"

The Chief smiles. Echoes the chuckle. He has to. It's a perfectly fine car. He borrowed it his first trip to the Sarcee, a little ten-mile jump, nothing like the hundred to the Bloods, where they are driving now. Howard insisted. Tomorrow's train out to Vancouver is train enough for any man, but a guest of honor ought to arrive in style, not wait around some backwoods whistle-stop to be hauled up and jounced another hour in some Indian agent's jalopy of a truck to the middle of God knows, the wilderness basically. No friend of Howard's gets treated like that.

The Chief thanks him again. Of all that crowd in the newsroom, Howard is the best, probably the youngest sports editor in all of Canada. Hangs on to the Chief's every word, about those bouts with Dempsey, how he used to run miles with Thorpe, played elbow to elbow with him in the Carlisle backfield. He told Howard he still didn't know why he took their managing editor's weekly thirty dollars, when he could have pulled five hundred per fight. Dempsey guaranteed it. He's thinking about telling that story again, but Howard is starting to say something, clearing his throat.

"So," says Howard. He coughs again, another dry one. "You ever get to say goodbye to Margaret?"

He pictures the Rolls-Royce. Silver-plated fittings, all the coachwork in aluminum paint, probably the only Silver Ghost in Calgary, in all Alberta. He loved driving it, engine humming like a sewing machine, Margaret gripping his free hand.

Howard is looking at him. Has to swerve a little to keep it up.

So he says, "Not really." And when the shrug isn't enough either, he adds, "Her husband's been in town all month."

That gets Howard's chin nodding. Eyes back on the road. It costs him another cough to manage: "Probably just as well." After he's said it again, he adds, "You know what you really need, don't you?" Howard holds his hand out, palm up, like he's trying to give him something, a mint maybe. "A squaw," Howard says. "A squaw of your own. That's what you need. You know that, don't you? "

He has no choice but to agree. He's said as much himself, to Howard, to the other *Herald* boys. Howard's free hand is on the shoulder of his coat now.

"A nice, educated Cherokee girl. One that's honestly looking to settle down, not sneak off on another weekend fling. You're better than that. You know that. You deserve better than that."

For the fourth time since slamming Howard's passenger door, he thanks him. "Who knows," he says. "Maybe tonight." He laughs one of his infectious laughs, the kind that can send the length of a restaurant table into a chorus of cackles, and the waitress scurrying for the next round. Maybe tonight will be his lucky night.

"That's the spirit, Chief. That's the spirit."

The Blood Reserve is a quick detour on his way west. That's what he told Howard, last week, after checking the assignment desk to see that Howard could get the day free. He was asked to be the speaker for the mission school's reunion dinner. A thank-you for that wonderful piece he wrote about the school and the reservation and all the hard work they're doing down there, the most progressive tribe in Alberta, a slap at the government and their land-leasing policies, forced impoverishment. It was an advocacy piece. That's what he is really. An advocate.

The sun is climbing out of his eyes, but his hands are numb from the rattle and the cold. The heater vent is no match for the hiss of the door cracks and windows. He would pull his scarf tighter, but it would be rude to Howard, whose gloves are the thin leathery kind they make just for drivers now. Though the suit rumpled under his coat is probably wool. All of Howard's suits are rumpled. That's the look in the newsroom these days. It was only a matter of time before Howard brought up his getting fired.

"It's just plain wrong. After the mayor said you shouldn't be. I mean, it's his call, right? If he can take a joke, why the hell can't Woods?"

As Howard sees it, and the rest of the newsroom, and the newsroom at the rival *Albertan* for that matter, it was the best prank in the history of City Hall. The *Albertan* published a ballad about it, in rhyming quatrains. Only Colonel Woods, who enjoys smearing burnt-cork on his face once a year with the other gentlemen of the Rotary Club, sees no humor in one of his *Herald* employees imposing indignities upon His Worship Mayor Adams and other officers of the city. The bruise the mayor received upon his forehead while colliding with his secretary in the conference room doorway could have resulted in a concussion. That Commissioner Samis was not seriously injured by the window he shattered with his bare fists nor by his second-story leap to the snowbank below was nothing short of miraculous. Commissioner Smith's knee-twisting dive under the meeting table was also a perfectly appropriate reaction to the sight of a gas-masked figure stepping into the room and tossing a satchel with an attached pressure gauge and a burning fuse.

When the Chief tells the story—and he's telling it all again now, for Howard, who's giggling, and swerving again, his face reddening as though every word of it were new—he plays up the suspense. His nod to the city engineer's secretary. The paper bag under his arm. Spreading the supplies out on the wash basin in the first-floor men's room. The assembly. The march up the rear stairwell. The voices from over the conference room transom. His hand on the doorknob. It's a great story, it really is. Nobody tells it better.

After Howard catches his breath, there's a silence, and he thinks maybe this time Howard is going to ask him. Why did he do it? It's an obvious enough question, but Howard's never asked it, and neither has anyone else. He might answer something about boredom, a year typing the City Hall beat, columns and columns of snowplows and sewers. Or he could play up the restless spirit angle, his nomadic blood calling him farther west. Since it's Howard asking, he might lead with Margaret, how she broke things off after he joked once about buying her a ring. One joke, that was it.

Maybe the conversation would shift to the philosophical next. They could chat about life, death, God. The Great Spirit. Tell me, Howard, do you believe in reincarnation? Reincarnation? Boy. I don't know. That's a little outside my beat. I mean, spirituality, isn't that your department, Chief? What do you believe? Can souls be reborn into new bodies? Are we just our old dead selves coming back again and again, trying to get it right this time, trying to get it right?

Howard isn't asking him anything. Howard's eyes are on the road. There's no danger of his telling Howard that he cooked up the gas bomb scheme after the reverend at the Blood Reserve invited him to the reunion dinner, and the special ceremony afterward. The naming ceremony. There's no danger of his revealing that.

Except for a lunch stop at a crossroads tavern, the rest of the drive is quieter. A hundred miles, an Indian can't be expected to chat for all of it. The Chief pretends to nap near the end, before rousing spontaneously, instinctively, when the roadster bumps across the border of the reserve. A sign marks it. He tells Howard which way when the road forks. He should double-check the directions scribbled on the *Herald* envelope in his pocket, but it would ruin the effect. That can't really be the same clump of cattle they keep roaring past. He just has to keep the ridge of mountains to the right.

He doesn't spot the mission right off, worries they'll have to backtrack, but then a cluster of white rectangles catches the sunlight, and the buildings emerge where the gray-white of the sky blurs into the white-gray of the prairie. There was no snow last time. No wind-carved dunes with snaking spines. Other spots are bare, or nearly, rows of hoed dirt and a string of frayed white down the centers. The school farms forty acres. In August the wheat quivered like fur, a great sleeping pelt of it. That's why the Rockies look taller today. The lip of them has been ratcheted up a gear or two. The whole range is puffed up and braced for him.

The entrance driveway is rutted, and the roadster's wheels slot into the frozen wagon tracks. Howard is craning his neck, taking in the hospital and gymnasium to the left, girls' quarters and dining hall to the right, boys' quarters and church up ahead, stables and granary in back, all of it done up in coats of identical white. It looked fresher last summer, like a movie set. Nothing like new coats to hide old sins, the reverend joked.

"So this is it then?"

He wants to tell Howard to park farther back, so the warp of the porch column isn't so obvious. The rot along the edge of the bottom step too. They're all frame buildings, same as the Vaheys'. One kick of a coal-oil lamp and it would all be prairie ash. He considers telling Howard not to judge by its skin, or that still water runs deep, something along those lines, but he can't. He's disappointed too. He likened it to Carlisle in the article, a scaled-down imitation. The reverend is a huge fan of Carlisle, of Colonel Pratt, the extraordinary work he accomplished there. The students speak English only, study from the same government-approved books as white children, receive a daily hour of religious instruction, plus both morning and evening prayers. Indian music and dancing is forbidden. They're moving into the twentieth century, the whole tribe is.

He lets Howard heave a suitcase to the middle step, no farther, before thanking him for the fifth time and shaking his gloved hand for a meaningful length of time. The leather isn't as soft as he imagined. Howard steps back and teeters there, one foot on wood, one crunching mud, both hands worrying his coat pockets. It's cold, and he could be inside already, but Howard has something he wants to say.

"You know the thing I most admire about you, Chief?" Howard has to tilt his chin up to meet his eyes. "I've seen you rub elbows with every kind of man, president of the board down to shoeshine boy, and I have never, I have never once seen you try to be anything but what you are."

It's fairly eloquent for a sportswriter, and probably he's been rehearsing it in his head for miles, maybe before they got in the car. The next part too.

"Forget Vancouver. Forget it. I give you a year, one year, before you're back home, back to Oklahoma, where you belong." He jabs his gloved finger at the ground, at the boot-shaped clods, to emphasize the point. It's a good gesture. "You think you're going to stick it out in the civilized life, but you're not. I know you better than you do. You're going back to the blanket. A squaw and a papoose, that's what you want deep down. I know it."

The Chief stares back at Howard a moment, a full measure, two half rests, before curving his lip into a half smile. "One year?" He cocks an eyebrow, the left one. "The right doesn't look as good when he practices in front of a bathroom mirror. "I got a hundred dollars says you're wrong."

Howard straightens, and then grins, right up to his gums. He loves this sort of talk. Man talk. It's why he went into journalism. "Deal," he booms back. And there's Howard's fist out there squeezing and pumping away again.

He waits until the roadster plumes a cloud of white fume above the entrance pillars, before turning inside. The dining hall is warmer, but not warm. The tables and chairs have been shoved along the windows, and a trio of boys is swabbing floorboards. He stomps clods of snow from his shoes, thinking someone—the reverend, one of the teachers—should be coming to greet him, but no one does. One of the boys looks up, then back down, the tendrils of his mop slapping a wet circle around his feet. Another struggles through a groaning side door with an armful of fire logs. When Sylvester asks him where he might find the reverend, the boy nods toward the back of the hall, at the kitchen.

The smell is good. The oven racks are deep in roasts and pies. He can unwind his scarf. Girls stand elbow to elbow at the chopping boards, with sacks of potatoes, turnips, carrots, upturned the length of the counters. The lone girl with the onion bag is twisting the back of her wrist into the corner of her eye. She blinks, tries to focus, blinks again, opens wider, focuses on the handsome man in the long coat, sees that she's staring, and smiles, laughs almost. He's smiling too. She's pretty.

Dusky daughters of the plains. His editor liked that phrase. Not yet a generation from savagery. He's unbuttoning his coat now, letting the air swim around his ribs. The girl is chopping again, but stealing glances too. She's still smiling, can't seem to help herself. Definitely the prettiest in the row. Howard's voice is in his ear, the high notes it hits when he wants to be emphatic. She looks old enough, probably graduating when the fields thaw. He tries to imagine her in an evening gown, instead of that shapeless mission dress and the finger-smeared apron, but he sees buckskins instead, soft as baby down, and a necklace of dyed porcupine quills, and then only the necklace on her.

"Mr. Long Lance!" The reverend is backing in the rear door, one end of what can only be a Victrola cabinet straightening his elbows. "Be with you in just a moment!" He waddles it to the wall and tells the boy at the other end to drop the front corner first, gently.

The English accent really is a great touch. It's hard not to imitate it. The whole life story, it's all good—orphan, quaint little mill town, heart of England, grows up on brave and noble tales of Red Indians, next thing abandoning grandfather's carriage business for a steamer ticket and the Canadian plains. Sylvester didn't put all that in the article, but he could have, if his editor had given him the extra column like he asked. Or a two-parter; it should have been a two-parter.

"Mr. Long Lance," the reverend bellows again. His cheeks are bright and the smell of wood smoke hangs on his black shirt. "So pleased you have made it safe and sound."

He forgot how weak the reverend's handshake is, a learned trait, Indian fashion. He has to remember that. He assures the reverend his drive was delightful, a final chance to relish the stark beauty of the Reserve in winter.

"I am sorry to hear you are leaving Alberta."

"It was a difficult choice, but it is time to move on to the next adventure."

"For your introduction, I'll say formerly of the *Calgary Herald*? Is there anything I should add in after that?"

Instead of the *Sun*, the smaller of the papers, he says, "*Vancouver Province.*"

"Oh, great news, I didn't know." The reverend is writing on an index card he produces from his shirt pocket. He tilts it sideways on his palm, scrawling up the column of his other notes.

"Their circulation is larger than both Calgary papers combined, than the whole population in fact." Sylvester doesn't mention that he introduced himself to the Vancouver editors as a Blackfoot, the language the Blood speak too. Not only will a new tribal affiliation give his reporting more credibility than continuing his bylines as an American Cherokee, but it will also bolster the image of the Canadian Plains Indian whom he is striving so very much to aid. He's confident the reverend would approve. Besides, he hasn't lived among his former tribe since childhood. The customs and legends of the Blackfoot peoples, they are as much his now as any in the world.

They put him in a room in the rectory, not the boys' quarters, which he only now realizes he was picturing, his old Carlisle room. Here he has a single, what only Thorpe and the other athletes got. According to the clock tapping on the nightstand, he has two hours to rest and wash up. The radiator is built closer to the wall than the ones at the Vaheys', but the dresser top is lower, so he opens the suitcase there. The Carlisle uniform gets a thorough smoothing as he drapes it on the bedspread like an emptied scarecrow. Then he takes up the scrapbook.

He is perched on the mattress edge and bends the glue-crinkled pages across his knees. He opens randomly. The American Indian Who Fought at Vimy Ridge. Lieut. Long-Lance of Carlisle Surprises Teachers with Note from Trenches. The photograph in the Canadian militia uniform is good. Firm chin, shoulders wide. A private's insignia mars the sleeve, but he regrets the smear in the caption more. The lettering was so small, he couldn't erase the erroneous "Cherokee" and pen in "Blackfoot" as he had in the other articles. He spent his last evening in Calgary doctoring newspaper font. Full-Blooded *Blackfoot* to Enter West Point. Fenimore Cooper's Romances Have Nothing on This *Blackfoot*'s Real Life Story.

Some pages stick, so he snakes his fingers along the margins before prying. The yellowing *Red Man* articles, these are a problem. "Among the interesting legends of the Cherokee," a column begins, "is the one concerning the naming of children." He could change it too, of course, transplant the whole tribe to the Northwest, or he could simply explain that he had been a curious chronicler in his youth, a gatherer of his fellow students' far-flung folklore. An anthropologist. What he is now practically.

Tonight he will put all past mistakes behind him. That week at the Sun Dance, trying to interview participants, how was he supposed to know the girl was a prostitute? No one else was talking to him, or posing for his camera. And teepee etiquette, those frowns when he ducked between the fire and his host, and then sat on his right side, the women's side. All of those failures, the humiliations, all of his old self, it will be overwritten tonight, as cleanly as chalk on a blackboard. He will make himself new again. He skims down to the last sentence: "From that day, the Indians have named their children after the first object they see on looking from their teepees when a child is born."

The water is not hot, but his bath is brief. He lingers longer at the sink, tapping black hairs from the razor on the white porcelain, leaning close, inhaling what threads of steam remain. He never shaves with cold water. It ravages the skin. There is time for calisthenics too, the whole routine. The floorboards creak under the heels of his palms as he exhales each number. His lips nearly touch the worn-smooth wood each time. Push-ups train the chest, shoulder, and triceps muscles. He tucks his toes under the empty dresser for sit-ups. The abdominals. His body rises and drops, rises and drops, the click of spine against wood muffled by the cotton of his undershirt.

The wagons and buckboards start clumping in at dusk, dozens of them. He watches from the window, with the drapes mostly pulled. An owner brushes snow from a pony's mane. The sun is setting behind a mountain peak, that one carved off on its own, like a distant castle almost. The Bloods have a name for it, but he can't remember what it is. He's dressed before six o'clock, every button bright in the lamplight. His shoes too, which sit by the foot of the bed, so they can't hear him pacing from below, if there's anyone even down there. When the clock on the nightstand reads quarter past, he slips them on.

The dining hall is a crowd of bodies and white linen tablecloths. Students and recent students stand in circles and half circles chatting in English, while the parents and grandparents keep to the edges, nearer their reflections in the windows, and whisper in Blackfoot. He pulls the door sealed behind him, listens to the wind tighten to a pinprick at the back of his neck, but he doesn't step farther into the room, not until the reverend hails him in that accent of his. He joins the teachers standing in the empty space under the center lights and shakes their hands. Loosely. He met some of them last summer, but he can't remember which or any of their names. The onion-chopping girl is standing there too, in an honest-to-God dress, hem halfway up her calf. It turns out she's last year's valedictorian, and she has stayed on as a teacher's aide. Her name is Mary Ghost Skin. Their hands meet in barely a whisper of a touch.

The reverend introduces him to Old Mountain Horse next, a tribal elder, and his son Michael Mountain Horse, who is a graduate and a veteran. He fought at Vimy Ridge too. When the father speaks, it's the reverend who translates.

"He would like to know if you were wounded."

He faces the old man, keeps his eyes centered on his. "Nothing very serious," he confesses, "a chunk of shrapnel in the back of the head." He's pointing, running his finger up his neck. Mary Ghost Skin's eyes widen. "And a broken nose. Sustained, I presume, while falling on my face." He timed the pause just right, and the circle is laughing. When the reverend mutters at Old Mountain Horse, the old man nods and allows a smile of his own.

The reverend, who did not serve in the Great War, compliments Mr. Long Lance's recent article on the Sun Dance, a too-often misunderstood religious ceremony. The public is wrong in its condemnation. The practice, like all Blackfoot religious practices, stems from a dutiful worship of the Great Spirit, the name his Lord God has taken among his Indian children. It's the son who has to keep his mouth tilted to his father's ear now. His father's face doesn't change. The portrait of King George behind his head doesn't change either.

Sylvester expected a taller man. The other wrinkled Indians tower a head above him. Mountain Horse. He wonders if the name was given as a joke, if Indians do that sort of thing. And where is the headdress, the eagle-plume headdress? They must have brought it and the rest of the ceremonial props. Set off in a bag somewhere, in a corner with the coat stands, or waiting in the washroom maybe, a quick change before the performance.

The teachers take their seats at the head table. He sits beside the reverend, who sits at the center next to a block of wood that's supposed to be a podium, something a student nailed together. Mary is a table over, but his eyes are on the old man. Trays are carried from the kitchen, but no lids are lifted until the reverend finishes his prayer, twice, once in English, once in Blackfoot, same as Sundays with the regular congregation.

The reverend and the rest of the room, even Old Mountain Horse, eat with the fork always in the left hand, and so he does too. After plates are cleared and teacups filled, the reverend taps his left-handed spoon against his half-full water glass. It's a brighter, rounder note than Sylvester would have predicted, and he has to stop himself from chiming his emptier glass to descend the scale. They're all standing up now, because the reverend's voice has dropped an octave as he proposes a toast to the king. Long may he live. Then they're sitting again, except for the reverend, who is standing at the little podium and trying not to use his index card more than he has to. He welcomes them again to the Ninth Annual Re-Union of St. Paul's Ex-Pupils and expresses his extreme pleasure in introducing tonight's speaker, Captain Sylvester Chahuska Long Lance, a role model for all that a twentieth-century Indian may achieve when he sets his heart and mind to the hard task ahead.

There's applause, and Sylvester nods through it humbly, before proposing a toast of his own, to all the proud graduates of this fine institution—they honor their parents and people in all that they aspire to. Chairs are scraping up and down again, and the thunk of glassware on muffled wood, and he waits for silence to resurface. And then he waits longer. Stretching it. The anticipation. Even Old Mountain Horse's face is a frozen stare. Sylvester clears his throat.

The average Indian walks daily between two worlds, his potential unrealized. He sees the pleasures and advantages of the white man in a haze that forever denies them to him. But these very same pleasures and advantages are, with a dash of initiative, grit, and determination, as available to each of us as they are to him. The white man's superiority is mere illusion, a mask that we may seize and pull over our own faces. It is but a costume, and in donning it, in adopting his ways of prosperity, we do not become the white man. We replace him. Let us seize his role and recast it for ourselves, outdo him in performance and so garner that grander applause we so rightfully deserve.

He goes on a little longer like that, but they get the picture. His eyes keep moving, taking in the breadth of the room, pausing table to table, on the next upturned face, on Mary's face, while keeping Old Mountain Horse and his son's tilted head always in his periphery. It's got to be a hard message for the old Indian, the obsolete past, turning your back on it. There might be something of his own father's face in him, not the nose obviously, but those grim jowls, the dark web at each eye.

There's more clapping when he's finished, a standing ovation if it counts when the teachers' table stands first. The reverend is patting his arm, leaning in with all kinds of heartfelt compliments. Dessert is good too. Not great, the peaches are canned, but the pie crust is fresh and crisp. It must have been planned that way, like a magician's trick, the distraction, pretty assistants in stockings, because when he looks up, there's the eagle-plume headdress. It's perched right there on top of the old man's head. Big gaudy feathers poking straight up. He doesn't know where they pulled it from.

But Sylvester's eyes are keen again, and he doesn't miss the buffalo robe getting spread out under the electric lamps, right there in the open middle of the room. Old Mountain Horse is gesturing at him, to come forward. The son gestures too, mirrors him a half-beat later, still translating. He thought there would be an announcement, a few words from the reverend, but that part of the show is over. Everyone knows what's happening.

His chair legs skitter back as he dabs his mouth with the napkin he finds still in his hand. Others are standing too, the men, all of the wrinkled men. They wait till he's almost to the robe before closing on him. Then there's a hand on his shoulder, pressing, shoving really. He's supposed to kneel. It's part of the ceremony. This is the ceremony. The adoption ceremony. They circle him hip to hip, so he can't see anything but denim, belt buckles, flannel shirts, barely a thread of tablecloth between elbow crooks. It's bad blocking, because the rest of the room, the audience, can't see him either. With the hide under his knees and the tobacco scent breathing around him, he could be in a teepee, a great pole-vaulted teepee, and the burn of fire and coal in the oven pit. He imagines he is inhaling bark smoke, and then he is inhaling it. Someone else's wrinkled hands are giving Old Mountain Horse a branch and the red coal smoldering in the crook of its fingers. There's an iron pan too, and the coal clomps and rolls to the blackened rim and hisses there, before Old Mountain Horse covers it, in grass clippings it looks like. Sweetgrass. Sylvester inhales twice, the second time deeply. It's not so bad.

The Indian's hand quivers in the smoke, splits it into rivulets. He wafts some up his arms, strokes his chest with it, like he's miming that he's in the shower. Old Mountain Horse is purifying himself. He says something, in Blackfoot, a prayer, the son's voice is translating, but Sylvester's heart is beating too much for him to catch the real words. The two voices sound the same, guttural, gibberish. The old man is lifting a buckskin bag, a nice one, and opening it. His fingers come out clay-stained, a shade of red Sylvester has never seen before, brighter, deeper, darker. The old man is reaching his daubed fingers toward him, toward his face. Old Mountain Horse strokes Sylvester's forehead first. The rising sun. The reverend went over it all with him on the telephone, the sun's path across the heavens. Only now it's not an Englishman's voice crackling a hundred miles away. It's the old Indian's calluses rubbing the grit of the clay into Sylvester's pores, his chin, the right cheek, now the left. Long life. The sacred paint wards off all sickness, all sins, all wrongs.

Sylvester is supposed to stand again. It's another prayer. He tries to listen to the son's translation, coming from behind him somewhere, but he's staring at the headdress. The old man is lifting it from his head. The feathers shift like there's something alive under there, something still breathing. The old man is looking at him. The headdress rests in his wrinkled hands now, flopped against his shirt, and he is looking into Sylvester's face. When the old man speaks, it's still Blackfoot, but not that chant anymore, not that chopping, memorized cadence. The old man is speaking for real.

Behind him Michael Mountain Horse says, "Buffalo Child's bravery is talked of daily among the Blackfoot and Blood Indians of these plains."

Old Mountain Horse's face is inches from his.

"And as you must henceforth be known by his honorable name among these tribes . . ."

Almost the entire bottom row of teeth is gone.

". . . you must ever endeavor to be the great Indian . . ."

The old man's breath smells of tea and canned peaches.

". . . whose spirit now comes back to earth and enters your body."

Sylvester bends his neck when the headdress rises in the old man's hands, so he doesn't have to stretch too much. Old Mountain Horse is placing the war bonnet, the dead Buffalo Child's war bonnet, upon Sylvester's head. The feathers are rustling. Sylvester is being crowned. The leather is brittle and scratches at his forehead as the band settles into place against his ears. It's lighter than he expected, lighter than the Sarcee chief's headdress he borrowed for the Calgary summer parade. If there were a mirror somewhere along the wall instead of all that framed royalty, he could peek over the old men's heads for a glimpse of himself. The reverend will have to take a photograph later, for the scrapbook. A whole new page.

Old Mountain Horse is chanting again, singing sort of. The reverend said they'd finish with the war song of Buffalo Child, of the new Buffalo Child. It's Sylvester's war song. He's Buffalo Child. He wishes he had the Sarcee chief's white buckskin costume on right now too, with the frilled sleeves, the one Sylvester wore when he and his war party galloped down Seventh Avenue to the steps of City Hall and roped Mayor Adams to a pony. You could barely see from all the flashbulbs. What great publicity. The mayor gave him a medal that time, literally, an honorary medal, promoted him to Indian Committeeman and Publicity Agent.

The old Indian finishes his song and then gives the new Buffalo Child a shove, in the chest, with both hands. It seems rude, but it's part of the act. Buffalo Child has been honored and now must return to his place among the other warriors as an equal. The warrior Buffalo Child. That's him. That's his name now. Old Mountain Horse turns away, all of the old men do, as they start winding their way back to their empty chairs and dessert plates. Buffalo Child stands alone on the muddy hide. That's it. That's the ceremony. He is a real Indian now.

The reverend is grinning at him, has his hand out for yet another shake, a surprisingly firm one, his other hand slapping his elbow again and again. Buffalo Child knew he wasn't going to get to keep the eagle-plumes, but he's still sad when Michael shuffles over with the canvas bag, slots the headdress in so all the feathers lie down in neat, flat rows. He wants to run his palm along their edges, but the head table is being moved back now, and he has to help. They're making room, lining rows of chairs along the walls. The Victrola the reverend lugged into the kitchen is under the portrait of the Queen now, and its horn is blaring a foxtrot. One of the teachers is cranking the arm. He can't see where the hide was spread on the floor before, but he's sure someone folded it up. They wouldn't just start dancing on it.

Before the record is changed a second time, Mary Ghost Skin is at his elbow, lamenting the state of her poor dance card. It's empty. He accepts her wrist-drooped hand, and they waltz into the parting crowd, the way no crowd in the Carlisle gymnasium would ever have parted for Sylvester Long. Look at him. He's got the prettiest girl, the way Thorpe and that quarterback used to grab up all the business girls every social. The heads turning, the smiles, they're all for him now. He's the star Indian here.

"So," says Mary. "The mighty Buffalo Child." She has to tilt up on her toes to talk into his ear. "How's it feel?"

He considers answering truthfully. It's a queer impulse, but so is the throb in his lungs, the way his ears are beating, blood filling cells he didn't know existed. He tells her it feels great. He feels absolutely great.

"Watch out, they'll make you the King of England next." She smells of canned peaches too. Of jars of strawberries, of plums and apricots and syruped pears. "You know you handled it better than he did. When Mike's father started smearing him up, you should have seen his expression."

"Whose expression?"

"The Prince's."

He's heard of princesses, of course, Indian princesses, but they're not called that, not seriously. He's still smiling at her, dumbly.

"Edward," she says.

"Edward who?"

She's giggling. She thinks he's putting her on. He's so funny. "Prince Edward! The Prince of Wales." She touches both of her hands to his chest when she laughs, to keep balance. "Remember when he did his tour of Canada? I was a first-year student, so I got to see his naming ceremony. He was kneeling right there, where you were." She kicks a heel up. "Right here." She jabs her finger at the floorboard running between their shoes. It's a different color than the others. A replacement board.

He feels dizzy. He tells her that, all the excitement. He should sit for the next dance, but really, she should go on without him, honestly, he doesn't mind. He finds his abandoned water glass, someone's water glass, and drinks it, empties it. When the girl finds him again, he pleads sore feet, and the next time a trick knee. She stops asking after that and dances with a boy from her graduating class. Sylvester probably couldn't have gotten her back to his room anyway. It's a rectory after all.

He begs off early, such a big day. The reverend understands completely. It is only a few yards between buildings, so Sylvester didn't bother with the coat. He steps outside and watches his breath congeal like a plume from Howard's roadster. The sweat along his collar goes frigid. The moon is sitting above that lone mountain peak, no stars around it. He scratches at his scalp with both hands, then smooths the hair back, fingers rigid as comb teeth.

The moon was in that Cherokee story, the one he typed up for the *Red Man*. The chief rode on an eagle's back expecting to find another planet, but instead he found that the moon was just a hole in a thick black crust. On the other side, his people, the dead people of his tribe, stumbled blindly, their eye sockets empty after the birds had eaten them out. It was punishment. The Great Spirit hid away the true heaven for the animals whom the Indians slaughtered to steal their names. His English teacher complimented him. Miss Moore said it was a highly spirited rendering of a legend.

He's still awake when the wagons start jangling under his window. He pictures Whippoorwill, the way his braids, his own real braids, flopped when he rode horseback in the Wild West Show. He scratches at the dried mud on his forehead, the bit that didn't scrub off in the basin. He can't see the clock in the dark. He can only hear it, how the mechanical beat deepens when he lowers his head to the pillow, as if submerging his body. He reminds himself that he is reborn. The whole world is. He imagines the clock hands clicking backward. The clock of the world spinning backward. He is Chief Buffalo Child. He is coming home, to the ancient plains, to the new past, to his new home.

Big Jim Becomes His Father

Although Charlotte—a Potawatomi and so naturally a Catholic—had vowed to love and obey Hiram Thorpe when they married that morning in the Sacred Heart Indian Mission, Hiram thought it best to send his other wives to the neighbor's farm for the night before bringing Charlotte to her new home. Hiram knew the priest's words by heart now, but it was the scent of the chapel's raw timber that lingered afterward, as did the startling heat and depth of his bride's mouth when he slouched to kiss her. Had she not spotted the bedding he would not have believed her a virgin after all.

Hiram was mounting her again when he heard Sarah's baby cry through the unlatched window. It was a sickly thing, and though nearly walking, it still woke two, sometimes three times a night to suck. Mary's children were older, and their cackles pierced like crow cries as the neighbor's wagon wheels moaned to a stop. Charlotte was nearly dressed when the door scraped open.

"My god," said Mary, "she's a child."

Charlotte was sixteen, older than Mary when Hiram brought her to the cabin six years before. He was thirty now, or thereabouts. His mother had not been gifted with dates, and after she joined Hiram's father in the Agency cemetery last winter, Hiram chose not to wonder anymore. He rose naked from the blanket and stroked the handlebars of his mustache.

"This is Charlotte," he said.

When he planted his heel against the trunk Mary was dragging across his floorboards to the open door, she draped the shawls and dresses onto her eldest daughter's arms and pushed the girl outside. The other two children she left.

They watched at the window as the wagon circled back to the double wheel path and the bleat of Sarah's baby dipped under the breeze. The neighbor agreed to take them as far as Okmulgee, where Mary had family and Sarah a lover.

"This is Charlotte," Hiram told his children. "Your new mother."

He had entertained notions of keeping all three women. Annuity checks from the old Kansas reservation plus profits from his herd would have kept them clothed, and there was no hunter in the Indian Territory better than Hiram Thorpe. Twenty miles with a stag on each shoulder he'd trudged once, or so the story at the Black Dog Saloon went. But even if he had pasture enough to graze two teams of horses and more cattle than he could count, a one-room cabin can't pen three wives at a stretch.

Charlotte was a Citizen Potawatomi too, and so not as easily broken. She talked Potawatomi to her mama, French to her pap, and Sac to Hiram. Nuns had taught her how to draw English, whole pages of pretty round letters. Mary couldn't scratch her name, and Sarah was refuse from the Civilized Tribes. Her people lost what became Hiram's ranch and the rest of their land for siding with the Confederates. Charlotte's family had known better. Not only had her grandfather, a fur trader's half-breed boy, made a Kansas judge call him competent and slice off his share of reservation, but he charged white men a dollar a head to cross his log bridge. Three hundred in one day, they said, while Hiram's grandfather was still huddling in a bark hut shaving his head.

Not that Hiram wasn't proud of his Thunder Clan. Black Hawk had warred when traders snatched up the last of the homelands up around the Great Lakes somewhere. The rest of the tribe loped down to Iowa, and then on to Kansas, like they were told, but Black Hawk fought to the death, or almost. That was Hiram's mother's clan, but since she married the blacksmith the government sent, Hiram was accepted mostly. Otherwise he didn't mind a white man for a father, though it had meant sitting mornings in the mission schoolhouse after the tribe let the Methodists build it. Only mixed-bloods showed, the Thorpe boys the rowdiest. They had lived in a frame house, beside the gunsmith shop, where hunting parties paraded Comanche scalps past the open windows. That was before the smallpox, and what the BIA man called flux, from eating green corn, he said. Hiram had been too young to help his father hammer burial boxes, six dollars each he charged, half price for child-sized. Multiply that by three hundred and you don't need a toll bridge to be the richest half-breed in an Agency town.

Now another three hundred dead wouldn't leave enough to do the digging. When the president of the United States said it was time to uproot again, it took seventeen wagons to haul the sick and old out of Kansas, another twenty-three for everything else that couldn't walk. Hiram was no child then, so he rode bareback and switched the packhorses and coondogs. Come spring they had him hoeing burnt prairie roots, women's work, but so were the other men, spacing out rows of pumpkins and beans.

The garden fenced next to the cabin was Charlotte's now, the hogs and chickens too, but Hiram liked picking pecans when the trees started sagging over the riverbanks. He didn't mind the government assigning him a quarter section after slicing up the last of the tribal acres, though it meant losing the rest to whites, neighbors he had to call them now, that tuft of a town sprouting not three miles upwind. Hiram knew enough to corral his herd at night, to keep cattlemen from rounding up stray stock. The floodplains below the cabin fed them all, the grass smelling sweet and green and thick in the dry gusts. What did he care about homelands?

When Charlotte's first twins died, girls, Hiram cribbed the frames himself, not three feet long either one of them. He built a sleeping loft for the cabin too, with sanded boards, not just cottonwood and hickory. Charlotte's second batch fared better, both boys, Charlie and Jim, and the next girl, Mary, what apparently every good Catholic mother has to name a daughter or two. Not that Hiram cared. He hadn't seen that first wife of his in years. This new Mary fell out of the wagon and stuck her throat on a cornstalk, so maybe that's why she could only talk Sac when she grew up and not a grunt of English. Anyway, it wasn't Hiram's fault, though he had been drinking and should have steered around the run-off ditch or at least slowed down some.

The girl rolled off one of the empty gallon jugs she was playing on in back. Other bootleggers covered theirs, said it was eggs they were selling, sometimes crammed their whiskey jars in the hollow wagon axles when they thought the BIA man was onto them. Not Hiram. He rolled in on payment days, parked his rig between the corn mill and the agent's eight-room brick house, and poured his goods into any flask he was handed. He looked good up there, same high-crowned hat as any Indian in the Territory, the scuffed boots too, but it was a white man's business suit he wore, with a silk scarf against his throat. He clamped the cigar in his teeth when he needed his other hand free, for pouring, or pocketing coins.

The BIA agent hollered from his doorjamb, and mailed letters to the Washington address where his paychecks came from, but the agent's manhood required nothing else of him, not with the holster on Hiram's hip and the tales coming downstream from Keokuk Falls. It wasn't much of a town, a couple of miles past Hiram's place along the North Fork River, but pushed up against the Creek Nation, what the government called "dry." It kept its seven saloons in business and more whores than a man could bed in a fortnight. Hiram slept off his hangovers on the front lawn of the justice of the peace, better than any room in the man's hotel, Hiram bragged. Even the hogs roamed drunk, gorged on the waste mash the distilleries dumped in the gullies out back. Stagecoaches dropped off enough newcomers to keep a pair of gravediggers employed, daily almost, but when the rails came in, the trains steered wide. The man Hiram killed he couldn't have named, much less said what they had been howling at the bar about. But he remembered the clack of the stranger's jaw against his fist and his expression, the wide almost laughing eyes, when he pulled the barrel of his gun away from the man's gut. The room had no business getting quiet as it did, as if they hadn't watched a body die before, or an Indian shove his fingers in the hole and rip them out dripping, up high, so even the nigger cook in the doorway could see.

He bought Charlotte a dress from the store window with his profits, told the counter girl, a busty Shawnee, to keep the nickel change. He was thinking about that first wife, dead of diphtheria, when little Mary toppled out of the wagon. The child cried some, but there wasn't much to be done, though Charlotte made him hitch a fresh team to the buckboard and rattle all the way back to the Agency to pay the doctor to tell them what any man could see himself. Afterward, the girl, too heavy now for her mother's arms, ran out ahead of them and clambered up the wagon edge, while Charlotte asked about the package in the back, the one Hiram kept hinting about. When the BIA agent trotted by on horseback, clucking and shaking his head, Hiram had to hurdle a railing and sprint the length of two alleys, but he beat the man to his stable and half dragged him from his saddle before the horse broke his grip with a gallop. He added a second sprint, neck on neck with the colt to the mission corner, and a lassoing, to the telling he gave Charlotte on the ride home.

"Would of beat him," he said, "if it weren't for the whiskey sloshing my gut."

Charlotte didn't believe him but giggled anyway as she smoothed the new dress in her lap. The calico she was wearing she'd sewn herself. It was shapeless, not bunched under the ribs like this one.

She didn't love the man, but there was something there a woman could take pride in if she had a mind to. Hiram hunted, smoked enough meat for them the winter through. He liked athletics too, the way a man's skull felt pinned under his elbow. Folks gathered in the meadow along Hiram's most Sundays while there was food enough to waste. The men wrestled, smeared their bare chests in dirt and blood, while the women cheered, even Charlotte. When Hiram raised his arms in victory, the sun quivered between them, burning, caught. His shadow stretched toward her, toward her legs open beneath her dress, and the bowl of wild berries clamped in her lap. Her children fought for mouthfuls and stained their fingers red. Little Mary elbowed past all but the boy twins, grunting to make herself known.

"Look," said Charlotte, "your father's won again." The neighbor, the man who drove the other wives over the border years before, hoisted himself to his knees, then to his wife's shoulder. His lips shone with blood. Hiram wasn't looking.

A son of Black Hawk, they called Hiram, though few remembered the old warrior's face, just the width of his hands, the block of his shoulders in the military jacket he was buried in. Two weeks he withered in his bed, in a cabin like Hiram's, on a river like Hiram's, and died. He lived between white men and drank at their picnics, made speeches when prodded. After the tribe got themselves marched off again, his neighbors scavenged his bones and sold tickets to look at them, until their little museum burned down. That happened the same year Hiram was born, someone claimed, and no one felt a need to disagree.

At his surrender, in a traitor's wigwam, Black Hawk had held his wrists to be corded and declared that his rival Keokuk was chief. Keokuk signed what was put in front of him, moved where he was told to move, swore never to return. He begged for Black Hawk's freedom too, brought him his family, pledged all that he had to keep the martyr from the warpath, even stepped down as chief to ease Black Hawk's pride. He never saw the falls on the North Fork named after him. Black Hawk and Keokuk were born back in Illinois, in the homeland, when the children never cried with hunger, when the people never were in want. The old chiefs were drunk when they scratched their marks on the first treaty. Everyone knows that.

When Hiram bent to kiss his wife, he tasted the sugar in her mouth and felt her tongue quiver, like an animal, a mussel pried from its shell. He remembered something else too, fleetingly, the queerness of the wafer Charlotte's priest set on his tongue, and the way it melted and clung to the spine of his mouth. It wasn't bread exactly, too white, too round, too thin. The moon if you were fool enough to pluck it down.

When Hiram didn't come home for a second year running and had a boy with the woman he was boarding with in Keokuk Falls, Charlotte wrote out a piece of paper with the word divorce spelled large near the top. She mailed the envelope to the address the Agency clerk gave her, but it didn't come to anything. Her people, her children's godparents, wouldn't hear of it. Hiram had moved back and was whipping the twins for running away from school before she gave birth again. Charlotte had lost a boy to fever that winter, but even if there was room in the cabin, Hiram saw no sense having loose ones about when they could be boarded in that three-story brick mission house in the Agency town. Problem was all the farm and freight wagons that Jim, the lighter-skinned one, could hop rides home on. Jim didn't like the Quaker women giving him kitchen detail because he was as big as any of the older boys for heaving iron pots around. He had Hiram's wide Irish jaw, Black Hawk's jaw, folks said. Some knew better, but none enough to argue.

The teacher prized Jim's brother Charlie, called him smart, and Charlie only ran away the once, after Jim's goading. Hiram raised a row of welts on Charlie's back, but not near as many as on Jim's, who blubbered the same excuses, the same sobs and promises, but with none of Charlie's earnestness, that spark of authenticity that neither pain nor fear can imitate. Jim muddied his uniform crawling under the house and getting dragged out by an ankle and twisting around snakelike, but Charlie's suit Charlotte had only to give a dusting, cooing under her breath as she handled the tiny matching vest. The second time, the tribal police hauled a wagonload of truants with Jim on his back on the groaning boards, shrieking at the branches overhead, every leaf red from the early frost.

Charlie didn't make it past fourth grade. Not typhoid, what had laid out the superintendent too, but pneumonia, the teacher said. Charlie shivered white-lipped as Charlotte spooned him blue medicine at the hour. She, and Hiram too, rode up for the night and let the teacher slip out to sleep in a bed, not just doze in the corner chair with the clock ticking by her head. Hiram was rattling her door before daybreak. He went for the doctor, knowing the man was useless, but it beat watching the women dip the boy's feet in mustard water and whimper as they stroked his cheeks. That one never had much of the look of his father.

After the preacher read his verse over the upturned dirt and the rest of the sickbeds had been emptied one way or another, Hiram gave Jim a full week at the cabin. Afterward, beat him all he liked, he could not make the boy go back to school. Drop him bruised on the mission doorstep and Jim would shave the twenty-three miles of wagon road down to eighteen of field and meadow, running every foot of it. Hiram recognized the squashed face glaring from the cabin window as he rolled in. With still more babies coming out of Charlotte, he told the school preacher to send the boy somewhere he couldn't find his way back from.

Three years the boy spent in Kansas, enough for Charlotte to lose a couple more little ones and waddle around the garden with her gut sagging with the next. Worse, Hiram was laid out with buckshot up and down his hip, from a cartridge that rolled too near the fire he set after dropping two bucks and emptying both of his boot flasks. He was supposed to die. By the time word reached the Kansas school, and Jim had hitched a ride on the roof of a freight train, Hiram was walking again but ugly about it, swinging his leg out like a block of wood, and in no mood to hear talk of his own funeral.

"They told me you were dead for sure," the boy said, and he got his worst drubbing yet. The edges of Hiram's belt were damp when he buckled it back on. Blood or sweat he didn't care. That kept the boy away another year, not at

school, but down in Texas, the Panhandle, ranch work, fixing fences and breaking horses. They liked him there. Thirteen only, and a runt, but he carried himself smart, knew what an animal was thinking before it did.

The owner asked who'd taught him horses. Jim said he was a direct descen-
dant of Black Hawk himself, the Sac warrior who beat Zachary Taylor and the
whole American Army if the British hadn't run out. He fought Abraham Lin-
coln, Jefferson Davis, and the son of Daniel Boone too. They buried him with
Henry Clay's cane, a row of medals John Quincy Adams gave him, a uniform
from Andrew Jackson, and a military cap hung with a plume of feathers. A picket
fence twelve feet high circled his mound. Black Hawk, said Jim, returned to his
land, to his birthplace, again and again, even after it was sold, even after the government warned him, and so they had to name a war after him.

The rancher had never heard of him. He was a half-Spaniard, said all the
horses, all the wild ones across the whole continent, had come from Spain, from
the conquistadors' ships, only a few hundred years ago, every last one of them.
Before that, he said, the savages just loped around on foot, like cavemen.

Next time Jim came home, he found his mother in the ground, and the baby
that killed her in the next plot. Hiram lied about the date, bumped it up a couple
of months, past the January cutoff so he could collect her annuities that spring.
He had a new wife lined up, Julia, and a new son on the way. Jim walked the three
miles to the Garden Grove public school every morning, and handled the little
ones better than the new wife, but she never took to him. When she wrote to the
BIA man, she asked about a boarding school way up in Pennsylvania she'd heard
of, a Great Lakes state. They civilized Indians, broke them if they needed breaking, and this one did. She signed Hiram's name, not that she fooled anybody.

"She wants you gone," Hiram told the boy. "They can teach you about electricity up there," he said. "And football."

Jim didn't fight. The children would miss him most, especially Ed, and little
Jimmie, his half-brother in Keokuk Falls. It wasn't a ghost town yet, but soon
would be, with all the talk of statehood and prohibition. His sister Mary rode him
to the depot. The neighbors were calling her a witch now.

She knew it before it happened, felt it, in her mouth, not a flavor but a weight.
Two weeks into term the superintendent's secretary called Jim out of the tailor

shop and says his father's been bit, blood poisoning, the wire called it, and sure enough there's no train in the world that can carry him home in time. His sister wrote later, said the wife put Hiram in the white town's cemetery, Garden Grove, across from the schoolhouse, with nothing but a brick of sandstone marking it, no name, no date.

Jim doesn't know his birthday either, not for sure. When asked, he says good things about his father. A strong man, a proud man, a man who chafed under the reins.

It comes up at the reception, the one Mr. Friedman holds in his white-pillared house out in front of the parade ground where the school band keeps blaring. And again in the gymnasium the next night, the dance they put on just for Iva and Jim, the bride and groom, like one of the old monthly socials, only they are married for real now. Gus is best man. It is Gus who says it, during the toasts. Big Jim and his Black Hawk blood. That's how Gus puts it. Big Jim, he's a Black Hawk. Just like his dad. And he claps Jim hard on the shoulder blade, and spills some champagne on his sleeve, and winks at Iva, or at one of the bridesmaids buzzing around her. Iva. That's what her name is now, how she started signing her letters after graduation.

Mr. Friedman volunteered to be guardian on the marriage license, because of Iva saying how both of her parents are dead. He writes "Red" next to her name, and "white" next to her mother's name, and "white Red" next to her father's, which Jim doesn't need Miss Moore's Commercial Math class to not add up. Both of Jim's parents Jim puts as "Red," which isn't a hundred percent of the whole truth either, but way quicker to write.

The wedding is up in big St. Patrick's, where Jim used to take Mass when he felt like it and wasn't away on games. He loves that high gray steeple and how on a gray day it looks like someone penciled it up there and didn't color it in yet. And the bells, the way they rattle up your leg bones, like it's Christmas morning clanging out or the Olympic parade the town threw him, before all that about him being a fake and Pop making him mail the medals back. Jim had to pen his name in longhand at the bottom of the letter Pop wrote for him apologizing. Jim tries not to think about that but how lucky he is Iva will still have him.

"Of course I will always love you, darling." That's how her letter began, the first she wrote after her brothers stopped intercepting Jim's. "What do we care about the rest of the world?"

Iva doesn't like it being a Tuesday, but next Sunday they will all be gone on the exhibition tour, and she couldn't schedule the wedding the Sunday before in case the World Series went longer like it should have. 4–1. Somebody tried to bribe the A's to throw the last game, for a cut of the next night's ticket sales, but the Giants still blew it. Jim didn't get to play. They hardly played him all season. A publicity stunt, that's all he is. The manager said so, out loud, not to his face, but to Pop's, on the telephone, and Pop still told Jim to sign the contract. It was good money, minus Pop's fee.

Pop says Ed, Jim's little brother, will never make the team, but Jim still likes how Ed and the other ushers look in their Carlisle uniforms. The bridesmaids are nice too, all puffy and frilly and walking like they have stilts on underneath. Only Iva doesn't wobble. He can't remember the maid of honor's name, Iva's best friend, the one Gus kind of dated. Gus just could not believe it on the telephone when Jim asked him to be best man.

"Ivy, Ivy Miller, you and Ivy Miller?"

Jim said, "She goes by Iva now."

Gus's voice was thick, but he got to laughing, asking if Jim remembered that coin flip they fought over, to see who'd get to ask her to the dance after the Penn game, was that two years ago? Three? Gus looks better in the suit. That high white collar keeps cutting into Jim's chin, his wide jaw. Iva looks comfortable enough, though regal too, with her hair parted in that fancy knot at the back of her neck and her puffy dress a wall between them. She could be queen of her very own country coming down the pews with those little flutter steps, her eyes that one-of-a kind color blinking behind the cloud of veil. She only closes them once, when she shout-whispers, "I do," like it is the last line in a poem recitation in front of the whole school on graduation day. It's hardly a kiss they have once the veil is up around her like a halo.

Iva absolutely adores the honeymoon. The Giants and the Sox have to go all over the world, even Japan, showing off what baseball is, helping the other countries assimilate into being American, which everyone is going to have to eventually. Jim gets himself on the roster, and gets his average up to where the manager starts noticing finally, even though he still scolds him for playing cards too much and ignoring his bride, like it's Jim's fault Iva can't go to the stag parties. When she watches Jim play in London, her box is right under King George's, the king of England. Jim squints and tries to wave from right field but can't really pick her out, just sees the wash of white faces knowing hers is mixed in there somewhere.

She makes him study French in their cabin the whole week before Paris. They stay in some ex-American's mansion, with footmen and butlers and maids and three-hundred-year-old wine and Iva knowing exactly how to hold her foot out with the toe pointed straight for one of the girls to lace up extra neat. When they tour the king's mansion in Rome, Iva says it isn't half as elegant or sophisticated. She sees the ruins of Pompeii and the pope and the Egyptian pyramids too. It's a fairy tale. She knows how to talk and smile and curtsy with every one of them, dukes and countesses and consuls and millionaires' wives. "Oh my husband," she brags and titters and squeezes Jim's cuff-linked wrist. It is like she was born for the part.

It doesn't take her a year to get pregnant. James Francis Thorpe Jr. The little fellow has the lungs of an athlete, a warrior, his scream swooping up and flapping around those high St. Aloysius ceilings after the priest splashes water in his face. A Catholic, like both his parents, since Iva converted for the wedding. She always considered herself a Catholic anyway. All those other denominations are really just imitation, she says.

They buy a house. Enough of the nomad sports-star life, the Thorpes need a home base. Iva approves of the name, Yale, but the town is barely a pinhole on the Oklahoma map, and the clapboard is only five rooms, just two with doors, a block off Main. She says the oak trim is stylish though, the white outside trim too, but her smile gets pinched if her eyes settle on the chips of gray too long. Jim agrees to repaint it. Chimney needs work too.

At least her sister's place next door is no bigger. It was Grace who wrote them about the house, after her old neighbor's funeral, a stroke of luck. No one told Jim that Grace was a teetotaler, the husband too, both of them squirming on Iva's new sofa at the click and hiss of the cap off of Jim's bottle. One beer. He never noticed the family resemblance so much, lips that can thin to nothing, until Iva and Grace both get frowning at the same time. Not at him, not directly, but at the lace doilies on the new maple coffee table and the sweat streaking their lemonade glasses.

"Me Injun," grunts Jim. "Me likum firewater."

He could stomach one of the Miller brothers better, even the one who shredded up his Stockholm letters before Ivy—she was still Ivy then—ever touched one. Iva is scraping new ice chips into the glass pitcher when Jim excuses himself to the backyard. He likes the backyard. Nothing dim and cramped and proper about it. The same dead flat horizon in every direction. Junior is barely walking before Jim is underhanding him pitches in the dirt, showing him to choke up on his swing because the bat is so big. Plus there's room back there to kennel two, three, as many as four hunting dogs, and time enough off-season to load a truck and take them barking along the North Fork River, Junior too. The hundred miles down to Hiram's old allotment isn't so bad, just ten miles more than Iva's dead mother's grave out east, the one Iva and Grace keep saying how they are going to visit one of these weekends soon, if there isn't some better church business to dress up for instead.

Raccoon isn't much for eating, so it doesn't matter how Iva won't cook one, let alone watch it getting skinned on the home plate stump. Pelts are money. Hiram used to make a killing, but she still makes Junior come inside, or at least stand on the other side of the kitchen screen. Jim can't see the boy's face through the mesh, just the shadow of a grimace, the way he flinches into the pleats of his mother's dress when the flesh tears loose from the bone. Hiram could do it better.

Junior likes fishing though, kicking his legs over a sunny rock and eyeing dragonflies as they slap circles along the edges of the stream. It's only really a stream most of the year. The same one where Hiram taught Jim to fish, only the fish are runty now. Not the two-footers he remembers. He almost has scars along his palm where he grabbed hold of one and the half-dead thing flexed and sliced its scales into him. "Stupid," Hiram said. Jim's neck stiffens for the slap, while Junior scratches river mud with a stick along the bank. Jim points out the very leaf-darkened spot where Junior's grandfather unloaded two rounds of buckshot into a bear's face, reloaded, and fired two more. It was a monster. Must have stood ten feet at least, and see, there's the root its claw dug out when it finally turned to lope away.

Baseball isn't much to speak of. Jim's manager still doesn't like him, and Iva can't travel as often with the team now, she says. Jim is playing football too, and gets news of his daughter's birth by wire. In Pittsburgh, he thinks it was, when he tries to remember. Gridirons all look the same. Even if it isn't much of a league, Jim is starring in it. The best of the college boys have to play under fake names, so their schools can still call them amateurs during the real season. They are decent enough kids, though no way should they have held him back from giving that upstart kicker the kick he deserved. One shot in the jaw, that's all Jim wanted, and maybe another for the ref going blue with that whistle in his teeth.

He isn't drinking as much as Grace makes it sound, not during weeks when he's home. Yale doesn't have more bootleggers than most towns, at least not towns with as many oil boys to sell to. Oklahoma is booming in oil. Used to be a forest of dinosaurs roaming the state, before the tropical plains shriveled up and the Indians got herded onto them. Now the government is making them all citizens, even Jim. The agent's letter comes with a patent signed by the president of the United States himself, or somebody hired to forge his name a thousand times a day. The paper says Jim is competent. Hiram's allotment is his now, legal and official. One hundred and sixty acres, most of them leased and fenced and cultivated, the Sac and Fox reservation, the crumbs of it. There isn't anything for Jim to do except hand over the envelope for Iva to file, along with the trinkets, a little eagle for his buttonhole, and a miniature arrow, representing the pride he must feel as a member of his most noble race, the first of all Americans.

There is hardly time between the two seasons anymore, just enough to shoot a few birds on an all-nighter or two. If Jim and a pal knock down more bottles in the process, that is no business of Grace's. It was probably her goading that got Iva looking for the empties in the rear closet. The way the town priest tells it back to Jim, you would think Jim was going into business, opening up a bar on his back stoop. There are already more speakeasies fronting Main than a man can favor in a night, and it's the pocket billiards he goes for anyway.

The priest keeps brushing his white hair back and explaining how Jim's wife is a lady, how Iva is a God-abiding lady, wife and mother in need of a righteous role model for her innocent and impressionable children. The same spiel Jim can hear from Grace's kitchen window whenever Iva goes over there for tea. Only the priest doesn't keep calling him an Indian. He just keeps thinking it real loud, and having to pause and start over whenever his syntax channels him back to the point he can't make, not to Jim's face. Jim is to seek God's help to rise above his natural, uh, his innate, his people's, uh. It has to have been Grace who made Iva complain to the old guy, shoving her up that little half-flight of church steps at the street corner. Not that Iva needs help with that prissy walk of hers, spine straight as a javelin, her head a shot put balanced on the point of it. He might not have realized it at the time, but that is the same walk, that is the exact same walk she had coming down the aisle, only with the veil invisible now.

He can't believe when he hears about Carlisle, the War Department closing it down. It's technically their land, the old barracks, and of course a veterans' hospital would be a good thing with the war, but still. There is something else about an investigation, how Pop and Mr. Friedman like to spend all that money the team earns them. Jim doesn't want to hear it. Those were good days in Pennsylvania. If somebody thinks it all really goes back to Jim stealing those medals, they don't say it, not with Jim in earshot, leaning over a whiskey, or popping the cue ball over the bumper again. Grace keeps her jaw tight too, every time Jim stomps through a room, every floorboard creaking between them.

Mornings he heads out to the yard, gives a shout as he rattles the kennel door. "Come here, Grace! You old bitch, get over here!" He named one of the dogs—the oldest, the ugliest, the one with the gimp leg where she took a piece of buck—he named her Grace. But he still can't help bawling over her when she's dying, and that has nothing to do with drink either. Poor thing stretched out on the kitchen mat, not moving but for blinks, cage of ribs barely able to heave itself up for a breath. Junior and Gail Margaret give the dog a last pat, and then another after Iva has them in nightclothes. Jim once stretched on the same spot on the kitchen floor, with those two giggling at his elbows, watching the mutt flop in the air and back to Jim's chest. The other dogs are hardier. They sniff the upturned dirt by the stump before trotting back to slurp at their bowls.

Junior dies at the end of summer. It starts in New York. Usually Iva has to pin him in her lap to keep him from running down the stands and out onto the field to join his dad. He wears a matching uniform, everything but the spikes, because he would gouge Iva jumping up and down. But when Jim squints over from right field, he can barely see the boy slumped in the seat next to her, not even a wave after Jim caught that fly, a tough one with the angle of the sun. Afterward, when Jim scoops him up, Junior's ankles are funny, his laces tight from the swelling. Their home doctor will know. They are all packed up and ready for the drive, because of the government cutting the season short for the war.

The influenza is supposed to be over, so maybe it's polio or something. The doctors can't decide. Jim keeps calling new ones, from neighboring towns, all the way from Stillwater, and Tulsa the last one.

"Jim Thorpe?" the nurse asks. "*The* Jim Thorpe?"

Two weeks later Jim is rocking the boy's body in front of the empty fireplace. The sun isn't through the windows yet. Iva is with the girl because she is squealing. The froth of spit on Junior's lips is pink. Jim is rocking him and watching the specks of bubbles cling at the corner of his mouth. They aren't bursting anymore. They aren't moving. He begged the hospital people, begged and hollered and sobbed, but none of them care. None did anything. The one who finally tries to pry the body away, Jim swears at him, curses him, curses his goddamn white God. Swings at him too, sort of, with his elbow at least, but Jim is kneeling, and off balance, and the man can't understand what he is blubbering anyway. Iva stands over in the kitchen archway, just standing there, her face wet, but her eyes the same blue-green as ever. That white-haired priest of hers is back there too.

"The Lord is mysterious," he says. "The Lord," he says, "the Lord has to test us," he says.

He makes it a little longer and more eloquent when everybody is sitting in the church with the squat little box dead center. Iva looks like a queen again, in the first pew. A perfect, dark-veiled queen mourning her prince.

When the second daughter comes, Jim wires back his love and congratulations. Iva names her Charlotte, after Jim's mother. He's playing in St. Louis. The Giants let him go, but there are plenty of teams, and it's coaching football he should really get himself into, like Pop and Lone Star, except the colleges hate anybody who goes pro. So he's stuck swinging at curves and chasing midfield bounces. He pounds any ball he can touch wood to, and he is still a steam-roller on the bases, no loafer in the field either. He lets that Akron editor know it too, shoves his way right up to the newsbox after reading his column. The louse deserved worse than a night with a steak pressed to his eye. And it takes two cops to pull Jim off that pair of hecklers in the stands after the ump kicked him out. It was worth the fine.

He rarely plays drunk, but off-days, it's whiskey afternoon to evening, wood alcohol if that's all anybody's selling. If he is home with the blinds down and one of the girls blunders into the dark of the bedroom, Iva shoos her back out. Daddy's sick. Iva keeps them next door mostly. Or somewhere. He doesn't know.

Switching down to the minors isn't so bad, not with a hefty signing fee, and if the West Coast dumps him a month later, it's nicer back east anyway. Jim is always ready to play. But he has principles. If a manager advertises how their new ex-Olympian is going to show off some field events, some pregame races and whatnot, and then they don't pay him, or even tell him first, well let the stands boo all they like. Every batter can pop up to right field—Jim isn't lifting a glove. Their loss, firing the best batter in their good-for-nothing league.

Iva names the third girl Grace. Like Jim might forget his sister-in-law's name now that she isn't parading in and out of his house every day, twice on Sundays. Jim had to move his family to Ohio, just down the road from President Harding's hometown. An old hunting pal hired Jim to front his new National Football League team, the Indians. Real Indians. Jim is hiring up a dozen of his old Carlisle pals, most of them in terrific shape for men in their thirties. Eagle Feather. White Cloud. Long Time Sleep. Running Deer. Long Wolf.

"Not Gus?" Iva asks. She is changing Grace's diaper, lifting the yellow-thick cloth by its farthest corner, before slopping it into the sink to soak with the others. "Where's he practicing law now?"

Jim drills his team four hours every afternoon in the field across from the boardinghouse where they all have to live, even Iva and the girls. It is the nicest in town, if you can call it a town, smaller than Yale. Locals think a tribe of wild and woolly Indians is swooping in from some pulp magazine cover. Granted, things do get a little loud for the baby's naps, for all the girls, not just with the team roaring back for showers and rubdowns and dinner, but then them all going back out again and hunting coons till midnight. That was part of the deal. Jim is kennel supervisor too. His hunting pal is a breeder, a big one, ships out more than a thousand dogs a month, his own mix, the most popular in the States according to the brochures everywhere. Apparently Indians will be the perfect trainers, that special bond, talk their language.

Iva agrees. "Animal to animal," she says.

She claims the top corner room, so no cleats grate over her bed. The front rooms have the view of the river, and that little wood bridge the team rattles like train tracks every time they cross to the field, but she prefers the back. When Jim limps in late, sometimes twelve-thirty or worse, scraping mud from his boots with the rusted butter knife he keeps by the tub, he wants to tell her how good the dogs are learning, best trackers he's ever held on a leash, but Iva is long asleep, usually in one of the girls' beds.

When she isn't asleep, she's asking him what's next, when the season's over, when they all get kicked out, since the team is only an advertising stunt, half-baked at best, and Jim doesn't say anything, because it's true. They have to stage a halftime show, a kind of Wild West thing, with the dogs, but also some knife and tomahawk throwing, and a few Indian dances, costumes too, naturally. Jim doesn't mind. He even likes the bear, Queen Mary. The dogs show their treeing skills on her for the crowd, but weekdays, it's Big Jim who has to get her into her other pen so they can hose out her piss and droppings. Worse stink than every one of Grace's diapers balled into one. Nobody else will set foot in there but Jim. He just shoulders her in her hairy ribs and drives her the direction he's looking for her to go, same game he plays every Sunday basically.

At least that's the story Freeda, one of the secretaries, heard. She asks Jim if it's true one afternoon while he's slouching in the office doorway, chatting up all the girls. It is, he says. It most definitely is. Freeda is a redhead. She works at the kennel afternoons, after her high school lets out. Saturdays too, when her father allows it. She is a cute little thing, perched at that little desk of hers with her knees crossed under her skirt. Jim tells her so. Cute little thing. What he called Ivy the first time they kissed out on the gymnasium dance floor.

Iva tries to throw Gail a fifth birthday party at the boardinghouse, wants the dining room all decked out in paper pumpkins and black cats, since it's October. Jim has to climb the ladder to hang them from the lamps, and again to snip the strings afterward. All the local kids get little pumpkin faces with candy inside, party favors Iva calls them. She telephoned the neighborhood newspaper to come and write it all up. The reporter, a woman, calls Iva regal-looking, stunning. Jim supposes it's true. The photograph is right there to prove it, though the article doesn't mention about some of his boys knocking chairs over as they poured in for a second "Happy Birthday to You." Jim joined in too, stomped his feet in time like the rest of the room, but he hadn't been off drinking in the parking lot with them, even though it was his day off too.

It's that night, after all the girls are down, that Iva tells him she is not an Indian anymore, never was, not a drop. It was all a cheat. She duped the government and him. He always knew she was no quarter-blood, that she never lived on any reservation anywhere. Eastern Cherokees, they civilized centuries ago, got themselves scattered into cities, but blood is blood. He assumed there was still something in her. Blanket Indians. That's what she's calling his pals, his team, what she's calling him. Just another drunk chief and his tribe of blanket Indians.

He may yell a few things back at her, and God knows the baby is always waking about something, or one of the girls with their nightmares. A man can't spend his life hushed-up on tiptoe. The world isn't a velvet rug rolling out in front of you. He never promised her that. Even if he did, a girl should know better. His mother did. Any real Indian woman would.

The whiskey bottle doesn't break the glass, just bounces off the cross of the windowpane and clatters on the floor, by Iva's foot. He wasn't aiming at her, but it shuts her up, and if that's a spark of fear in her eyes, her spine is no more rigid than on the day she was born. A white lady's spine.

He doesn't stay to watch the whiskey gurgling out. He is stomping down the hall, down the back stairs, shoving the back door out into the cold. No wonder she doesn't understand him. Her and her bitch of a sister. Indians. They told the whole world they were Indians. Anybody could see Ivy was just as good as any white girl, smarter even, and prettier. She proved it. She got him. She got Jim

Thorpe, the Olympian, the All-American, best athlete of all time, and he picked Ivy Miller. From all the girls in the entire world, he picked the one fake one.

The wood of the bridge is rattling under his feet before he stops to notice where he is. The grass of the field spreads out gray in the moonlight. All the gouges and ruined spots are smoothed over black. It isn't so cold he can see his breath, just the idea of it, a ghost scattering itself before it can appear. Past the field, past the black of the tree line he can't see, the sky collapses into black-blue where no stars can sink to. It looks like water. He thinks maybe that's north he's looking at, and so Lake Erie over there. Probably not even that many miles. The Great Lakes. He thinks the Fox and Sac might have lived around here. He's pretty sure. His tribe must have come from somewhere. His homeland, the one Black Hawk fought for, would still fight for, to this day he would, forever. This field should be his. Everything around it, the bridge, the water mumbling under it, the black trees, the town, the sky and the stars and the wide-open moon. It should all be his. He got tricked. Keokuk let them carve it into a gridiron, into quarters and innings and seconds left on the clock. It wasn't right. He shouldn't have gotten born into this. The world should be better. It should treat him better than this. He's shouting it. He's bawling the words back at the field, feeling them pulse and vanish into the dirt, into the vacuum of the air. Nobody's listening. His face is soaked, his throat is raw, and nobody's listening. His Ivy, his very own Ivy, she's not listening.

Next thing she and the girls are shipping themselves out to California, with a trunk of his memorabilia, minus his face snipped out of the fanciest photograph album. She wants $125 a month child support, and is trying to run it through the Indian Bureau, but the Bureau isn't having it, since the two of them are both competent and educated now. The room is quieter without the baby hollering, and the bed as big as it ever was. He pays the landlady the same every month whether he sleeps in it alone or not. When he asks for his security money back, she says it's not his, because of the cost of the repainting and the scuffed floors and all, and Jim doesn't fight about it. He doesn't need it all that bad.

Jim promises Freeda he'll marry her just as soon as the divorce is official and legal. Freeda is working full-time at the kennels since graduation. He hates being away from her so much, but when the Indians lost their second season, half the games shutouts, some of them by forty, even fifty points and more, the breeder was done with the NFL. There are always other teams though, and more triple A in summer. He writes Freeda every week, twice sometimes, wishing she could be up in the stands, her and her pregnant belly. She's such a skinny thing with that bulge in front, like a football tucked under a jersey for a trick play. Junior was only three months the first time Iva brought him out to see his papa on the field. If it's a boy, he'll teach him all about Hiram, about the Black Hawk clan, about his people's proud and noble blood thumping through his heart. That's all that matters to Jim. That's all Jim has ever really cared about.

The Greatest All-Around Athlete
in Modern History Adds a Word

Although I have received literally hundreds of requests in the course of my multi-faceted sports career, never before have I given permission for my name to be used in a product testimonial. The fact that I now break from this personal precedent should demonstrate my wholehearted sincerity in endorsing the Chief Long Lance Shoe as simply the best sports footwear I have ever encountered, on or off the playing field.

Had B.F. Goodrich manufactured this running shoe some twenty years ago, I am convinced that I would have made All-American half-back before 1908 and that I would have exceeded the 25 touchdowns that I earned during my final collegiate season with the Carlisle Indians. Indeed, with Long Lance's natural muscle-building shoes supporting me, there is no knowing how many track medals—in addition to my Golds in the Pentathlon and the Decathlon—that I might have brought home from the 1912 Olympic Games in Sweden. During my professional football career, which spanned seven teams and two decades and included three unofficial world championships, my teammates and I depleted an incalculable supply of rubber-soled canvas shoes, while benefitting not at all from the unique Long Lance design that allows for free exercise of the foot and leg. As the first President of the American Professional Football Association, I regret only that I could not have equipped every team with Long Lance's moccasin-inspired footwear. Of course the shoe's benefits apply equally to all athletes, including baseball players, who—as a pitcher in the summer leagues of my youth to my six years as a fielder for the New York Giants, Cincinnati Reds, and Boston Braves—I am proud to count myself among. With the Long Lance shoe under me, perhaps I would have retired after my final season of Major League Baseball with a batting average even higher than .326, and now at the age of forty-one I might not be bidding goodbye to the great game of football as well.

Dillard pinches his tear ducts, draws his head back to blink at the flecks of mucus on his thumb and fingertip, then shoves the ad copy to the middle of the meeting table. He's blind to it. He can't keep editing.

He drove in early, to be ready for the New York call, to give his damage assessment to the Client Executive, but it was Resor's secretary who telephoned with a schedule problem after Dillard had paced within arm's reach of his desk for twenty minutes. Same time tomorrow. Have the Long Lance numbers ready, the current ones, not projections.

He tips back on the wooden chair legs till his head touches the window glass. Traffic exhaust seeps in with the heat and a skirmish of car horns from the intersection below. He should be shoring up accounts after the October crash, reminding clients how the upswing's coming, this summer at the latest, guaranteed, the natural ebb and flow. The J. Walter Thompson Agency is the surest anchor for turbulent waters. That's what Resor wrote in last month's *News Bulletin,* and that's what Dillard told the Goodrich people, told them to push harder on the Long Lance promotion, drive the summer delivery orders up. Now look at them. Pulled the radio spots Monday, withdrew the first Thorpe testimonial before it ran.

Across the table, tacked onto the corner easel, is the promotional poster. That goddamned Indian blocked up in black and white. Dillard liked the original mock-up, one-tone, sharp lines, a tight two-inch graphic for the shoe tags, but he didn't realize how it would translate big. The hair and shadows merge too much, all that negative space, the geometry of the face off somehow. It's the eyes that bother him the most. They should have gone more cartoon, standard cigar Injun. It didn't matter if it actually looked like the guy, or anybody. What were they thinking—the Indian was a celebrity?

"Mr. Dillard?"

Angela is in the doorway. She's pointing behind her, at the receptionist desk, at her telephone probably.

"Is it Resor?" He should have stayed in his office, kept the file at hand. But it gets so claustrophobic in there. The meeting room is the only room on the sixth floor with any space, any air, a wall of windows to remind you where you are.

"No, sir. They're calling from the lobby. Mr. Thorpe is waiting down there."

Dillard looks off, remembers his eleven o'clock appointment—is it eleven now?—and looks at Angela again, at the little lavender hat pinned to her hair, what all the promotion-minded girls are wearing to the office these days.

"Well, send him up."

"He's waiting to pay his taxi, sir. They said he forgot his wallet."

Dillard considers scowling, or chuckling maybe, but does neither. He pats his rib instead, then realizes that he's not wearing his suit jacket, that his suit jacket is on the back of his office chair, and that his wallet is inside the jacket. Angela is still looking at him.

"Could you . . ."

She stands there, heels touching, hands poised, longer than she needs to. "Of course, Mr. Dillard."

Her clicking gait recedes as Dillard turns to the window, stands so his cheek almost touches the warm glass. He can't quite see the curb down there, or a parked taxi, just the moving ones, the string of cars gunning through the intersection, the yellow light climbing soundlessly to red. When he steps back, his foot comes down on one of the Long Lance shoeboxes and caves in the lid. They're lined up under the windows, a row of them, the leftovers from the samples the staff didn't take home. Dillard kicks at the dented cardboard, nudges it with his toe, but it won't pop back into shape.

> *But to understand fully the revolutionary nature of this new yet time-honored sports shoe, the reader must first understand its creator. It was in the quaint, historic town of Carlisle, Pennsylvania, where I attended the United States' top non-reservation Indian boarding school that I first became acquainted with Chief Buffalo Child Long Lance. At the time, my fellow classmates and I naively knew him by his adopted name, Sylvester Long. Even our teachers and coaches were not*

*aware of his true heritage, thinking that he, like his foster parents in North Caro-
lina, was of Eastern Cherokee descent and so an Indian youth long familiar with
the ways of the white man. As a baptized Christian, born in a log cabin in an area
of Oklahoma ceded by the Five Civilized Tribes, I too assumed that Long Lance
shared my history of modern ways. Imagine my surprise when I learned that my
new friend had only then recently stepped from the prehistoric plains of the North
West, where his people, the proud Blackfoot Indians, had romped wild and free
until the final decades of the last century.*

*It was on those vast western fields—fields now accustomed to cattle ranching
and minor league baseball—that Long Lance witnessed and, despite his youthful
age, participated in the last buffalo hunts ever to take place on this great continent.
He grew up straddling the naked backs of black-and-white pintos, watching his
clan's braves combat ancestral enemies by arrow and tomahawk, and listening
to his wizened elders share tales of mythic lore over blazing teepee fires. None of
us in Carlisle then could have predicted that our quiet classmate would someday
captivate readers across the nation with his astonishing articles in such prestigious magazines as* Cosmopolitan, Maclean's, *and* Good Housekeeping, *
and then ultimately in his own book-length autobiography—now in its second
printing, with British, Dutch, and German editions on the way—detailing the lost
world of his vanquished tribe.*

He considered ducking into his office for the suit jacket, but this isn't a client, and what does Jim Thorpe care about business attire? Dillard unbuttons his
sleeves instead, rolls each twice, and pulls at his Windsor knot, so he won't look
like the generic exec type. He keeps the vest buttoned though. He's at the table
again, fountain pen hacking, when Angela appears at the door.

"Mr. Dillard? Mr. Thorpe is here, sir."

Dillard raises a finger before raising his head, then he's all smiles, knocking
the chair against the wall as he stands. "Jim Thorpe," he booms. "What a pleasure."

Dillard is halfway around the table before he gets a look at him. Not such a
big guy, not tall at least, just wide, a scrap of yellow tie lost out there in front of all
that chest. It's not the brightest face, not the jowls of a sports star either, but it's a
solid smile, some warmth behind it, better than Dillard's. The suit is cheap, but

not as cheap as the haircut. Dillard shoves his hand at him, and the Indian takes it, lets him pump his arm, lets him test his grip against a legend.

"I was a real fan of yours back in the day."

This is almost true. Dillard does remember the broadcasts, the headlines, the way his father joked about the Olympic committee, called them Indian givers. Their minister cited the athlete in one of his sermons, proof the Lord punishes liars.

Thorpe thanks him, mumbles something else, an apology it sounds like, about the taxi. Doesn't know how he walked out of the house like that.

"My wife," says Dillard, "she says I'd forget my head if it weren't attached." He laughs too loudly, and Thorpe matches him note for note. The Indian's not at ease. His silence afterward is searching. Dillard lets him hang there a second or so. "Ever been married, Jim? You don't mind if I call you Jim?"

Thorpe tries to answer both questions at once, so his nod is too vigorous. He gets out the word "twice." Maybe it's the Indian thing, or a whiff of infamy still dogging him, but the guy is older than he should be, older than Dillard will be when he hits his forties next year, the second half of his career still to climb. It's like a smell on the Indian's breath. Dillard doesn't know what he was expecting, but this is pretty close.

"So," Dillard says. "Have a seat." He gestures along the whole row of chairs, to see which Thorpe picks, the closest, or the center, or the one opposite Dillard's nest of papers. Dillard always sits with his back to the windows, so he can imagine his own silhouette while the other man squints. Thorpe hesitates, then settles in at a corner. His side of the table is bare but for his big brown hands. The left one is tapping soundlessly. Dillard takes his time sitting down.

"Okay," says Dillard. Thorpe meets his eyes, brows raised, and then leans forward, can't seem to help himself. Dillard plants both his elbows on the table. "Let's talk about this Long Lance pal of yours."

As his readers know, Long Lance's people had legends for everything, from the great shame befalling those who lie, to the proper care of feet. I remember one such legend that Long Lance repeated to me during our days running with and against one another on the Carlisle track team, a tale which I now recognize as the ancient wisdom that inspired the new Long Lance shoe. Once a great warrior was being pursued by his enemies, and after a tremendous sprint, his speed began to slacken. To his feet he called, "I shall be killed if you do not help me! More speed, I beseech you!" But his feet scoffed. Never before had the warrior acknowledged them, never had he anointed and rubbed them. "You neglect us," his feet called back. "Why should we help you?" The warrior pleaded further, declaring that should his enemies overtake him, they would chop off his feet and throw them to their dogs as scrap. To this the feet responded and began kicking of their own accord, carrying the warrior far out of reach of his pursuers. Thus afterwards, the warrior anointed and rubbed his feet every day, just as Long Lance's own mother warned him and the other youths of his tribe to do also. "In our primitive life," Long Lance told me, "nothing was more important than our feet. I wonder if the white race would not be sturdier if they too took better care of their feet in childhood."

Though a superb football player, Long Lance's true athletic skill emerged on the Carlisle Indian School track team, and it was this ability he attributed to the traditional footwear of his youth, the ancient moccasin known to all tribes of Red Man. "Our lives," Long Lance explained as we sprinted side by side, "depended on the endurance of our legs and feet in hunting game for food. Without moccasins, many more of us would have perished." I had grown up wearing white man's clothes with my feet bound in unnaturally stiff leather, a practice I now recognize as so detrimental to proper muscular development. I wonder, as I began to then, how much greater my sports career might have been had I started running with Long Lance not on the circular track of the Carlisle athletic field but on the grassy plains of his ancestral Wyoming.

Fortunately, today's youth will never have to ask themselves such a question because B.F. Goodrich has made available the wisdom of Long Lance's elders to all Americans. Every bit of canvas, every stitch of thread, every ounce of rubber of this new sports shoe emulates the venerable Blackfoot moccasin, and it was Long Lance himself who explained the design so that white men could understand and reproduce it. I commend the B.F. Goodrich Company for seeking out Long Lance and requesting that he develop, test, and endorse this improved canvas running shoe. I do not know anyone better fitted than my old schoolmate to know what a man most needs in a shoe of this kind. It was Long Lance who helped me to pre-

pare for the 1912 Olympics, and when the games were over at Stockholm I told him
that it was the stiff competition that he had given me in the mile run which had
enabled me to win the World's All-Around Athletic Championship that year. He
was an intense trainer, using up dozens of pairs of the rubber-soled shoes we and
our teammates had to wear in our athletics then. Once after a particularly gruel-
ing jaunt through the picturesque streets of Carlisle, we spent most of an evening
soaking our feet and discussing the kind of superior running shoe we wished to see
someone turn out. Little did I think then that Long Lance himself would someday
design it!

Dillard's going over the basics, repeating some points, because he wants to
see how long the Indian can keep his head bobbing. "We did fine on the fall delivery—those orders were taken late summer—but with the slump and these crazy
rumors now, we got to circle the wagons. We're thinking of going article-length
on the testimonial. We're going to run it like a newspaper column, like an editorial. From you." Lansdowne, the Creative Director, dictated the new strategy over
the telephone to Angela yesterday, never even asked to speak to him. It's no extra
cost to Goodrich, except the space of course, newspaper inches cost plenty, but
Dillard will never see a bonus from that. "You following me?"

Thorpe says he is, absolutely, an editorial, great idea. What's he got to do?

Dillard has the draft in front of him. The pages are wet with his slash marks.
It's bad. That new copywriter isn't working out. The whole account is cursed. If it
weren't for the talkie, Resor would never have handed him Goodrich, but the L.A.
branch handles Hollywood, even second-rate Hollywood. They thought Long
Lance was a star. Somebody at Goodrich saw his autobiography, heard the movie
was in production, thought they would get the Indian while he was cheap.

Dillard slides the open file across the tabletop and watches Thorpe rotate it,
lean down, squint, bend the row of corners up to see how many pages there are.
He asks if he should read this all now, and when Dillard doesn't answer, he starts.
Normally Dillard wouldn't have brought him in, would have mailed him the finished copy, but after Dillard talked with that producer at Paramount yesterday
and heard what his private investigator was up to, Dillard isn't taking chances. It
was Long Lance who suggested Thorpe.

"You know, my son," says Dillard, "he's fifteen this month, he thought this Long Lance character was really something. We got him that book last—no—two Christmases ago. He loved it, wild about it, wanted to be an Indian. When I told him I was handling these shoes, he couldn't believe it. You really knew him, right? Long Lance?"

Thorpe is trying to read and listen at the same time, so his head keeps lifting and dropping, lifting and dropping. He says Long Lance knew him back at Carlisle.

"Really well, right? You were close."

Thorpe shrugs.

"But you were buddies, on the team, back when Carlisle won all those championships. Long Lance played—what was it?" Dillard is reaching forward, flicking his finger at the pages. "Tackle, right?"

Thorpe doesn't say anything. He isn't reading anymore. He isn't doing anything but sitting there, face blank, eyes everywhere but on Dillard's.

But perhaps the reader is wondering how a simple Indian could have achieved the intellectual feat of engineering a modern shoe, and I readily admit that such a task is beyond my own mental prowess. My former Carlisle classmate, however, is no average Indian. Not only did Long Lance graduate as valedictorian from our all-Indian boarding school, but he went on to excel in white education too, in such fine institutions as Conway Hall and St. John's Military School, and then to became the first Indian appointed by the President of the United States to attend West Point. He represented his people honorably during the Great War and returned a decorated officer and hero. Afterwards his achievements have only continued to rise: international journalist, best-selling author, dauntless aviator, celebrated movie star, esteemed spokesman for our proud race, and now he has chosen to direct his keen intellect back to the realm of the athlete where he began his extraordinary journey upward.

Despite his achievements in the white man's world, Long Lance remains deeply rooted in his tribal past. Hunger—that silent enemy that dogged his childhood and threatened his people with extinction—was the force that compelled the hunters of his clan to develop their bodies into athletic paragons. Little wonder then that Long Lance's portrayal of Baluk, the manly Ojibwa hunter in The Silent Enemy *released by Paramount Pictures last year, has received such lavish praise by critics from the* New York Post, *the* Wall Street Journal, Variety, *and the* New Republic. *Renowned sportswriter Grantland Rice, a man who once championed my own athletic abilities, reported that Long Lance's battle with a bull moose in the film rivaled "the first round of the Dempsey-Firpo match" with "enough action through a minute to last three or four modern fights." Douglas Burden, the film's producer and a naturalist and explorer himself, selected Long Lance for the leading role after seeing the striking frontispiece portrait in his autobiography. Burden needed to read no further than the first chapter to realize that Long Lance's childhood duplicated the story of the Ojibwa Indians he wished to dramatize. Just as Long Lance's tribe narrowly escaped starvation by chancing onto a herd of mountain-sheep, Baluk and his hunger-ravished people are saved when the migrating caribou are sighted in the movie's final frames. Had Long Lance been able to remain among his people and live out his life in their primitive ways, there is little doubt that he, like the fictional Baluk, would have become his tribe's champion hunter-athlete and their venerable chief's choice for successor. The* Silent Enemy *is a magical window into the life Long Lance would now be living, a born hero in both the red and white man's worlds.*

Who, then, in terms of mental intellect, ancestral wisdom, and athletic aptitude, is better fitted than Chief Buffalo Child Long Lance to revolutionize the modern sports shoe? The answer is obvious, and our testimonial should end here on so happy a note. Circumstances, however, dictate a further word. At this point in so luminary a career as Long Lance's, perhaps it is inevitable that detractors and gossip-mongers should begin to swarm around his bright path. It has been suggested—and I blush to repeat so scandalous a slur—that Chief Buffalo Child Long Lance is in fact not an Indian at all. The absurdity of this charge should be self-evident, but at the request of the B.F. Goodrich Company, whose stockholders stand to lose unfairly should this rumor continue to escalate, I will address it. That any defense of my dear old schoolmate is necessary saddens my heart and recalls to me my own struggles with the Olympic committee and the newspaper media that turned against me that cold winter of 1913. I will therefore speak out in order to end the pain now being inflicted upon my noble friend.

So he was never a tackle. Thorpe swears the guy never played tackle, or any position, except on Intramurals maybe. Unless it was third string. He guesses maybe it could have been on third string. That's possible. Two decades is a long time to remember. The rest of it he has no idea.

"But you think so? West Point and all that. In your opinion, it's all true, right?"

Thorpe is scratching at the back of his scalp, digging at it with both hands, like he's trying to uproot something. It's got to be true, he says, if his pal says it is.

"But I'm asking you—I'm asking you whether you can vouch for him or not."

Thorpe says Long is a good guy, that Long lent him money a couple of times, when he was between jobs, and got him this Goodrich spot too. Then he goes on for a while about that, about the work he's doing, studio jobs now, doubling and filling in as an extra in some Westerns. Plus, just like Long Lance, he's got his own motion picture on the way, sold the rights to his life to M-G-M and they already wrote it up. *Red Son of Carlisle*. Only with the slump and all, they had to postpone production. So right now he's just painting filling stations for an L.A. oil company. It's fine, he says, it's fine work. His fingers are rubbing at the wood finish.

"Look," says Dillard. "There's talk, okay? I know you know. I get that you don't want to talk to me about it. And that's good. It means you're still looking out for him, which means you're not going to talk to anybody else about him either. Like a reporter. Frankly the guy means zero to me. I'm looking after my client, and bottom line, that means Long Lance was an Indian. The best god-damned Indian that ever was. Right?"

Dillard slaps the table, and Thorpe agrees, practically repeats him word for word. Best goddamned Indian. Dillard wonders if this is really the smart move, a fraud vouching for a fake, but it's Lansdowne's call, and Resor's problem. Goodrich is a big account—not the shoes, the tires, the part Dillard will never see, that and the General Motors contract he got beat out of when they transferred him out here. Dillard rubs his eyes, pinches them again, focuses back in on the Indian blinking at him.

"The way I heard it, after the rumors started up, Paramount sent a man out to the guy's family, North Carolina, I think. Supposedly they got the real story there, but they're keeping their hats on it. They have an investment. They had Long Lance out on publicity already. It's the same for us. It's a matter of promoting the version we want, the Long Lance that sells the most shoes. No one's got evidence about anything, and even if they do, they're not buying ad space for it. We just have to get our version out there in front. It's like a race. We're pushing our Long Lance out there in front."

Thorpe lets out a single blunt yelp of a laugh. He must like the metaphor. He's forward in his seat again, hands braced hard on the table. He'll push his buddy Long Lance all the way, he says. To the finish line. And then he asks what the rumors are.

To understand Long Lance, the reader should first know something of the way in which our government defines an Indian. It is not so simple as lifting a teepee flap! Gone are the days of half-naked savages prowling the prairies in breechcloths and berry paint. My family lived in a log-and-timbered farmhouse with a separate sleeping loft and hog and chicken pens outside. My siblings and I were baptized at the Sacred Heart Church in Konawa, Oklahoma, where my mother's family lived and my grandfather served as godfather. We Indians have lived beside the white man for so many decades now that our path to civilization has mingled many times with yours. You may be surprised to learn that even I, a proud member of the Sac-Fox and Potawatomi tribes, am only five-eighths Indian. My father's father was an Irish blacksmith, and my mother's great-grandfather a Canadian adventurer and fur trader. Few of my Carlisle schoolmates were full-bloods either. Some were only one-eighth, the minimum government requirement that Long Lance must have met to enroll. I do not doubt that the Long Lance family tree, like mine, branches in and out of the larger Caucasian forest which surrounds us. And even if more white than red blood pumps through Long Lance's veins, he nonetheless has the heart of a full-blooded Indian.

White ancestry, however, is not the most scurrilous of the attacks against my former teammate. Some will go so far as to suggest that he is actually a Negro masquerading as a Red Man. Although laughable, the charge is hurtful to Long Lance and to Indians everywhere. Are we to believe that a Negro could rise to the very top of the Indian educational system and graduate first in his class from the most prestigious of all the government schools? Why would a Negro even apply to Carlisle when schools such as the Negroes' own Hampton Institute, Booker T. Washington's alma mater, stand ready to educate him? And are we also to believe that in the course of Long Lance's three-year term that not a single one of his nearly one thousand schoolmates or the dozens of experienced teachers, coaches, and administrators noticed his deception? And could a Negro have gone on to achieve all that Long Lance has since? What of the endorsements he has received from learned white scholars? Anthropologist Paul Radin stated that there is no "better corrective of the ridiculous notions still prevailing about the Indians" than Long Lance's invaluable autobiography. Madison Grant, President of the New York Zoological Society and author of The Passing of the Great Race, *called* The Silent Enemy *"accurate in every detail." Grant's book warns against the dangers of black-and-white marriages and the pass-for-white mulattoes attempting to dilute the Nordic race. So surely the author would have spotted one such Negro projected onto a thirty-foot screen during his private viewing!*

But when it comes to Indians, the best judge is always another red man, preferably a venerable one such as Chauncey Yellow Robe, great nephew of Sitting Bull, one of the first graduates of the Carlisle Indian School, and Long Lance's co-star in The Silent Enemy. *In the months that Yellow Robe worked beside Long Lance, playing Chotega the wise old chief, he had every opportunity to detect an imposter. Yet afterwards when Chauncey took ill with pneumonia, he implored Long Lance to replace him on the Hollywood publicity tour. When the full-blooded Sioux passed away, Long Lance was grief-stricken as if he had lost his own father and offered to pay for Chauncey's youngest daughter's education. This is the Long Lance I know and love, a true friend and a true Indian— whatever his dappled ancestry.*

After the Indian promises, gives his word he'll stick to their story, there isn't much else to be said. Thorpe tries to go over the copy some more, give some suggestions, but Dillard says his people are on it. He'll mail Thorpe a copy, tomorrow probably, after legal goes through it. Dillard has an early lunch with Fairbanks's agent, trying to get him to reconsider Resor's new television gimmick, but before

Dillard sends the Indian out, he wants to hear firsthand about those medals. It's not hard to get him talking.

First off, says Thorpe, the six-month regulation passed, and his professional play wasn't in track anyway, so they had no right taking his Golds. That summer team paid him nothing, especially compared to salaries Pop used to sneak the older boys at Carlisle. Thorpe got some bonuses too, loans Pop called them, plus all the presents and clothes from the school and town merchants. Pop knew all along, but he dictated the letter to his secretary saying it was just ignorance, that Jim Thorpe didn't know better. He signed above where his name was typed. Dillard watches how his hand moves when he says it. And it's like he's still holding the medals when he describes them, how the fronts had a picture of two ladies setting a wreath on an athlete's head, all of them naked but with cloths over the ladies' laps. He says Pop wrapped them up and wrote the Swedish address in big letters on the front of the box. Then he isn't saying anything, just sitting there, leaning on his elbows and looking past Dillard, at the window, though not really looking. With his face angled like that, chin up slightly, he's not a bad-looking guy, handsome still, in that Indian sort of way. Dillard turns toward the window too, but he doesn't look out either.

"Hey," says Dillard, "you want one of these?" The Long Lance boxes are stacked two deep, the dented one in arm's reach when he leans over the chair arm. "What's your size?" Thorpe tells him, and Dillard flicks a few lids off. "This is pretty close." He pulls out a pair by their unstrung laces. They do look a little like moccasins, the way the stitching meets along the ridges, plus how they dyed the canvas that leather color. Thorpe is reaching for them.

"You know," says Dillard, "it's too bad really, that crazy buddy of yours must have really had something going for him. I mean the temerity, you know, to pull it all off so long? Then he winds up with a bullet in his head. It's a bad way to go out."

Thorpe has taken the shoes by the laces, but his arm stops there, so the shoes are swaying above the table as his mouth opens. His lips are pursed, a little "o" in the center, the syllable "who" or "what" caught there. He's breathless.

"You knew, right? They found him dead on Monday, in some millionaire's house. They're calling it suicide, but it's fishy. There's supposed to be an inquest."

The shoes drop and Thorpe drags them toward him as he stutters. Thorpe just got a letter from Long Lance a week ago, and he goes on about it, what Long Lance was up to, how he can't believe it. It doesn't make sense. Is Dillard sure?

"I'm so sorry to be the one to break it to you, Jim." He's coming around the side of the table, his hand out. He shakes Thorpe's hand again, grips his shoulder. "It's too bad, it's really too bad." Thorpe wants to talk about it, starts up about Carlisle, the old track, and as sympathetic as Dillard is, he can't help but look at his watch. The agent said Fairbanks is in town, might be joining them, if he's free. He apologizes for cutting things short. "See Angela about taxi money home," he says. "She'll take care of you. And, again, really, I'm so sorry. All the more reason to help him out now, you know? We're fighting for his memory. The world is going to remember him the way we do."

Thorpe neither agrees nor disagrees. He's looking at Dillard, eyes sharp now, like a drunkard jolted into clarity. Dillard doesn't like his expression, not a frown exactly, as if the effort isn't worth it, as if Dillard isn't worth it. Dillard's hand is still on Thorpe's shoulder, or just above it. He was patting his sleeve, giving him a hearty send-off, and now Dillard has to remove his hand, or rather withdraw it from where it's hovering. He doesn't like Thorpe's expression.

"Angela will take care of you." He points, since his hand is up there anyway. "My receptionist."

The Indian knows who he means. He gives Dillard a last glance over, takes the room in too, the windows, the canyon of buildings pushing back at them. And then his back is turned, those wide shoulders, and Dillard is watching until he rounds the frame, surprised by the lightness of his step. He's gone.

Dillard has to backtrack to the chair on the other side of the table to get his suit jacket, before remembering it isn't there, that the suit jacket is in his office. Thorpe's voice is ringing in his head, not any specific words, he never had that much to say, but the sound of it. It's a deep voice, richer than he noticed at first. It's like someone is breathing in his head. When he gathers the papers and the folder and caps his pen, he glances up, and the other Indian is staring at him from the easel. They're not really eyes, just triangles, and the spaces suggested between the triangles. It shouldn't look like a face at all, but it does, and that annoys him right now. It makes him grip the pen. It makes Dillard want to chuck his fountain pen at the promotional poster. But he doesn't, because that would be stupid, and he's got to focus on his lunch strategy, on selling the agent on the new promotion, on selling everybody on it, the world. Angela's heels are clicking toward him.

Sometimes I look back at my halcyon days at the Indian School fondly and wish that Long Lance and I could once again kick up those cinders along that bleacher-lined track. Alas, dear old Carlisle was converted into a military hospital during the Great War, and the years and injuries since are a defensive line I can never batter through. Worse, reports of Chief Buffalo Child Long Lance's unexpected death are just now reaching me. I am shocked and sorrowed by the news. Words cannot express the turbulence of my emotions. I knew that Long Lance had retreated from public scrutiny to wrestle the twin demons of alcohol and despondency, opponents I have battled so long myself, but his last letter gave no indication of depression. He spoke of the thrills of flying his new Lockheed aeroplane and of a planned trip to Central America to discover a lost Mayan city. The notion that Long Lance could have taken his own life is ridiculous. He was too proud, too resourceful, too Indian. My Carlisle teammates and I dubbed him "Sly," short for his adopted name Sylvester, but also for the mythological Indian trickster so ubiquitous in our far-flung tribes, that half-animal god who spit the world whole from his mouth. We knew even then that our pal Long Lance would ascend a luminous path after he left our humble boarding school behind.

Although I can never return to those glory days of our shared youth, my beloved schoolmate has bestowed to me from beyond the grave a prize in some ways greater than any I have ever received. I have just tried out my first pair of the Chief Long Lance Shoes and find that they remove the last objections he and I had to this type of footwear. I can think of no better crowning achievement to Long Lance's short but magnificent career than these. I will go the limit in saying that in all my years of athletics, I find this shoe the smoothest, the best, and most natural foot and leg-muscle builder of any shoe of any kind that I have ever seen. As I now wear my complimentary pair, I feel the thrills of old Carlisle rushing back to me, the thump of the track beneath my legs, the roar of the stadium, the flutter of tickertape across my bare arms. Long Lance has captured all of these sensations and in magic worthy of an ancient Blackfoot medicine man transformed them into canvas, thread, and rubber for every athlete in America to share and cherish. I thank you Chief Buffalo Child Long Lance, and I thank you B.F. Goodrich Company. Long may his spirit run.

Phyllis Thaxter Becomes Ivy Miller

There are reporters in the parking lot when they pull in, and a few fans too, some scattered along the curb, most in pairs leaning on car hoods and sipping coffee. Somebody points, and then there's a muffled shout, and then the glass doors of the lobby are opening and a cardboard sign is jiggling over a girl's head. Phyllis has to press against one of the beauty queens to make out the lopsided letters: "WELCOME TO CARLISLE, BURT!!!"

Mrs. Brown laughs. Her husband, singing cowboy Jimmy Brown, is asleep in the front seat. "Wouldn't have been room for him anyhow," she drawls.

Hendricks, the studio rep, is sitting up there too, but he doesn't say anything, just scratches at his bald spot, and elbows the driver toward the overhang. The Molly Pitcher Hotel, a four-story mock-Tudor, looks passable, despite the ragged glow of neon in the morning haze. Phyllis had hoped Hendricks would splurge on one of those new luxury high-rises around the National Airport. After the canceled flight out of Oklahoma, and the midnight detour into D.C., they deserved better than five hours hip to hip in a backseat. The beauty teen, "Miss Carlisle," wheezed and drooled on Phyllis's sweater as the sunrise glared through the side windows. The darker one, "Miss Oklahoma City," was all questions and chatter, pointing at the highway signage as letters loomed in the headlights. She wanted to know where the Mason-Dixon Line was, had they crossed it yet, is that it, is this?

When Hendricks announced it would be a double premiere—"Tale of Two Cities," the press release bragged—Phyllis assumed New York and L.A., not a pair of backwater towns nowhere near either coast. Carlisle at least makes sense, an inevitability, but Oklahoma City? Thorpe never even lived there. Still, of the two, Oklahoma City is the metropolis, and Phyllis wishes she stayed back there with

Burt and Bickford, but Hendricks booked her here. I need you in Carlisle, he said. He calls her the co-star. She would love to believe it, but she knows how low her name is on the poster, what font size her agent settled for. Carlisle is second string. The town only gets Thorpe because Warner Brothers wouldn't pay the $500 speaking fee his wife kept demanding for a cameo on the Oklahoma stage. It would have been Thorpe and Burt tonight stepping side by side from a limo, the waving movie star and the remains of the ex-Olympian he impersonates—the waving star beside a vicious funhouse mirror.

Hendricks bounds out first and arranges the fans and the reporters and the single photographer into a miniature gauntlet between curb and lobby door. He shouts each name like a circus barker. Carlisle's own teen beauty, Virginia Parlin! On loan from her southern tribe, a bona fide Indian princess, Miss Oklahoma City! The girls scramble out, grinning and squinting, followed by Brown and his wife, leather frills swaying. Phyllis runs her fingers over her hair, hopes the spray didn't flatten in the back, and fixes her smile. Miss Phyllis Thaxter! Starring tonight as Jim Thorpe's first wife and boarding school sweetheart Margaret Miller!

The fans nearest the curb clap and nod at her, before their eyes surge back to the car door. They want Burt Lancaster, or Charles Bickford at least ("Bringing the beloved Coach 'Pop' Warner to life on the big screen!"). Phyllis turns too. The backseat is a long plush cavern, empty of course. There is no one to follow her, no dark double, no Ivy Miller—certainly not "Margaret." She was never called "Margaret." Phyllis doubts Hendricks knows that, or cares. Phyllis's name changed when Ivy, the real Ivy, wouldn't give up rights to her own. The photographer aims grudgingly at Phyllis's face. She beams at the flashbulb, doesn't flinch as the world bursts white, and now she is coasting forward, feeling for Hendricks's arm, for one of the girls' sleeves, for anyone.

There's only the one elevator, and the Browns take it first. Phyllis waits with the pageant queens—the two are sharing a room—while the second bellhop blushes and fingers the luggage cart. The monument unveiling isn't until this afternoon. Hendricks told Phyllis to grab some sleep, drew her aside in the lobby, a solicitous hand at her elbow, another at her back where her bra fastens. He said it like he was giving her something, just Phyllis. If Mrs. Brown hadn't shooed her husband to the front seat—for the other girls' sake, she said, a modicum of privacy—Phyllis would have endured the ride thigh to thigh with her studio boss. He sat beside her on the plane too, leaned into her lap to point through her window. Oklahoma City's crossroads bisect at ninety-degree angles at every one-mile stretch, like a football gridiron, see? Phyllis smiled for him, said yes. A checkerboard for giants, she thought. He went on to lecture about pre-1912 field markings, as though she hadn't spent a month last year sitting in a college grandstand of extras, clapping and waving a Carlisle pendant every time the assistant director blew his whistle at her. It only took four days to shoot her speaking parts. Once she and Burt finished their one on-screen kiss, Phyllis never saw the camera again.

The elevator quivers as the number 4 clicks above the panel. Something groans beyond the moving walls and then stills. Phyllis and the girls stare at the seam between the doors, waiting. The bellhop says it's normal. It just takes a second sometimes. He says it to Miss Carlisle, almost raises his eyes to hers, as she yawns, a wide jaw-aching yawn she pats with the tips of her polished nails, before grinning in apology. She's pretty enough, but a little short. Her chemically blonde curls are sagging. Phyllis prefers the Indian girl leaning in the opposite corner, her tinted reflection leaning back at her. She doesn't really look all that Indian, just a hint along the cheekbones, and the hair of course. That's how Phyllis imagines Ivy.

She regrets never meeting her. Hendricks said he tried a few times, even mailed her a draft of the screenplay for her comments, but she mailed it right back, and the check too. After she gave an earful to a PR secretary on the telephone, long-distance, a studio lawyer sent around a memo forbidding further contact, for fear of a lawsuit. Ivy's name is "Mrs. Harrison Gray Davis of Chicago, Illinois" now. Hendricks said the husband is a retired oilman, former president and owner of Superior Oil before the '29 Crash, and a bit jealous of his wife's first husband. Imagine, he chuckled, living under that Paul-Bunyan-sized shadow, some twerp as pale as a sheet of company letterhead. You just got to pity him, Hendricks said, his head wagging in contradiction.

The bellhop stops at the girls' room first, takes his time placing each bag at the edge of each bed. Miss Oklahoma City finds the bathroom switch and clicks the lock behind her. Phyllis doesn't know whose idea it was to rent out the beauty queens, but she can guess. Hendricks got a pair of state governors too, but the girls are the poetic touch. They are Ivy's two halves. That was Phyllis's first surprise. Her agent's secretary delivered the script with a penciled note: "Great news! No redface make-up for you!" It turned out Big Jim's girl was white on the inside and Indian on the outside. Or, no, would it be Indian on the inside and white on the outside? The photographs the studio dug up didn't help. The one was a long shot of "Redskin ladies" in Victorian dresses ready for their monthly waltz in the Carlisle gym—the one they named after Thorpe after he left. It would have made a gorgeous sequence, Big Jim swinging her across those floorboards, dress hem swishing in widening arcs. The writers didn't see it that way. A few choppy scenes, and it's back to the gridiron.

The bellhop wheels the cart into the hallway and pulls the door shut after touching his hand to his uniform cap, tipping it, bowing almost. Neither girl is looking. Phyllis isn't that much older than they are, is prettier in fact, but the boy is only one-half a fool. He thinks he might have a chance with the local girl. Phyllis waits until the cart is moving before she speaks.

"Has Mr. Thorpe checked in yet?" she asks.

The kid blinks and then nods. "Yes, ma'am." He still can't look at her. "They both are."

"Both?" For an instant Phyllis thinks of Burt, she can't help it, a last-minute change, she and her co-star ascending the stage arm in arm.

"Sgt. Thorpe," he says. "Mr. Thorpe's son? They got in yesterday."

Phyllis catches herself before correcting him, before she can declare too firmly, no, his son is dead. He was just a little boy. She forgets how much the writers cut out—the daughters, Thorpe's second marriage, his four boys, the third marriage. It's more tragic if Jim Jr. is an only child. It absolves the hero of his boozing, the squandered baseball career, the way he drove poor Ivy away.

The bellhop is pointing. "They're just the next room down from you, ma'am."

Phyllis looks at a door identical to all of the other doors. It was infantile paralysis, or something like that, not influenza. They made that up, made the boy old enough to throw ball with his dad, ride on his shoulders like a little bronze god. Writers can do anything. Phyllis understands why they axed Ivy's daughters, to simplify the plot, but that was no reason for Hendricks not to invite them to the premiere. It could have been a reunion. Maybe Ivy—maybe "Mrs. Davis" would have come, if they had approached her the right way. Imagine passing back into her own world after years as an Indian school Indian, and then all the years afterward, the endless aftermath, having only the memory of it, no proof anywhere in your lakeview house, the neighborhood of suburban retirees, your husband puttering in the lawn. You don't slide a check across a ticket counter and think the old lady is going to whip out her braids and moccasins again. Ivy is no circus attraction. Phyllis knows that much.

After the boy hefts her suitcase onto the bed, she asks about Thorpe's wife, the current one. She thinks her name is Patty. Or Patsy.

"I believe her reservation was canceled, ma'am. Illness or something."

She nods, accepting the secondhand lie. At least Hendricks will be happy. He's had run-ins with the woman, Thorpe's business manager, a harpy apparently, wrings every cent out of the old guy on the lecture circuit. Plastic plaques, inscribed watches, gold-painted keys crowd his suitcase as he shuttles between award dinners. Phyllis heard he'd been destitute, so maybe it's a good thing. Maybe it was better for both of them that Ivy packed her daughters up while he was out bingeing and minor-leaguing. Phyllis wonders if Ivy understood everything she was leaving then, not just a husband, a decade of marriage to a broken Indian, but that part of herself she had spent her life inventing, her tribe of one. Her story was over, at least the parts anybody else was watching.

Phyllis tips the bellhop, watches him blush a final time, and waits until he pulls the door closed with an almost inaudible click. When she was Ivy, Phyllis got to slam it on her way out, while Burt raged and crumpled with an empty prop bottle in his fist. The camera should have followed Ivy. Thorpe's plot was dead anyway. No one wants to see a ghost scrounging for Hollywood work as a B-movie extra, or hocking his name to that all-Indian song-and-dance troupe "The Jim Thorpe Show" opening in Philadelphia next month. Ivy's story has dignity at least. Divorced mother of three working clerk shifts in a Tulsa hotel, finally putting those business classes to real use. If it hadn't been a regular stop-off on Mr.

Davis's business rounds, she might still be there, a fifty-seven-year-old orphan, working the same job her father had when he abandoned her. When Ivy said yes to Davis, Phyllis wonders if she thought she was going home finally, or was she just accepting what was offered to her, what she had always accepted? If Davis hadn't purchased so widely on margin and bankrupted his company, the two of them would still be in Oklahoma right now, in the capital probably, where the lights from the Warner Theater warm the skyline at night, recessing the stars outside Ivy's windows.

Phyllis unfastens her suitcase locks, watches the metal springs clack against the shell, but she doesn't lift the lid. She doesn't want to change into her night-gown. The bed creaks as she sits. The air-conditioning is cool, falsely autumnal, except where a rectangle of sunlight slices her calves and the paisley pattern of the carpeting. A metal-framed mirror hangs in front of her, and Phyllis reflexively arranges her hands atop her crossed knees, and then drops them because no one is watching her but herself. When she hears a noise through the wall, she leans forward, tilts her ear. Not quite a voice, but more than a footfall, something skittering across a night table perhaps. She's not sure whether she is facing the beauty queens' room or the Thorpes', so she doesn't know what to picture on the other side of the mirror. She tries to retrace her steps to the room, the direction the bellhop pointed, the spatial relationship of door to hall to bed, but it's a jumble. She could be anywhere. Her Oklahoma room had the same wallpaper.

What she's looking at is her reflection, which makes her think of Burt. The actual shoots were nothing compared to their private rehearsals. It's strange an actor, a star like him, hating the camera so much, needing to hide from it, hide his feelings, he said. He meant the love scenes. They met in the dressing room, in front of the wall-length mirror, the largest anywhere, and choreographed each movement, every gesture, his hand on her cheek, the turn of her hips toward him, till the blocking was perfect, more nuanced than the slowest, most lingering waltz. It wasn't the same under the weight of the lights. She couldn't touch his face for fear of smudging foundation, ruining those high cheekbones the make-up girls painted in every day. The director shot two takes, a third for safety, and it was over.

There is another clomp and shuffle behind the wall, and Phyllis is certain it's Thorpe now. She pictures him pacing, then dropping into a chair with a newspaper, or maybe an autographed copy of his new biography. The publisher released it this week to capitalize on the Warner Brothers' movie promotions—a dirty trick, Hendricks said, but he was grinning. It's the face on the jacket cover Phyllis is picturing now, Thorpe at his prime, the dapper brute Ivy fell for. He was almost as handsome as Burt then, with no toxic whiff of dye darkening a once-blonde scalp. Phyllis has to blink, actually clenches her lids as though forcing a slide into a projection slot, before she can remember him, the Thorpe she met on location, the pudgy gray-haired man who watched from the empty bleachers while Lancaster practiced. Thorpe had sold his story rights twenty years before, but Hendricks listed him on the payroll as a consultant, a "technical advisor." It was the UCLA team and track director who did the coaching. Burt was twelve years too old for the part, but he only had to look good doing it. The camera faked the distances on the shot put and discus throws. Thorpe came down from the stands just the once, to show how he used to hold the pigskin for a dropkick. That's the kind of stunt Patsy has him doing now, a between-games exhibition at the New York Polo Grounds, a crowd-waving gig as "coach" for the Israel National Soccer Team. They say he beat all of Carlisle's track records with a fifth of gin in his gut, that he never trained, never practiced at all, not even for the Olympics, but that's just another myth. Burt nodded and nudged the other players into clapping as the football flopped and rolled toward the distant goal line.

Phyllis pulls the yellow curtains, but there's no keeping the sunlight out. It pulses when she closes her eyes. She drapes her dress over a wooden chair back and stretches across the bedspread in her slip. She likes the chill, the tiny hairs bristling on her arms. Her head is thick, her eyes ache, but she can't possibly sleep, not with that crack in the ceiling plaster. She traces it, loses it, finds it again, or another just like it. She thinks about Ivy, what her first day in Carlisle would have been like. Phyllis just traveled the same path, by airplane not train engine, but she had to cross the same borders, squint at the same sun. Ivy had to sleep too, eventually, lie down somewhere soft, turn away from the windows, ease her eyes closed. She must have dropped her guard, pretended she was somewhere she wanted to be. Phyllis feels her breath slowing. She imagines that she is Ivy,

Ivy in her dormitory room, Ivy on her cot, in the old barracks, Ivy slipping into someone else's dreams. She considers opening her eyes, to place herself, to grasp at something already beyond her, and then she doesn't.

Hendricks promised a crowd, and fifteen thousand is pretty good for this town, the number they mustered forty years ago for Thorpe's Olympic parade. Warner Brothers hoped to publicize *Jim Thorpe: All-American* with a joint announcement from the Amateur Athletic Union and the U.S. Olympic Committee, stating that Mr. Thorpe's 1912 amateur status would be reinstated and his medals returned, but the studio got snubbed, same as his wife and all the congressmen and sportswriters on her petitions. Instead of gold medals, there is a hunk of marble to unveil on the courthouse lawn, a sports monument to the man the Associated Press declared not just the best football player of the half-century but all-around male athlete too. That's something at least. Plus Hendricks wangled another name for the dedication photo caption: Gen. Trudeau, acting commandant of the Carlisle Army War College, site of the former Carlisle Indian School, closed since the First World War. Phyllis is there too. And Thorpe, of course. His uniformed son slouches at his other shoulder.

Hendricks promised it would be good for her, the extra publicity. Phyllis's career could be on the up and up now—this, plus two other premieres this year, and those two last year. *No Man of Her Own* may have been a Barbara Stanwyck vehicle, but Phyllis was the linchpin to the plot, a small but "haunting" performance, according to *Variety*. Moments after meeting the pregnant and destitute Stanwyck on a train, Phyllis and her new aristocratic husband die in a derailment, and Stanwyck steals Phyllis's identity. She passes as the daughter-in-law the bereaved family had yet to meet. Of course they want to believe her. Of course they take her in. Phyllis's body is never found. Phyllis hopes Ivy saw the movie, hopes Ivy heard her name before. She wonders what she will think of her performance as "Margaret." Ivy's little-used first name, Margaret Iva Davis née Miller—hardly a change at all.

Inscribed on the curb of Carlisle's downtown square are the words "Whoever drinks from the old town pump, though he wander far from Carlisle, will surely return." Phyllis reads them a dozen times, while smiling and sweating in her evening jacket, her heels punching slow divots in the grass. No one said it would be this dank, or that the mountains, the Appalachians, would look so stunted. She claps after each speech and contains her wince when the podium speaker trembles with feedback near her head. Ivy must never have sipped from that pump, or Phyllis wouldn't be substituting for her, both on and off screen now, posing here beside her schoolgirl beau. Thorpe's not as tall as Phyllis keeps expecting, not as tall as Burt. It's easy not to look at him. They stand shoulder to shoulder, their faces toward the crowd-thick street, eyes glazing over a smear of bodies, the banners and streamer-wound telephone poles. Sometimes their elbows touch. Sometimes Phyllis catches a glimpse of his too-short hair, the curve of his belt, the pudge of his chin. It could be anyone beside her.

It's strange for Thorpe too. It must be. Phyllis is a ghost of his first wife, younger than when they divorced, prettier than when they met. Phyllis doesn't look much like Ivy though, no cascade of black hair, no bewitching "cat eyes." That's how the socialite column described them, "prone to shift chameleon-like with the whims of her wardrobe, first green then blue and next a penetrating gray shimmer." That was back when Ivy was honeymooning, still accepting the kisses of Japanese ambassadors on the flesh of her chilled knuckles. Phyllis's agent mailed her the strip of grainy newspaper, and Phyllis pinned it beside her dressing mirror, hoping the exaggerations were at least half true. Thorpe probably prefers Phyllis anyway, her blonde waves, her pretty English nose. His next wives were both white, no exotic family lore, no funny business on school application forms.

Phyllis marvels at that, how a little girl hoodwinked the United States government for a free home. Sure, she had a hint of ancestry, the proverbial Cherokee grandmother, but no Miller relative appears on any tribal registry. Not that Phyllis blames her, her mother gone, her father worse than dead, her big sister fending for them both. Ivy was an innocent, a blank slate. She played the part she was given. How did the screenwriters put it? "A sort of mix-up." "A special exception" due to "unusual circumstances." When "Margaret" thinks no true Indian like Jim could love a white girl, "Margaret" flees Carlisle, and her sewing teacher is left to break the news: "Margaret's not an Indian." Phyllis would like to see the original scene, the one erased by this fiction, but maybe that's a fiction too. Maybe there was no confession, no great unmasking. Maybe Ivy believed. Maybe now, lost in some suburban back room, she is still pretending, a wayward squaw imagining her return to her secret tribe one day, wondering when precisely it was she left it, when if ever she completed her initiation. Phyllis is a romantic too. She wants to fool the world into believing she's a star.

When the governor's metallic voice stops rattling the speaker, and the crowd slows its lazy clapping, and the photographers inch forward and kneel at the lip of the lawn, it's time for the unveiling. Someone introduces Sgt. Carl Thorpe, and then Sgt. Thorpe pulls the string, and then everyone, including Phyllis, is clapping again. It's just a block of dark marble etched with rows of letters. It looks like a tombstone. Phyllis doesn't want to, but she thinks it looks like a hulking tombstone, and now one of Hendricks's stories is flashing through her—how Thorpe was rolled in unconscious after his second heart attack and confined in an oxygen tent, and how after three days he tossed aside his bedsheets and strolled out of the hospital under his own steam. Hendricks barked his staccato laugh. He didn't believe it either.

The clapping sounds like barking too, and the flashbulbs are blotting out the sun's glare. Phyllis keeps beaming. She feels Thorpe at her side, her hand on his elbow, his palm at the small of her back. They're turning toward each other. It's spontaneous, the way she tips onto the balls of her feet, and wavers that slow instant, chin high, lips pursed, wavering between his cheek and his lips. The cameras keep clicking. She chooses lips. It's the better shot. She barely notices the surgical incision where Thorpe's doctors removed a tumor that summer and promised no cancer cells were lingering after the infection.

Phyllis pulls away, lowers the leg she raised, for balance, and avoids Thorpe's startled eyes. She tries to feel the tingles that must have swept up from Ivy's toes when he first bent his massive frame to her breathless mouth. She wonders which version is the real one, the first kiss. The screenwriters send in Pop Warner to play Friar Lawrence to the star-crossed lovers and soon Phyllis is in her nurse's uniform bending backward into Burt's arms in the infirmary. *The Jim Thorpe Story* is more scenic. Phyllis skimmed a copy in an Oklahoma City bookstore, ignoring the *Collected Poems* of Marianne Moore on the neighboring table. She paused for minutes on Ivy's two pages. The biographer stages a starlit confession at the edge of the school grounds. It's poor Jim who worries that his Ivy won't marry an

Indian, but his girl sets him right: "I was afraid, Jim, afraid you wouldn't want to marry a girl who wasn't the Cherokee she said she was."

Phyllis would ask Thorpe, but she doubts his memory and all the layers written across it. Besides, the ceremony is breaking up now. It's time for the ten-car motorcade to carry them the few blocks to the Dickinson College gymnasium for the prescreening banquet. It's Ivy whom Phyllis wants to ask. She wants to be with her right now in her six-room ranch in Wicando, Illinois, helping her dust knick-knacks and run the vacuum, while Mr. Davis pushes a lawn mower or pokes in the front beds, a new hobby for the ex-executive. Maybe they will take a stroll around the lake after dinner and admire the shallow waves splashing the pebbles. It's a quiet life, one that prodded the former vice president into a stint as a local car salesman, but he has settled into the home routine now, content to finish his days with his bride of a quarter century—longer than Ivy lived as an Indian. Ivy has no regrets, no loss, thinks Phyllis. She misses nothing. Maybe sending the script back was her idea. She's sure it was. Though her youngest daughter, one of Jim's daughters, now divorced with two children of her own, could have used the cash, the Warner Brothers check stirred waters Ivy has spent her second life stilling.

Ivy has no desire to sit at a head table in a banquet of five hundred admirers and listen to speeches by college presidents, football coaches, the latest All-Americans. She would rather finish baking the casserole for her oldest daughter driving out from Chicago tomorrow and watch her grandchildren throw a ball in the yard. It requires an actress like Phyllis Thaxter to maintain so bright a smile while signing yet another immaculate football and standing with her substitute co-star to present it to the governor's adult son. No one at the banquet, not Phyllis, not even Jim seated in the first chair beside the bunting-draped podium, thinks how Ivy and Jim met in a room like this, a gymnasium, the same dull glare of ceiling fixtures on varnished boards. Only Ivy could remember how he literally swept her off her feet, how thankful, how ludicrously thankful she was that the superintendent didn't cancel the monthly socials.

What this story needs is a reunion, a final atonement, the moment of redemption, that reconciliation between the time-tossed Jim and Ivy. It was still "Ivy" when Ivy skimmed the script at her kitchen table. She'd opened the mail while Mr. Davis was out gossiping at the hardware store. She soaked her blouse with sweat, smeared her make-up, laughed until she coughed, almost gagged, holding onto the sink edge. Her hands were shaking when she poured herself a second cup of coffee, but she didn't spill any that time. She doesn't need Warner Brothers to give her a happy ending. The ruse is over. She's home. She sacrificed nothing to get here, nothing she has ever tried to give a name to, no word she can form in her mouth, a sound she will hold there indefinitely. Ivy read the breakup scene five times, but she could not find her name on any page that followed. When Phyllis Thaxter flees from her husband's alcoholic fury during tonight's screening, it will be the last the audience sees of her character.

When Phyllis looks across the lake of faces, she does not recognize the forgotten Carlisle players, Indian stars now thin-haired and hobbled. Phyllis doesn't recognize Lone Star Deitz or know that the gray-bobbed woman at his elbow is his second wife, some white woman. Angel DeCora died of the flu two months after their divorce. The new wife never gave him any children either, and he will be struggling soon, painting portraits mostly, when the commercial art school he just opened goes bankrupt. He quit coaching years ago. The Boston Braves changed their name to the Redskins, in his honor, and then moved to Washington.

Phyllis does not scan the tables for Gus Welch either, the Carlisle quarterback Big Jim beat out for Ivy's starting lineup. Gus was Jim's best man, second string at the altar. A distance runner on the 1912 U.S. track team, he missed that boat too, when he was forced to stay home with the flu. He beat Jim to proposing, but Ivy gave her heart of gold to the Olympian. Gus fumbled the replay too, marrying the daughter of an Oklahoma congressman, a year before Ivy and Big Jim made their divorce final. Gus's wife is descended from a Connecticut man who was captured in an Indian raid as a child and raised in the wild, before marrying into his new tribe as a consenting adult. Someone should make a movie about that. The Welches have no natural children, but they did adopt a niece, a pretty little Indian maiden who modeled for the canning labels of Pocahontas Foods. Gus, a lawyer and lifelong coach to children, exchanges letters with Ivy to this day. Theirs is a purely platonic correspondence, but who can say what might have been? It's too dangerous for Ivy to think about, but if she could, if Warner Brothers could replay the clock, tonight's premiere might be titled *Gus Welch: All-American*.

But now is not the time for speculation. The meal is over, and the motorcade is on the move again, to the Carlisle Theater where a throng of spectators over-flows West High Street, and the platform beneath the marquee awaits its stars. Soon Jimmy Brown will serenade the crowd. Phyllis Thaxter will smile and call them all "All-Americans." Pretty Miss Oklahoma City will crown Governor Fine with an Indian headdress, making him an honorary chief, and the governor will declare in a triumphant shout: "If we had more Red Men like Jim Thorpe and fewer 'Reds,' this country would have nothing to worry about!"

The world is black-and-white now. Jim thinks, yes, this is how it happened. This is how it should have happened. The father takes his son aside. He does not whip him. They speak of the old ways and the changes and the changes still to come. The boy will go to the white man's school. He will make his people proud. See him study. See how he works. He reads books until the words pursue him in his dreams. Awake, he is still running. Pop sees him, begs him to join the track team, but it's football, football that catches the girl's eye. She smiles at him from the bleachers. Jim is in love. The fact fills him with a simplicity and wholeness impossible in life. He tells her, watches as he tells her, and he is giddy. His palm is rubbing the wood of the arm rest. He is telling Ivy that he loves her.

His heart aches, literally aches, and he squirms in his seat, rubs his chest. Heartburn, he whispers, to no one since Patsy is not here to be lied to. Phyllis, the girl on the screen, the girl beside him now, leans closer, touches his arm in the flickering half-light. What? He smiles, apologizes, waves her hand away, nothing.

Patsy will not be there next spring either, in California, as he wheezes over a plate in their trailer home. She walked out again, fed up. Jim's hair will be wet from the shower. The sun will have already crested, the hillside and power lines etched in red. He will spit back the mouthful of sandwich. He will knock a picture from a nail, careen against the counter. It's the trailer park manager who will find him. The man yelling into the phone, those are the last words Jim will recognize. When the doctor arrives he will register the prick of the needle, but he will not understand.

He will not think of Ivy. No montage will reel through him. He will be beyond even the redemption of Hollywood. If he has regrets, and surely he does, he will not feel them. He will no longer blame Ivy's sister, that teetotaling Methodist, the

Indian hater who turned his wife against him. He should never have bought the house next to hers, but they needed a home somewhere off-seasons, and Ivy had wanted it. He saw his daughters so little after he remarried the first time. They still meet, sometimes, in Chicago, in New York, every few years or so, far from Ivy's suburb.

He doesn't know her husband's name or where they live. He's never seen the stars through her kitchen window, the ones Ivy is staring at now, sipping tea in her bathrobe, sleepless. Her husband is snoring. It's nearly midnight. The premiere will end soon, and the five hundred in the Carlisle Theater will applaud and linger until the celebrities vanish behind car windows. Outside the Warner Theater a dwindling Oklahoma crowd paces the Grand Street sidewalks hoping to glimpse the absent champion. Ivy does not know this. It will be two weeks before her oldest daughter calls and describes the movie to her. *Jim Thorpe: All-American* will be repeated every football season, for years. One day she will find herself in a room in one of her brothers' houses, where a grandchild has left the TV mumbling, and she will sit in the dark of a couch, half daydreaming, and watch herself as a stranger would, watch this white woman, some second-rate actress she has never seen before—until her chest catches in recognition.

Ivy does not know that Jim's remains will be sold by Patsy to a small Pennsylvania town two hours from Carlisle. Neither Jim nor Ivy ever heard of Mauch Chunk. Once considered the wealthiest town in America, its railroad is closed, its mines are boarded up, its historical downtown papered with foreclosures and for sale signs, but it will soon have a proud new name: Jim Thorpe, Pennsylvania, final resting home of the Olympic hero. Patsy was won over by the town's pluck, the citizens' weekly nickel contributions to their economic development fund. Jim Thorpe unites two rival boroughs, Mauch Chunk and East Mauch Chunk, under the champion's name, guaranteeing their mutual return to economic prosperity. Tourists will visit the athlete's tasteful burial monument a short hike from the shopping district. Although his medals were never restored in his too-brief lifetime, their facsimiles will forever decorate him in the afterlife. Three flags snap at continual attention above the marble-etched paraphrase of a king: "Sir, you are the greatest athlete in the world."

Ivy doesn't know that her second husband will not live out the decade either, and that she will move to California again, to be near her sister, and that she will die alone, except for the nurse those last years, after the stroke, when she is paralyzed, speechless, comatose, or nearly. Three years she will have alone with her paling body. Then she will cross over one last and irrevocable time. For now, she twirls her teaspoon, watches the dollop of cream swirl and vanish. I am home, she tells herself. I am exactly who I am. My performance is flawless, unassailable. She is not thinking of the script a Hollywood man named Mr. William Hendricks mailed to her or how she read it a final time, like this, at night, with her husband's breathing audible through the crack of the bedroom door. How queer to imagine this other Ivy and her other Jim holding hands and sipping punch, serenaded by the tattoo of Indian drums. It made her dizzy, literally, this alien self, this most modern of vertigoes. She has been written over again. She is still a chalk-smeared slate.

In her attic is a shoebox. It has traveled with her from her homes in Oklahoma to her homes in Illinois. It will travel with her to California. Her daughters will find it. It rests, right now, on a board of plywood her husband laid crooked over the attic floor beams, almost but not quite over her head, unless she leans backward, balances herself on the rear legs of the kitchen chair. Inside are Jim's school medals. There are clippings and photographs. Some have slipped from their scrapbook pages to leave stains of brittle glue. She has his varsity letter too, the great golden "C," the one Phyllis Thaxter sews onto his sweater as he waits and blinks at her, lovestruck. When he threads his arms through the sleeves again, she notices a loose string. She steps closer, pulls the fabric to her mouth, and bites it with her teeth.

Jim feels the tug in his chest. It is the only moment in the movie he needs to be real. The games, that fool Lancaster shuffling over the same field again and again, while the voice-over pretends we're in some new city after each cut, it's nonsense, even the historic footage, the Olympic stadium, the real vice president spliced in. Now it's another of those endless awards banquets, some man droning on, detailing the moments Jim's learned to exaggerate too, to keep the faces nodding, smiling. He is who they want him to be. Here comes Lancaster again, only they've grayed his dyed hair, cropped it the way Patsy shears his. The applause begins, at first from the theater speakers, those black-and-white people beaming at his double, and then from all around him, all the clatter merging.

He expects that rise of blood, the thrill of it, however slight, but this time he does not know if they are applauding him or the screen. His face warms. The lights have not risen yet. For an instant he is lost, drawn into the plot, the way a good movie should draw you. Forgive him, Phyllis, if for a moment Jim's hand fumbles over your arm rest, if he keeps reaching toward your lap, uncertain whose chilled wrist it is he's touching, whose hand he hopes to find there in this dark.

Sports Illustrated
Interviews Marianne Moore

antwell is lucky. He's scored a parking spot, a bit tight but right across from the apartment on West 9th, practically across from it, the same block at least. He punches reverse, skims the Edsel's rear tire on the curb, punches drive, taps bumpers, punches reverse again, ratchets his neck higher, a bad angle, but he manages to wedge himself mostly in. He tugs his coat sleeve back to see how early he is. Midmorning, so traffic was light on the bridge, even lighter on this side, so barely twenty minutes getting here. Interviewees usually prefer a meal on the magazine, and so does Cantwell. He could be treating the both of them to a Manhattan brunch, could be sucking down a screwdriver and Camel before omelets, but instead he's out here, in Brooklyn, the old lady's home turf. The so-called *Waterfront.* As if Marlon Brando would set foot in Red Hook without a camera crew watching his back.

Cantwell elbows the lock down while shuffling out of the seat but gives the handle an extra yank, to be sure, his head swerving, car keys jangling to his coat pocket. The street is empty. Just a jalopy idling at the intersection. Marianne Moore told him on the phone, actually warned him, be careful, before going on about break-ins, a subway mugging, the bum she found sleeping it off on her stoop the week before. What does she expect? Al Capone grew up around here. And now all the jobs gone to Jersey, the longshoremen projects filling up with Negroes. Even the Dodgers jumped ship. She should move to Manhattan like the rest of the civilized world.

His shoulders tighten as he crosses the street. Not cold for January, but cold all the same. He's nearly to the curb when he glimpses a figure, someone right there, rounding the other edge of a parked car. He doesn't startle, not exactly. But he can't help his neck jerking like that, even after he sees it's only a woman, a black woman, a short one. Her head is down, so she can't appreciate the scowl she deserves; probably was eyeing him the whole block, shambling on her little panther feet.

He steps in front of her, listens to her stride waver and fall back, while he squints at addresses: 30, 33. And there it is, 35, the number scribbled on the notepad in his pocket. He's halfway up the brick steps, his finger rising for the bell, before he feels the woman at his back again, still following him. He turns, and there she stands, frozen now, in the middle of the private walk. Followed him right off the sidewalk, like a little brown dog.

"What do you want?"

His voice shouldn't sound so defensive. Annoyance would be better. Let her know she's got no business with him, no handouts. If it weren't for the safety of the stoop, the wall of mortared bricks behind him, he might be scanning for other figures, for heftier shadows sifting from the alleyways at his sides. And now he *is* looking, between parked cars, at the empty porches, at the lampposts casting no shadows through the pale air. It's just him and this Negro woman pointing, not at him, but at the door at his back.

"I work here," she says.

Cantwell glances at the decorative knocker, at the bell he hasn't pressed yet, and back at the woman. Her coat is worn, but respectable, the fringe at her neck a little mangy. She looks about forty, fifty maybe, his age. A cleaning girl. Of course an old lady would keep one.

"For Marianne Moore?" he almost says, but the cleaning girl is already bending over, tucking a pair of parcels from the welcome mat into the crook of her arm, both too big for the letter slot. It's a lazy hour for a morning shift, but there's a key sparkling in her other hand, and then Cantwell finds himself stepping back from the door. The lock is large and just as shiny, the gouged wood around its edges newly varnished, the color almost but not quite matching the rest of the door. Break-ins. Marianne Moore is in his ear again, his right ear, his phone ear.

The cleaning girl shoves the door and is stepping inside, a breath of warmth escaping. Cantwell hesitates. He hasn't rung the bell yet. "I'm here to see Marianne Moore," he calls out, as though she were sealing the door closed between them, which she's not.

"You have an appointment?"

There's nothing necessarily disrespectful in her tone, so soft and flat she's barely audible over the car passing at Cantwell's back. But he doesn't like the way her eyes skitter across his face.

"I'll tell her you're here," she says.

She lets him in but leaves him to close the door himself, which requires a surprisingly rough thrust, a manly thrust, before the evidently new lock agrees to click. His coat is already unbuttoned. He left his gloves on the passenger seat, so he has nothing to do but study the foyer. The foyer of one of the finest living American poets. No, America's greatest living poet, that was *The New Yorker*'s phrase. Cantwell may have used it himself when he was still at *Newsweek* and Marianne Moore kept winning that grand slam of poetry, Pulitzer, National Book, the Bollingen maybe, some other he can't think of. He might use that Eliot quote this time, enduring contribution to the English language, something like that. He'll look it up again. Literary editor of the nation's top sports magazine is not entirely an oxymoron.

A mechanical crow stares down from a high shelf. Marianne Moore's foyer is a cluttered alcove of bookshelves, a menagerie of bric-a-brac, a cacophony of book spines. A wooden lizard winds its tail along a jagged row of leathery book tops, its wood the same grain as the wood behind it, tones blending so you can't see the animal unless you're looking at it. A black bowl of coins rests on the shelf beneath. No—Cantwell leans over the puddled shadows—they're subway tokens.

He's swirling his fingers in them when the cleaning girl returns. Only it's not the girl. It's a slight and pear-shaped silhouette, pale window glow framing her in an inner doorway. A halo of tight braid, white even in this light.

"For visitors," announces Marianne Moore. "Help yourself."

Cantwell's hand snaps away from the tokens, almost topples them. "Oh, no, no, I drove. I'm parked right outside."

Marianne Moore keeps pointing at the bowl. She and her mother, she is explaining, they used to keep errand money by the door that way, in a little red box. With pretty porcupine quills on the lid. She doesn't know where the bowl came from. She's had it for years, decades actually. Would Mr. Cantwell like to come in and sit?

She'd sounded old on the telephone. She is old. But the voice, the papery hoarseness, he thought that was the static. Cantwell is very careful when he accepts her bird-light handshake. A frail and elderly lady. That's what he'll call her. And he'll have to mention something about her costume too, always that white blouse, the pleated skirt—a private uniform, in every photograph he's ever seen of her. Minus the cape and tricorne hat, indoors. Did she wear those on Jack Paar's show? The White Sox were ahead, and there she was, the greatest living American poet accurately forecasting a Dodgers' victory. I bet she has some predictions for next season, or advice at least. That's how Cantwell convinced his editor she was worth an article, a short one at least. A spinster poet's love of sports, of athletic excellence, the irony of it really, that sort of thing. She threw out the first ball of the Yankees' season last year—that's a paragraph right there.

They sit in her front room, amid a tiered drift of half-sorted envelopes, most unopened, this morning's packages commanding their own corner of the coffee table. He hopes she's not paying that cleaning girl too much, because there are breakfast dishes still out, the remains of an avocado, something orange staining a glass bottom. Moore lifts a postcard, at random, an amusement park on the front. From *The New Yorker* editor, she reads, hoping for a poem apparently. It takes her an hour and a half, every morning, she sighs. Books to be signed, requests for interviews, blurbs, petitions, academics with their little niggling questions, as though she could remember what she could possibly have been thinking the first time she penned this or that line, twenty, thirty, forty years ago, fifty. Whole lifetimes. She returns the postcard to the crown of the straightest pile.

Cantwell smiles indulgently, arms spreading. "The burdens of maintaining so august a reputation." This is all very nice, but it's not a story. Old lady opens mail.

Reputation. Moore flinches at the sound of it. She is no longer a poet, she declares, if a poet is a creature who composes poetry. She's only a dutiful curiosity now, to be taxied to readings and banquets and libraries, kept out much too late, always a dinner forced on her, guest of honor, certificates, medals, when she simply wishes to be returned to her home by five o'clock. She has one this very afternoon in fact, a reading, at a women's prison of all things, a house of detention, if she's well enough to appear. She sincerely hopes she is not contagious and won't send Mr. Cantwell home to his wife with the flu, the one forever stalking her.

"Oh, don't worry about me. I'm healthy as an ox." Cantwell draws his yellow notebook from an inner pocket. "A complete ox," he repeats, flipping the cover, pen in hand, glimpsing some ancient scribble of his, a box score it looks like. He tries not to write too much during interviews, lets what matters stick in his head, but the notebook is a good prop. An opening bell, a whistle blow. They're officially starting.

"So Miss Moore. The Dodgers. That poem you wrote for them—I can't imagine the rest of the literary establishment was very pleased. Rather lowbrow for us highbrows, no?"

Okay, not his tightest opening pitch. The "us," where did that come from? As if the finest living American poet has read his Hawthorne biography, or cares he was a novelist himself in the thirties. Marianne Moore runs a palm along the pleat of her skirt. She has been aware of being disapproved of for most of the century. Lester Littlefield, she says, does not like any of her occasional poems, Dodgers-themed or otherwise. Ephemera, he terms them. She can only imagine how he will describe her foreword, the one she is slaving over, for the *Marianne Moore Reader*. That's what her publisher is going to call it, a tombstone of a title. Sometimes she wishes she could be like her friend Hilda and simply run off to the Alps and hide with her poems.

"But," says Cantwell, his pen up like a conductor's baton. "You don't. You're much more—of the people. I mean, you don't see T. S. Eliot ringside at a Cassius Clay fight, do you?"

Moore coughs a throaty laugh, mumbles "Tom" a few times. No, she admits, it's true. She does love her athletes. Exemplars of art, really, of self-possession. Cantwell starts writing the phrase, then stops. He'll ask her opinion about the designated pinch hitter experiment if he can't get anything better going soon.

"And what exactly do you attribute your passion to? What novels lead you down this path?" He ticks off a few, *The Natural*, *The Southpaw*, but she waves them off. Her interest was never literary. She has read almost nothing of sports. But she did grow up surrounded by it all, in Pennsylvania, following the Indians every year, her whole town did. The parades, you simply would not believe the parades Carlisle threw, after the games, the victories, the pride they felt. A total sports immersion—how could she help but assimilate?

"Carlisle?" Cantwell's pen has stopped. It was just a doodle, a baseball pendant. "That was your hometown?" Marianne Moore nods. "Carlisle. Carlisle, Pennsylvania. Home of the Carlisle Indians." She's still nodding. "I had absolutely no idea," he says. He would have mentioned it to his editor when he pitched his idea for this interview, would have someone in the filing cabinets already, the photo archives. "Chief Bender," he blurts, "of the A's, he came out of Carlisle, didn't he?"

Charles Bender certainly did, but a little before Marianne Moore's time. She had still been a student herself when Charles started in the majors.

"The school turned that Indian into a heck of a ballplayer. A pitcher," says Cantwell. "That's more than just a savage arm, you know. It's amazing what the government could do back then. A wild Indian like that, how they could turn them into something so worthwhile." Maybe one of the interns can unearth an old shot of Bender, or some other Indian, when he first arrived, in dead animal furs and whatnot, war paint, to show the transformation. His editor will love this, another two pages easily.

Oh, and Marianne Moore taught there herself. At the school. She was a teacher.

"Where?" says Cantwell.

Carlisle.

The pen turns horizontally in his fingers, centered like a balance. "You don't mean you taught at the actual Carlisle Indian School? You taught—you actually taught Indians?"

Yes, in fact, she does mean that. English, typing, that sort of thing, for, how long, it couldn't have been five years, could it? If she started in 1911?

Cantwell stammers, arms rising like goalposts. "During the Olympics, the 1912 Olympics? The Jim Thorpe Olympics? You were there when Thorpe was there, when Pop Warner was, when they won all those championships?"

Yes. Yes, Moore was there. James was one of her students.

"Thorpe? You actually taught Jim Thorpe?"

She taught the whole backfield. She begins naming her spindly fingers: Joel Wheelock, James Baker, Alex Arcasa, Gus Welch. Oh Gus, he was such a fine fine boy, so handsome, so intelligent, hardly a hint of Indian about him. Almost Grecian, his looks. All of the students were, in a way. Moore twists on her couch cushion, her eyes scanning the interminable shelf clutter. She has a card somewhere, a honeymoon card, from Iva.

"Weren't you afraid?"

Cantwell simply can't imagine it. This fragile bird of a creature, a child then, her perfumed hands and girl-white face lost in the musk of savages, Neanderthals practically. He's seen pictures. They arrived off the trains like animals. It was still the nineteenth century almost, Custer and Geronimo. They ate buffalo off the blades of their tomahawks. Actually, it's Natalie Wood he's picturing in front of a classroom, from *The Searchers*, in her Comanche ponytails and buckskins, which makes no sense because it was the Indians they dressed up like students, and Marianne Moore, Cantwell seriously doubts, could ever have passed as a Hollywood starlet.

Moore is smiling her ancient spinster smile at him. It never occurred to her to be afraid, she says. Although it certainly occurred to Moore's mother and Moore's brother. The superintendent who hired her, his name was Friedman, a nice Jewish man, or half-Jewish, or ex-Jewish—it occurred to him too. But really he had no choice, with his business department teacher quitting so abruptly, off to sell typewriters somewhere. Moore had no choice either, a salary of two thousand dollars, twice as much as the men teaching in the industrial buildings, and she barely out of commercial college, barely twenty-four years old.

"But they were Indians," repeats Cantwell. "Actual savages. Did they even know how to speak yet? English?"

Moore laughs. She was teaching them commercial law, you know. It wasn't just the quick brown fox jumps over the lazy dog. They were to go back home and turn into entrepreneurs. Into Americans. Businessmen. It's what the government said it wanted. She laughs again. There's something in her tone, the inscrutable echo of a flat, midwestern twang, that gives him pause. He's never heard another voice like it. A British accent, only reversed somehow. Inverted. A nation of one. Is the old lady toying with him?

"But," he says. He can't keep his pen tip from tapping the paper on his thigh. "They couldn't possibly have been smart enough." It's like the Democrats now. Throw a Catholic in the White House and all the Negroes are suddenly supposed to be able to earn a college diploma and fly to the moon? Probably better to steer clear of politics though. "You can't simply erase the past. They were born as God made them. With the souls of Indians. They must die as Indians too, as God made them."

Marianne Moore blinks. Slowly. She wouldn't know anything about that. Her brother is the minister of the family.

"I simply mean the expectation was rather grandiose, wouldn't you say? A little naive really?"

She can't speak of the larger student body, but the business department was selective, a kind of graduate program, in theory. She took only the cream of the crop. The phrase halts her, tugs her tight little-old-lady mouth into a frown. She's thinking something, something unpleasant. The cliché, assumes Cantwell. Even poets get trapped in them.

"But Jim Thorpe," he says, "look what happened to his career. He just stayed out there getting pummeled for years because he couldn't do anything else. It was a tragedy."

Marianne Moore is still frowning. She looks off, toward the gloom of the window. James was in a little over his head perhaps, she admits. She'd spoken about him to her principal, the irregularity of his presence in her department, considering his grades, the lack of them, and her principal had spoken to the superintendent, but of course nothing was ever done. Hers were the only classes James attended. To be with his future wife. Iva Miller. Though not at first, Iva was Gus's girl. They practically wrestled for her, that complexion of hers. So pretty, and smart too, quite the prize. Moore's eyes rise to a different wall of clutter, her head bobbing sideways to see past Cantwell's shoulders. She must still have that honeymoon card somewhere. From Japan.

"But you've never written about any of this," protests Cantwell. "In any of your poems. How is that possible?" He's read most of them, the *Collected Poems,* dense and thick-tongued riddles about chameleons and zebras and little scaly, armored things, all eminently poetic and impenetrable.

When he looks up again the poet's neck has gone taut, her spine, every hollow bone of her. Why ever should the school have become a part of her life? And what does poetry have to do with self-expression? Marianne Moore has never written about herself. A poem is a thing, not a person. It's a mask. A poem is a mask. Marianne Moore says it a third time, a mask, and Cantwell understands that he has been scolded. A crack on the knuckles from a nun's wooden ruler. He has embarrassed himself. There must be a cloud outside, because the room has dimmed. He's back in the murk with the other young savages, watching the prim Miss Moore breathing through her nostrils.

He flips a page of his notebook, smooths it flat, for no reason. A bell. A new round. He exhales and smiles.

"So. They were never any trouble to you then. The Indians. Discipline-wise?"

Moore listens to the question, sits a silent moment, as though waiting for her brain to finish translating his words from some exotic language, and then begins to tell a story. Her hands are folded on her lap. One day she was chaperoning a trip to the circus. It was Memorial Day. The students had spent the morning cutting the grass in the Indian cemetery with scythes, and now it was time to go and see the circus. It was cloudy and it looked like it might rain, so she brought her parasol with her. James Thorpe approached her as they were walking. Miss Moore, James said. Miss Moore, would you like me to carry your parasol for you? That was the way James was. James Thorpe was chivalrous and cooperative and helpful and kindly. He was a gentleman. Her hands are still folded when she finishes speaking.

Cantwell is writing, getting the list of adjectives down. It's a nice story, and he knows he's probably going to use it. But he also knows he's lost her. Her eyes aren't focused anymore, all that blinking, her gaze adrift. It wasn't just his insult to the integrity of poetry. She's gone elsewhere, back to Carlisle presumably. Which appears to be located just beyond his left shoulder. He keeps wanting to follow her eyes, see what's back there in the doorway. Savages in secretary skirts. He has to make do with the telegram of her body. Not that he can't lure enough anecdotes out of her to fill this sheet and the next two. It's been half a century, but there's nothing wrong with this old lady's memory. Apparently Thorpe was a gentleman in the classroom too, he and Welch keeping the recalcitrants in their places. Some hoodlum called Loud Bear. Literally. Loud Bear. Cantwell's editor isn't going to believe this stuff.

Next he gets her chattering about General Pratt, the school's founder, up on his high horse—literally, he rode a horse—and now the article is simply writing itself. Ten, maybe eleven pages, counting ads and photographs of the athletes, some of Marianne Moore back in the day if she has any. She must. That's a bookshelf of photo albums lurking behind the floor lamp. Cantwell has fallen into a gold mine.

He eventually gets her to crack one open, a scrapbook, dust motes swirling in the wake of each turned page, and there she is, the young Miss Moore, tennis racquet in hand, hat brim shadowing her face like the mask of Zorro. But it's the classroom shot that will haunt him later. Not her face, not her body either—she was no Natalie Wood—yet there's something about her. Maybe the angle of that elbow. The high waist of the skirt, black of course, the square of the shoulders, the white front of her high-necked blouse. And those spindly fingers stroking the desktop at her hip. It arouses him, the ghost of this girl, dead half a century.

The cleaning girl comes in, from behind him, doesn't know enough to knock on the door frame first, shambles over to clear that plate finally, the browned avocado bits. Maybe it's carrot juice staining the glass. Moore tries to introduce them—or did Mr. Cantwell meet Gladys already, when he came in? Cantwell grunts. The cleaning girl's eyes never come near him. Though she's all grins with her employer. Mrs. Berry has been taking care of Marianne Moore for a long long time now, a decade at least. Moore would simply starve without her Gladys— she'd be entombed in envelopes. They both laugh. The cleaning girl should be on her way back to the kitchen, not stalling by the typewriter stand. Then suddenly Moore is standing too, her gnarled hands smoothing pleats, explaining how avocado keeps her hair shiny, and the bottled water her Lebanese doctor recommends for her, and it dawns on Cantwell that his interview has ended. He checks his watch, half wonders if the cleaning girl timed it this way, but there's no guile, no intelligence in those dark, doe eyes.

"It was a pleasure, Miss Moore." He cradles her spindly hand in his own once more. "An absolute pleasure."

He manages one more question in the foyer, an observation really, as he buttons his coat. Marianne Moore is standing at the bookshelf, the wooden lizard half-hidden at her shoulder. "I suppose ultimately it was a failure though, the school. Since they had to close it. A grand idea and all, educating Indians in the ways of civilization, but it did fail in the end."

It's not quite a frown that darkens her face. And she recovers quickly enough, her hand reaching past him for the doorknob, which of course Cantwell must take himself. Carlisle became an army medical school, she tells him. She left when it became an army medical school. She doesn't say anything else.

Cantwell jerks at the door. "Good morning, Miss Moore. And thank you again." He's got records to dig up, football stats, has to send an assistant to the library. Half the article can be Carlisle recap, the heyday, historical snippets to space out the anecdotes. Cantwell's coat recedes down the cement steps and into the gray of the street.

Marianne Moore clicks the new lock behind the interviewer, clicks it twice, to be sure. The new shiny lock. Her niece insisted. It was Gladys who called the man to install it. Marianne stands there, fingertips on the cool metal.

The angle of the door pane is the same as the old one on Hanover Street, or nearly, framed up high so it's mostly the gray wash of sky she can see, the glass warping it. It could almost be Carlisle out there. The sounds are wrong, but not utterly. No trolley clatter, but the crest and ebb of car engines is not so very different from that remote, hivelike hum of Carlisle air. A street is a street. She does not have to close her eyes to imagine it, but she does anyway. Shuts them tight, to fend off the queer beat of her heart, the pulse of her reddening blood.

A failure. Yes. Certainly the new superintendent had thought so. The one who replaced Mr. Friedman after the hearings. The one who fired her. Fired Friedman, Mr. Stauffer, Coach Warner, even that horrid head matron. Discarded the business department entirely, cooked up Domestic Science instead, and a lower-paying position teaching the general classes, should Miss Moore pass the examinations. Her mother had her decline. It was an insult. But no less a release.

She had promised she would not quit, and she had not. No one could blame her in any way at all.

Since she finds her fingers still resting on the metal, she twists the bolt once more, for no reason. She knows it's locked. Nothing can get in. A muffler grumbles outside—Mr. Cantwell's perhaps, that personal embarrassment of an automobile she spied through her bedroom sheers while he bullied into a parking space. The Edsel. Really she had nothing to do with the name, whatever the rumor. Would a Ford Turtletop have been any less a fiasco? At least Mr. Cantwell did not interrogate her about that. She listens, but he's gone, he and his dissolving exhaust. Behind it, a ferry horn perhaps, distant, like a gull cry.

It's not true of course. There is nothing of Carlisle in Brooklyn. No student brigade marches shoulder to shoulder past this stoop, no bright inner cape hems flashing red from their black folds. If she rode her bicycle—if she still owned a bicycle, if she could work her hobbled body around its gears and spokes—no half-mile ride would find her at the mouth of any stony entrance bridge. The clack of bicycle tire over trolley track, that's probably not even a memory. Her brain could be making that up. Though she can still picture it, or map it at least, Coach Warner's house on the right, after the entrance pillars, the arts castle there on the left, the Deitzes' wolfhounds prowling behind their pickets. Only the steeple of the boiler house smokestack stands beyond the orchard turn. She pedaled toward it every morning, never looking up, and away again each night, the soot steam invisible in the black air. Back home to her own bed in her mother's house, after student study hours, her fingerprints black from typewriter ribbons, the endless repairs, keys eternally jammed.

Especially her own. Upstairs in her room, typing away on the tiny second-hand desk her mother bought for her when she turned nine. All the writing she did, all those poems, trying to invent herself, the poet she wished to become, a new self to inhabit. Anything to escape the school, those lonely children, staring at her from their black eyes, their masked-in bones. There was something so horrible about it all, even then she knew it, and practiced the unknowing of it every night in her room. She had faked her way through Bryn Mawr, and there she was, posing as a teacher, still a child herself. Barely six months older than James. Of course he never completed her assignments. They were peers, a kind of couple practically, the oldest boy and girl in the room. She had to grin and turn her reddening face to the blackboard whenever he reprimanded a younger student on her behalf. It didn't mean anything of course. It was simply James's nature to be a gentleman. There was no secret bond between them. Even afternoons when he lingered by her desk after class, after the hall had stopped echoing. When there was no one else to see them. She remembers the pink of his hand resting on her desk blotter. Her hand was practically the same color, with the blotter glowing underneath it too. She remembers thinking that, but not speaking it, choosing not to speak it. Her pen rested in her other hand, beside the new sheets of old problems. Commercial Math. It was ridiculous, her brother mailing her back proper answers from his seminary, her columns of figures forever riddled with errors. She did not belong there. None of them did. They were all pretending. There was no choice.

"I'm still an imposter," Marianne says aloud.

"What?"

Mrs. Berry is moving from kitchen to hall toilet, wastepaper basket in hand.

Marianne's head swivels, forces the face into focus.

"Oh, Gladys, I am sorry. I was thinking. You must ignore me, you know." And then remembering Gladys's husband and his fall at the construction site: "Wallace, how is he? What did the doctors say this morning?"

The woman's frown is pained but not panicked. "They think it could be a week, but he's doing well enough, the bones are set right. He'll be fine."

Marianne advances for a hug, a half-hug, one hand pressing the small of Mrs. Berry's back. "Of course he will, of course he will, dear."

Both women smile glumly, their hands touch, wrinkled skin on wrinkled skin, and then Mrs. Berry is all business again. "What would you like to wear this afternoon?"

"Wear?"

"For the reading? The taxi will be here after lunch."

"Oh." The inmates, Marianne had nearly forgotten the women inmates. "The black taffeta, I suppose."

Mrs. Berry's face falls. "Not the navy?"

Marianne pictures the arsenal of her wardrobe, searches for it.

"It's just been washed, you know, and didn't shrink or fade any," assures Mrs. Berry.

She finds it. Blue with the crystal-and-gold buttons and zigzag gold belt. "Yes," Marianne says, "yes, that will be perfect, won't it?"

Another smile and Mrs. Berry is off with her wastebasket, and it's back to the mail. Marianne settles herself in her corner, plumps the pillow at her back, and stares at the jagged stacks of envelopes. An hour at least today. The photo album, the one she took down for Mr. Cantwell, sits open beside the larger packages. The ones she really can't bear to open just now. She simply hasn't room for more knickknacks, more gifts from beggars. She is under no obligation to respond, as her friends scold her, but of course she must. A printed return card would be nice though. Miss Moore regrets that she is unable to respond to requests for interviews, petitions, etc. Gladys could slot them into the envelopes for her. She should be at her desk, finishing the foreword, proofing the Henry Ford correspondence her editor insists on. The *Reader* is a testament to something, to her presumably, some new mutation, Marianne Moore the celebrity. Not the poet. She culled the prewar poems—the pre–World War II poems—to a half dozen, an unhinged skeleton of her youth. No growth, no primordial struggle, just the seamless, grandmotherly end product. It's a book of omissions she's making.

"And omissions," she says aloud, "are not accidents." She gives a theatrical turn as she makes this announcement, gestures to the missing guest at her elbow. A ghost of Cantwell fidgeting on his empty couch cushion. It is easier to embody oneself in the presence of a half-stranger. He is only a swirl of motes in the window light now.

Why did she lie to Mr. Cantwell? If not a lie exactly, then more omissions. The same species she once performed daily for Mr. Friedman. She couldn't very well have revealed her politics—the suffragist meetings possibly, but never the Socialist, not with students being expelled for less, his vendetta against that poor boy with the ice cream wagon. She can picture the superintendent so easily still, the gray-spackled goatee, that Hebraic nose, those myopic blinks, as if he were always just then raising his gaze from his desk blotter to look at you, permanently book-blinded, straining to find his way three-dimensionally. He did have a way with words though. Sowers of sedition, he termed her students. A fomenter of dissent, he called her. She can see him, right there, frowning at her, his thumbnail rapping the edge of the coffee table. Or is that Mr. Cantwell again?

She has no business being haunted. She was not responsible for anything, not personally. She seized no bawling infants from any mother's papoose board. She was abetting the children, building them armor against the white swindlers preying on their reservations. And it was not her fault the school closed, not directly. She had moved away before the War even began, the first War. It simply was not true what Mr. Friedman said. She provided her students with extensive instruction in political honor, crushing out rancor wherever she spied it.

She had not encouraged a single one of the petitions that originated from her classroom. How her students adored petitions. Petitions to expel that poor colored boy, to ship away the pregnant girl from the infirmary, petitions requesting the reconsideration of other expulsions, to amend the meager portions of dining hall meals, the unjust reduction of evening socials in the gymnasium, the ungentlemanly savagery of Mr. Stauffer's spankings, Coach Warner's abusiveness, his betting on games—anything they could think of, the food, the mattresses, the moral depravity. Of course she applauded their initiative, she was their teacher, she encouraged free thought, mental growth. It was her job. They thought the world could be rewritten one brazen sentence at a time. Rolled forward on the hinges of grease-gummed typewriters commandeered while her back was turned, her knees bent at the desk of some dutiful student, an Iva Miller. The next chapter of drills, that was the real work at hand. The business department was built on ticket profits. Football paid her salary. She had no choice but to hide. First from the inspector, then from the senators who followed, assembling their court of folding tables behind the gymnasium foul line. They interviewed everyone. The whole town was a-twitter with the gossip of it, the side-taking, a grand new game, its rules more bewildering than Coach Warner's playbooks. Stay in your igloo, her brother warned, and Marianne did.

The poet smooths her skirt, smooths the fabric of the couch cushion, a pattern so familiar it has worn itself invisible to the eye. We all must choose who we are. From whole cloth, as it were. The scrapbook is open on the table, the wide black page framing each white-bordered photograph. Except for one. Mr.

Cantwell asked to borrow it. A coil of crusted glue marks the empty space. She can't remember which it was now, which image of herself. Omissions are natural, are a necessary outcome of choosing. There is no need for regret.

Did they all die Indians? It is not a question she can mail her brother, and she would not open his envelope had he the audacity to attempt an answer. Her math is as good as anyone's now. That Iva, she was Marianne's salvation, all of those children were. The colored boy, that pompous and frightened colored boy, whatever was his name? Marianne should get up now, should dress while Mrs. Berry assembles something nice for her lunch. She must finish the foreword as soon as possible, after today's reading. Or tomorrow. Miss Moore never wanted to be a part of anything, Modernism, Imagism, Objectivism. She never wanted to be one of those beautiful, unfathomable children.

Sylvester Goes Home

Bessie's letter was later found crinkled inside Lance's jacket pocket. She'd mailed it before telephoning to say she'd married an art student named Tom Hayakawa. Tom was Oriental. Could they visit?

Lance was living at the Glendale Hotel by then, at Anita's expense, and had stopped bringing girls to his room after the night clerk tipped him off about the private detective Anita had hired. Any more philandering and she would yank Lance's Glendale airfield tuition. The promised Lockheed airplane was already out of his reach. Anita did not approve of his new L.A. drinking crowd. Lance didn't think much of them either, brats mostly, but they beat chatting stock figures over colas in Anita's library, rising to stoke the fire whenever she eased beside him on the settee.

Lance told Bessie on the phone that no, unfortunately, he would be out of town then and would miss them. Maybe on their return? Bessie was looking forward to the honeymoon and meeting all of her new Japanese in-laws. Bessie had told him once, if a girl loved a man she should marry him, whatever his heritage. She'd thought she meant it too, not that it mattered now. Lance knew how quickly her grandmother, a coal baron's niece, would have annulled their marriage. Someone would have tipped the family off sooner or later. Still, he would have enjoyed scribbling his name across the bottom of a wedding certificate. His signature was nonsense, but he rendered it with such flourish, each curved letter and slash and that final thrust of ink off the page edge. He'd wanted to tell Bessie, of course he had, but she was only a kid. He pictured her eyes as she babbled over the receiver, the spokes of green coral threading each iris, the milky glow of her

tan lines, her spine's pebbled trail against his fingertips. He hung up first. Have
to go, he said, and congratulations again, really.

Anita didn't know about Bessie, or didn't differentiate her from Lance's other
women, a dozen in one month, he bragged once. Lance liked to watch the wrinkles along Anita's jaw tighten. He could make her smile too, grin like a girl, her
whole face stretching with a trill of giggles at her dining room table, that obscene
twelve-footer set for two under chandelier glare. She was fifty, twice divorced.
Dogs, she called them, her ex-husbands, all men. Anita was a philanthropist now.
She had never encountered a specimen quite like Lance, a full-blood, born on
the blanket, a noble nomad ascending the white man's world.

It wasn't easy, but he had shaken her last summer, gotten her to dump him
in New York after the fiasco abroad. He wasn't suicidal, though once or twice
after tilting a bottle dry he had climbed through a porthole, halfway, but always
on the lounge deck, a dozen hands to haul him back. The carving knife was
different. He let someone coax it from his fist while their hosts and the roasted
pig gaped. It was a show. The Germans, all Karl May fans like their new chancellor,
wanted to shake hands with Anita's educated Indian. They wanted translations of
his autobiography signed with personalized notes. A bona fide best seller and
the aboriginal had written it himself, no anthropologist's daughter scribbling
shorthand beside his teepee fire. Lance was considering *Last of the Mohicans* for
his next movie, Anita said. According to her accountant, he was her secretary-
bodyguard, but she told him to write "pleasure" on the passport application. Her
real guards she left at home with her hounds and barbed-wire fence. Communists
could storm the ranch at any moment.

Lance had preferred New York over L.A anyway. This was last fall. He'd still
had his eighth-floor room at the prestigious Explorers Club, and though most
members were snubbing him in the library and the smoking lounge by then,
technically the only rules he broke were the bottle of vodka labeled "hair tonic"
in his medicine cabinet and the .45 in the shoebox under his bed. Rumors
couldn't expel him. Still, his publisher's crowd was done with him, and his editor at *Cosmopolitan* refused his calls. The option on his second book, a "novel,"
vanished. He still had the occasional private screening or banquet, but his lec-

ture fees had gone the way of the market. At least his flying lessons were paid off, but after he wired another money order to North Carolina, to help with his father's year-old hospital bills, the dregs of Anita's salary lasted only another month, not quite to Christmas.

Rain froze against his trench coat when he trotted the two blocks to the telegraph office. The bald man behind the counter didn't glance up from his typewriter, so Lance spread his shoulders and a trellis of ice splintered onto the tiled floor. He had come to send a telegram to Anita, asking for the second chance she longed to give him. Anita had a soft spot for Indians. She cluttered her mansion with illegal artifacts and employed two Hopi housemaids to dust them. Plus it was California. She didn't know the East Coast had stopped inviting him to cocktail parties, to benefit galas, to anything.

His final month in New York was a good one. Lance dined again with that rich girl flyer he'd met at Roosevelt Field the summer before. This time he was the one bragging about Continental climates and stately ruins, plus the Toulouse-Lautrec paintings Anita's son hung in his Paris apartment, how the boy had abandoned a wife and children to live with a French tennis star. Oh, you've heard of her? The aviatrix slept with him this time, not in his room, but at a roadside inn across the Hudson. The wilds, she called it. She made cat noises, a kind of mewling, then a bark when she gripped his body still. She wasn't so special balled in the sheets and snoring when he rose to pee and smoke one of her cigarettes outside. Lance slept with a Broadway girl a few times that month too, after evening movies, a matinee once. She was a Chickasaw with "exotic" braids, but couldn't break past her string of minor roles, never would. She didn't believe the gossip about Lance, not when he held her eyes, his voice rumbling in his chest that way, Indian to Indian.

The fake Scot who rented the room next to Lance's and took his calls when he was out, always from women, introduced him to Bessie. She was dancing in a chorus line and sharing an apartment in Greenwich Village with a girlfriend. She was eighteen. Lance liked her. She didn't brag about Paris, or the private girls' schools her parents had routed her through. She wanted a taste of the real world, to grip it in her own fingers, she said as she squeezed his. Her fingers were tiny. They smelled of lotion, of lavender. She called the Village "Little Africa," apparently a forgotten post–Civil War name she'd heard somewhere and believed. After strolls in the Park, she loved to ride the subway north, not into Harlem, but near it, or east, to sip warm beer in Mexican diners. Best food on the planet, she said. The waitress, a dark-skinned Mexican lady, mixed-blood probably, almost certainly mixed-blood, eyed Lance as Bessie ate her tortillas and beans. Lance wasn't hungry.

Her great-granduncle's mansion stood on Fifth. He was dead, so it was a museum now. Anita's ranch was bigger, more sprawling, but that was California. The moon rolled along the museum roof as Lance turned and looked, turned and looked. Bessie was chattering. The cold had broken, so they strolled with their coats loose, the flesh of her hand hot inside his.

"I'm Indian," she said. "I must be, I'm certain of it." How else to explain her animal attraction to him?

Lance laughed. He didn't mean to, but he did. Bessie's heels dragged as she squinted up at him, not with anger, her round white face haloed in fur. She couldn't have seen much, not with the street lamp at his back, headlights slashing her face. Lance pulled her in, closed his mouth around hers, till her breath quickened against his cheek.

His last night in New York he took out the blonde who worked the Explorers Club switchboard. She was pretty enough. He grinned back at her over the twitching table candle as she reported how the club president was writing to the Commissioner of Indian Affairs. Was Lance really a Blackfoot chief? The president had written to West Point as well, about one of the lesser rumors. The girl's breasts spread against the tablecloth as she leaned to whisper. What does a cadet have to do, she wondered, to be expelled for conduct unbecoming? Lance offered to escort her to his room for a demonstration. He'd broken things off with Bessie anyhow. He'd had to, though Bessie really was a great girl, and he liked her, he really did.

Bessie still insisted on goodbyes at Penn Station, gripping his hand as a baggage boy loaded Lance's suitcases into the luggage car. She teetered against his chest as they kissed. She was crying. I will never love any man but you.

Lance waved from his window seat. It could have been Lovie, his first girl, the shape of her there on the platform—if he squinted or let his eyes blur on the glass. Bessie's hair was almost dark enough, but not kinky, and his family wasn't huddled around her gaping at the last passenger car in the North Carolina heat. That was twenty years ago. His brother said Lovie had quit her teaching job at the Negro college and married a druggist. They had kids. She was a virgin back then, same as Lance, and she kissed his lips as chastely as his mother had before he climbed the metal steps. He never saw her again. He never saw any of them again, except his brother, just that once, last spring.

Lance stopped an afternoon in Chicago to meet a married friend before continuing to California. The girl kept all of his postcards in the inner pocket of her purse and spread them across the table in the hotel restaurant, the clippings and photographs too. Her favorite was the bare-chested portrait she tore from the frontispiece of his autobiography. She couldn't lug the whole book around. When Lance was dressed again and absolutely had to leave, she rode with him in the same taxi, a risk, and clenched his hand on the platform, before she caught an eastbound back to her suburb alone.

Lance spent the next day writing letters, short ones, just time enough to dash a few lines between ports, he explained. An underage girl grinned and lingered in the Pullman car as he sipped his complimentary drinks, whiskeys, but it didn't lead to anything, just her perfume in his head as the scenery plodded on. He'd seen it before. The conductor asked for an autograph after pulling down his bags. Lance was the lone passenger for the empty Santa Anita station, but the express had to stop. Anita's father had stipulated so in the right-of-way deed across the estate. Lance tipped the luggage boy, a Negro about his own age, and felt the platform slats quake as the train receded. No chauffeur idled beyond the sealed ticket booth this time, so he called a cab from the pay phone and waited.

The first time Lance visited Anoakia—an Indian word meaning haven, according to Anita—he squinted through a Rolls-Royce window at the ten-foot walls bricking the grounds. Electric wire braided the tops. Past the guardhouse, the driveway wound to a glass peacock-etched doorway, which opened at his approach. A butler hoisted his bags from the trunk.

That time Lance slept downstairs in a guest suite nearest the bathhouse and columned gymnasium. The mansion's second floor was closed. Anita, house-poor she called herself, could barely pay the taxes, not with the Crash cutting her holdings in half. The president was to blame. She wanted to sell it, all three thousand acres, and settle into her Lake Tahoe estate, but where would she find a buyer now? Anita touched Lance's arm, his biceps through his cotton sleeve, as she pointed at the ocean, the vaguest haze of ocean, far beyond the descending valley.

She was too old for him of course, closer to his mother's age. Anita retired early and ordered the head watchman, the sergeant, to keep an extra eye on the maids' rooms, lest the Chief think to exercise certain tribal rights after hours. Chief Buffalo Child Long Lance. She wrote her son about him at her desk in her nightgown.

They had met the first time in Hollywood during Lance's publicity tour, at a Paramount party, before Paramount backed out of his film. That was the year before. The producer hadn't set his lawyer on Lance's trail yet. No one had unearthed his Indian school application. During the orchestra break, Lance improvised an arm-flailing translation of his tribe's death song at the micro-phone, and then transcribed it, more or less, on the back of Anita's program while sipping champagne on the balcony. We must record it, she said. Anita adored aboriginal music. In fact, many of her own compositions were inspired by them. Lance must come see the Indian murals she commissioned for a hallway in her home. The house itself was an Italian Renaissance design, only larger. Had he ever been to Italy?

Anita's first letter, an invitation to join her on a paid three-month tour of Europe, arrived at the lobby of the Explorers Club the same week as one of Lance's old schoolmates, an out-of-luck Sioux. They used to sweat side by side in the boarding school printshop, blackening their palms with ink. His trousers were marbled with grime now, and he smelled of mildew, perhaps urine. Lance welcomed him upstairs, to his shower, then dressed him from his closet, before sending him back out with the contents of his billfold and a full stomach. Lance paraded Loud Bear around the dining room first, introducing him as an old res-ervation chum, a fellow full-blood making good in the white man's town.

Lance's brother Walter showed up the next night. Lance wasn't hard to find. He was booked for an appearance at a theater near Roosevelt Field, not Times Square where the film premiered, but still an enthusiastic crowd. He gave a speech afterward and performed Indian sign language for the single newspaper photographer. *A forest. Many trees.* If Paramount hadn't pulled promotion, the movie might have made something. Reviewers loved it. Educational, they called it. Lance was a tribute to his race.

Walter waited under the marquee, just out of the rain. He didn't try to buy a ticket. There was no colored section. Maybe the usher girl would have given him a second look as she tore his ticket but not challenged him, not called the manager over. It wasn't worth the risk. He'd already seen the flick. It starred an authentic Blackfoot chief from the frigid Canadian plains.

Walter had never been this far north before, so he didn't know how queer the fog was, or that it should have been snowflakes, or sleet at least, as the wind kept snapping against his trousers. Lance didn't recognize him. Lance had a girl on his arm. She was grinning, eyes unfocused. The theater was empty behind them, had been for a while. Walter waited until his brother had almost passed before addressing him, before saying his own name.

"'Walter'?" echoed Lance. He hadn't looked at the Negro's face yet. "'Walter' who?" Lance was polite, almost chivalrous, the way well-dressed white men pretended to be when they spoke to Walter back home. They liked Walter, the way he cupped one hand over the other, bent forward when he answered them.

"Walter *Long*," he said.

The girl was placed in a separate cab. Lance said she was a light-opera star. He kept talking about her, craning his neck toward his blurring window, and talking about her. Twenty, over twenty years.

"It's Pop," said Walter. "He's been sick. I wouldn't come up here and bother you if it wasn't serious. I'd have wrote or phoned, but it's even riskier, you know? Leave a trail right back to you that way, and soon anybody's finding out where you're from."

On his passport application, Lance had declared that his father, Pitah, a full-blood, died in Sweetgrass, Montana, thirty years before. Anita had witnessed.

"At least that lawyer never came round again, that one asking about you. The one from Hollywood."

Lance wasn't listening anymore, the details, stray news, the secret scrapbook Mama still kept. When he saw the steps of Penn Station slowing behind the streaked glass, he shoved out of the cab door. The wind plumed into his trench coat. He looked back, once, at Walter digging into his pocket to pay the cabbie. His brother's face was tight against the pelts of rain. Slivers of white mottled the black kinks above his ear. His suit—anyone would have said it was perfectly respectable, anyone.

On his second arrival at Anoakia, the sleeves of Anita's peacock gown swayed as she embraced him. Reformed, she declared. He inhaled through his mouth to avoid the vapors of perfume. That night they sipped mineral water on her screened-in porch as she fretted over headlines, kidnappings, Asian aggression. The dogs' barking rose through the wire mesh. A rabbit probably. The country needed fewer laws, fewer taxes, more vigilantes, she said. The spotlight on the mansion roof revolved. Lance counted each time the bars of the aviary glistened behind Anita's head.

He received the use of her home, her library, her rare collections. He stayed often, went riding, dined, but insisted on a room in Glendale to be near the airfield. Eastern weather had hampered his pilot training long enough. He hankered for that blue vastness, like the ancient plains before the deluge of the paleskins. Anita squinted from the runway grandstand as he improvised loops, rolls, tailspins. The mob jostled her as a dark speck of a man plunged from the airplane floor and hung, as high and heavy as the sun, before he was caught in parachute wings. The red man will always emulate the way of the eagle, Lance told the cluster of reporters. He drank too much afterward, in a new L.A. restaurant Anita had not heard of. The maître d' addressed him by name. Tomorrow Lance was taking a scientist up thousands of feet, to photograph something, an eclipse, a comet, he couldn't remember.

He wrote his brother again with more apologies, and a check, the last. He so wished to visit, but it was simply impossible at present. Please don't respond. The hotel staff reads the postmarks.

He wanted to try Central America next. Anita had already studied the tribes of Arizona and New Mexico, and she should push farther south, to the Aztecs, the Mayans, Lance told her. There were entire cities scientists had not unearthed. Ruins mired in jungle vines. Sometimes he showed up drunk at Anita's. He taunted the guards, shoved the sergeant in the chest, laughed when the man's hand twitched above his holster. The gate hinges groaned when Lance threw his boot, his whole body against it. You wait, muttered the sergeant, you wait. Someday. You wait.

The hotel switchboard put Bessie's call through to his room. She laughed meaninglessly during the pauses, but her voice was thin. Her husband was Japanese. He was an artist. "I could have married you," she said. Lance paced an arc between the desk and window, stretching the phone cord to its length. He was in his underwear, marring the window glass with his fingerprints and breath. The sky was moonless, starless, a black lid. "You and your damn Indian honor," she said.

He had explained it all in New York while holding her in the twilight of his drawn curtains. His obligation, a girl from his own tribe, an ancient arrangement between clans, for the good of his people. Bessie shivered. He remembered the way her sobbing grew breathless, how she sucked air through her teeth as he pushed in and out of her. He imagined the boy she would have raised for him, a white boy. Lance was probably half-white himself, and a good bit Indian too, though not half, not in Winston. He could have lived his whole life down there.

"What's her name?" Bessie's breath was constricted, brittle through the tiny phone speaker. She had not asked until now.

Lance studied the hiss. It wasn't a single string of static, but several intertwined. "Ivy," he said.

It was the first name that came to him, a girl he had barely known in the boarding school, had barely thought of since. She was a white girl, or nearly, an orphan passing as Indian. Everyone knew. She was popular, made accomplices of the whole school. In his yearbook, next to tribe, she had scribbled, "Same as yours."

Bessie's letter arrived two days later. The clerk signed for it. The envelope was leaning in the mail slot when Lance returned from an evening show. He was alone. His L.A. crowd, a younger brood, bluebloods mostly and a fake or two feeding off them, had dispersed for the weekend, the girls too. So he took in a stag flick. It was hilarious. A bogus Congo expedition splicing decades-old jungle footage with California-bright close-ups. The white hunter squints, shoots, and a rhino's grainy blur collapses in authentic dust. The audience, all male, hooted as a fake gun-holder rolled under the paws of a geriatric stunt lion. But it was the final reel they had come for. The lobby poster promised sex between a colored girl and a gorilla.

Once a year the tribe sacrifices a virgin, bound, topless, in a clearing. The gorillas understand. Barren women stalk them in the hopes of coupling, of reentering the tribe as mothers. The ape approaches through a tangle of shadows. His bride does not shudder, does not shriek as the beast lugs her body into the brush. But the white hunters have arrived. There are gunshots, a knife blade between the girl's wrists. She's free. The audience boos. All the camera can show now is the slow crawl of a naked Negress from the branches. She prods her mate, smooths his matted chest. Prods him. His maw is rubber.

The night clerk called his name as Lance stalked toward the elevator. The letter contained nothing new. Bessie had posted it before phoning. It was signed "Dakatowin," the nickname he'd given her. It meant "Indian maiden," he said, in Sioux, and it probably did. If he had told her, and she had listened, to all of it, there would have been a chance, a chance, maybe. He could imagine that now, what that life might have felt like.

He was drunk when he came down an hour later. "Ever see one of these?" He angled the .45 Colt from his jacket pocket. The clerk had already phoned his taxi.

Lance always passed the same theater marquee on the way to Anoakia. He didn't recognize the new title, which surprised him, but the actress he knew, had met her once, had flirted. He never did sleep with his own co-star, a pretty girl the producer had found dancing in a bar, half-white but the right tribe, or just about. She didn't have much of a part. When Lance vanquished the evil medicine man, of course he would get the chief's beautiful daughter. But he had been off his mark in Quebec during the shoot last year, no, almost two years ago. The Commissioner of Indian Affairs had already returned his editor's letter thanking them for the copy of Lance's autobiography, quite readable, he said, a delightful work of fiction. The book had gotten him the acting gig, authentic Northern Plains Indian, just what the producer fantasized. But that reservation Indian playing the chief, he kept studying Lance, his punctuality at the mess tent, the way Lance's laughter stoked the table into roars. Lance could small-talk anybody, actors, crew, locals. He entertained them all, jiggling his chicken dances across makeshift floorboards, while the assistant director thumped a soup tureen with a pair of metal ladles.

It was the waitress in town who outed him. Never saw an Indian like you, she said. Must be a different kind. Probably she didn't mean anything by it. Lance slapped the plate from her hand. What did a little half-breed know about full-bloods? She was the cook too, and the dishwasher. A whore practically.

Safest to stick to white girls, married, though single could be fine too. No one was going to settle down with an Indian. Lance was a fling. A savage. After his first, when he was still writing for the *Herald*, carving out his tribal niche, he sent a snapshot home to his parents. Smiling young white lady posed on the park grass, her blonde curls against their son's shirt pocket.

They picnicked, took long drives, rented rooms. Girls adored him, the curves beneath his ironed suits, that ramrod spine. Name any tribe, they were all the same to a white girl, even Bessie. But he really was Indian, part of him was. That should have mattered for something. Someone should understand that.

He shaved a year and then another from his age, a half decade, more now. A man peaks at thirty-four. He told a Hollywood reporter that. Between film scenes, he had chopped wood, dove through holes he chiseled in the frozen lake. Anita's pool was heated. Her gymnasium smelled of dry, fresh leather. He shadowboxed. He had turned forty-one in December, before telegramming her, swearing off squaws and firewater for a ticket east. It was over.

It wasn't the sergeant in the guardhouse. Anita had sent two of her men to her daughter's estate, to defend her granddaughter from possible kidnappers. It was midnight. Lance tilted his head through the open window, hollered, and the watchman flagged him through. That's what the man testified during the coroner's inquest. The hearing would be brief. Anita represented half the county's tax base. She would send a signed statement and a letter from her doctor, full rest, no additional strain.

Anita answered the bell as the taxi circled around. The butler was sleeping. "Lance, what is it? Is something wrong?" She stepped backward to avoid the thrust of the door. "Really it's terribly late."

He mumbled something. Anita caught the word "Charlemagne." She'd told him once that she was descended from the emperor, that her mother was, almost certainly was, despite the murkiness of lines through those Flemish counts. Maybe that's what he said. He was mumbling. She shut the door.

"Why don't you come to the library? I was just reading."

A paperback curved around a chair arm, with the dregs of ice in a tumbler beside it. They looked like props. The table was leaf-shaped, an oak leaf. A translucent hem dangled below Anita's bathrobe. She was barefoot.

"Do you want something?" She meant the drink trolley. Lance didn't answer. He was stalking the edge of the Oriental rug, sliding his fingertips along a row of spines, all even, all leathery dark. He wondered how much each cost. A whore, a Negro whore, went for a dollar back at the boarding school, but that was two decades ago.

"First one," Lance said, "he left you, you told me that. After your babies died. But the second husband, you paid off, right? So you'd get custody. How much he make you pay?"

He pulled a book at random, opened it, *The Conquest of a Continent*. He skimmed a few words, vertically, before dropping it to a table, another oak leaf. Anita loved oak leaves. Her arms were folded in front of her breasts.

"I'm going to bed now."

"Now your daddy, he had a harem full. Your mama was, what, number three? One of the mistresses he married when you came out of her. She was sixteen, right? Younger than your half-sister. Then she dies and he finds another just like her. That man knew what he liked. Gotta respect that. Imagine, a farm boy getting that rich. That's America, now ain't it? That's America."

If Anita had not fled to her daughter's mansion before the police arrived, someone might have noticed the bruise on her arm, a red mark at least. It didn't darken until morning. Lance squeezed until she cried out. Though not loudly, not enough to bring a servant. She didn't want that. The library doors hung open at his back.

Anita's private dick would later write: *Subject's father retired janitor Winston-Salem, NC, Negro district.* He added the bit about the rouge and hair-straightening fluid to please her. When Anita ran her hand across Lance's scalp that night, her fingers tangled, but the hairs were straight. Nothing smeared from his cheeks. Her hands were clean afterward. Only his scent lingered on her.

Lance gripped her face between his hands, pressed the joints of her jaw into his palms. "Three hundred thousand," she rasped in the whisper she imagined was sexy. "My second husband was cheap." She said it again. "He was cheap." She would have said more, but Lance pressed his mouth around hers, to shut her up. He didn't have to shove her onto the sofa. She was already sinking backward. She knew about him, she must have, probably.

Anita would tell the deputy sheriff she heard the gunshot from her bedroom, which was true, since the bath adjoined it. She was scrubbing herself, still shivering from the savagery, the pleasure of it. The watchman investigated. Lance sat in the library, in Anita's chair, legs crossed, head back, what was left of it. The watchman had never seen a hole that big. The butler had to dial. The testimony was conclusive: the trigger released when the deputy pried the revolver from the hand, one bullet, suicide.

Walter would come to see the grave and contest the will. The last of his brother's money went to some Indian charity, for mission school scholarships, up in Alberta of all places. The Longs wired to postpone the burial, but didn't have cash enough to ship the body home. Ten days in a morgue drawer, that was it. Bessie was still en route to Asia.

Afterward, Anita closed her bathrobe and then the library door behind her. Lance wasn't watching. He reached into his pocket and unballed the envelope, flattened the wrinkles against his chest. He had not tucked his shirttails back yet. His belt hung loose. That's what Anita saw, not the letter, before the door clicked. He didn't read it again. He'd forgotten it was there. Bessie's great-uncle had been a store clerk, he remembered that, and a farmhand first, before there was a corporation to be chairman of, before there were unions to thwart, land to buy up. What did Indians know about iron ore and oil? Of course they lost everything.

He settled himself in front of the fireplace. The logs were unlit. Mild air seeped through the window screen. He wanted a fire anyway, but the logs were decorative, no matches, no kindling, unless you counted the books. The watchmen smoked, but the walk to the guardhouse was too much. Lance leaned back, crossed his legs far in front of him. He daydreamed headlines, the way he used to at the *Herald*, and in the school shop before that, real words, rows of metal letters arranged inside the printing press while he cranked the metal wheel. He rubbed his eyes, pinched them. The tiles in the fireplace hung in streaks of pink and violet, amber and blue, in the shapes of peacock feathers, which resembled flames, or nearly.

Coda: Ivy Poses

"Don't look at me," said Angel. "You're not an Indian princess."

Ivy blinked, from a daydream. She was thinking about Jim, the Halloween dance tonight. "What?"

Angel's paintbrush sagged. "Ones in ads? The girl is always smiling at you. She wants you to look at her."

The silver earrings jingled when Ivy nodded. They were the teacher's, Angel's, though her name wasn't really Angel. That was a corruption of some Sioux word. Angel had told her her real name once, but Ivy could never remember.

"Look at the beads," said Angel. "You know you have to give them up when you leave for school tomorrow."

She meant in the story. Angel was painting an illustration for another story. Ivy looked at her hands, at the silver rings and the bracelets, how Angel had arranged them on her lap, the beaded dress and belt just so. It was a pretty dress, with the fringes, and the deerskin so smooth. All the embroidery, the dyed quills, that showed the maker's love, a mother for a daughter perhaps. The moccasins were embroidered too. Ivy's toes twitched inside them.

"What's this one about again?" Ivy meant the story. She had posed for Angel before.

"It's not very good," said Angel.

Ivy smiled. Angel had written it. Angel wrote lots of stories for magazines, but Ivy remembered only the true ones, the ones Angel told about herself. A man had asked her if she wanted to ride on a train. She was twelve. She said yes. She rode for three days. It wasn't this school, but one just like it. She didn't know

English. Most of her family died while she was gone, and she felt lost for the rest of her life. But the girls in her make-believe stories usually wanted to go to school. Ivy's character would have too, but that was different.

"Does it have a happy ending?"

Angel dabbed her brush, kept painting. She was studying a point just below Ivy's left eye. Her gaze narrowed, her mouth too. Maybe it was a mean question. Everyone knew Angel's husband was leaving her, or she was leaving him. Stories varied. They were never seen around school together anymore. Mr. Deitz walked their wolfhounds by himself. One had jerked loose last week and chewed up a neighbor's terrier. He had to pay for it. He had a coaching job lined up at Washington State. Imagine a lady in her forties wanting to be divorced, or a husband willing to abandon her. It wasn't Angel's fault she couldn't have any babies.

Angel was squinting at Ivy's throat now. She had her littlest brushes out. "You're fidgeting," she said.

"No I'm not." Ivy held her hands still. "I'm not."

Angel waited while Ivy breathed, swished her shoulders around, primped her neck, pressed her back flat against the school chair. The chair wasn't in the picture. She was in a teepee. She was out west. She couldn't remember which reservation.

"Am I Cherokee?"

Angel was squeezing a glob of white from a tube grimy with her fingerprints, blue, yellow, green. She grinned but didn't answer.

"I mean in the story."

"Apache," she said.

Ivy nodded as though taking direction. Apache. Not that it mattered. Sometimes Angel only outlined her body, a penciled white space in the center of the canvas. She always changed the face. But Ivy was a good sitter, dead silent for a full hour, or could be sometimes. Who else would give up her free time after chapel? Plus today she had to go finish setting up the gym. In a few hours she would get to dance with Jim. If Mr. Friedman didn't cancel at the last moment again. He had already cut back socials to once a month. The risk of contagion was too great, he announced. Miss Ridenour would keep the Girls' Quarters quarantined year-round if she could. A few cases of flu and they think it's the plague. They almost canceled tonight, because the town minister complained, the sacrilege. It wasn't the girls' fault the thirty-first fell on a Sunday.

Angel wiped her eye with the back of her wrist. Her cheek was already smeared. So was most of her wrist. She got so messy when she painted.

"Guess who I invited," said Ivy.

Angel finished the patch of canvas she'd been struggling with, which meant staring at it a long time, with the brush tip poised just above. "Invited to what?"

"You know what."

The girls' literary society was hosting the Halloween dance. Each member selected one boy. It was a secret. The boys didn't find out until the end.

Angel leaned back, cocked her head at the easel. "Gus," she said.

"We broke up *weeks* ago."

"I give up."

"*Guess.*"

"I give up."

"Big Jim."

"Thorpe? You couldn't settle for the quarterback—you have to go after the star player too?"

"I wonder what he'll come as."

Last year the team was away, in Syracuse—Ivy had the newspaper clipping in her scrapbook—so all she could picture was Jim in that Santa outfit at Christmas, handing out gifts from St. Patrick's and Second Presbyterian. The girls' choir sang from the balcony, then the team unmasked Jim, and Mr. Friedman gave him an American flag all folded up tight in a triangle. Everyone was cheering. Ivy tried to get the beard afterward, but it got trampled under the children, then vanished.

He would probably be a gypsy. Athletes always dressed as gypsies, or tramps, whatever was easiest. Once the backfield came as girls, in hobble skirts with enormous peach-basket hats, but it was Angel who made all of those, because Mr. Deitz asked her to. He was still on the team then. It was too bad the Deitzes weren't coming. They always won best costume. Except last year the printshop came as darkies, a whole chain of them in rags and blackface, and they looked so funny waltzing that Mrs. Friedman said she simply had to give them first prize. The old plantation days, she chimed, as though following some melody in her head. Ivy imagined Jim as a pirate, or, no, a wolf. That would be perfect.

"Jim's grandfather was white," said Ivy, "on his father's side, I think. Maybe both."

"Is that why you like him?" Angel was squinting at her, but she spoke as though addressing someone else, someone across the room or just outside the door.

"I just mean you wouldn't think looking at him. Gus, he's full-blood, and Miss Moore thinks he's Greek or something. She says Ulysses sailed west before he died. Maybe all the tribes are Grecian."

"She's joking."

"I know."

Julia had said the same thing to Ivy about Gus, that Ivy didn't like him anymore because he was too Indian. But it was Julia who complained about Ridenour, that she was used to her old Pueblo dorm, smacking around full-bloods all day. Ridenour didn't appreciate that Carlisle girls were part-whites. They were ladies. She and Julia weren't talking anymore, not since Julia heard about Gus proposing. It wasn't Ivy's fault.

"They used to think we were wandering Jews," said Angel. She rattled a brush in the jar on the table. The water was a brackish gray, with splashes of brighter color around the glass rim. "They must have known what they were doing," she continued, "when they made Mr. Friedman superintendent." Angel grinned but kept her eyes low. Ivy knew she didn't like Mr. Friedman. Most of the teachers didn't. They said the coach and the bandmaster ran the school. All Friedman cared about was pomp and appearances, and the cash the head clerk siphoned out of the student travel accounts and left in a white envelope under his desk blotter every week. That was the rumor. Mrs. Friedman got free vegetables from the school gardens every morning too. That was a fact.

Mrs. Friedman was no lady. Julia said so. Mrs. Friedman was a flirt. She kicked her legs so high at the last social her knees showed, and once Julia saw her playing peekaboo with Mr. Friedman between their porch columns, and another teacher spotted her with a lady guest smoking a cigarette, right there out front, where the beer wagon stopped the first Monday of every month. The Friedmans used profanity too. At night, with their windows open, it could be the Deitzes' hounds barking in their bedroom.

Ivy didn't care. Her grudge was against Mr. Deitz, how when he got so old other teams complained about him playing they had to find him more work. Angel was the better artist, everyone knew that, but Mr. Friedman promoted him right over her, and Mr. Deitz had been her student. Plus the coach still snuck him in sometimes anyway. Like when that tackle got his nose broken, it was Mr. Deitz who came out the second half in the torn jersey and his face taped up. It wasn't fair, especially now that the new commissioner was closing Angel's Native Arts program.

"Who got the elk-tooth collar?" Ivy was looking over Angel's shoulder, at the empty cabinets.

Angel dabbed at the canvas and shrugged.

There were only a couple of vases left and some tidbits. The quartermaster was giving them to teachers to take home. Miss Moore got a black Zuni bowl, to go with the birch box in her mother's house, she said. They lived downtown. Other teachers lived in the Quarters or bungalows, the ones with families, but Miss Moore bicycled in alone every morning, and again for evening study hours. She was quiet. She wrote poetry that no one read. Julia said she was a Communist, and so maybe an atheist too. Miss Moore never said anything bad about anybody, even Mr. Friedman, or Big Jim, who didn't belong in her or anybody else's business class, even if he was the nicest student. It was good of her to chaperone tonight. Ivy couldn't imagine her in a costume though. Her suits were so sharp and plain.

In the corner of the art room, Ivy saw her Pima basket squashed into a row of boxes. It was one of the first things she'd made in Angel's class. The smaller baskets intimidated her with their tight weaves and fancy markings, little geometric plants and people. She wanted to make a storage bin. Something big and useful couldn't be as hard to fake. Angel was so patient with her, showing her how to weave herself into the center, and then praising her afterward, before telling her to uncoil it all and start again.

Angel always said how important it was to practice the old ways, that each tribe's crafts were priceless, that every weaver had her own design, a variation of old and new, the sort of improvisation each of them would have to achieve. There was some interest in Indian art then, even from the government. The old commissioner thought the schools could ready the Indians for the white world, while preserving a few fragments of cultural value. For a while Miss Moore assigned arithmetic problems using the prices of rug materials. Bulk was best. Think like entrepreneurs, she said. The reservations need businessmen.

Once Angel told Ivy how hard teaching was, how the students resisted. For decades the schools had marched and drilled them, paraded them in uniforms, hair shorn, eyes straight. She said each new class was like looking at creatures from an alien race. Ivy couldn't be sure she was serious. It was Ivy she was talking to. And it didn't matter now. The new commissioner banned traditional songs again, and nature study, all the curriculum that came in with Angel. She had demanded complete freedom before taking the job. The best Indian artist in the world, the old commissioner bragged. So did Mr. Friedman then. He was a Jew, but he believed in Jesus like everybody else.

When the door clattered behind Ivy, she spun in the chair, arms across her chest, as though caught undressing. The boy looked startled too. It was Long Lance, Sylvester Long Lance. She knew him from Miss Moore's typing class.

"I—I—," he said.

"*Osiyo*," said Angel.

Sylvester's mouth mirrored the first sound, a round pursed *O* of panic. It meant "hello," in Cherokee, the tribe on Sylvester's student form, same as Ivy's. They looked nothing alike. Sylvester was coppery and chisel-faced, and Ivy pale and green-eyed, mostly. Angel's beads were drawing out the green just then, or Ivy hoped they were. Ivy couldn't see. Sylvester dressed better, pants creased, not a wrinkle on his shirt. She knew the store where he bought them. She'd seen that tie on a window mannequin, headless and white-handed, literally white, like their typing paper. Sylvester didn't have any more money than she did, but he didn't splurge, didn't loiter at the bakery or nickelodeon Saturdays. He didn't have friends.

"Mr. Deitz," he said, "Mr. Deitz told me I could come up here and get some paint. For my costume." He held a bundle under his arm. It looked like rags.

"If Mr. Deitz said you could, then it must be fine," said Angel. "But these are my personal property." She swept her hand around the desk and easel. She was still smiling, sort of. "Did Mr. Deitz tell you where you could find any of his paints?"

Sylvester looked frightened. Ivy almost laughed, though she felt bad for him. He was a nice boy. She saw him stick up for some first-years once, little ones. The costume surprised her, that he had a reason to make one. She couldn't imagine who had invited him. None of the girls in the literary society ever talked to him. Julia was very particular about membership.

Angel selected a fresh brush, the tiniest of them all, and smacked flecks of water against her palm, before pointing to a row of drawers. "You can try back there. Mr. Deitz may not have cleaned those out yet."

Sylvester nodded and obeyed. His thank-you was so soft Ivy could only see his lips move. He rifled through the cabinet and eventually produced two ink bottles. Their sides looked dried, but they brightened when he shook them. Ivy smiled as he turned.

"What are you going to be?"

"A scarecrow. I already got straw from the livery." He hesitated then, his expression flattening. "Mr. Friedman said I could go, as a reporter. He wants an article in the next *Red Man*."

Ivy's head bobbed, defensively. "That's great," she said. Why would she mind? The school magazine hardly printed any student writing these days, all official press releases, and whatever scraps Mr. Friedman allowed. Mr. Friedman liked Sylvester. He was giving the valedictorian speech at commencement in the spring. Ivy was graduating too. She didn't want to. She wasn't lining up scholarships like Sylvester. She'd probably end up with Grace again, or out in California with one of her brothers, and a secretary job if she were lucky. She would have the nursing certificate too. That's what she'd come for. There wasn't any other reason for Ivy to be here. It would all be over soon, the pretending, the game of it, and then she would just be a white girl again, with nothing to hide, nothing special about her, except the story she could tell. It was a good story. She wondered if getting caught would have made it a better one.

Sylvester mumbled a goodbye and moved toward the door. Angel didn't look up. She was painting.

"*Osda iga*," said Ivy. She said it too loudly. Sylvester hovered on the threshold, uncertain whether she was making fun of him. She wasn't. Of course he knew what it meant. He'd picked up more Cherokee than she had.

"We shouldn't talk to each other," he said. "In Indian."

"Two Cherokees?" Angel's eyebrows rose amid wrinkles. "No palefaces in sight? Who will tell?"

Sylvester stared at a space above her shoulder. A portrait of George Washington, the same one in every room in the schoolhouse, hung crooked above the blackboard, with a clean rectangle to each side. Mr. Deitz had already taken down the good pictures.

"The rules are for our own good," Sylvester said. "They teach us self-discipline."

As he turned to leave, the bells of the chapel began to chime. Angel had propped the row of windows open to air the fumes and enjoy what breeze there was. It was an odd October, so warm. All three paused as the strokes sounded, clear and loud and deep. There were twelve.

Everyone knew Sylvester wasn't Indian, but it was Gus who told her outright. Almost have to admire the nigger, he said, sneaking through like that. She and Gus weren't talking anymore, except in class, while he was drafting the petition, not against Sylvester but Mr. Friedman and Mr. Warner this time. The whole class helped, their business law class. Miss Moore had to pretend not to notice while frittering at her desk and vanishing into the hall every few minutes, on errands, she mumbled. Ivy helped with the wording. She crossed out Julia's sentence about Mr. Friedman being ungentlemanly, how he never tipped his hat to lady students, and said "Hello" instead of "Good morning." That's not going to convince anyone of anything.

Congressman Rupley ran a hotel in town and would be home from Washington this weekend. Gus was walking the petition right to his doorstep, after lights-out. The athletic dorm was lax that way. The athletes complained about that too. They thought they wanted an investigation. It was another sport to conquer. Everyone signed, except Jim. He wasn't there. He had an awards banquet with the coach. Gus said they could get the whole school shut down if they wanted. There would be government inspectors, and hearings, congressional hearings. Just you wait.

Sylvester vanished before the last knell.

"Maybe that's enough for today," said Angel.

Ivy was staring at the empty doorway, her pose forgotten. "All right," she said, so quietly she could barely hear herself.

Angel carried the brushes to the sink, like headless stems in a vase, as Ivy tugged at the jewelry. The rings came from the box on the desk, beside the easel. She studied the painting as she unwound the beads.

The girl didn't look like her, though more than other times maybe. The black hair, sure, the length of it, and the curve of the shoulders, but the face was rounder, chubbier, prettier. Her eyes were low. You couldn't tell the color. The girl was thinking something, but Ivy couldn't imagine what. She never knew what anybody was thinking, not for sure. The shadow on the wall just behind her, that was Ivy's, though it wasn't cinder blocks in the painting. It was a teepee liner, flat and abstract, reaching around the frame, literally. Angel's strokes spilled over the canvas edge onto the sides, where tiny nails gripped the canvas in place. The girl was lit by campfire, by flames. Ivy would be standing in them. Angel's stool would be burning too.

Ivy liked the background best. Angel only worked on it while Ivy was gone, tall brash patterns to the right of the girl. The left side was murkier. Something less linear was merging in the browns and grays. When Angel finished, she would sign it twice, once in each corner, her English name, then in Sioux at the girl's other elbow. Angel was standing beside Ivy now, toweling her hands.

"So what are you going to be?"

"Little Red Riding Hood," said Ivy. Then she shrugged, embarrassed. It was better than Julia's little Swiss girl. Ivy had borrowed the muslin from the seamstress weeks ago, and worked every study hour on it. Jim would have to notice her.

She stepped out of view of the door, before changing back into her Sunday dress. It rested on a cabinet ledge, far from Angel's paints. She looked at the door, at the wedge of hallway, but no sounds came. Sylvester wasn't coming back.

"Are you still coming tonight?" Ivy had asked Angel to chaperone, and then Julia had asked Mr. Deitz, or sort of asked him, through Gus. It got all muddled.

"Wouldn't miss it for the world," Angel said.

Ivy pulled her head and then her hair through the deerskin collar. "What are you?" she asked. "I mean, what are you going to be? What are you coming as?"

She knew Angel's grandfather was supposed to have been a Winnebago chief, an important man among settlers, with many wives. Angel was born in a wigwam. When she came home, her reservation was half empty. Ivy pictured the bedroom her own mother died in, and how big it looked after her father sold the furniture. He took them to the orphan home the next morning.

"I'll think of something."

Ivy looked at the Indian dress, where she had let it drop, formless and empty. She scooped it up and folded it into a tight square. Angel had said it was expensive. She'd found it in a collector's store. Ivy flattened every wrinkle.

"When should I come back?"

Angel was scrubbing a spot on her wrist, frowning. "No need to. It's almost done, the sitting part. But thanks." She rubbed so hard, the rag jerked and snapped against her blouse. Ivy imagined the skin turning raw, the pores speckled with blood. Angel didn't really look anything like Ivy's mother, what Ivy could remember of her. She hadn't seen that photograph in years. "Thank you so much," said Angel.

Ivy nodded, then waited, then nodded again. "*Osda iga.*"

The other girls were already at the gym. Julia was pointing where she wanted the piano wheeled to, away from the windows, and angled the other direction, to hide the gouges in the wood. Julia was Potawatomie, same as Jim's mother, but not a chieftain clan. A quarter-blood. Any less and the school couldn't have taken her, not unless a commissioner wrote a letter, or she faked the application. They couldn't check everybody, not thoroughly. Ivy was late, so she was handed one of the buckets and scrub brushes. Dirt and tobacco spit spotted the walls and pipes. It would take hours.

She kneeled before the last radiator, where she stood during calisthenics, out of view of the teacher, and leaned the brush into it. It was too bad no one invited Sylvester, not properly. He was a handsome boy, and so smart too. She'd heard he was an orphan, like Jim and her. She almost wished she had asked him. Though imagine what her sister would say. Grace had trouble enough stomaching Indians. Imagine if Ivy had said yes to Gus. He only liked her because he knew. Everyone did. She was the prettiest girl in the school, he said.

Everything was mixed, thought Ivy. Everybody. None of this had cost her anything. The government paid for it. Ivy never chose this home, this self, not exactly. She only chose not to resist it. And now it would fall away from her just as completely, without her having ever understood it, having ever felt it was hers. It was only the government she fooled, white people, like her. They thought in blood quanta and tribal rolls, mathematics and geometry, lines that converged or did not.

Next year, after she was gone, then she would be a white girl who had pretended to be something else once. But she was not that yet. She was still just a girl, a pretty girl, in an Indian school.

Julia was shouting at one of the new girls, a first-year. She had strung the streamers the wrong way. Julia wanted tighter loops. "Ignorant," said Julia. "You're so ignorant." Ivy didn't turn to watch. She kept scrubbing and squinting. The day was bright through the windows. It shone everywhere, every streak of filth. This was an ugly room, but it could be made beautiful. With the sun gone and the music loud, Ivy might pretend it was beautiful.

Acknowledgments

The characters and events of these stories, while based very closely on fact, are ultimately fictional. My depiction of the Carlisle Indian School and its students and employees is drawn from dozens of historical sources, including a range of texts on Indian schools generally and the Carlisle Indian School specifically; on the records of the 1914 joint commission of Congress investigating administrative corruption at Carlisle; on phone interviews with Iva Miller and Jim Thorpe's daughters, Grace Thorpe and Gale Thorpe; on Marianne Moore's unpublished letters at the Rosenbach Museum and Library; on memoirs of various Indian school teachers and students; newspaper and magazine articles of the period; and on numerous biographical studies.

For information on Sylvester Long, I am deeply indebted to Donald B. Smith for his biography *Chief Buffalo Child Long Lance: The Glorious Imposter.* Because no biography of Ivy Miller exists, I relied heavily on her Chilocco and Carlisle school files housed at the National Archives and Records. For information on Jim Thorpe and his relationship with Ivy Miller, I am fortunate to have shared research and drafts with Kate Buford as she was writing a new, comprehensive biography, *Native Son: The Life and Sporting Legend of Jim Thorpe* (Knopf, 2010).

I owe my deepest thanks to Kathryn Lang, whose commitment and guidance has brought this manuscript to publication, and to Christopher Tilghman for his invaluable mentoring. I also appreciate the many readers of these stories in their various drafts: Ann Beattie, Laura Brodie, Kate Buford, Deborah Eisenberg, Cliff Garstang, John Gavaler, Paul Hanstedt, Barbara Landis, Christopher Matthews, Deborah Miranda, Molly Petty, Don Smith, Asali Solomon, Linda Waggoner, Gordon Weaver, Lesley Wheeler, Steve Yarbrough, and the University of Virginia's MFA fellows of 2005, 2006, and 2007.

I thank the editors of the following journals for selecting versions of these stories for publication: "Ivy Works for Strangers" in *Prairie Schooner* (under the title "The Bones"); "Ivy Becomes an Indian" in the *Southwest Review* (under the title "Ivy Miller Poses"); "Sylvester Runs in Circles" in *Aethlon* (under the title "The Shortest Distance"); and "Sylvester Pretends to Search for a Missing Child" in *South Dakota Review* (under the title "Indian Finds Blood on Trail of Lost Child").

Finally, I thank my family for their support and love: my wife, Lesley; my children, Cameron and Madeleine; and my parents, Judy, John, and Margaret.

Jeremy Leadbetter

CHRIS GAVALER's fiction has appeared in many literary venues, including *Shenandoah, Prairie Schooner,* and *Black Warrior Review.* He's the author of *Pretend I'm Not Here,* a suspense novel, and a four-time winner of Outstanding Playwright awards from the Pittsburgh New Works Festival. A visiting assistant professor of English at Washington & Lee University, he lives with his family in Lexington, Virginia.